EM

I GAVE MY HEART
TO KNOW THIS

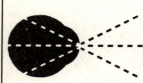

This Large Print Book carries the
Seal of Approval of N.A.V.H.

I Gave My Heart to Know This

Ellen Baker

WHEELER PUBLISHING
A part of Gale, Cengage Learning

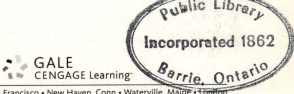

GALE
CENGAGE Learning™

Detroit • New York • San Francisco • New Haven, Conn • Waterville, Maine • London

GALE
CENGAGE Learning

Wheeler Publishing Large Print Hardcover.
The text of this Large Print edition is unabridged.
Other aspects of the book may vary from the original edition.
Set in 16 pt. Plantin.

LIBRARY OF CONGRESS CATALOGING-IN-PUBLICATION DATA

Baker, Ellen, 1975–
   I gave my heart to know this / by Ellen Baker.
     p. cm.
   ISBN-13: 978-1-4104-4348-9 (hardcover)
   ISBN-10: 1-4104-4348-5 (hardcover)
     1. Families—Fiction. 2. Wisconsin—Fiction. 3. Domestic fiction. 4. Large type books. I. Title.
   PS3602.A586313 2011b
   813'.6—dc22
                               2011033285

Published in 2011 by arrangement with Random House, Inc.

Printed in the United States of America
1 2 3 4 5 6 7 15 14 13 12 11

To Jay

Love, love, the low smokes roll
From me like Isadora's scarves,
I'm in a fright

One scarf will catch and
anchor in the wheel.
— **SYLVIA PLATH**, "Fever 103°"

And I gave my heart to know wisdom,
and to know madness and folly:
I perceived that this also is vexation
of spirit. For in much wisdom
is much grief:
and he that increaseth knowledge
increaseth sorrow.
— **ECCLESIASTES 1:17–18**

PROLOGUE:

November 1925

Violet set out from the little white house walking, but, when the pains came, she was brought to her knees. Watching the puffs of her breath make steam, she willed herself not to make a sound, not to give in to this sensation that wanted to strand her and her baby on this lonely road.

She studied the gray horizon and imagined a car was coming toward her.

But that was just a trick of her eyes. There was no car, no person on horseback. Nothing at all moved that she could see, though she envisioned hunters with long rifles tramping through the distant woods, a deer dipping its lips into the ice-crusted creek. She recalled the bright summer days when the cutover fields had been cleared of stumps with dynamite and pulling teams of horses.

But everything in sight now was as colorless and frozen as the gravel that indented her knees and hands. Her limbs were numb. She wondered if she would see her home again. If the spiders would win the battle over the upper corners of the rooms.

She'd been in the kitchen working on the collar of her husband's shirt when her water had broken. Alone on the farm in the house that her husband, before he was her husband, had won in a card game. No telephone. Jago had been gone four days with the car; she didn't know when he'd be back. There was nothing to do but to go for help.

She retrieved the mop and bucket from the back porch and cleaned up the mess on the light blue painted wood floor; in the bedroom, she selected a clean dress, stockings, gloves, her cloche hat. Her best coat, with its worn fur collar, wouldn't button closed over her. She adjusted the dampers on both stoves, then stepped out into the frigid afternoon. When the door latched behind her, she felt the familiar shock of being orphaned.

Now gravel dug through her stockings. Her coat trailed at her sides. Sudden misery rolled through. She clenched herself against it, almost grateful for its heat.

When the worst had passed, she leaned back on her haunches and yanked her cloche over her ears.

She would crawl down this road and up the neighbors' driveway. She would get to her feet, knock at the door, and ask Mrs. Tuomi for help. *This is my first baby,* she would say. *And Jago's out of town, and we don't have a telephone.*

It was unthinkable that her home would be left to the spiders.

Mrs. Tuomi had insisted on fetching a doctor. Now he was turning away from Violet, wiping his hands on a towel. The little girl had been born and the cord cut, but Violet's body still felt like a snowplow had run through it. Mrs. Tuomi had taken the baby away to clean her; Violet knew she hadn't dreamed the birth. Why was her breath still so frantic? "The pains," she puffed. "Haven't stopped. Doctor."

"Don't worry, Mrs. Maki, it's just the afterbirth." He peered under the sheet to check. After a moment, he said, "My heavens. Another one!"

Soon, a baby girl in one arm, a boy in the other. Mrs. Tuomi helped Violet set them up to nurse. Afterward, both babies fell asleep, and Violet marveled at their miniature eyelashes, their tiny fists. "Your daddy's going to take good care of you," she whispered. *Lena Hannah,* she had told the doctor to write on the girl's birth certificate. *Derrick Carl* for the boy. "You're never going to be alone, or disappointed."

"What's that, Mrs. Maki?" said Mrs. Tuomi, who had stepped into the room to collect a pile of dirty linens.

"Nothing." Violet sighed. She hadn't meant for the first words she'd spoken to her children to be lies.

At least, though, they would have the farm. Violet hated to be away from it, but Mrs. Tuomi, promising that her husband would care for Violet's animals, clucking over how Violet could have managed Jago's outside chores in addition to her own work, refused to let her and the babies go home until Jago returned. Violet wondered what her neighbors would do if he never came. She held the babies until her arms throbbed. She tried to discern their personalities. Lena fussed more than Derrick did. Maybe the girl was going to take after Jago, though Violet hoped not.

Lying in bed, she remembered their first summer on the farm, when he'd bought a pair of overalls and worked to clear stumps from the fields. Each evening, he'd bathed and dressed in his white pants and starched shirt to play his accordion and sing, or smoke and read his gold-edged *Complete Works of Shakespeare.* That winter, he'd outfitted himself in head-to-toe wool and was away all season cutting lumber, like any Blackberry Ridge farmer. Jago, though, had stopped in Hurley on his way home and doubled his winter earnings. Having had his fill of farming and lumberjacking, he bought the Blackberry Ridge General Store, a piano and a ukulele, a white suit, a straw boater, a black fedora, and a gray suit with the sheen of slate in water. For Violet, he brought home fabric and impractical hats, a milk cow, and the gelding, which he named Jolson.

She realized: without her produce, jams, and homemade pasties — meat-and-potato-and-rutabaga pies with their crusts folded over to be eaten like sandwiches — Jago's store would probably go under. He was too generous with credit. He preferred entertaining people to selling them things.

And this week, he'd decided to close up shop, telling her to "take a break": he was going to Milwaukee to buy gift items for Christmas.

She'd been dismayed. "What if the baby comes?"

"I doubt it will!" he'd said, stacking socks

in a valise. "Isn't it too soon, ay?"

I look like a snake that's swallowed a ten-pound cat! she'd wanted to say, but the restlessness in his eyes had stopped her. Now she couldn't help wondering if he'd gone to Hurley to play cards again. Speeding away, the Model T had trailed a tremendous cloud of dust.

She'd known he was nervous about the baby, but this seemed ridiculous.

Still, he and the babies and the farm were her family: the first and only one she'd had. She wasn't about to deprive her children of their father on account of her foolishness in choosing him.

So when he finally appeared at the Tuomi farm, she said nothing about his bloodshot eyes, or about the fear that flashed across his face at the sight of her and the babies. She made no comment on his rumpled suit, or the way that even his unwashed hair looked alarmed when he tiptoed into the room to whisper, "Twins?" She didn't object when he told her that in all of Milwaukee he hadn't found a single item worth buying.

She sat wordless on the passenger side of the Model T, Lena in one arm, Derrick in the other. Both babies felt heavier than sacks of gold. Jago tugged on his hat brim and shot them a glance, a quivering smile.

"Twins, ay? What're the odds? And healthy!" He was driving smoothly, inching forward, the most cautious she'd seen him.

So that when, some minutes later, they pulled onto the yard of the little white farmhouse, *home,* she felt almost optimistic.

September 1999

Standing in the yard of the little white farmhouse, her aunt and uncle's idling RV causing the earth to rumble under her running shoes, Julia had a momentary sensation of panic, of *how did I get here, really? As easy as — just — showing up?*

The farm had been in the family for generations on her grandma Lena's side; Julia had agreed at first only to consider the idea of house-sitting. But the moment she arrived, she'd been captivated by the tranquil yard, the red barn, the pasture, the garden; the diffused light. The shivering leaves of the birch and aspen surrounding the pasture had seemed to call to her.

Now her mother's sister, Alice, with strands of graying blond hair escaping a single braid, frowned at Julia from the RV's passenger window. Julia stood on her tiptoes and called, "Alice, don't worry, everything's going to be fine, the house, the barn, the horses — I'll check their hooves every single

15

day, twice a day, I promise —"

"I'll call you," Alice said. It was hard to hear her over the RV.

Julia clutched her hands under her chin. "I'll tell you everything, my progress on redecorating, I promise. Don't worry! Go and have a good time, have the year of your life, really!"

Alice nodded, then turned to her husband, George, in the driver's seat. The RV shifted into reverse and Alice's hand shot out the window and she smiled while she waved, as if Julia had really reassured her, and the horn tooted and they turned the corner and were gone. And then Julia thought: *Now I am really alone. Because how could I be more alone than here, this place, how? Thank God, really — but how?*

She began moving boxes and old furniture from the attic to the erstwhile chicken coop. Alice had warned it would be colder than an unheated ice-fishing shanty upstairs come winter, but Julia felt the downstairs bedroom too cramped, and she liked the light that slanted through the tiny windows in the peaks of the attic gables. She had a vision of a space of her own: the walls and vaulted ceiling painted stark white, the plank floors refinished with the lightest possible stain. All the dust, gone.

It mystified her why some of the things had been saved. A pile of *National Geographics* from the 1920s and '30s; a stack of *Farm Lifes* from the forties. She found an empty box and loaded in the dusty heap, a handful at a time. And then, how strange: between two ancient *Farm Lifes* was a hand-tinted, unframed studio portrait of a glamorous blond woman. Restlessness and determination were visible in her full mouth, grand dreams and a sense of irony in her blue eyes. Julia wondered who she was, if her dreams had ever come true.

On the back was written in flowing handwriting, *To my darling, If you insist! Love, Grace.*

Julia had never heard her family speak of anyone by that name. Not that they spoke much about the past at all. Still, she decided to bring the portrait downstairs and use her leftover supplies to frame it. She'd given up on portraiture the first year of her MFA program. Maybe this image would be inspiring — one way or another.

With the magazines cleared away, Julia recognized an antique steamer trunk from the few times she'd visited the farm as a child. Alice had said the trunk held ghosts, terrifying Julia. She fingered the ratty twine encircling it, wondering if something inside might explain why her mom, Marty, didn't like to talk about the family, or who this woman Grace was.

She dropped the twine. She had her own problems, and if she got lost in all this old junk, she'd never get the attic done.

She ran downstairs to call her "in case of emergency" person, George's brother, Isaac, who lived on a neighboring farm, to ask if he'd come over and help her move the trunk out to the shed, and she put on an old Ray Charles LP — Alice and George had made so few changes to the farmhouse in thirty-plus years that everything was retro. She turned up the volume and then vacuumed the living room's orange shag carpet until every strand was at attention. When she shut off the noise, "I've Got a Woman" was playing and she lunged to lift the needle and left the record spinning and spinning and banged out the door to wait, realizing that the air was tinged with the smoke of autumn, hating the smell of it and wishing she hadn't called Isaac, because she had the impulse to run and run these long, rolling roads, to erase from her brain the thought of the empty house, the coming winter, the ancient trunk and that old photograph. To erase her memory entirely, if only it were possible.

■ ■ ■ ■

PART ONE:
WORK

■ ■ ■ ■

January 1944

Grace Anderson stepped out into the biting wind, clutching her father's old lunch box. In the muted light of nearing dawn, the Superior Shipbuilding Company's vast parking lot was so full that some latecomers' cars were half on snowbanks, tilting at precarious angles, and the men emerging from them were sheepish or angry or chuckling, and other men were joshing them, the sounds carrying across the stillness as if across water. She heard the far-off banging of metal on metal, the creaking of cables, the screaming of machinery — the night shift finishing up as the day shift came on.

She saw Violet and Lena Maki, the mother and daughter who'd started as welders the same day as Grace last November, getting out of their neighbor's truck; they made the long journey to town every day from their farm. She waved, but they didn't see her.

23

Not surprising, in this crowd of shadowy men in their dark wool coats, scruffy pants and boots, with pin-on buttons on their hats — MEMBER LOCAL NO. 117; BOILERMAK- ERS AND SHIPBUILDERS; SOLIDARITY. Grace's muscles ached against her heavy clothes as she merged with the mass, moving toward the gates. She'd been working here only two months, but the smells of smoke and metal and worn-too-often-too-long clothes, the sounds of lunch boxes thunking against legs and boots crunching on packed snow seemed eternally familiar. Ahead, floodlights brightened the skeleton of a four-story-tall ocean-going cargo ship, the nearly completed hull of another in the opposite slip, the cranes hulking above both. In the farthest slip was a just-christened frigate with its sleek, pointed bow, proud superstructure, and low, flat stern — Grace's favorite. The Coast Guard crew took this ship on near-daily test runs on Lake Superior; she would soon be heading for Lake Michigan, the Illinois Canal, down the Mississippi River to the Gulf of Mexico, and, from there, anywhere in the world.

Grace turned up her collar against the wind, thinking what a far cry this life was from what she'd dreamed.

But she laughed when she caught sight of

Boots Dahlquist unfolding her six-foot frame from underneath a blanket on the floor of a Ford V8 — Boots lived across the harbor in Duluth, Minnesota, and the fellows she carpooled with had elected her to hide out to save on tolls when they crossed the bridge to Wisconsin. "Worth the nickel, Boots?" Grace called.

"Don't you know there's a war on?" Boots said, unkinking her back.

Grace saw Lena hurrying toward them, cutting against the grain of the foot traffic. "Grace, I've got something to show you," she called, and she was clutching a piece of paper in her gloved hand, waving it above her head.

The cold made Grace's smile slow motion. "A surprise? You didn't have to, kid." When Grace had first met Lena, she'd worried that the girl's billiard-cue wrists might break under the strain of the job, but she'd quickly learned how stubborn Lena was. She and Boots had started teasing that Lena's bones were made of steel. "If you break, we won't worry — we'll just weld you back together!" Lena's mother, Violet, didn't seem to think that was funny, but there wasn't much that she did.

Lena reached them, her pale skin flushed, her eyes the color of a low winter sky. When she smiled, her nose dipped like a divining rod. "I got a letter," she said, and her voice was the chirping of a bird being carried away on a strong breeze. "From Derrick."

Grace and Boots let out automatic groans. Lena and Violet often discussed Lena's twin brother's evidently limitless merits — one of the few subjects on which daughter and mother agreed.

Lena stamped her foot and pointed with a gloved finger at the text. "I sent him a picture of the four of us, and he wants to meet you! I mean, write to you."

Grace was trying to shield her face from the wind. "For Pete's sake, Lena, it's *cold* out here. Let's not just stand here."

"He says, 'She's every bit as pretty as you described, and if she's as sweet and funny as you say, I sure would like to hear from her, if she wouldn't mind helping "boost the morale" of a poor, lonely sailor, sniff, sniff.' "

"Morale!" Boots said. "Now you're in for it!" Everyone knew that any girl who refused to do her part to boost a serviceman's "morale" was not only heartless but practically handing victory to the enemy.

Lena was serious. "He's just joking with that 'sniff, sniff,' part, he's got plenty of pen pals, but you're from *home,* Hollywood."

26

Lena had come up with Grace's nickname supposedly because she looked "just like" the movie star Lana Turner, but since Grace imagined the real reason was that she always wore red lipstick and black mascara to work, it was a reminder not only that she hadn't been blessed with Lena's flawless pale skin and shadow-casting long eyelashes but also of the dream she'd deferred of going to Hollywood to become a costume designer. "Forget it, Lena. You know I have a boy-friend."

"Alex Kowalski, Mr. East High 1942," Boots supplied.

"Very funny," Grace said. Her friends had given her a hard time because she'd draped her work locker with pink organdy and pasted up photos of Alex in all his uniforms — Marine, baseball, basketball — as well as of him and Grace together at the spring dance, graduation. "This isn't *high school,* Hollywood," Lena had scoffed, while Boots laughed and Violet frowned. "You've got to admit the place needed a little dressing up," Grace had shot back, thinking there was no reason for anyone to be jealous. Alex's pictures were nice to look at, but she hadn't seen him in a year and a half. She still wrote him daily, but she didn't tell him much. It wouldn't do to complain about the cold weather and hard work of the shipyard to a boy who was off living in mud and mosquitoes, fighting a war.

Lena handed Grace a snapshot from the envelope. "Derrick's the one on the right." Two sailors in work dungarees squinted into the sun. Derrick, shorter and leaner than the other fellow, with light blond hair and a straight nose like Lena's, leaned all his weight on his right foot and tilted his head with a just-perceptible smile, as if he was on the verge of asking the prettiest girl in the room to dance.

Written on the back was: *Me and Grabowski in Calif. sun getting ready for our next big "starring roles," Dec. 1943. Note authentic-looking "sweat."*

Lena said, "They're in California, training in the desert."

"Well, I guess I don't need to hear about it, when I'll be there soon enough," Grace said, shoving the snapshot to Lena as Violet approached.

"Oh, Derrick's picture!" Violet said, smiling. Grace didn't know how Violet always managed to look like she'd just stepped off a propaganda poster, her pants and even her wool jacket pressed and clean, her boots shiny, the red bandanna covering her hair as bright as a rose. "He looks just like his

28

father looked when he was young," she said, her mouth relaxing into its typical frown. She'd made no secret of her anger at her husband, Jago, who'd signed Derrick's enlistment papers so Derrick could go into the Navy at age seventeen, last summer. They hadn't told Violet until it was done. "Except that Derrick actually is as nice a boy as he looks."

Grace started again toward the gates, rubbing her face with her free hand. "Are we standing in this wind for our health?"

"I don't see why you'd ever want to go to California," Lena said, catching up. "You might be something special around here, but, out there, girls like you are going to be a dime a dozen, honestly."

"Thanks, kid."

"I just mean, you think dull old Alex is what 'home' means, but what if you met someone from here you liked better? Besides, it wouldn't hurt to have a new pen pal."

Behind them, Boots whistled; Lena must have given her the picture. "I'd say it wouldn't hurt one bit. You do realize he's not *really* a movie star, though, right, Gracie?"

Violet laughed; sure, she'd think *this* was funny, of all things.

"Alex isn't *dull,* Lena," Grace said, her stomach tightening. "I don't know why you even bothered telling your brother about me."

"Well, we like to know everything that's going on with each other, so of course I told him all about you, and now he wants you to write to him, and I just want him to be happy. Would it *hurt* you to do it?"

Just what Grace needed: another boy to tie her to this town. Obviously, he was only in California because the Navy had sent him there. Even worse, he was a farm boy, short, and too young besides — just eighteen, compared to her almost twenty. "You never know."

"Derrick wouldn't hurt you," Lena said. "Never. Besides, I bet he'd tell you everything about California, and you'd find out it isn't nearly as great as what you think."

Grace got in line to punch her time card, tuning out Lena's breathy voice going on to Boots and Violet about how ridiculous Grace was to dream of California, where they didn't even have *seasons.* As far as Grace was concerned, that was a main selling point, as it should have been for anyone standing in this bitter wind in the dark on the crusted-over snow. On the billboard above the gate was the image of a soldier lying facedown, his stiff hand outstretched like a claw, showing the agony of his death. AND YOU TALK OF "SACRIFICES"! CANCELING BOND PLEDGES WON'T HELP.

She shivered, wondering, as she did every morning, standing here, if she was wrong to keep telling Alex they shouldn't be exclusive, when he was off risking his life for their country. Talk about not doing her part for "morale." Of course, when he'd left for the Marines, she'd been headed for fashion design school in Chicago, planning not to give her hometown a backward glance, and she hadn't thought he should be made to feel beholden to a girl who had the whole world in her sights. But then, a month into school, she'd received the telegram from her mother about her father's stroke, and the summons to come home to take care of her younger brothers and sister — her mother had to go to work. Riding the train back north to Superior, watching out the window the red leaves drifting to the ground, Grace had thought: *A temporary sidetrack. He'll be better in a month.* But when she'd walked into her parents' house and smelled the boiled coffee and rye bread and lingonberry jam and seen her father stranded in his bed, his body and face slackened, only his sparking blue eyes familiar, even as an apology lingered in them, a *looks like we won't be dancing to* Your Hit Parade *this Saturday night, Gracie,* she'd known this was no drill, that she was in it for the long haul.

She'd taken care of him, her siblings, and most of the housework, for a year. Radio broadcasts of war news and FDR's Fireside Chats seemed her only connection to the actual world. And then, last fall, her uncle, Jorgen Anderson — who, as chief loftsman, was one of the most important men at the shipyard — had called with the news that the yard was going to be hiring girls as welders, and paying them more than a dollar an hour. Her dad had grown well enough to shuffle around the house and keep an eye on ten-year-old Susan and six-year-old Ted when they got home from school; Pete, at fourteen, was old enough to look after himself, mostly. So her mother had encouraged her, saying the family could use the extra money, and Grace, tired of being the only girl in the whole USA not doing anything for the war effort, and wanting to save some money besides, for when her dad was finally back to normal, had signed up for the six-week training course, and now here she was, day after long, cold day. Yet she kept holding out on Alex, unable to stand the thought that she might end up stuck in this town forever.

It was her turn to punch in. She shuddered at the noise the machine made, handed her card to the attendant, and dragged her feet through the massive gates. The slab — the low stage in the yard's center where all the beginning welders were assigned — was visible in the distance. Here, after burners had cut the steel into the sizes and shapes indicated on the ship's plans, welders like Grace and her friends worked to fasten immense flat pieces of steel together, forming the large sections of the ship's hull. Lying down on the below-zero steel was the worst part. No matter how many layers of scratchy wool and stiff leather Grace wore, the cold always seemed to shoot straight into her bone marrow. After an hour, she'd be so frozen that, when she tried to get up, her legs wouldn't want to bend. Even in wool socks and work boots, her feet would burn like she'd soaked them in ice water, a disconcerting contrast to the hot stickiness under her arms and around her collar. Her head and neck would ache from her welding helmet and the intermittent bright flashes. Eventually, she'd get up and shuffle to the warming shack, elbowing between hulking men, peeling off

33

her two sets of gloves, holding her filthy hands an inch from the black stove without feeling the warmth.

But the monotony of drawing flat seam after flat seam was almost worse than the discomfort. She'd asked her uncle if she might work for him in the loft, where he supervised the transferring of the engineers' drawings into full-size paper patterns, which were then used to cut basswood templates of the ship's pieces. Grace had thought the loft would be the perfect place to employ her three-dimensional imagination, but her uncle had told her girls weren't being hired there. "The skills it takes, Gracie, and the amount of training," he'd said with a shrug.

Lena caught up to her. "Did I tell you Derrick's a really good dancer?"

"Very funny," Grace said. She'd told her friends about Alex's enormous feet, as graceful as canoes out of water; how, every school dance, she'd wound up taking her own bruised feet to the floor with a series of less handsome, less treacherous boys while Alex leaned sheepishly in the corner, drawing longing looks from girls who didn't know any better than to wish he'd ask them to dance.

"I'm not trying to be funny."

"Forget it, Lena, I told you, I don't want

the distraction." Crossing the railroad track, Grace thought of the supply train that stopped at the shipyard daily to drop off gondolas full of steel and pick up empties; how she always imagined swinging up onto a boxcar's ladder and riding to the main rail yard, then somehow finding a car that was on its way to California, stowing away . . .

Well, for now, she had to be content with trying for a promotion. The good welders got to do different jobs all over the yard, and she could imagine the many locations that would be more interesting than the slab — not to mention warmer.

Probably not as interesting as the loft, and not as warm as California, but still.

The clamor of the anchor was unmistakable.

"Lena! We're going to get fired!" Grace said. A promotion suddenly seemed like the last thing she could hope for. Lena had told her they'd been invited by a crew member to have lunch aboard the frigate, and Grace had trailed her up the gangplank. But, with the anchor chain clattering, whistle blowing, and a voice blaring over the loud-speaker, "Last warning to unauthorized personnel," Grace knew there'd been no invitation.

Lena winked, pulling Grace from approaching footsteps. "Relax, we'll be back right after lunch," she whispered. "Besides, they wouldn't *fire* us." She started up the nearest ladder; Grace surrendered and followed, fighting to keep her equilibrium as the frigate's engines churned.

A long corridor, another long climb, the ship picking up speed. Around each corner seemed to echo a new set of footsteps; Grace's nerves were high voltage. When Lena tried the handle of a heavy door, it opened, blasting them with arctic air. "Come on!"

The steel door slammed shut behind Grace. Clenching her teeth, she followed Lena up one more ladder, to the topmost deck, and caught up to her at the railing. Her face and lungs burned in the frigid air. "Lena, I cannot believe you —"

"Look," Lena interrupted, gesturing to the horizon.

The frigate was cutting through churning ice chunks, passing through the swing bridge that connected Duluth and Superior. Across the harbor was the miles-long sandbar of Minnesota Point, doll-size houses dotting its length; beyond it, four ore boats clustered on Lake Superior. To Grace's left, an immense freighter was taking on grain at

Superior's new elevators, said to be the largest and tallest in the world. Some distance to her right were the coal docks, where two ships were being filled with black cargo. The ore docks, where her father had worked, poked into the harbor beyond them. And when she turned to face south, she could see the whole busy city of Superior, spread out like it was bowing at her feet, darting cars and tiny houses bleeding into the distance.

It suddenly seemed possible: someday, she just might get out of this town.

"See how beautiful it is?" Lena said. "Why would you ever want to live anywhere else?"

Grace laughed, shaking her head.

Lena grinned. "Now, don't think I was going to make you go hungry," she said, pulling a wax-paper-wrapped pasty from her pocket. She tore it in two and handed half to Grace. Even cold, the combination of flaky dough, tender venison, and potatoes was as delicious as anything Grace had ever tasted — she understood why Lena scorned cafeteria food. Despite the freezing wind, she actually felt happy, standing here with Lena, watching Superior shrink in the distance as the proud ship forged its path through the harbor.

■ ■ ■ ■

"What is she, crazy?" Grace's high school friend Hat said that night, when Grace related the afternoon's adventure. Along with another girl, Char, they were celebrating Hat's twentieth birthday at Lonny's Cabaret, so solidly back in the heart of Superior that the cruise aboard the frigate might as well have been a dream.

On the bright side, Grace and Lena had managed to get off the ship and back to work without being caught, which Grace figured had to be Lena's luck, since it certainly wasn't typical of hers. And she hadn't seen her high school friends in a while — both worked long hours cleaning locomotives at the Great Northern roundhouse. So even if Lonny's was smoke-choked and gin-soaked and she wouldn't have wanted to see what the red upholstery and carpet looked like with the lights on high, at least being out with them, listening to the band onstage, was a break from her typical evening with her family — the constant demands of her brothers and sister, her mother's crankiness and exhaustion, and her father's best efforts to help, which often ended in spills and tears and frustration.

"Oh, I don't think she's *crazy,*" Grace said. "But did I tell you she's all up in arms about me writing to her twin brother?"

She filled them in, but even when she laughed as if there weren't a more ridiculous idea in the world than her writing to Derrick Maki, Hat just raised her thin eyebrows over her drink, while Char said pointedly, "Have you heard from Alex? How is he?"

"He's fine," Grace said, though it had been three weeks since she'd had a letter.

"I don't know why you didn't grab him while you had the chance," Hat said. "He'd probably have married you before he left."

Alex had looked at Grace sometimes like she was his favorite flavor of ice cream on a hot summer day. It puzzled her that she'd never been inspired to share her soul with him. Her body, yes. Once. (Her friends didn't know about that.) She guessed some girls would have demanded at least an engagement ring first, but when he'd asked her, just before graduation, if she'd do him one great favor before he left, he'd been so awkward and sweet about it that she'd decided to make him happy in what ways she could. He'd insisted the experience be more meaningful than what could be had in the backseat of a car, so, one spring Sunday

39

morning, with her family heading to the Lutheran church and his to St. Mary's, each pleaded a headache, and she ran over to his house. He met her at the back door and took her upstairs to his bedroom. He was more nervous than she was. He admitted he'd asked his married older brother what to do to make it nice for her. The brother had evidently given good advice.

And she'd never regretted it, except for feeling a little guilty they'd done it while they were supposed to be in church.

But committing to spending the rest of her life with him — that was different. "Well, what if one of us decided we wanted to . . . you know, do something unexpected? And then we couldn't, because we were stuck with each other?"

Char giggled. "Hollywood dreams."

" 'Somewhere over the rainbow,' " Hat said, rolling her eyes.

Grace frowned. "I don't see what's wrong with having dreams."

"Nothing," Hat said. "Until you're done dreaming and you look up and you find you missed out on everything you had a real chance at. Look at the way this town pulls at you, sucks you down. You think you're actually going to get away? Even if this war ever does end? You might as well marry

Alex. Chances are, he's going to be the best thing to come along. And let me remind you, he isn't half bad."

"You're so cynical," Grace said.

But Hat was busy scanning the room. "You know what I'd like for my birthday? A dance partner between the ages of nineteen and thirty-two."

"There're some cute boys," Char joked, indicating a group dressed in work clothes. They were probably sixteen or seventeen, trying to look older with beers in their hands.

"I'm not a cradle robber."

But the boys saw their opening and approached; Grace told the one who asked her to dance that she had a boyfriend who was a Marine. Char, sliding off her stool with her hand in a boy's, said, "Oh, come on, Grace, we all have boyfriends."

Grace shook her head and watched them fade into the crowd.

It wasn't really just Alex that made her not want to dance with an adolescent. She wondered if Char and Hat remembered two years ago, January 1942, when they'd come to Lonny's — along with another friend, Marilyn — to celebrate Hat's eighteenth birthday. That night, they'd paraded into the smoky dance hall wearing dresses Grace

41

had designed and sewn, plus jewelry and silk stockings and pumps and hats that she'd picked up at Roth's, where she'd worked part-time in the shoe department and — fortunately, since she never could seem to resist so many lovely shoe styles — got a discount. The band onstage played "Darn That Dream." Hat, with much fluttering of her eyelashes, convinced the bartender to serve all four girls gin fizzes, and they settled at a high table in the corner. Char raised her glass. "To the birthday girl!" They drank the toast, laughing like they were already tipsy.

"Did I hear you say it's someone's birthday?" said a man's voice.

He was dark-haired, wearing work clothes. His body was as compact and lithe as a trapeze artist's, his expression like he'd just flung himself from the high bar in the hope of his partner catching him.

"Why, yes," Char said, resting her hand on Hat's wrist. "It's Miss Hattie Gudowski's birthday today. She's twenty-one." The girls giggled at Char's lie.

"Well, Miss Hattie Gudowski," the man said. "I'd say that calls for a dance."

Hat placed a manicured finger on her red lips; the girls egged her on. Then the man gestured to the taller fellow behind him, who was sandy-haired with an outsize Adam's apple and a broad smile. "Meet my friend Hank."

"Oh!" Hat said. But when Hank's brown eyes lighted on her, she laughed. "Well, sure!" He reached for her hand, and they were gone. The band broke into "Chattanooga Choo Choo"; the dancers whooped and started to jitterbug.

"Do you dance?" Char asked the dark-haired man.

"No." He smiled. "But I'm an ace at sitting." This with a pointed look at the seat Hat had vacated, and an even more pointed look at Grace.

Char exchanged glances with Marilyn, the two of them like a prom queen and her attendant confronted with a freshman member of the chess club.

Grace's face was hot. "Go ahead."

He came over and sat, thunking his beer bottle onto the table. He had a reckless smile, and when he turned it on Grace, she felt her heart amp up.

"What's your name?" he said.

"Grace." She kicked Marilyn under the table, not wanting their age to be betrayed by giggles. "You?"

"Joe," he said, and she saw that his eyes were indigo blue, not brown as she'd thought. "You from around here?"

"Yes." The word came out sounding like a question.

He smiled; she felt as if he'd put his hand on her waist, three notches too high. She jerked her gaze from his, and noticed the dirt under his fingernails and in the creases of his skin. Her father's hands were always filthy from the ore docks; she'd planned to marry someone with clean hands.

She scolded herself: *I'm not* marrying *him!*

Two men came up and asked Char and Marilyn to dance, leaving Grace alone with Joe and feeling much like she had the previous summer at the fair when she'd walked the runway in front of the fashion judges. "Are you from here?" she said, trying to sound calm.

"No, I've just lived here a couple years." His eyes pinched, making her wonder what had gone wrong to bring him here.

But she didn't want to be nosy. "What do you do?"

"Work on the railroad. Not for long, though. I'm going into the AAF."

"Really? Are you going to be a pilot?"

His mouth crooked. "Sorry. Just a plain old airman."

"Oh." She found herself puzzled by the tone of his voice: all the boys leaving school to enlist acted like the war was going to be some grand adventure, but Joe didn't seem to be looking forward to it at all.

"You don't have to sound so disappointed," he teased.

"Oh, no, I'm not!"

He laughed.

For Pete's sake, Grace, lay your cards on the table, why don't you? She tilted her chin and smiled. "I mean, of course every girl prefers a pilot. But I wouldn't want to be rude."

"So that's how it is."

"Of course. I'd bet you'll find the same thing wherever you go."

"You know I'll be risking my life for you, just the same as any old pilot."

"Well, yes. That's why I don't want to be rude."

His eyes glinted. "I guess the question is, just how far does this get me?"

She blushed. "Not as far as you might like, I guess."

She sipped her drink; he swigged his beer.

Then he said, "Would it help if I told you, when I saw you I thought: there's a girl worth fighting a damn war for."

"Not a bad line, if it wasn't so obvious."

His face reddened; the visible hurt at the

corners of his mouth made her stomach clutch.

"For Pete's sake, you weren't serious, were you? I'm sorry, I — I thought it was a joke. I mean, me?"

"Chattanooga Choo Choo" ended with a flourish. The dancers cheered and the band started in on "Body and Soul," the slow tones wafting toward Grace and Joe like the smoke in the air. He smiled — the brightness of it flooded her with relief, and that she cared so much surprised her. "I guess I could forgive you," he said, "if you'll dance with me."

"I thought you didn't dance."

"Not with just anyone, I don't. And — well, I'm not too good on those fast numbers."

"Very funny," she said, smiling, and she held out her hand to him.

One dance turned into another, and then another, and Grace forgot his dirty hands, because at least on the train he went places, not like her father, who'd always been stuck on the docks, and Joe's arms were warm, and up close he smelled like soap and something underneath the soap that made her nose wish for more. During the songs that he declared too fast for his comfort — and it was true he was a bit awkward, even on the slow songs, but she found herself in a forgiving mood about that — they retreated to the table in the corner. She found out he was the oldest of five children, that he'd grown up on a small farm in north-central Wisconsin. After his mother had died, three years before, Joe had wanted to implement new methods that had been proven more efficient, more productive; his father had refused to consider change. *That explains the pinch around his eyes,* Grace thought.

He told her he didn't have a girlfriend; she admitted she had no boyfriend. He bought her another drink, and when they walked to and from the dance floor, he kept his hand on the small of her back, like they were really together, and she started hoping he would ask to see her again. When they danced, her eyes were level with his mouth, and she wondered what it would be like to kiss him. He smiled like he knew what she was thinking, and her embarrassment was a pleasure because he seemed to be thinking the same thing. And he had to be at least twenty-two!

After a couple such pleasant hours, they returned to the corner table to find Hat there with Joe's friend Hank, who gave Grace an innocent smile. "I'm trying to convince Hat to come back to me and Joe's place. What do you say? You want to? All go together?"

Grace felt Joe's arm tense against her back.

"Life's short," Hank said, holding Hat's hand in both of his. She was flushed, her eyes shiny, her hair escaping its careful pins. He looked at Grace. "And Joe here's about to go off to the war and make his a lot shorter."

"That's enough, Hank," Joe said, which fortified Grace to think, *At least he's not like his friend.* But when he turned to her, she sensed in the sudden curve of his smile, and in the heat of his fingers on her back, his hopeful question: *We've been having such a nice time — and I am going off to the war. . . .*

All of this *a girl worth fighting a war for* — he probably used the same line on a different girl every night. Well, Grace wasn't about to succumb like that, not to some man she'd just met.

"We can't," she said, grabbing Hat's hand to pull her off the stool. "We have to be getting home. Our parents are waiting up for us. They're going to be worried."

"Your *parents?*" Hank said. "I thought you said you were twenty-one."

"We're seventeen," she spat. "Or, well,

Hat's eighteen. Today. We're in *high school.*"

Dragging Hat away, she heard Hank say behind them, "Well, that was a damn waste of time." She could only assume Joe felt the same way as she gathered Char and Marilyn. The frigid night air was cleansing, a shock.

The next evening, when she and her friends donned their glamorous outfits again and ventured to Bridgeman's for ice cream with the four boys they were good friends with, she decided not to mind the slightly predatory, curious looks Alex gave her, or the way he seemed to hope she was impressed when he and Harold Ostman talked about joining the Marines. And when he drove her home and walked her to the porch, she stood shivering, waiting. Maybe the war had changed her mind. Or maybe she was reckless because of her new dress — or because of Joe. But when Alex finally kissed her and said, "I know we're supposed to be just friends, but sometimes I —" she interrupted, smiling, to say she agreed, and that had been the start of things with him. And then, of course, she'd ended up losing her virginity to him some six months after being so offended at the proposal from Joe — but it had seemed different, somehow, since she'd known Alex for so long and truly cared for him.

But now it appeared that Alex would, unfortunately, be forever tied in her mind with Joe. And so would Hat's birthday, and Lonny's Cabaret, and dancing, and more things altogether than she wanted to admit. And she didn't even know Joe's last name.

Scanning the crowd again, she realized she was looking for him.

Ridiculous. He wasn't even a good dancer. Besides, it was two years later, and he'd long since gotten out of town. He was probably in Europe. Or maybe even dead, for all she knew, though the thought made her shudder.

Well, anyway, he certainly wasn't here. The crowd was all filthy dockhands and shipbuilders and railroad men and too-old young boys, mixing with women with callused hands and hardened hearts — all, in their own diverse ways, settling for what was in front of them in this moment. Only Grace sat in the corner, hoping for something better. She wondered how long she could keep it up.

Winter 1944

"Can you believe they'd make a movie star stand out in this weather?" Lena said, blowing into her gloved hands and glaring at a grimy man ahead of her who'd obliviously banged her head with his elbow. The four women were waiting in the crowd that packed the shipyard's vast center; Ingrid Bergman was scheduled to appear to promote the latest bond drive.

"War is hell," Boots said.

"Then again," Lena said, winking at Grace, "*our* Hollywood bears it every day."

"Don't remind me," Grace said, craning to see over the men in front of her. She didn't want to meet Lena's eyes; it seemed like every time she had, the past month, another reminder had come of how much Derrick wanted her for a pen pal, and another story: how he used to run outside every time an airplane flew over the Maki

51

farm; the summer when they were eight and he'd gotten so mad at Lena because she'd killed a frog he'd caught; the fall when he was twelve and he'd shot his first buck and his face had gone white at the sight of the blood, and how much he'd hated to hunt after that but never said so because their dad had been out of work for years and they hardly had two dimes to rub together, much less to buy food; and the time he'd loaned Lena his small stash of change so she could order the Champion Bullseye Shooter for their marble games, and how she'd learned to adjust her shooting to the slight tilt of the attic floor, but he'd always been too busy reading *National Geographic* to practice, so sometimes she'd just let him win, but she'd had to be crafty about it because he'd get mad if he thought she'd done it on purpose.

Grace had held out so far by saying that he probably wouldn't stoop to exchange letters with a mere mortal like her anyway, which drew sputters of happy protest from Lena. But Grace, to her dismay, didn't seem to need prompting to think of Derrick's picture; she'd even dreamed of being with him in the desert sun. He'd stepped close and put his hands on her waist; his eyes had been the color she imagined the Pacific

Ocean to be. When she'd awakened and realized what she'd been dreaming, she'd punched her pillow. Then willed herself to dream it again.

She didn't figure that was her fault; she had so little real diversion, and so little hope of any in the foreseeable future. She and her friends had been promoted off the slab a week ago, only to learn that everywhere else in the yard was just as cold — even colder, sometimes, on top of a hull in the wind. At least, though, the view of the city and the harbor from up there always made her feel optimistic, just as it had that day on the frigate with Lena.

"There she is!" Boots crowed. Grace, clutching her hands together, stood on tiptoe to see Ingrid Bergman walking onto the stage.

"She's so beautiful!" Lena said over the cheering crowd. "I wish Dad could see her. He was so jealous this morning when I told him she was going to be here."

"If he came to work here, he could see her," Violet grumbled as the actress waved and smiled and stepped up to the microphone.

"You know he couldn't possibly, with his back," Lena said. "It's all he can do to get the chores done."

"He doesn't get them done. I do. And you."

"He does his best. You never give him any credit. Just because he can't work for the war effort, it doesn't mean he doesn't care about Derrick."

Grace turned. "Hush, you two, I can't hear!"

Violet's bright blue eyes met Lena's soft gray ones; each raised an eyebrow. Grace laughed, facing the stage again to listen to the actress exhort them in her charming accent to buy more bonds.

Afterward, Grace made her friends wait in the crush of men who were spit-smoothing their hair, hoping to speak with the star. Grace was as bad as any of them, rubbing at her grimy face, at least until Lena teased she was only making it worse. Then, she just tried to think what she might say. Did she dare ask whether the actress needed someone to sew her gowns?

But soon it was announced that Miss Bergman had to leave to catch her next flight. She waved goodbye and was escorted out; those who hadn't had the chance to shake her hand put on their hats and faded away in disappointment. Boots tugged Grace's sleeve, and the women headed back to work, Grace feeling like her feet were encased in twenty-pound blocks of ice. She thought of the hot sun in Derrick's snapshot. "Is your brother still in California?" she asked Lena.

Lena nodded. "Not far from San Diego."

"Do you suppose he'd . . . describe it to me? If I wrote to him?"

Lena grinned. "Sure he would."

One evening last week, Grace had spent two hours making Alex a valentine, so she didn't feel bad about the fifteen minutes she spent writing a note to Derrick. She'd first thought to enclose her graduation portrait but, at the last minute, decided she might as well really "boost his morale" with a copy of a snapshot from last summer that she'd sent to Alex, one of those silly bathing suit shots that all the girls were taking lately to send overseas.

In the morning, she showed Lena the envelope, depositing it in the office's mail slot after they'd punched in. "Are you satisfied? Now, watch, all this fuss, and he probably won't even write me back."

Lena laughed. "Oh, he will."

An hour later, all thought of Derrick and the letter was gone. Grace's head pounded from the weight of her helmet and the echoes of hammers on metal in the small hold as she contemplated the overhead weld she'd just been assigned. It was the one type of weld she was still uneasy about. If you moved your stinger over the metal too fast, the weld wouldn't hold. Too slow, the metal would melt and drip right on you.

She sensed the surrounding men watching her. "You want us to lose this war because of *you?*" her new foreman had said the other day, when she'd hesitated an instant too long.

She flipped down her helmet's visor, then fired up her stinger, raised it above her head, and touched it to the metal. There was sudden heat like she'd stepped into a bread oven. A shower of orange-red metal rained down, sizzling burns into her coveralls. Her shoulders and neck strained. She hummed a tune, trying to keep her rhythm. She felt herself shrinking into her boots, her knees starting to buckle. A fragment of burning metal dropped between her glove and sleeve. She yelped, kept going. Her arms trembled. And then there were shouts — "She's on fire!" — and men were slapping at her legs, and she fought to keep her balance. The last thing she wanted was for this weld to have to be chipped out and redone.

When she finally finished and flipped up her visor, she shook the now-cooled piece of metal from her sleeve and licked the burn mark it had made on her wrist, while the men smiled and shook their heads and pointed to her legs. She looked down at the black marks on her coveralls where they'd started to smolder; she smelled dissipating smoke.

"Tough cookie," said one of the men, laughing.

"Hotshot," said another.

Grace forced herself to smile. "Well, what did you think?"

"Hold on, girls," Violet said. "Hold on!"

"We're holding *on*," Lena said. "And they haven't even started the countdown yet."

Grace, Boots, Violet, and Lena clutched the railing on the high side of the slanting top deck of Hull number 31, as snowflakes drifted from the dirty-cotton sky and a man's voice on the loudspeaker spoke of patriotism and sacrifice. The bunting-draped bleachers were populated end to end, and so many people packed the ship-yard's ground below that Grace couldn't see a square foot of earth. In the distant opposite slip, workers swarmed the scaffolding that encased the hull in progress there.

"Are you holding on, Hotshot?" Violet said to Grace, who blushed as she nodded. An article had appeared in the shipyard's newsletter about her welding while her pants burned, along with a photo captioned *"Hotshot" Anderson.* All over the yard, men she'd never met had been grinning at the sight of her and exclaiming the nickname.

"Her name is Hollywood, Mom," Lena said, then turned to Grace. "I hate when those men call you Hotshot. Like they own you or something."

"You're sweet to worry, Lena, but you don't need to." The newsletter photo had prompted six men to ask Grace to the next Boilermakers and Shipbuilders Union dance. Of course, she'd refused them, but it was a wistful moment when she saw the next issue of the newsletter, which reported: *Slow down, boys, we have it on good authority that our famed and favorite little welderette, "Hotshot" Anderson, is 100% committed to a Marine in the Pacific.*

"Course, she *is* a hotshot, so it's only fitting they'd notice," Boots said. Grace grinned.

Lena said, "Have you heard from Derrick yet?"

"No." Two weeks had passed, and Grace tried not to think about the letter and picture she'd sent, which was hard to do when Lena kept asking. "Now, pay attention, it's time."

A new voice on the loudspeaker had begun counting down from ten; the crowd joined in.

"Hold on, girls!" Violet said.

"Three . . . two . . . one!" intoned the voice, and the crowd roared as the sponsor smashed a champagne bottle against the ship's prow. Grace locked her arms around the railing, imagining she could feel the lines being whacked with axes: *wham, wham, wham.*

And then the ship was sliding down the greased timbers like a kid's bottom on snow. Grace screamed as her boots slithered on the deck and heard Violet: "Hold oooooon!"

The ship crashed into the icy water; Grace, hugging the railing like it was a lover going to war, felt cold spray and screamed as the ship bobbed, then bobbed again. Finally, it straightened, settling into the water upright, as though having never had another intention.

As the yelling on deck died down and Grace caught her breath, she could hear the crowd cheering below and a band playing "Anchors Aweigh." She saw Violet, checking to make sure her bandanna was still in place over her hair. Then she met eyes with Lena and with Boots and the three of them screamed again and laughed and laughed, Grace feeling certain that everything would, in time, right itself. That her dad and Alex and all her friends would be just fine. That she'd make it to California, soon.

When she arrived home one evening to finally discover a letter from Derrick, Grace tore it open before she'd even washed her hands.

A photograph and a cocktail napkin fluttered to the floor from between the pages of stationery. She knelt to examine the napkin first: on it was printed HOLLYWOOD CANTEEN; sprawling handwriting — she made out: *To Grace, Judy Garland.*

She screamed; her mother and sister came running. She tried to explain, was too thrilled. But they finally understood, and laughed and exclaimed over it.

As the excitement died down, Susan picked up the photograph from the floor. "Is this him? Oh my gosh!" Taking it from her, Grace drew in a quick breath. From the distant snapshot, she hadn't realized what an adorable, smooth face he had; those dimples in both round cheeks; that little smile; clear, calm eyes; slicked-back, light blond hair.

She collected herself. "All right, you two, a little privacy while I read this."

Mother and sister took a step back; it was plain that was all they were going to allow. Grace gave up and read:

March 11, 1944

Dear Grace,
Well, Lena said you were pretty, but she should have been more specific. You're a *"knockout."* I'm glad you decided to write to me. (It's lucky for me that my sister's a first-rate arm twister!) As for the picture she showed you, I can understand why it didn't 100% impress you, so I'm upping the ante and enclosing my "portrait," which, thanks to some trick lighting and fancy lenses or something, turned out all right.

So, not to make you jealous or anything, but, on leave earlier this week, we went to the Hollywood Canteen and met Lana Turner "in the flesh" — she does look a bit like you, but from your letter I think you've got a sweetness she lacks. Judy Garland, on the other hand, danced with us all (me twice, I'll fess up — did you know her parents met in Superior?

So she was real keen to talk with me, "a boy from home," as she called me, and she was impressed to hear about you and my mom and sister working at the shipyards there). She was a real peach in general. I'm enclosing an autograph, which I hope will help to make up for your not being able to meet Ingrid Bergman before.

Don't think it's *all* "roses" out here, though. We spent quite some time close to the Mexican border. Sunshine all the time and during the day we couldn't touch the airplanes without getting burned. (I got to be about the color of a baked ham — an attractive picture, I know.) You wouldn't guess it, but the nights were cold enough to make a fellow shiver even in a jacket. Maybe my sister told you that I'm a gunner aboard a "TBM Avenger" aircraft. I recently experienced my first takeoff from a carrier deck. Much puttering and sputtering, and then — wham! The catapult launched us and all I could do was hold on, put my faith in my pilot (Lt. Nelson) and "God" — then there was no deck below, I was looking down at the water and realized we were actually sinking toward it, and I could see (I face "backward") we were *below* the ship's deck and I was looking up at it! I swear we skimmed the top of the waves before we (finally!!!) began to rise.

(Here I am trying to impress you, forgetting you know my mom. Keep this under your hat, all right?)

You asked me what sorts of things I like, so here goes. Steak and eggs, strawberries out of my mom's garden, wild blackberries, pancakes. Oh, did you mean other than food? Well, let's see. Flying. Music (Duke Ellington especially). I listen to the radio when I can. I sing "almost as good as Bing Crosby," so the fellows tell me (I don't believe them, and neither should you). Don't tell my mom, but I'm getting to be an "ace" at cards. (I can see her shaking her head and complaining I'm turning out "just like my father," which actually I hope never to do.) I'm a dog man (but I don't mind if you like cats) and a leg man (yours are *plenty good*). Favorite machinery: the *TBM Avenger* aircraft! Hero: all the fellows who've given their lives so far.

Now you — what do you like? Tell me

everything, Grace.

Sincerely yours,
Derrick

P.S. How tall are you?

Grace was smiling as she looked up to see her mother and Susan watching her. "Nothing to see here, folks, move along."

"You're blushing," Susan pointed out.

"Who is this boy?" said her mother.

"Just a pen pal." Grace sighed and creaked to her feet, gathering the letter, the picture, and the precious autographed napkin. She trudged upstairs, thinking he seemed much older than eighteen, and more sophisticated than your average farm boy; musing over how to begin her next letter to him; and ignoring Susan, who trailed asking questions.

Standing at her locker the next evening, Violet could hear the girls. Lena was teasing how she'd known Grace would be crazy about Derrick, while Grace laughed and Boots quipped, "Miss Matchmaker 1944." Violet's hands were trembling. Her skin was dry and cracked. She'd been shivering, aching, all day. Maybe she was just too old to be a welder. She would be forty this summer, but she felt she'd lived so many lifetimes already.

And chores ahead this evening, as always, unless Jago had done them. The small chance of it felt heavier on her than her leather coveralls.

Years ago, whenever she'd gone out to collect the eggs in the morning, she would look at the little white house and the red barn and the rolling, troublesome, stump-scarred land and laugh with glee: *All mine?*

That was back when Jago had sung solos at the Lutheran church. How proud she'd been that he was *hers*. Ladies brought out their handkerchiefs to dab their brows, his rumbling voice raising chills, while Violet held the twins, one on each knee, Lena squirming, Derrick enraptured by the music, both so clean-smelling and new in the clothes she'd sewn and starched for them and their matching white-blond hair. Back then, the services had been in the Finnish language; Violet had found them a comfort even if she didn't usually understand the words.

They hadn't been to church in years. After Jago's store had gone under, in 1931, it had seemed all Violet could do to keep everything from slipping through her fingers entirely. Underfoot at the farm, he sometimes tried to help, but there were things he flatly refused to do, like picking tomatoes. He said he couldn't stand the smell. Other times he was too lost in his books and music, occasionally writing songs that he promised would be published and make them rich. More often, he was gone, "looking for work," or out in the woods to hunt and fish. Violet worked at Ma's Kitchen café in Blackberry Ridge six days a week, took care of the farm and the house. She supposed she'd hoped that he would come to see the value of their home and family — that nothing else could ever come close.

But when the war began, and the shipyards begged for able male workers, Jago could have made a hundred dollars a week; instead, he'd claimed his back was too bad from long ago shoveling rock in the copper mine, clearing the farm of its stumps. And then, last year, he'd signed those papers, allowing Derrick to join the Navy. Violet had been praying that, by some miracle, the war would end before her boy turned eighteen. Instead, they saw Derrick to the train. On the platform at the depot, he gave them a little wave and grin, then leaped aboard like he was heading for summer camp, unaware he'd made off with her lungs. And all Jago did was smile.

When the yards finally started hiring

women, Violet had realized she could make four times the wages she'd been making at the café. And Lena had begged to drop out of school and become a welder, too, because she wanted to feel she was somehow helping Derrick. And Jago had only sat there and watched them go.

Whenever Violet found herself short of breath, Jago said it wasn't reality that Derrick could have taken her lungs. "You were the one always encouraging him to 'see the world.' Paying for all those magazine subscriptions and those goddamn maps. What did you want me to do, deny him?"

"I wanted him to see what he wanted of the world — not fight a war!"

Jago shrugged, called the doctor for her. The doctor said her lungs were fine. No, she didn't have asthma. He couldn't explain why she so often felt short of breath. "Sometimes these things are only in our minds," he said.

If only these men knew how near Violet felt herself to disappearing. It would take just a slight bending of the light. If only they knew how long she'd felt that way — and now, how much sharper the premonition. Her mother, Hannah, had died giving birth to a stillborn boy when Violet was two. Her father, a Swede lumberjack named Carl

Carlson, had left Violet with a neighbor "temporarily." There were occasional stilted letters stuffed with cash. Violet saw him once a year, on her birthday, the third of July. He was missing two fingers on his right hand and emitted a pickled, sweet scent even from across the room. His flat blue eyes were cool as glass; his beard and mustache, the color of fresh-cut pine, were so thick that she couldn't tell if he smiled at the sight of her. On her "sweet sixteen," he didn't appear, didn't send a letter. She realized then that he was dead: that in all the world there was not a single person connected to her.

Now, with Derrick away, Violet felt her grip on everything more tenuous than ever. Jago said that she just shouldn't have ridden that ship down the ways if it was going to scare her so much: Violet had seen herself sliding off that slippery deck, spinning and falling as the earth lost its hold on her. Only the pounding of her heart, after everything had settled, told her she had not succumbed.

But even Lena seemed to sense that things were off balance without Derrick. He had always been the steady one. Violet remembered one time, when the twins were about six, she'd sent them to collect the eggs, only to hear a subsequent chorus of clucking and squawking. She'd looked out to see Lena skipping through the upset chickens, poking any she could reach with a stick, Derrick standing in the door of the coop with his hands on his hips, his little cowlick standing on end. "Lena!" he'd said. "Focus!" And Lena, after sticking her tongue out at him, had. She'd calmed right down.

Maybe that was why Lena was so intent on Grace and Derrick becoming pen pals. To bring Derrick home more quickly.

But when she glanced at the girls again and saw the way Lena's eyes sparked at Grace, Violet found herself unsettled. She hoped that a boy would soon come along to capture Lena's attention. She spoke up. "Lena, Derrick's a long way away, and he probably will be for a long time, as much as we don't like it. He might meet another girl, somewhere out there. And Grace has Alex, remember?"

Lena considered Violet for a moment, her gray eyes impervious. Then she grinned and nudged Grace's shoulder. "I don't think Grace really likes Alex that much."

Grace pretended to be appalled, blushed deeper. "You know that isn't true."

Violet felt the aching in her lungs. "Everything isn't up to you, Lena," she said.

And Lena gave her a little smile.

At home, the chores weren't done, but at least there was a letter from Derrick. In the kitchen, huddled up to the stove, Violet finally managed to stop shivering. Lena read out loud: *"Dear Mom and Dad and Lena: Sorry I can't write you separately this time, training is sure keeping me hopping. Just wanted you to know I got your letters, and I am doing well and getting plenty to eat, Mom, so don't worry about me. Lena, thanks for making Grace write to me. Too bad I didn't have enough charm all on my own to convince her, but it's a good thing I've got you. It's way too soon to answer that question you asked, as I've only seen two pictures and one letter from her. 'Hold your horses, Nellie,' as the saying goes."*

Lena giggled at that, then went on: *"I know you like her bunches and that sure means a lot, and anything you can tell me about her I'll be glad to hear. But you know I'm not looking to settle down anytime soon. Though she does seem swell. What do you think of her, Mom? Have I mentioned lately that around here I am pretty much revered (ha ha) based on the fact that my mom and sister are shipbuilders? Roughly half or three-quarters of the boys have asked me for your address,*

Lena, but don't worry, I have no intention of setting up my sister with anyone low-class like a sailor." She looked up. "What a hilarious brother I have." And back down again. *"Dad, I guess you'll be proud to know I'm ahead in the pool and some of your tricks have paid off nicely. Well, sorry this is short, but it's lights out so I have to close. Write as soon as you can and tell me what's new at home. Your son and brother, Derrick.* That's all. It's good news he's winning at cards!"

Jago was looking sheepish — a memory of a long-ago day twitched in Violet's heart.

"Chores, Lena," Violet snapped. "I'll be out after I talk to your father."

With a roll of her eyes, Lena was gone, leaving Derrick's letter on the table, thumping into her boots and coat on the back porch. Violet got up to load the stove.

"You taught my little boy to gamble," she said, after Lena had banged outside. The stove wood was rough on her callused hands.

Jago blinked. "He wrote that only so you'd be angry with me."

"He wouldn't do that."

He shrugged, his fingertips resting on the swirls of Derrick's words. "You know, it never seemed a problem for you when I was winning. You took it all. The horse. The cow.

The clock. This goddamn farm."

"I raised them to be honest."

"And how honest have you been, ay?"

Violet sat down.

"All the stories you've told. How I was right outside the room when they were born. How we bought the farm with the money from my lumberjacking and your little tips from your waitress job in Ironwood."

"I told them that so they wouldn't hate you!"

"You can't control the feelings of people," he said. "Not when you don't know the half of it."

Her heart seemed to crack, to flame. "Then why don't you tell me? Tell me, if you're so wise, just how everything is. Cure me of my ignorance."

He got up. "It would take a lifetime. Now, I suppose you're not going to cook."

"I've been working all day, Jago. Since before you were up this morning!"

He sighed, lifting a skillet down from its hook on the wall. "Yes, the poor patriot girl, running off to work in her pants every morning, leaving me here with the chickens and the cats."

"Do you think I like it? Do you think I'm not tired?"

"I can tell you a man requires comfort," he said. "More than you give, ay?"

Violet picked up Derrick's letter. She folded it back into its envelope. Her hands were shaking. "I've done everything for you. Everything."

He shrugged. Ran a knife through an onion, the scent exploding.

Violet caught sight of a cobweb in the corner. She jumped from her chair to knock the thing down. She slammed outside, shoving Derrick's letter into her pocket. The cold air burned.

Two weeks after sending her reply to Derrick, and having heard nothing in return, Grace climbed the long ladder down Hull 33 for her break, reflecting how, in the two months since its keel had been laid, the hull had risen to its full height; in two more months, after being outfitted with plumbing and electrical and steering systems and pumps and diesel engines and generators and insulation, it would be christened and launched. Then would come the superstructure, the gun mounts, gratings, railings, refrigerators, heads, berths, and on and on, until finally it was ready to sail the world.

Well, at least the ships she worked on would get somewhere, even if it seemed she never would. Crossing the yard, she cast a longing glance at the train, which idled on the track while men switched out its cars.

She scolded herself, thinking of her poor dad, who was still so helpless in so many ways, and of Alex, fighting in the Pacific, and Derrick, training to do the same. They didn't have the option to hop a train and run away — why should she?

A man stepped out from between the cars, his back to her. He was wearing a leather bomber jacket, painted with rows of little white bombs. Strange, for a railroad man.

When he turned in her direction, she almost tripped. It was Joe. The man who, more than two years ago, she'd danced all night with; who, then, had been about to leave his railroad job to join the AAF. Now his face and clothes were smudged; under the dirt, his face was the color of paste. But his reckless smile was the same.

She shoved her hands into her pockets, ruing the sorry state of her face and clothes, and wondering why anyone would come back to this town once he'd managed to get away. Or had he lied from the beginning and never gone into the service? But then, why the jacket with the bombs on the back? They didn't give those things out for nothing. Yet she'd never heard of them sending anyone home in the middle of things, either. He didn't look wounded.

He tilted his head, as though he recognized her.

Not that he'd be the type to remember a girl's name.

He started to cough, ducking his head, covering his mouth with his arm.

"Excuse me!" she cried, before he'd recovered, and she hurried away, not looking back. She imagined smoke trailing from her legs, as if she'd set herself on fire again.

Excuse me? she thought then. *When he should be the one to say he's sorry!*

She found herself wishing she'd gone up and kicked him in the shin when she'd had the chance.

"So, who was that railroad man?" Lena asked at the end of the day, as Grace and her friends stood near the matron's office, drinking their required daily glasses of milk, which management thought necessary to fortify the women.

"What?"

Boots grinned. "We saw you when you saw that brakeman. You just about tripped all over yourself."

Grace hadn't stopped to think she'd been in perfect view of most of the yard when she'd seen Joe.

"Who was he?" Lena said again.

"Nobody!" Grace set her empty glass on the matron's metal cart and shuffled to her locker, shrugging off her jacket.

Lena followed. Her eyes had softened; the look on her smudged face reminded Grace of her mother's *I know you're sorry, but I'm still disappointed in you* look.

"He's nobody," Grace said again, letting her coveralls collapse around her ankles. She sat on the bench to tug the legs over her work boots as Violet and Boots came over. "Just someone I met once, a long time ago. I was just surprised, that's all. It wasn't anything."

"Well, I won't tell Derrick," Lena said. "*This* time." She winked and walked away, leaving Grace staring after her in disbelief. Violet caught her eye, shaking her head as if to say, *Don't mind her.*

"Oh, Grace," Violet said then, frowning. "Did you see this afternoon's newspaper? We didn't know if you might know the boy on the front page, from your high school."

The front page could only mean the boy had been killed.

"It isn't Alex!" Violet said.

Grace closed her eyes, trying to stop her vision from swimming.

76

But when Lena handed her the paper, she knew the face in the picture. It was Harold Ostman. Alex's best friend, and Char's best guy. When they'd bid him and Alex good-bye at the depot just after graduation, Char had cried a downpour. "They'll be back!" Grace had assured her. "And he'll still love you, too, you just wait and see."

But now here was his picture in the paper, a caption underneath stating he'd been killed somewhere called Ebon Atoll, in the Marshall Islands.

Lena and Boots sat on either side of her. One of them rubbed her back, the other held her hand. She didn't know which was which as she stared at Harold's grainy picture, her gaze blurring with tears.

She went straight to Char's house and sat with her and Hat on Char's shaggy bedroom rug, and in a way it was like old times, except that Char couldn't stop crying. Hat pulled a bottle of vodka from her coat — a sympathy gift from their railroad co-workers — and the three friends told funny Harold stories and cried and got drunk. They'd planned to get together tomorrow to cel-ebrate Grace's twentieth birthday; the thought of it was ludicrous. Finally, Char leaned against her bed and closed her eyes.

Grace didn't know if she'd passed out or fallen asleep. Maybe it didn't matter. Grace and Hat lifted her into bed and tucked her in, then stumbled downstairs, half tripping over each other, drawing a raised eyebrow from Char's mother, who was knitting in the living room by a single lamp. "Is she all right?" she asked.

Hat held a finger to her lips. "She's sleeping." Vodka sloshed in the near-empty bottle she'd stashed back inside her coat.

Outside, the sky was as dark as if black brocade had been dropped over the city; snow was falling like rain. Grace clutched Hat briefly, then turned toward the whirling darkness. The layer of white under her feet seemed to tilt with every step. Her eyes watered from the cold, or maybe she was crying.

When she finally got home, the house was hushed and dark. Her coat, hat, and scarf were covered in snow. She hung them up to dry, pried her feet out of her galoshes.

On the kitchen table, the white rectangle of an envelope glared. "Alex!" she said. But then she saw it was from Derrick.

Dear Grace,
It sure was good to hear from you and you're certainly welcome about the

78

autograph. I'll be glad to do the same again, if I have a chance with any other big "stars."

I was really happy to read that you like to dance. I don't mean to count chickens and all that, but maybe someday we could go dancing. (I'm five foot seven and a half so we could truly dance "cheek to cheek," which I have to say is nice to picture.) What do you say? Can we make a date of it? Either I'll come back home to take you, or we can meet up in California or wherever you've managed to get to. (Don't worry, Grace, I think you'll have the chance to get away. All you have to do is set your mind to it. I'm planning to see the world myself, and, who knows, maybe if we hit it off, we'll end up hitched and seeing the world together.)

Hold on, the sailor is getting ahead of himself. And here I told my sister I wasn't ready to think of settling down. However, as long as we're discussing these things, do you have one particular boyfriend? To be 100% honest, I had a girlfriend when I left home, but she has since found someone else she likes better (he isn't "halfway around the world"), so I'm "free and clear." (In case you wanted to know!)

Tears streamed down her face. She carried the letter upstairs, fell onto her bed, and slept immediately, clutching it in her hand.

The next morning, Grace dragged herself out of bed barely in time to get to work, and she was embarrassed to punch in with a few other hungover stragglers. Rushing into the locker room, she was thinking only of how late she was, so she was taken aback when all the women broke into singing "Happy Birthday" and Violet brought her a cake, twenty candles burning atop it. "And happy April Fool's!" Boots added at the end of the song.

"Very funny," Grace said, dismayed at having forgotten her own birthday. For the first time in her life, she wondered whether its being on April Fool's made her whole existence some kind of joke.

But, at Violet's urging, she made a wish — that the buoyant feeling she'd had a month ago, after riding that ship down the ways, would come back — and she blew at the flaming candles. Only half of them went out, the first try; the women groaned in sympathy. She looked up at them and

thought, *You have no idea.*

But that wasn't fair, she realized. They did. They all did.

"I got you something!" Lena said, handing over a prettily wrapped box. Opening it, Grace discovered a length of purple fabric — crepe georgette, the fancy three-dollars-a-yard stuff.

"Lena, you shouldn't have! There must be five yards here."

"I thought you might want to make yourself a dancing dress."

Pain stabbed Grace between her eyes. Did Lena know what Derrick had written? "Thank you," she mumbled. "That was very thoughtful of you." She ran a hand over the fabric; her calluses caught. She drew back like she'd been burned.

"Service cake," Violet said, as she cut into it. "Only three-quarters of a cup of sugar. Say, Lena, why don't you bring a piece to that boy who was making eyes at you in the cafeteria yesterday?"

Lena grimaced. "No, thanks, Mom."

"Cake for defense," Boots quipped, "and the sure way to any young shipbuilder's heart."

Grace felt sick at the thought of eating. She wished Violet and Lena weren't being so nice. The minute she'd awakened to see

81

Derrick's letter crumpled underneath her, she'd known she was going to have to tell him they couldn't be pen pals anymore. As much as it pained her to think it, she knew she was just lucky Harold had been killed instead of Alex. God couldn't possibly take two boys out of the same group of friends, could He? Still, she thought she'd better behave herself, to be safe — to make up to God about what she and Alex had done that spring Sunday morning; to show Him that Alex had a good girl waiting for him back home. *I'll even marry him, if that's what You want,* she prayed, hating the warmth in Lena's and Violet's eyes, hating to think how disappointed they would be.

Spring 1944

"God doesn't *care,*" Lena had said this morning, after Grace had explained why she'd broken off her correspondence with Derrick; he'd evidently told Lena all about it. "Do you honestly think, with everything else going on in the world right now, He really has time to worry about every last detail of *your* life?" Now, in the noisy, cavernous engine room of a recently launched hull, Grace hoped Lena was wrong. Her new foreman, Russ, was pointing to a ceiling beam, shouting, "We're goin' up on the catwalk, Anderson. I'm gonna hold on to you while you lean out and do these welds." There was nothing below but a twenty-foot drop to the engines.

Well, whether or not God was watching over her, Grace was going to do the work. She wasn't about to give anyone cause to think she didn't deserve her "Hotshot" nickname, not to mention today's surprise promotion to an elite "odd-job" crew. Frustratingly, ever since she'd spotted Joe that day the news had come about Harold, the train's allure had actually increased, which she wouldn't have thought possible. If this work didn't put the idea out of her mind, she didn't know what would.

Not to mention, if she faltered, no doubt the men would start calling her "Potshot" — or worse.

"Boss," Les, the crew's burner, yelled, "don't you think we'd better build a platform for her? Those welds are three feet out. She'll have to be leaning way back."

"*I* can do those welds," said the crew's other welder, Sean O'Connor. He was tall and burly with hematite black eyes and a way of looking at Grace that made her feel like something had just crawled down her back.

"No time for that," Russ shouted. "And I'd rather be holding on to a hundred and thirty pounds than two hundred, O'Connor. Come on, Anderson."

As she followed him up the ladder, she couldn't help wishing he'd guessed she weighed one-twenty instead.

Last night, she'd received Derrick's reply; she'd read it enough times to commit part to memory. *Now that I know about your Marine, Grace, I wouldn't try to interfere with things between you. Besides, we're really just "pen pals," aren't we? I'm still just hoping you'll help see me through this.*

"And if God *is* checking up on you, Hollywood," Lena had said, "I bet He'd much rather have you supporting more boys, instead of just writing to one. How selfish can you get? I mean, Derrick's really homesick. Not that he'd ever admit it. But I *know* he is. So of course he likes to hear from you, since you're from *home*. Besides, how can you disappoint someone who's been so nice to you, getting you that Judy Garland autograph and all?"

Now, on the catwalk, face-to-face with Russ, Grace could smell the cigarettes on his breath. He unbuckled his belt, whipped it out of his belt loops — she scarcely had time to be alarmed before he encircled her with it, buckling it over her heavy jacket. He clenched the thick leather band in his fist, wrapped his other arm around a support beam above, and turned his foot sideways in front of her boots so they wouldn't slip forward. "Ready? I'll yell when you're at the right place."

Grace, hoping he was trustworthy, flipped her helmet down. Its shade made the world black. She heard pounding, shouting; smelled smoke. *Maybe you're right that God is in control,* Derrick had written, *but from what I've seen, it's a little more random. We lost a pilot who missed a landing and crashed into the water. He was the noblest guy you'd ever want to meet, and religious, too, and his two crewmen were, you might say, not. However, they got out with hardly a scratch. I guess I've been doing my share of trying to get God more familiar with my situation, but sometimes I can't help but think that the only thing that can be counted on is that some of us won't get through and others will be left to pick up the pieces.* Despite the burn marks that peppered her neck and wrists, Grace honestly hadn't imagined it would end up such a strong possibility that someone would have to pick up pieces of *her.*

She thought of Alex's latest letter: *I think of you in the quiet times and it helps me through.*

Maybe Lena was right — maybe everyone needed to stay connected with as many people from home as they could, in these strange, harrowing times. Besides, if Grace was going to think about anyone other than Alex, better it be a boy who was far away than a man who came into and out of the shipyard every day on the train.

With aching arms, she lifted her stinger to the beam; Russ's belt dug into her back as she reclined over the chasm. She decided: she would write to Derrick tonight. *Of course you're right, we're just "pen pals," and I'm glad we are, for the time being, because we all need a little help getting through the days. And I don't suppose there'd be any harm in planning to go dancing for a "welcome home" maybe just* once, *when you get back, as it would certainly give us both something to look forward to. . . .*

Russ shouted for her to go ahead, and she made the weld, sparks showering her.

There was no marking time by the May weather, which blew from snowy to sunny to foggy to rainy to just plain sweltering. And there seemed to be no marking time by work. Every morning, Grace waited in line at the rod shack with Sean O'Connor to pick up the welding rods they'd need for the day, ignoring his snide intonation of "Hotshot" and his comments about her lack of experience: he liked to rub it in that he was worker number 201, meaning he'd been the two hundred and first man hired, while she was number 6223. Every day, at least if she was in a position to, she watched the distant train puff into the yard, watched a faraway Joe in his bomber jacket switching out the cars, and wondered where he might be getting to next. Every evening, she plodded back to the locker room, filthy and sore and satisfied and happy for the chance to chat with her friends. And every night she dreaded going home to her dad's glacial improvements, her mother's exhausted distraction, her siblings' screeching demands, and the constant drone of the war news on the radio that, for all its worrisome details, never told her what she really needed to know, like where Alex was and if he was going to make it back home.

It was late May when she realized she'd begun marking time by Derrick's letters, which usually arrived once a week. In the letter she received on Saturday, the third of June, he wrote, *I know what you mean about monotony, but it looks like on our end it's about to let up. I can't tell you much except that in the near future my letters might not arrive like clockwork, even though I'll continue to write often.*

So he was setting out to sea, going to see the world. She smiled at the thought.

On Wednesday, June 7, the sun was so hot that Grace felt close to fainting — not that she could actually have fallen, with the bond rally crowd pressing her on all sides, Lena holding her arm, Boots and Violet behind her, and Sean O'Connor looming too close on her right. But she was weak-kneed from not sleeping the last two nights; she'd stayed up listening to the radio reports from the beaches of Normandy. The "losses" from yesterday's long-anticipated D-Day invasion had been "less than expected," and the Allies were reportedly making good progress. *Losses.* The word massed the thousands together, but Grace couldn't help thinking of all those boys like Alex and Derrick, with families and girls back home.

Now the veteran onstage was talking of an earlier battle. "The German fighters picked us up just after we passed the French coast."

Grace couldn't seem to listen; instead, she heard the voice of the man on the radio describing the scene at Normandy. Her mother had awakened everyone, the first night, and the family had gathered around the radio in dim lamplight, little Ted in their mother's lap, Susan leaning on Grace, Pete on the arm of their father's chair. The smell of strong coffee lingered; her mother sipped long after the liquid had gone cold.

Now the crowd cheered; Grace didn't know for what.

At the shipyard yesterday morning, the

workers had gathered in the rain to pray, thousands of voices rumbling as one. And then, in the afternoon, the loudspeaker had relayed the radio broadcast of Philadelphia's mayor ringing the Liberty Bell. The shipyard had stilled as the deep gong reverberated and a man's voice intoned: "The inscription on the bell reads, 'Proclaim liberty throughout all the land, unto all the inhabitants thereof.' Today, let it indeed proclaim liberty throughout the land and the return of liberty throughout the world."

Even Sean O'Connor had wiped a tear from his eye, and Grace, rain-drenched, had started to shiver, and couldn't stop, and then the men around her had begun to applaud, and soon, all across the shipyard, men were cheering and stomping their feet in the pounding rain. And then, quickly, back to work. It seemed like everyone had their keys turned up three notches higher. *Get the ships done, the boys need them.*

And last night, listening to the radio again with her family. Susan — whom Grace had caught more than once gazing dreamily at Derrick's photograph and reading his letters when Grace had specifically told her "hands off," Susan saying in defense, "Well, you've never even met him, and, besides, you already have Alex" — now looking at her suddenly wide-eyed and saying, "So this is why you've got two of them. So that, if one of them dies, like all these boys in France, you'll still have someone to marry." And Grace yanking Susan's braid and Susan crying out and Grace still pulling, now screaming, "Don't say that! Don't *say* that!" And her mother slapping at the back of Grace's head until she let go — and her mute father, horror in his blue eyes.

Now the speaker onstage enthused: "We need your help — buy bonds and keep 'em flying!"

The crowd's wild cheers were muted by a sudden, thundering roar behind them. Grace turned to see an airplane coming in fast and low. It zoomed overhead; she whirled with the crowd as it barreled straight for a narrow space between two immense cranes, tipped on its side and whooshed through, drawing yells and gasps. Lena jumped up and down, squeezing Grace's arm and screaming. The plane straightened its wings and headed out over the harbor.

"That was Major Bong!" said someone onstage into the microphone. "Flying his famous P-38 fighter! Unbelievable!"

The men were cheering, some bending to pick up hats they'd lost, as the P-38, piloted by the local boy who was the USA's number one flying ace, rose, veering into a bank of clouds. Grace had read in the paper that Major Bong had promised to part people's hair down the middle buzzing the shipyards while he was home promoting the Fifth War Loan Drive, but she hadn't realized he'd meant it literally. "Oh my gosh!" Lena said. "I can't believe it was really him!"

"He's engaged, kid," Boots said, laughing. All around, tough shipbuilders were grinning, giggling; when they tried to walk, their knees wobbled and they laughed more. Grace saw Sean and another man congratulating each other as if they'd performed the feat themselves.

"I know," Lena said. "But still. Anyone want to come out to the airport with me after work and see if we can meet him? I heard the P-38 is going to be out there all week."

Violet said, "You were going to help me in the garden, Lena. You said you wanted your dad to rest and you would do it. We don't have time for fripperies. Now, if you wanted to date a *real* boy, instead of daydreaming about someone who's so clearly unavailable, we could discuss it."

Lena frowned. "All the *real* boys are gone, Mom."

"Well, then. If that's what you choose to

believe."

And Grace suddenly felt she couldn't bear the memory of her own mother, last night: "What on earth, young lady? Susan's a child! She doesn't understand! For goodness' sake, what are you, some kind of a caged animal?"

And Grace had said, "Yes!"

And her mother had looked at her like she was a bug on the bottom of someone's shoe.

Now another man onstage was urging the crowd again to support the work of Major Bong and other heroes like him; Grace heard men around her stating their intentions of a thousand dollars and more. Of course, they worked some ninety hours a week, much more than the sixty the women were allowed to work, so they could afford that much. Grace invested fifty percent of her pay in bonds; after taxes, union dues, insurance, and what she gave to her family, there wasn't much left.

But she had saved a little. For her California fund, but — for emergencies, too.

"Boots," she said, "you're looking for a flat in Superior, aren't you? How would you like a roommate?"

Boots grinned. "Just fine, Gracie! As long as we can find a place in this crowded town. I'll step up the search!"

"What about you, Lena?"

Lena's face brightened a moment. But then her smile faded; she glared at her mom. "I can't. *Someone's* got to take care of my dad."

Violet just shook her head; Grace had never seen her look so sad.

Saturday afternoon, Grace was feeling the effects of a sixty-hour week with hardly any sleep as she sat gripping the bench of a rowboat that was parked on the shore of Superior Bay. She'd wanted variety in her job, and now here she was, about to "weld on water" — and there was nothing religious about it. The rowboat was loaded down with iron plates that were to be tacked to the side of the *Westchester,* an oceangoing cargo ship being readied for its trip to New Orleans. "Here we go," Russ said, and she felt the sliding vibration in her seat as he pushed, then the buoyancy underneath. He jumped into the stern, grabbed the oars, and started rowing.

The sunshine on her face made her think of California, of Derrick; the rippling water reminded her of blue silk, dancing.

And if those dreams weren't going to come true, for the time being, she'd settle for the flat with Boots. She still planned to give her mother money, and to stop in at her parents' every day to check on her dad, but at least she'd have her own address, the chance sometimes to escape. Best of all, she wouldn't have to share a bedroom (or Derrick's letters) with Susan. She'd decided to speak to her mother only after Boots had found a place, so she wouldn't be able to stop her.

She'd decided not to think any more about the train.

"Any questions about the job?" Russ said.

She stifled a yawn. "No." She really shouldn't have stayed up so late last night, especially after being so short on sleep all week, but yesterday she'd received a note from Alex that said:

Your letters seem to get shorter and shorter. I can't help but want to ask you if everything is all right, or if you've had a change of heart. I know we didn't make any certain plans, but I want to tell you, my heart is still entirely yours. Remembering the times we had, and thinking of the times to come, has gotten me through an awful lot. I guess I've pretty much seen all I want to of the world, and I've learned along the way that you're really the best thing in it.

When I get home, there are a few things I plan to tell you (or should I say ask), unless you tell me now you'd rather I didn't.

It had taken her more than an hour to compose her reply, chewing on the end of her pencil until the taste of eraser dust coated the inside of her mouth:

I'm so sorry if I've made you doubt me. I guess I've been a little preoccupied, between work and home, the family, etc. But that's no excuse because I'm sure you have much greater things to pre-occupy you and it's only fair that you expect a bit more from me on the letter-writing end of things. I haven't wanted to burden you with all the details of home life, my dad, the long hours at work, yet my life consists of nothing else, so it can be hard to think of things to write. If I've lost my gumption for writing, it's not because of you, but because of everything else. I hope you can forgive me. I think of those times we had, too, and I dream about seeing you again. So to sum up, darling, don't worry about me. I'll be here with bells on when this darn war is over! You just worry about keeping yourself safe and getting back home.

All my love,
Grace

Reading it over, finally, she'd decided it was about eighty-five percent honest — not too bad a ratio in wartime. She wasn't about to break his heart for no good reason at all, not when he'd been gone too long for her to have any sense of how she would feel when he came back home.

Russ interrupted her thoughts. "I'm gonna be watching the boat traffic so we don't get caught off guard by a wake. We're gonna both be standing, so we'll have to watch our balance but good. I'll hold the plates up to the ship and you'll tack 'em on there, three or four good tack welds. Then we'll go back and finish 'em."

"All right," she said, craning her neck at the huge ship as their little boat cruised past its bow, like a bobbing duck circling a whale.

Soon Russ had the rowboat parallel to the cargo ship; it nudged the vast steel hull with each rhythmic wave. He dropped the anchor and hollered up to Sean, Les, and Al, who were on the big ship's deck, to lower Grace's cable and stinger.

"You guys look like Munchkins down

there," Les called, leaning over the rail, and, even from such a distance, Grace could see his toothy grin.

"You guys look like idiots up there," Russ called back, "but what's changed?"

Grace laughed, reaching for her stinger. She got it fixed up with a rod and put on her helmet while Russ gingerly stood to retrieve an iron plate. When he lifted it, Grace felt the rowboat's rocking in her stomach. Russ looked out to the bay. "No traffic, so we'll get this one done quick. Go on and stand up."

She stood, felt for an instant like she might topple. But she got her balance, and she and Russ stayed still until again the only motion of the boat was from the waves. Russ lifted the plate so its edge butted the hull. She raised her stinger, flipped down her visor, and braced her shoulder against the wall, like she always did.

Except it wasn't a wall — it was a ship, and her leaning pushed the rowboat away from it.

She felt her center of gravity sliding from her hips to her chest and then her shoulders, and she couldn't move, couldn't see anything through the visor and she felt herself falling toward the water —

A shocking force yanked her collar, and

then she was flat in the bottom of the rowboat, jarred up her spine, feeling only the mad rocking and trying to breathe.

She heard voices from above: her crew, cursing in disbelief and alarm.

She raised her helmet. Russ was still on his feet, knees bent funny, holding out his arms to keep his balance. As the rocking slowed, he lowered himself to the bench, reaching for her arm. "You all right?"

"I — I'm sorry. That was stupid. Habit." If she'd gone overboard with her heavy equipment on, she would have sunk straight to the bottom. She imagined the cold blue water closing over top of her until there was no trace left.

"I should have warned you," Russ said. "I know you always lean that way."

All she could think of was being underwater. *I've got to get out of here,* she thought. "I wasn't paying attention. I was tired."

Russ studied her. "Well, maybe you're not the hotshot you thought you were. But I need you on this crew. Now, are you ready to do this?"

She wanted to object: "Hotshot" was never her idea! And then she realized: there was no getting away. The war would keep going and going until it decided it was done, and Derrick was right, it would simply take

99

who it wanted: Harold, maybe Alex, maybe Derrick. Maybe her. Not today, but maybe another day. If not a fall, she might set herself on fire again.

But these ships had to be built, and they had to be delivered. If she gave up, how could she expect Alex and Derrick to make it home? "All right, yes," she said, and she straightened up, forced herself to stop shaking.

"Next time we have a job like that, I'd suggest you take me out, so nobody gets killed," Sean was saying, as the crew sped back toward the main yard in the pickup truck, toward banks of low gray clouds that were rolling in across the water. "She doesn't have the brains to realize what can happen in certain situations."

"You've got at least seventy-five pounds on her," Russ growled from the driver's seat. "Those damn plates are heavy enough for that little boat. And, O'Connor, what happens on the crew stays on the crew — or you don't."

Sean grumbled; Grace just hoped he would keep quiet. If everyone found out what she'd done, she'd probably be demoted no matter what Russ said. So, at the end of the day, when her friends commented on how wrecked she looked, she just said, "Guess I forgot to refresh my lipstick," trying to hide that her hands had started quaking again.

At home, Susan met her at the door with another letter from Derrick. Grace shook off the unease that struck her at the sight of her sister's braids; she grinned and made a show of checking to see that the envelope hadn't been steamed open. "I wouldn't!" Susan said. "But can I see what he wrote?"

"Very funny," Grace said, and she took the letter out to the front porch, shutting the door behind her. The rain had started and was pattering on the roof, streaming down the downspouts, turning the grass a darker shade of green.

There was a ten-dollar bill inside the envelope, which unnerved her. She stuffed it into her pocket and read:

Well, Grace, one of my good friends was killed yesterday. I don't want to worry my family, so I hope you don't mind if I "get it off my chest," because here goes.

The weather was rough and the deck was pitching badly. All of us planes got off fine and did our thing (training, don't worry) and finally came back around to land. It was a real white-knuckle time and I was reminding God that, although I may have my shortcomings lately, there were those times as a kid when I gave my precious nickels to the collection plate at Grace Lutheran in Blackberry Ridge, Wisconsin, U.S.A. ("I was the little blond kid whose sister kept poking me in the ribs to make me laugh so I'd get in trouble, remember?") As much as I might have told you things seem random out here, I'd like to see the man who could turn from God in moments like this. Lt. Nelson later said he thought the LSO — that's Landing Signal Officer — had to be crazy, the signals he was giving, that we were going to hit the back of the ship, but the deck pitched down at just the right moment and caught us. So, you can imagine me and Grabowski, after we landed, slapping each other on the back, and even Lt. Nelson, every few seconds, happy to be on the deck and sure everyone would make it since we had. But the next plane to approach fell short. We heard the shouts and ran. (They said later that a tremendous wave had reached up just as the deck pitched down — if he'd managed to get fifty yards ahead, the deck would have caught him — but the wave grabbed the tail and forced it into the water.)

So then we were shouting and leaning over the rail, screaming to "get the h*** out of there!" The pilot and gunner opened their hatches and got into the water, and they were able to inflate their lifeboat and climb in. But there was no sign of my friend Carter. The tail section was sinking. We yelled his name over and over.

I really don't want to think about the way that plane disappeared a little at a time and then all at once, or the sight of the pilot and gunner bobbing on the waves in their rubber boat, staring at that empty spot in the ocean, but it feels like all I can see. It's strange a man can exist for eighteen years and then in only a moment there's no single trace of him left. Today, Carter's replacement was up in the air with that same pilot and gunner. Hard for me to swallow just how little a fellow's being lost seems to matter out here, except to his friends, and even we are having a lot of trouble believing that it's really done and there's no taking it back.

Grace, I know this is a lot to ask, since we are only just getting to know each other, but from your letters I think you're one of the best girls out there, and I know my sister and mom think the same, and I've been thinking — if for some reason I don't make it through, will you do me a big favor and "look after" them for me? (Don't tell them I asked, it would only make them mad!) It would mean a lot to know I could count on you. I think they'd take it pretty hard if something were to happen to me, and my dad is not what you would call "reliable." One thing I have always wanted is to be a better man than him, and hopefully I will have the chance in the future to prove it. All right, enough said on that.

So, I still look forward to going up in the air! You probably think I'm nuts, but it's true. Besides, a guy doesn't want to think his friend lost his life for no good reason at all, so this makes the stakes even higher.

Speaking of "stakes," I'm going to send you ten dollars ("hard-earned" — I'm not so different from my dad, after all, am I?). Will you hold on to it so I can use it to take you dancing when I get home? (Money is not safe on this ship!) This way, even if I've lost my last dime,

when I get back we can still go dancing!
(I think about it a lot, Grace.)

Please write as soon as you can and tell me everything.

Yours,
Derrick

The letter trembled in Grace's hands. She looked up, out into the street, and saw a little girl in a pink dress riding by on a bicycle, her beribboned hair wetly plastered to her head. The girl was grinning, pumping the pedals hard, then she stood on them and coasted, for a moment throwing back her head, closing her eyes, and opening her mouth to catch the rain.

Summer 1944

All summer, working long hours on the odd-job crew, sweating in her coveralls, and getting a new sunburn on her face every time an old one had about turned to tan, Grace went home at night to sleep fitfully with dreams of choking on smoke and darkness, of falling into water, sinking down and down.

She did her best to keep her letters to Alex long and cheerful, to keep her eyes off the train. But what seemed to take no effort at all was writing to Derrick. She'd stowed his ten-dollar bill in her jewelry box, with a note clipped to it that said, *DERRICK! DANCING!* Despite knowing now just what dangers he faced, and despite the fact that she couldn't quite forget Susan's thoughtless comment, she was pleased he'd started telling her things that he hadn't even told Lena or Violet. In return, she'd told only him about her near miss in the rowboat, swearing him to secrecy, in the same letter that she'd written: *Of course I'd "look after" your mom and sister for you, but I'm counting on you to take me dancing, and I know you're too sweet to disappoint me, so I won't consider anything to be possible* except *that we will go dancing, and soon!* I didn't fall, *and neither will you.*

He'd replied, *Holy Cow, Grace, do you mind if I tell you to please be careful? But all right, your confidence is inspiring, and you'll have to forgive me for having my doubts about my "future," after seeing what happened to Carter. It really does help to know that you'll be there waiting (your Marine notwithstanding!) when I get back, but, Grace, you have to promise me that you're going to run a "safety check" on all your future jobs to the tune of "Would AOM2 Maki approve?" I am serious about that! And seriously, too, it does seem impossible to think that we wouldn't meet someday, you're right about that.*

The only things she didn't share with him — aside from her involuntary lingering fascination with the train — were Susan's comment and her own nightmares. She didn't want him to worry, or to regret telling her how his friend had disappeared into the water; she was sure the nightmares were more results of her own near miss. But she was tired of suffering alone, so, one morning, when Lena mentioned how tired she looked, she confessed, "I just keep having these dreams — I fall overboard and the water's so cold and dark, and I'm so heavy, I just keep sinking and sinking."

Lena smiled. "I don't see how anything bad like that could happen to a nice person like you, sis."

"Oh, so it's 'sis,' now?"

Lena winked. "Well, you know, if everything goes well . . ."

When Grace wrote to Derrick that Lena seemed to be getting some big ideas about them, he replied:

I guess you should know, Grace, my sister has this notion that she and I will split the farm, build a new house on a section, and be "next door neighbors" the rest of our lives. She thinks my time in the Navy should be plenty of "seeing the world" for anyone. (She's twenty minutes older than me, and because of this she's always thought she knows what's best for me — ha ha.) I think the longer I'm gone, the more she'll realize she can be just as happy without me, and that we aren't kids anymore and don't have to be "inseparable," when we want such different things in life.

Anyway, to be 100% honest, she has written to me her idea of how you and I will get hitched and the three of us (along with whoever she marries, I guess) will live "happily ever after" on the farm. I guess she probably set us up as pen pals with that in mind, since the two of you are such good friends. Maybe she didn't know we'd thwart her by planning to meet in California!

Seriously, Grace, I don't see myself coming back home to live, at least not for some time. Anyway, don't worry, my sister might be planning your life, but I intend to leave everything up to you as far as if you want anything to do with me after this war is over! I will make one promise, and that is I would never "in a million years" tie you to the farm, if "seeing the world" is what you want. For the time being, I want to see it, too, even if imagining my mom's cooking does make my mouth water even from a thousand miles away, ha ha. I'll admit that sometimes I do imagine stepping out the back door in the morning and the air in the fall (which smells like smoke) and the spring (the dirt and the rain) and the summer (hay that's just been cut) and the winter (ice). I guess I probably never have told you about the tree stand I built in the woods a few years back. It was where I would go to get "away from it all," even sometimes when I wasn't hunting, and, to be 100% honest, whenever I get a little "down and out" about Navy life, I picture the view from up there and (you might think I'm crazy) I feel peaceful again. So, anyway, I guess Lena's right that it's "home" and where I belong, and I suppose it's "inevitable" I'm bound to get back there "someday." Now you probably do really think I'm crazy, and wishy-washy at that, Grace.

But when she moved out of her parents' house, into a flat with Boots, and found herself reveling in the privacy and the freedom — and lying awake at night missing the sound of Susan's breathing and wondering how her dad was making it through the night and why her mother hadn't put up a fuss about her leaving and had offered extra linens and old furniture instead — she knew exactly what he meant.

Violet settled into the rocking chair, picked

up her mending. The scent of the fresh air coming in through the open window portended summer's inevitable fading. Lena was outside, finishing up the chores, so when the door banged, Violet supposed it was her. But then she heard Jago's humming.

"Any luck?" she called. He'd gone out fishing after supper.

He came into the room. His face was flushed. "Not tonight. Getting dark soon."

She pursed her lips. "Why don't you wind the clock?" It was one chore he'd insisted on taking full responsibility for; he rarely remembered to do it.

"Later." He sat down at the piano, played a few flourishes. "Say, what's going on with the kids and that girl Grace, do you think, ay?"

Violet felt heat rising in her face. Another letter had arrived from Derrick today; he'd asked several questions about Grace, and Lena had seemed triumphant at his growing interest. Though Violet still tended to wonder over Lena's motivations, she had, despite herself, begun to wish that Lena was onto something. Maybe the idea of Grace really could entice Derrick to come home, and they could all be together again. "Well, you know how she is when she sets her mind on something," she said carefully.

Jago nodded. Started playing a song she didn't recognize. Her hands made awkward stitches. She was always cautioning Lena against getting her hopes up, and yet, here she was, doing the same thing.

When Lena came in, she went to stand by Jago. "Let me sing with you, Dad. How about 'For Me and My Gal'?"

Her thin soprano sounded like the far part of the sky; his rumbling bass was as disconnected from it as the earth from heaven. When they were through, Violet set down her sewing to applaud. His voice could still get under her skin. Anyway, she was always happy to have her family's songs filling the house. And anything was better than listening to their new radio, the unending reports about places she'd never heard of, reports that only made her wish Derrick were there to explain where in the world places like Saipan and Saint-Lô and Guam were.

Lena twirled across the living room. "I can just imagine Derrick dancing with Judy Garland at the Hollywood Canteen, can't you? And to think, he was thinking of Grace even then. Getting her that autograph."

Jago laughed. "Now, kid, 'The course of true love never did run smooth,' remember."

Lena sighed, brushing her hair off her

face. "I know, Dad. It's just — well, I just know how much they'd like each other, that's all. I just want them to be happy."

Violet picked up her mending. "We miss him, too, Lena. But you do have to let those two live their own lives. We don't want to see you disappointed."

Lena rolled her eyes. "Excuse me, Mrs. Doom and Mr. Gloom, I have a letter to write." She ran upstairs.

Jago shrugged and turned back to the piano.

Later, in bed, Violet's chest was aching. "You should have thought of her, at least, when you signed those papers," she said, staring up into the darkness.

"He would have gone anyway." Jago's voice was wistful. "A boy has to make his own way. And it isn't easy, at that age, you know. You want so much. You want so much, and it's all so possible and so out of reach, at once, ay."

Violet said nothing. It occurred to her: the clock hadn't chimed. Had Jago neglected again to wind it? Or, in Derrick's absence, had gravity truly lost its pull?

Fall 1944

September had its share of dazzling blue skies and crisp nights; leaves began down-shifting their greens to hues of orange and gold. October commenced with a cold drizzle, and a windstorm stripped the trees, leaving skeletons. Grace dragged for two weeks with the flu, Violet bringing her homemade chicken soup in a Thermos and Russ telling her to go home. She wouldn't; Sean would have used her absence to argue that the crew could do without her for good. In the meantime, though, her correspondence lagged, and she worried that Derrick would imagine she'd had a change of heart, that Alex would think her faithless. But, after just a few days, Derrick wrote, *My sister tells me you've been battling the "flu" in your own private war, and you haven't taken a sick day yet. Patriotism is one thing, but there're enough people dying for it these days, don't you think? Seriously, I want you to take good care of yourself. I'm going to be coming home to take you dancing before you know it, remember, and if you're not in shape for it, I'll have some pretty hurt feelings, I can tell you. There, how's that? Are you going to eat your chicken soup now?*

On the first evening that she actually felt capable of staying upright, her friends came into the locker room as she was changing. Preoccupied with the letters she intended to write when she got home — she'd sent Derrick a quick note this morning in response to a letter that had arrived yesterday, but she wanted to say so much more — she didn't even hear them until Lena called, "Hollywood! You look half alive instead of half dead."

Grace laughed. "Isn't that the same thing?"

Boots had picked up the afternoon newspaper. "Uh-oh."

"What is it?" Violet said.

Boots passed the paper to Grace, who stopped taking off her coveralls to read, FIERCE NAVAL BATTLE IN LEYTE GULF; AIRCRAFT CARRIER SUNK BY JAPS.

She scanned the article and found the name. Derrick's ship.

"What is it?" Lena said.

115

"Grace?" said Violet.

They scrambled for the paper. When she saw, Violet leaned against the lockers, color draining from her face; Lena skimmed for information. "Seven hundred out of the nine hundred men survived!" Her eyes were fevered. "He's all right, I'm sure of it!"

Grace hid her face in her hands.

As much as it seemed to Grace she should just be constantly praying, it was some relief to work, to feel she was making some progress on something, as time crawled and no answers came. The few days since they'd seen the news felt like an entire season, especially after a storm came, freezing rain slicking up the steel beams. With the wind bitter off the lake, warmth seemed as distant a memory as dancing with that railroad man, Joe. It was back again to itchy wool underwear sandwiched between the smoother cotton underwear, to thick wool pants and shirt upon shirt upon shirt under her heavy wool jacket and heavier leather coveralls, to the feeling that her fingers wouldn't bend and her face might crack in two if she smiled.

Not that she felt much like smiling.

Lena kept saying she was certain Derrick was one of the seven hundred survivors, that she'd feel it in her bones if her twin was gone. "He probably wasn't even on the ship when it went down!" she'd insisted. "He was probably in the air, shooting down Jap planes." Violet, though paler than ever, appeared somewhat reassured by Lena's certainty, and by the fact that a few days had passed without their receiving a telegram. But Grace couldn't seem to shake the feeling that maybe she was going to be punished for her folly.

She'd been trying to write to him as usual, but it was so hard to know what to say.

"Anderson, you up to going in?" Russ didn't wait for an answer. "You lower yourself down in there and we'll pass you your equipment. You'll have to pull it all the way through with you, all the way to the end, and you'll see the place, all right? There aren't any air hoses, but it's just one small weld, you'll be fine."

The inspectors had found an unsatisfactory weld in this nearly finished ship, in the bilge, where cubelike structures with cutout circular openings about twenty inches in diameter tunneled to the tip of the prow. After everything was assembled, getting down in there was nearly impossible.

"Boss, I can go," Sean objected.

"No way would your shoulders fit through

there, O'Connor. You ready, Anderson? You'll want to take off a few layers of clothes, so you don't get stuck."

Sean smirked at that. Grace glared, started unbuttoning her jacket.

Fitting, she thought, to descend into a place where she couldn't breathe.

Down to her pants and long underwear, plus her two long underwear tops, her welding helmet, and two pairs of wool socks, she crawled into the hold and had soon inched her way on her elbows almost to the end of the white steel tube, holding Russ's flashlight in one hand, towing her equipment and electrical cords with the other, sure that at any moment her hips were going to get stuck. The light reflected like ghosts haunting the tiny passageway. The smell of paint was almost a solid thing. Russ called encouragement to her, his voice echoing.

Reaching the final cube, she rolled onto her back and brought her stinger to her chest, using the flashlight to locate the place overhead that needed the weld. Sparks were going to come down all over her helmet and shirt. She said a little prayer that she wouldn't catch fire, or that she'd at least be able to finish her weld before it got bad. If she didn't complete the work, the inspectors wouldn't let the ship leave the harbor.

She heard her first supervisor: "You want us to lose this war because of *you?*"

She flipped down her helmet and fired up her stinger. When she touched it to the metal, sparks flew and smoke billowed, filling the chamber.

She inched out backward, coughing, dragging her equipment. She'd finished the weld without catching fire, but all the smoke in such a confined area had been overwhelming. As her crew hauled equipment to the truck, she expended her remaining energy putting on her clothes and boots, and ended up propped against a railing, too weak to continue. Sean came back and slung her over his shoulder to carry her. If she'd had the strength, she would have fought his touching her, but her limbs flopped like a marionette's. When he slid her onto the truck's seat, she nearly toppled. He caught her, and, as he climbed in beside her, he said, "Lean on my shoulder, that's right."

She wanted to protest, but she had to lean on something.

She heard Russ say, "I guess I shouldn't have had her go in without the air hoses. But I don't know if she'd have fit through there."

"You should have had me go in," Sean said.

"You wouldn't have fit at all."

"We'd better take her to the nurse. Take some deep breaths, Hotshot."

I'm going to be fine, she intended to tell them, but she must have passed out instead.

She opened her eyes to her crew looming over her with hats in hands, as if they were paying their last respects. Recognizing their surroundings as the nurse's office, she coughed. "Fellows, I'm not dead."

Relief dawned on their faces. Russ grinned and swooped to kiss her forehead, his beard tickling her. Then he caught himself, blushed bright red, and straightened. "All right, Anderson, glad to see you're up and about. We're going back to work, but you take as much time as you need, the whole afternoon if you want, that was a tight spot and I'm sorry. Come on, gang."

As they filed out, Grace overheard Les saying, "Gee, boss, you've never kissed *my* forehead, even that time I was in the hospital."

She spent a few hours swimming in a nightmare-laced sleep. She couldn't help wondering how many near misses she would be granted. If Derrick would be granted a crucial one.

When she finally awoke, she was hungry. Ignoring the nurse's protests, she dragged herself up to cross the windswept yard. The warmth of the cafeteria was a comfort. She sat down at one end of a long, empty table with her coffee and doughnut, blinking to soothe her smoke-dry eyes.

Derrick's latest letter, the one that had arrived the day before the news of his ship's sinking, was in her coat pocket, and she took it out of its battered envelope, smoothing the pages next to her coffee cup. She'd read it at least a dozen times; it seemed the only ground on which she had to stand.

Dear Grace,

Wow, was I happy to get your last letter. I've been awfully busy, but it hasn't seemed to do any good toward the problem of not being able to stop thinking about going dancing with my favorite "pen pal." I only wish I had more time to write. I'll make it up to you someday, I promise! Meanwhile, I hope you'll keep writing as much as you can. Your letters mean more than I can say.

You asked what we've been doing. For now let me just tell you that I will have quite some stories to tell my grandkids someday. I'll tell you someday, too, I promise.

Now you'll have to forgive me, because there's something serious I want to say to you. (Ahem.) I want to tell you there's never been any girl who's fascinated me for any period of time the way that you have. To be 100% honest, I've always been the type of guy to crash and burn, meaning I fall hard for a pretty face and later learn the substance behind it leaves a lot to be desired. I guess maybe I feel different about you because you want to see the world, too, and what makes it perfect is that if you were with me I'd have "home" with me, too. (Maybe my sister does know best, after all!) Most of the girls I knew in Blackberry Ridge didn't have dreams beyond maybe getting to Superior on a Saturday night, which to me was only the bottom rung of the ladder, not the top, as it was for them.

Now, I'm sure your Marine is taller and more handsome than me, Grace, but from what you've told me, he seems to be one of those who doesn't ask what more the world has to offer. I wonder if you have considered this. I guess what

I'm saying is that I hope you will. (I know I promised not to interfere, but sometimes a sailor has to stand up and say something.) I'm not perfect by any means, but it's possible, I think, that I could be perfect for you, and you for me. Maybe that's strange to say when we've never met in person, but I feel I know you, Grace, from your letters, and from what my sister has told me, and I think you're coming to know me better than anyone. I don't plan to be limited by "where I come from" as much as I plan to look ahead to where I can get to, and I believe you want to do the same, but you seem shy about breaking free of what you see as your obligations. I want to encourage you to see that obligations to "family" and "Marines" (ha ha) may be honorable, but there are other ways of being honorable, too. Maybe I'm "reading between the lines" too much in your letters, but I'm going to go out on a limb and say I think you are beginning to like me "a little bit"??? Grace, I believe that if you devote your life to something or someone that you aren't 100% passionate about, you will regret it. I think the "sky's the limit" for you, Grace, and I want you to believe it, too.

Write me and tell me you believe it, Grace.

Yours,
Derrick

Folding the letter back into its envelope, Grace remembered what she'd written in her initial quick reply. *I want to try to believe it, I do, and sometimes it seems all I can think of is the day when we finally meet, because I think I'll know immediately then what to do. (I hope you don't think me a coward in the meantime.)* In all the days since his ship had gone down, the post office hadn't returned this letter — or the ones she'd sent after, explaining she was praying and praying, and, if only he'd be all right, she was pretty sure she knew exactly what she wanted — which really was a hopeful sign.

Now her head still ached, and she was coughing sporadically, but reading Derrick's words had restored her. She took another sip of coffee, a bite of her doughnut. And then a personnel manager was standing at the end of the table. Grace, conscious of his clean white shirt, hid her filthy hands. Was she going to be fired for ignoring safety protocol in the bilge? But that had been Russ's call! And they didn't fire skilled welders these days, did they?

But the manager said, "Grace Anderson? You know Violet Maki, don't you?"

Grace wished for an instant that she didn't, that he was talking to anyone else. She could barely nod.

"I need you to do me a favor," the manager said. "We just got a phone call from her husband. They got a telegram about her son. Will you go find her and tell her he's missing in action? We're busy in the office."

"What?" Her voice was a whisper.

"Sometimes this news is better coming from a friend. Tell her she can come to the office and sign out for the day." He turned away.

"Wait," Grace managed, but he was gone. She coughed until tears streamed down her face.

In a cargo hold of Hull 41, every pound of every hammer felt like it was directly on her forehead. She asked a man where she could find Violet; her vision blurred when he pointed. She didn't know how she was going to say the words. But she shuffled over and waited, watching the sparks fly. Finishing, Violet raised her helmet; her eyes crinkled when she saw Grace.

Grace took one step closer. Then one more.

Violet's brow furrowed; her mouth pursed.

Grace stood there, tears burning tracks down her cheeks.

"Tell me," Violet said.

Tell me everything, Grace thought. She blinked. Swallowed. "Your husband got a telegram," she managed. " 'Missing in action.' "

Violet stared, her eyes welling with horror.

Violet asked Grace to come with her to tell Lena, and though it was the last thing Grace wanted to do, she couldn't say no. *He asked me to take care of them.*

But she couldn't believe it had come to this.

At the news, Lena's lip trembled; her usually breathy voice was like steel. "Then he'll be found soon. Where did you get that information?"

Grace explained.

Lena shook her head. "He's going to be fine," she snapped. Grace had never seen her gray eyes so dark.

The three women went to the office for more information, but all anyone could tell them was what Jago Maki had said when he called: a telegram had arrived at the farm stating that Derrick was missing in action

126

as of October 25, when the airplane he was manning had disappeared in the midst of the battle. Violet and Lena were excused from work for the afternoon, along with John Tuomi, their ride. Grace went with them to the locker room. Lena kept insisting that Derrick would turn out to be fine. "I'd know it if he were gone," she said, shoving her helmet into her locker, running a dirty hand through her dirty white-blond hair. "I would."

After seeing them off, Grace crossed the yard, intending to search for her crew. But with Violet and Lena gone, she couldn't stop crying, and she wasn't watching where she was going. The train idled on the track, but all she could seem to see was Derrick at the bottom of the ocean, her nightmare of being swallowed by water come true.

She didn't hear the footsteps approaching, but she had no strength to be surprised by the hand that gripped her elbow. "Hey, are you all right?"

She focused her eyes. She hadn't seen Joe up close since the first time she'd recognized him in the yard, months earlier; she had almost stopped thinking of him. Still, his indigo eyes seemed familiar. "I'm fine," she said, wiping at her face. She could hardly imagine how smudged and wrecked she looked; she found she didn't care.

"You don't look in any condition to work." He reached into his pocket and handed her a handkerchief.

She used it. "Thanks."

He smiled. "Have you been out fighting fires?"

"Something like that." She coughed.

He touched her elbow. "What's the matter?"

"My pen pal. He's missing. His plane disappeared. And his aircraft carrier sank."

Joe's eyes softened, went dim. "Oh. Jesus. I'm sorry." He turned away, covering his mouth to cough.

How dare he be home safe in Superior when other boys were going missing, dying? "What are you doing back here?" she snapped.

His face reddened. He wouldn't meet her gaze. "I see you're not seventeen anymore."

"Twenty." So he did recognize her. She still doubted he'd recall her name.

"You look different in your work clothes."

She wished the ground would steady; she felt seasick. She gripped the letter in her pocket.

"Do you think we could bury the hatchet, Grace? I honestly — I mean, I think you

128

got the wrong idea about me, that night — I didn't want to offend you."

She shrugged. Her astonishment annoyed her. "It makes no difference to me, *Joe.* I have a boyfriend, a Marine. And my pen pal, the sailor —" Her vision clouded.

She felt him step closer, like he was trying to shield her. "I'm sorry," he said.

She stood, blotting her face with his handkerchief, conscious of the warmth emanating from him. She remembered how she'd felt dancing with him, so long ago; how she hadn't wanted any song to end.

"Look, I got rheumatic fever," he said. "I flew twelve missions and then they sent me home from England. I'm supposed to be on bed rest."

She glanced up. He really did look awful: that pasty complexion. "You have rheumatic fever? That stuff could kill you. Why aren't you home resting?"

"How could I stay in bed and rest when my friends are out there dying?"

She felt something pass between them, almost as if they'd touched.

And then in her mind again was the image of a little plane spiraling from the sky, sinking below the vast surface of the ocean. She turned, hurried away. She could see Derrick, fathoms deep, his face expressionless, the rocking of the current making him look as if he were shaking his head in gentle protest.

The next morning, Violet and Lena were back at work. Violet was as ashen-faced as oxygen-deprived Grace, but Lena just looked tired. Every time someone offered their hopes and prayers, she'd smile and say, "Thanks so much! He's fine, really; we'll hear from him any day, I'm sure. Or hear something from somewhere, from the Navy! Imagine all that has to be straightened out, after a big battle like that! All the people that have to be sorted and found!"

But when Grace went into the restroom late that afternoon, she found Lena leaning on the sink, gazing into the mirror with vacant, reddened eyes.

"Is there anything I can do, Lena?" Grace ventured. "Anything at all?"

"You believe he's still alive, don't you? Promise me you do."

"Of course, Lena!" Though, at the sudden brightness of the girl's eyes, Grace almost regretted saying it.

A tear broke free, trailed down Lena's cheek. "As long as you believe, too — then I can stand it."

Grace felt that like an immunization shot:

a pinching, deep pain.

Lena turned back to the mirror, meeting Grace's eyes in their reflection. "It's hardest when I'm alone. And at home. His chair at the table. His empty bed." She slipped her arm through Grace's; her mouth quivered. "I know he's going to end up being fine, but — it's just so hard."

So that evening after work, the sky nearly full dark already, and a sleet-rain mix falling, Grace crammed into the cab of John Tuomi's pickup truck with John, Violet, and Lena. Both women had seemed grateful when she'd suggested that she could spend the night at their farm. "Maybe there'll be news today," Lena had said. "Then you can know he's all right the very minute we do."

Grace had focused on her bootlaces.

The yellow light radiating from the farmhouse windows didn't offset the loneliness Grace sensed hovering as she stepped out of the truck under the dark expanse of sky. The barn in the distance looked haunted. Mist coated her face, and she shivered, thinking of the bottom of the sea.

Lena ran for the house, but Grace, nervous — and not wanting to be rude — stayed with Violet, who moved stiffly, clos-

131

ing her eyes every few seconds, as if in brief prayer, trusting her feet to keep moving without the benefit of sight.

When they finally stepped into the warm kitchen, Lena was sitting at the table, chin in hand, eyes cast down. The man in front of the stove turned. Grace had to swallow her shock: it seemed Derrick's photo might just have come to life before her, aged cruelly, the face wrinkled like crepe paper, the belly and jowls distended. "Nothing today," Jago said, in a rumbling voice that seemed to rise all the way from his heels.

Grace wondered if Derrick's voice was as deep. She hadn't imagined it that way at all.

"Tomorrow," Lena said, her fingertip tracing an invisible line on the table.

Conscious of Violet, deflating, next to her, Grace gazed down at her ratty wool socks and was embarrassed to realize that her toes were wiggling in pleasure at being free from her boots and in the kitchen's warmth. She stopped them. She wished she hadn't come; she felt that this place had already swallowed her, that she'd never been so helpless in her life.

At the supper table, Lena went on about what might have happened to Derrick: his plane had landed at sea and he was floating on a raft or washed up on some shore, or his plane had crashed on a remote island and he was being cared for by a native tribe. Or maybe he'd been rescued by the Navy but had lost his memory and clothes and couldn't be identified.

"Mom and Dad, you remember, when we were nine and he broke his arm down by the creek?" She turned to Grace. "I was in the barn and I felt the pain in my arm, and I knew something had happened, and I went to find him." She took a sip of milk, wiped her mouth with her hand. "If he were dead, I'd feel it, and I don't. I know he's still alive. *Se ei pelaa, joka pelkää,* right, Dad?"

While Grace wondered what that meant, Violet shoved back her chair, stood, and walked stiffly to the kitchen.

Grace had the impulse to go to her, but she heard the creak and slam of the back door: Violet, going outside. Wanting to be alone. So Grace stayed still. In the other room, a clock chimed.

"I know you feel that way, kid," Jago rumbled, as if Violet hadn't been there at all.

"I know it's true." Lena turned to Grace and translated: " 'He who's afraid does not gamble.' "

"I know, kid," Jago sighed. "I want to

believe it, too. Just — keep a twenty percent window, ay? So it doesn't kill you if —"

Lena cursed. She blinked back tears. "I will not, Dad."

"Fifteen percent, then. Something."

"You've got to be on my side, Dad," Lena said, drumming the table with her fingertips. "You've always said you would be. Always."

"I am. I am on your side." He squeezed his eyes shut, as if trying to conjure magical powers.

Lena slammed her hand flat. "Then you have to believe."

Tell me you believe it, Grace. Grace pressed her fist to her mouth, and, when Lena's gray gaze flashed onto hers, she couldn't bear the longing in it; she closed her eyes, too.

Later, with the dishes done, Jago outside to coax Violet in, and Lena upstairs to change into her pajamas, Grace found herself alone in the living room. It was sparsely furnished but very clean, with large rag rugs strewn across the pine floor, walls of exposed logs and chinking, a grandfather clock marking time in the far corner, and a pretty arrangement of dried flowers mounted on the wall next to a fiddle. An upright piano was stationed against the wall, an accordion on the floor next to it, a ukulele on top. Stacks of sheet music overloaded a small shelf; books were crammed on a larger one, along with scrapbooks labeled PLANTS, 1932–34; TREES, 1933–36; and so on. The furniture was run-of-the-mill Sears catalog stuff, probably years old, but well polished. A wood-burning stove stood next to the wall that hid the steep stairs to the attic.

Despite the rustic feel of the place, it was cozy and warm, and Grace thought she'd been wrong, upon first arriving, to sense loneliness hovering, to feel so trapped.

She didn't hear Jago behind her until he said, "What you expected?" She turned to see him smiling his wrinkled smile, a cigarette smoldering in his hand.

"I — I'm sorry," she said, hating that he'd assumed she was judging the place. "I was just thinking. It feels like . . . home. Like Derrick said."

Jago stubbed out his cigarette. "What else did he tell you, ay?"

"Oh, I —"

"He might not care about me, but he wouldn't do this to his mother, would he?"

Grace swallowed. "Violet . . . is she all right?"

His face contorted. "Out in the barn with the animals. Says she feels less alone out there, can you beat it?" He squeezed his eyes shut again, opened them. "That kid. Had to be a hero and go in early! Had to have me sign those goddamn papers. As if I could have refused him. And now this. Hurting his mother this way . . ."

"Mr. Maki, he never would mean to . . . I mean, it really isn't up to —"

"Goddamn, the war, I know!" Jago said. "We're 'fortune's fools'! You want to think you can control it, or that he . . . that there's some way to predict . . . And I don't know what Lena'll do, what any of us, if —"

Grace cried, "The odds are good! Seven hundred out of nine hundred!"

"Seventy-seven point seven percent! I know! Goddamn. Odds!" He took a deep breath; his eyes went flat. "You two with your hearts on your sleeves. I'm sorry to see you suffer this." And before she could think what to say, he turned from her, crossed the room, and sat at the piano. She recognized the tune of "I'll Be with You in Apple Blossom Time"; a few measures in, his warm voice quavered to life. Lena came downstairs and stood at the foot of the steps to listen, looking like a child in her pajamas and robe, tears streaming from her tired eyes.

They assigned Grace to Derrick's bed, in the unheated attic, on the opposite side of a

136

heavy red velvet curtain from Lena. Grace crawled into it gratefully, but she couldn't sleep. Despite the many blankets piled on her, she was shivering, remembering the events of the day and thinking despite herself of all the times Derrick had slept between this same set of sheets and what he might feel like, lying with her.

"Whenever we got into trouble, he'd be able to get us out of it," Lena had said. "Not that he's dishonest at all. Just naturally innocent. I mean, people believe he doesn't mean any harm, and, really, he never does. He just likes to make everyone happy. And he's always been lucky. Getting out of scrapes, you know? That's why I know he'll be found. 'Missing in action' just means they don't know exactly where he is right now, that's all. And how could they, when the ship where he was living is gone?"

Lena's various scenarios played out in Grace's mind. She tried to imagine him resting in a Pacific island hut, a native woman smoothing a cool cloth over his forehead. The vision alternated with the persistent, horrific one of him dead and rocking at the bottom of the sea.

Downstairs, Violet was awake, too, cold to her bones despite the quilts and Jago's heat next to her, clenching her teeth against the sounds of his snoring. Her thoughts swung from misery to misery. Insomnia. Jago's noises. Yesterday's telegram. A sinking ship. A tiny airplane vanishing into clouds. Derrick! She would want to scream. Then she would say to herself, *Sleep!* And the thoughts would begin again.

The snoring! There might as well have been a jackhammer in bed with her. And he thrashed like a fish in the bottom of a boat. An elbow in her face. A kick to her leg. If ever she came close to sleep, she was jarred out of it.

She flopped onto her stomach and yanked her pillow over her head.

She hated him, *hated him.*

If Jago hadn't signed those papers, if Derrick had waited to enlist until he was eighteen, he wouldn't have been assigned to that ship. He probably wouldn't have been in that terrible battle at all. And Violet wouldn't be lying here now barely able to breathe and counting the chimes of the grandfather clock that Jago, today, had finally wound. Yesterday, they simply hadn't believed the news. Today, they were counting down toward something, counting away from something else. One more hour gone. And one more.

She remembered another long-ago night. The blood, the clutching emptiness of her womb. The eight-year-old twins had been asleep in the attic. She could imagine them even now, the way she'd pictured them that night: sleeping sweet faces, quilts to their chins, in their two twin beds with the red velvet curtain hung between.

That night, Jago's eyes had been like silver dinner plates in the moonlight. He'd come out wondering why she hadn't returned from what should have been a short trip to the privy. He found her sprawled on the dew-damp grass and dirt behind the house. On his face was the horror of realization.

"My fault," he said, reaching for her. She bowed her head. The air smelled of smoke from the chimney. Jago's store was sitting empty, spices waiting in their tins. He was gone for days at a time, said he was looking for work. But she'd see his bloodshot eyes and notice bills of her egg money missing, no matter where she hid it. The last time, he'd taken all but two dollars. She'd fumed, while part of her wondered: *Why not take it all, if he was going to take it?*

But she'd hoped the new baby might make him stay home again. When the twins were infants, he'd come home early every night to hold them and rock them and sing

139

to them.

Had she killed it with her hard work? All those hours in the fields, the barn, the steamy kitchen with the canning kettle? Selling her pasties out of the kitchen, to those few who could afford them? (More often, giving them away, grudgingly, to hungry hoboes who'd stumbled off the train in Blackberry Ridge, looking for food, like locusts.)

She wanted to tell him how he'd hurt her; how she hurt everywhere. But the words that came were: "You have to help me. We can't lose our home!"

"I know," he said, wide-eyed, still reaching for her. "I know!"

The haze of memory now. Was it true that by the time Lena and Derrick came scampering downstairs the next morning, Violet was at the stove stirring a pan of Cream of Wheat, melting butter in the skillet for their eggs?

Lena: "Look, Mom! Derrick's a pirate. He's got a glass eye!"

And Derrick, smirking, holding something to his left eye. Then Violet saw: between his forefinger and thumb was a marble, the exact cool blue shade of his eyes.

She gripped the oven door handle. Thinking of her long-gone father and his flat-glass eyes; Jago in the moonlight, the night before.

"He won't even need a patch, now!" Lena went on.

Violet set down her spoon. Clumsily, she picked a waiting egg off the butcher block and cracked it on the skillet.

The contents slid into the sizzling butter. In the yolk was a spot of blood. Violet dropped the shell and staggered back.

"What's the matter?" Lena asked, coming to look.

Violet blinked. She'd planned to act as if nothing were different, and now she'd ruined everything, and they would know.

But Lena scoffed. "Oh, gosh, Mom. It's nothing." The egg was congealing; Lena picked out the pieces of shell with a fork.

Violet, watching, was unable even to say, *Be careful! You'll burn yourself!*

"We can't waste *food,*" Lena said, echoing Violet's habitual refrain.

Derrick tugged Violet's skirt. "Do you want my marble, Mom?"

Lena fixed him in a cool look. "Mom doesn't collect *marbles.* Besides, you can't give away your *eye.*"

Was it Violet's imagination that, as Lena turned back to the skillet, there was something ghostly about her? That Derrick, gazing up at Violet, was a blur?

That afternoon, or sometime shortly after, the telephone rang. The Makis' ring on the party line: two long, one short. Violet listened as Irma Warner, the owner of Ma's Kitchen café, chattered on about her health: gout, a swollen foot, doctor's orders to *stay off,* and maybe she was ready to retire anyway. "So, I need some help at the café. I thought, you don't have little kids, and I *know* you can cook. Wait tables. Didn't I hear you used to?"

That evening, as Violet sat in the rocking chair mending a pair of Derrick's pants, she told Jago that she was going to be working in town from 5:00 A.M. till 2:00 P.M., Monday through Saturday, and he would have to get the twins off to school in the mornings. He looked up from the newspaper. His eyes filled. Or was that a trick of the light? "Violet," he said, "you have to trust me, ay?"

She just kept pushing the needle in, pulling it out, thinking of the empty jar her egg money had been in. If she was hurting him, it was for the sake of the farm. There was still a mortgage on the defunct store. No one was going to buy the building, not in these dark times.

"I don't see how I can — without you —"

In and out. In and out.

Now Jago was shaking her awake. She hadn't realized she'd drifted off; had believed she never would. "Violet, I can't sleep," he said. "Is the shipyard still hiring?"

Am I dreaming? she thought.

But he was waiting for an answer. She found herself recalling her astonishment when the twins had turned out to be serious coffee drinkers by age nine, albeit with liberal cream. "Dad makes us sing for our breakfast! Or recite Mr. Snakes-spear," Lena had explained. "We have to be awake!" A less happy Derrick described how Jago would stand at the roaring stove, teaching new verses and lines and Finnish vocabulary words while he scrambled eggs, wearing what they all termed his "city slicker" clothes, a flour-sack towel tied around his waist to protect his once-fine pants, which were, by this time, a little threadbare. "I don't know why he can't just feed us like you do, Mom," Derrick said.

"He does *help* us, though," Lena said. (Later, as tonight, she and Jago would speak their Finnish phrases when they didn't want Violet to understand.)

Now Violet could imagine him coaching

them: "All that glitters is not gold. Tempt not a desperate man." And his young bass: "This old man, he played one." The twins, half shouting, half singing in reply: "He played knickknack on my thumb!"

This old man, he played two.
He played knickknack on my shoe!

She remembered the evenings when he would help Lena identify and preserve the plant specimens she'd collected in the woods, while Derrick nearby studied his maps. Violet had always used what egg money remained to spring for Derrick's magazines; Jago had scraped together enough to buy Lena a plant guide and scrapbooks. He'd encouraged his daughter to share his passion for languages, but he'd been willing to learn about what fascinated her, too. And sometimes Derrick would pipe up with a tidbit for Violet: "In Mogok, the monsoons wash rubies right out of the ground! And Burmese warriors put the stones under their skin to protect them from being wounded in battle!"

Violet wondered how they all could have drifted so far from the things they loved. Was it her fault?

How she wished she'd had a ruby to give to Derrick. Anything that might have protected him. Though maybe she'd foolishly imagined that her love would be enough. When had it ever been? "Yes, they're always hiring," she said now. "I think they're looking for painters. You shouldn't need any special training for that. A lot of motion, though, painting."

"I'll endure it."

Her eyes welled. She tossed off the covers, tried to get up, but he grabbed her. There were tears in his eyes, too.

"Lena," she choked, struggling against his embrace, falling into it.

He clutched her. "Yes, all right. We just won't tell her. We won't tell her we're afraid."

■ ■ ■ ■

PART TWO:
TIME

■ ■ ■ ■

May 2000

Julia reached the crest of the last hill loving the rhythm of mile six, her sheen of sweat, the crunch of her shoes on the gravel road, the springing of roadside wildflowers around lingering patches of dirty snow. All winter, in the muted light, the horses' moist breath on her hand when she'd offered a carrot or apple had seemed the only evidence of actual life — that or her own breath making steam as she ran the frozen roads, pulling her hat lower over her ears to fight the wind. Now, unthinkable as it sometimes seemed that time just went on, she had to acknowledge her relief at the lengthening of the days, at not having to suffer any longer in the cold.

She was feeling good, thinking, *I could do seven miles, just keep going,* when an old blue pickup turned the corner from Blackberry Ridge Road, coming toward her —

and then turned in to the driveway at Alice and George's.

She slowed, dismayed, annoyed. She'd been imagining an invisible fence around the place, imagining she'd have it to herself until her aunt and uncle returned.

She considered running past, pretending the visitor was no concern of hers — but maybe it was something important.

As she veered in to the driveway, a tiny woman, her hair a wispy cloud of white, climbed stiffly out of the truck. She was old-looking even from a distance, and she wore a tucked-in plaid shirt and too-big jeans, secured around her narrow waist with a rope belt.

"Hello?" Julia called, taking her hair down and twisting it up into a fresh knot as she approached, with effort slowing her legs, which seemed to want to keep going.

The woman swung the truck door closed; it creaked, slammed. Her spotless white Keds planted like a rooted tree, she lifted her hand to shade her eyes. "Alice?"

That stopped Julia; she lodged her fists on her hips. *She knows my aunt,* she chided herself, *so she must be a friend.* "I'm sorry, Alice isn't here," she said.

"But she does still live here?"

"Yes, but she's traveling. She's not going

to be home for a few months."

The woman frowned. "Well, that could be far too late."

As if *Julia* were the one intruding! "Well, if you give me your name, I can tell her you stopped by, maybe she could call you —"

"Some good that will do —" The woman pressed her hand to her temple.

"Are you all right?" Julia ventured. The cool breeze was raising goose bumps on her sweaty skin.

The woman's hand lowered, trembling; sunlight glinted on her glasses. "What about Grace?"

"What?"

The woman flinched as if in surprise. She reached for the truck door handle, but her eyes rolled back and her hand fumbled at air as her legs gave way.

Julia lunged and caught her; she was heavier than she looked, and Julia was brought to her knees, lowering the woman to the grass, registering the slack mouth, the glasses askew on the bridge of the sun-mottled nose, the map of white lines on the weathered face. She feared the worst.

But when she saw the chest rising and falling with steady breaths, she jumped up and raced for the telephone.

■ ■ ■ ■

She followed the ambulance in her Corolla, clutching the wheel with both hands, realizing she hadn't driven anywhere in weeks, except rarely to the tiny market in the eight-block-square town of Blackberry Ridge, where she bought her staples of apples, peanut butter, and Death by Chocolate ice cream, giving brief answers to the cashier's questions about Alice and George's travels, trying to ignore the comments on how skinny she was getting or how so-and-so had seen her run past their place. Even more rarely, she would drive the twenty-five miles to the big hardware store in Superior and fill a cart with paint, stain, rollers, brushes, tape, putty, sandpaper, spackle, sponges, buckets, how-to books. If they were getting to recognize her there, no one ever acknowledged it.

When the paramedic told her that someone would have to bring the woman back home, Julia had protested, "But this isn't her home! I don't even know who she is!" Of course, her objections had done no good.

Now she wondered, if the woman was a friend of Alice's, how could she have mistaken Julia for Alice, when Alice was thirty years older, forty pounds heavier, and a couple inches taller, too? Besides, Alice's friends all knew about Alice and George's RV trip, and when Julia had spoken with her yesterday, there'd been no mention of potential visitors.

And Alice wasn't going to be calling again for almost a week. She'd said yesterday that she'd finally convinced George to leave the comfort of the RV, and they were going wilderness camping in the Sequoia National Forest. Julia had actually been pleased at the prospect of a few days without Alice's questions and instructions.

At the hospital, she parked and watched the paramedics wheel the old woman in on a stretcher, then she took a deep breath and went inside; the sliding doors whooshed behind her like a final judgment. As she settled into the waiting room, the wan fluorescent light, the antiseptic smell, and the mallard duck paintings on the teal-papered walls made her stomach hurt. On the reception desk was a page-a-day calendar, proclaiming it to be Sunday, May 7. She had thought and hoped it was still April.

In only two weeks, an entire year would have gone by since that night.

Chewing a thumbnail, she stared at a "find the differences" puzzle in a crumpled *High-*

lights magazine. She thought of a picture of her life last year; a picture of now — finding similarities would be more of a challenge. A year ago, she'd never have imagined housesitting at her aunt and uncle's farm. Small town life was what she'd run from, leaving her mother, Marty, and younger brother, Danny, behind in Devil's Bend, South Dakota, when she was eighteen to go to the U in Minneapolis. Her longest visit back there since had been a day and a half, and she'd stopped going at all about four years ago, after Danny married his pregnant high school "sweetheart" (not an apt term for Nicole, in Julia's opinion) and joined the Army, while Marty had moved to North Carolina to marry a "cabinetmaker" she'd met on her first-ever beach vacation. Julia's new stepfather, Tom Callahan, didn't actually make cabinets — he owned six Super Cabinet Outlet stores and designed upscale kitchens, flashing his toothpaste-commercial smile to convince customers that upgrading in the planning stage would save a "boatload" in the long run.

Now, Marty was often giddily nostalgic about having spent "practically a lifetime!" supporting two kids on a fifth-grade teacher's salary and intermittent child support. (Once, when Julia's dad, Dan Abraham, had treated her and Danny to one of their infrequent suppers at the Hellfire Griddle in Devil's Bend, Julia had confronted him on his being such a flake, maybe because his earnest hazel eyes, too-long red hair, and three-day beard had reminded her of the needy, inconstant Irish setter whose poop she'd been scooping at her after-school job at Dr. Fricke's, or maybe just because she'd morphed into a know-it-all since she'd last seen him, and he'd flinched a little, eyes still wide, and said, "No one ever said I was perfect, kids, and I've never aimed to be." Marty, when this was reported, had laughed wildly. "The man finally said something true!")

"Find the differences." Marty and Tom's brand-new McMansion; Alice's old farm. Ryan's beautiful loft apartment last year; the farm this year. Last year, Julia had been just finishing her MFA in photography, having spent the two years shooting the vari-colored fur of zoo animals, the intricate machinery of bicycles, the odd corners of buildings. Everything so close-up it became abstract. Her final show was titled "Close/so far: Perspectives," and there was a wine and cheese reception, which she'd spent on Ryan's arm, so happy she didn't mind the pinch of her high-heeled shoes.

She remembered his crisp maroon shirt under her fingers, his smooth voice when he'd chimed in on her conversations with what had seemed just the right blend of admiration and humility and teasing. Her mom hadn't flown in for the show; Dan Abraham hadn't even replied to the invitation. But Ryan's parents had come, and they'd actually refrained from insulting her, which in itself qualified the evening as a success. She'd been with Ryan two years, and they thought her spoiled, the way she indulged in her "frivolous" photography while freeloading off their hardworking banker son. They were fond of telling how they'd grown up so poor that they'd had to go barefoot all summer to save their shoes for the school year (Julia thought this a possibility for one of them, but both?), and how they'd had to struggle for every dime to pay for their own business-oriented educations and, finally, for their brick rambler in the suburbs and the educations of their children. Art, they propounded, was something that could be done honorably only "on the side," the way Ryan did his charcoal sketches — not that they were too pleased he'd met Julia when she'd been a nude model for one of his night classes.

She'd noticed him right away, sitting in

the second row: the smooth, dark skin of his shaved head, his deep eyes, sculpted face, too-long legs bent awkwardly under the desk. She'd hoped he wouldn't think her too hideous — funny how you always worried more what the pretty people would think — but there was nothing to do but stay perched on her stool, since she needed the sixty bucks. Tying her robe afterward, she'd been surprised when he approached to show her his drawing — people *never* did that — and it was a side perspective in which her eyes were cast down, one hand rested on the opposite shoulder, and her curly hair spilled down her back. She'd laughed and told him she wasn't that beautiful, and he'd said, "Yes, you are."

Some months later, her days of posing nude were through when she succumbed to a small fit of optimism and moved into his loft near the Lake of the Isles, which included a darkroom for her, a king-size bed and walk-in closets, a gleaming kitchen. There were nights at the theater, days at the Institute of Arts, winter evenings lying curled together on the leather couch watching his giant flat-screen, leisurely Sunday morning runs around the lake, endless laughter over her attempts to dance to his vintage Ray Charles and Earth, Wind & Fire

LPs. She remembered how soft her hands had been, how her legs had always been meticulously shaved and moisturized, and the unfamiliar certainty she'd come to feel — that Ryan always thought her beautiful, no matter the light.

Now, someone said, "Miss? You're with Amelia Carlson?"

That had been the name on the old woman's driver's license, and Julia looked up to see a white-coated man with deep-set green eyes, high cheekbones, a strong jaw, and short blond hair gelled into the spiky texture of a plastic welcome mat. She dropped the *Highlights* onto the table, realizing what she must look like to him: tangled, curly ponytail, ragged fingernails, ancient shorts and running shoes, and the sweatshirt she'd grabbed when she rushed out to follow the ambulance, oh-so-attractively adorned with horsehair and hayseeds and dried swaths of paint. "Find the differences" indeed.

He made no comment — thank God; she'd been planning her escape, but the chances of the sliding glass doors actually transporting her to another dimension seemed slim — and his eyes sobered when he said that Amelia might simply have fainted out of sheer exhaustion, but that she wasn't clear about the date or the day of the week (and Julia thought, *Ha! That makes two of us!*). Amelia was also unable to explain why she'd taken such a long drive from her home in central Minnesota to Blackberry Ridge; *he* was unable to explain how she could have a valid driver's license at her age. It was possible she'd suffered a mini-stroke, but she was adamant about not staying in the hospital. "So, I'm going to release her," he said. "She'll be more comfortable resting at home. We'll have you set up an appointment for her to see someone tomorrow for more tests."

Julia wanted to run out those sliding doors and just keep running. "You don't understand. She doesn't *live* with me — I don't even know her. She just showed up at my house this afternoon, looking for my aunt. I can't take her home."

The doctor's eyebrows shot up; he looked bewildered, and then almost ashamed — for her, Julia had to imagine, as, beyond his shoulder, she saw Amelia approaching, walking next to a wheelchair being pushed by a nurse, the nurse trying to convince Amelia to sit down and let herself be wheeled.

"Is it possible you might get in touch with your aunt?" the doctor said carefully.

"No, no, I can't, because she's camping in

California."

He nodded in practiced understanding. "But Amelia knows her?"

Now Amelia had stopped, was standing in the middle of the waiting room, her eyes expectant for a moment. Then, the expectation flickered and went dark; her shoulders fell, and she looked at the nurse, whose face turned overly kind and blank.

The doctor was waiting.

"Oh, my God, all right," Julia said finally, unable to stomach the sight of such abject aloneness. Besides, Amelia did know Alice, and Julia didn't want to seem heartless. "I'll take her. Just until tomorrow!"

The doctor's smile was bright; briefly, Julia felt expectation of her own rising within her, and she smiled back. Then she tamped it down and went to collect Amelia.

"Crying is a waste of time," the old woman said, surveying the farmhouse kitchen, a fat teardrop coursing down her cheek. "But I just don't — Did I forget to start something for supper? And where is my stove?"

Julia clutched the handle of Amelia's antique suitcase. She'd argued with the nurse for ten minutes but hadn't been able to get an appointment for the old woman's tests until Tuesday — as if just having her till tomorrow wouldn't have been way over Julia's head.

"Supper?" she said. She supposed the sight of the room *would* bring someone to tears if they weren't used to it. She'd put off redoing it, not relishing the idea of repainting the sky blue cabinets and refinishing the light blue painted wood floor. Besides, whatever she did, the thirty-year-old refrigerator, stove, and sink would dull the room, and she kind of liked the intimacy of the old white wallpaper with the tiny blue flowers and the way the morning light streamed through the window above the sink on the east-facing wall. She'd anticipated the pleasure of eating her meals at the little table, but whenever she'd tried, everything had tasted of cardboard — most of the sit-down meals in her life had been with Ryan.

Amelia was still crying.

"Come on, Amelia," Julia urged, "the bedroom's this way, and the doctor said you should rest, and I have your suitcase, so maybe you can get into something more comfortable."

"Everything looks so different. I don't know how it could look so different."

"Well, I've done a lot of work, a lot." Julia, her muscles twitching at the indignity of

161

moving so slowly, led Amelia through the empty dining room. Here, Julia had stripped and refinished the two original log walls and the plank floors, chosen a lace window treatment, and sponged two dark tones of green onto the plaster south wall, which she understood had been added in the 1950s to create the walk-through pantry/laundry room and bathroom, accessed from the kitchen.

Amelia made no comment until they stepped into the living room. "Who did this?" she gasped.

"Refinished the logs and floors, you mean?" Julia snapped. She couldn't seem to stop herself. "Got rid of that horrible orange carpet and chose this awesome bright white for the walls?" For furniture, she'd left only a rocking chair, a floor lamp, and, not by choice, an ancient grandfather clock — immovable since she'd had a falling-out with George's brother, Isaac. When he'd expressed seemingly mild concern that she was making such drastic changes to the house without permission, she'd told him Alice had given her full discretion. He'd shot her a glassy blue look, turned on his heel, and walked out, and whenever she'd phoned after that, his wife had said, "Oh, dear, you just missed him, he went to town and won't be back for hours!" Julia had finally cut out the carpet (four orange tufts remained around the clock's feet, like cheerful weeds), and she'd waited what seemed an eternity for the damn thing to wind down — though, actually, its chiming every quarter hour had been a good impetus to keep running the sander.

"That blasted clock," Amelia muttered. "And where did these pictures come from?"

"They're mine." Julia had hung her MFA show in one long row, like a belt around the waist of the room. Some part of her had wanted these reminders of her former life in plain sight — even if there was one black-and-white shot of Ryan's muscular back that made her queasy every time she walked past. She'd also framed and hung the hand-tinted portrait she'd found mixed with the old magazines in the attic.

Amelia's eyes lighted on it. "Grace!" she said.

Julia hadn't thought, earlier, of the name on the back of the picture. "Amelia, is that the woman you were looking for? Who is she?"

"Why do you keep calling me Amelia?"

"— Isn't that your name?"

"My middle name. My first name is Violet."

Julia thought of the doctor with his ridiculous gelled hair, the way he'd pressured her into taking Amelia home. What had he been thinking, releasing someone into the world who was so addled? She remembered he'd mentioned the old woman was confused about time, too. "Can you tell me what year it is?"

"Why, 1947, of course. I'm afraid I don't remember your name?"

Her head aching, Julia could think only to leave the woman in the bedroom, encourage her to sleep, and hope she'd come to her senses — she'd asked for Alice at first, so she'd obviously known then that it wasn't 1947.

Outside, the horses paraded into the little red barn, their indignation at their late supper evident in the switching of their tails, and Julia weighed out their pungent grain and brought them fresh pails of water, trying not to think about the old woman, though she was as impossible to forget as a sliver under a fingernail. At least Julia hadn't been using the bedroom; she'd survived winter in the restored attic with the help of two down comforters, a space heater, flannel pajamas, and wool socks.

And then she realized: *Violet.* And remembered, from vague and long-ago tellings of family lore, who that was: her grandma Lena's mother. Julia had always thought she was dead.

Julia ran inside to call her mom, but the teenage stepsister who answered said that Marty and Tom had gone to Spain and would be there the rest of the week. *Of course,* Julia thought, hanging up. Then she remembered the trunk. It had been in the shed, untouched, since last fall. Maybe there was something inside it that could help determine if the old woman really was Violet — had anyone ever *said* Violet was dead, or had Julia just assumed?

In the shed, she moved boxes and furniture aside, cut the trunk's twine, and let it fall away. The lid creaked as she raised it, releasing the smell of dust. The top tray contained an antique gilded *Complete Works of Shakespeare,* an old volume on plants of the upper Midwest, and a couple of tattered scrapbooks labeled PLANTS, 1932–34; TREES, 1933–36.

Earth-shattering, Julia thought.

But the lower compartment was stacked full of old shoe boxes. For a moment, she imagined wild possibilities: cash, jewels, treasure maps? The first two boxes she pried out were stuffed with canceled checks from the 1950s; her excitement waned. The third box, though, was promising: shiny black-and-white snapshots. The evening was deepening, the unwired shed's interior growing darker; she stepped outside for better light.

She appreciated the pictures' starkness, the light and the shadows, but she couldn't seem to recognize any of the long-ago faces or scenes — women in work clothes and bizarre-looking helmets? Ice and snow and . . . ships?

Then she found a weathered newspaper clipping tucked in the stack. She unfolded it gingerly and read:

Superior Gazette
January 25, 1945

ENTIRE FAMILY LABORS AT SUPERIOR SHIPBUILDING CO. IN HONOR OF SAILOR LOST AT SEA

By Harry Mickelson

When Jago Maki of Blackberry Ridge received the telegram two months ago that his son, Derrick, 19, was Missing in Action after the sinking of his aircraft carrier in the naval battle against the Imperial Japanese Navy off Samar, he decided that his crippling disability wasn't going to stop him any longer from taking a larger part in the war effort. Despite a chronically bad back, Mr. Maki had been operating the family farm while his wife, Violet, and daughter, Lena — Derrick's twin sister — labored as girl welders at the Superior Shipbuilding Company. With the news about Derrick, an Aviation Ordnance Man Second Class and gunner aboard a TBM Avenger aircraft, Mr. Maki applied for work at the same company as a painter. Now the entire family is doing its part locally to wipe out the Axis abroad.

Sister Lena took a break between welds recently to say, "We've written to several of his shipmates and they all say that Derrick's plane took off when the battle started, so we know he wasn't on the ship when it sank. We just have to track him down." When Derrick broke an arm at age nine, Lena felt pain in her own arm from a distance before she knew what had happened. Feeling no pain now, she is certain her twin is alive.

Mother Violet, working nearby, said, "I pray she's right. We haven't heard from him since the ship went down, but the twins have always been very close."

Mr. Maki also exhibited a cautiously optimistic outlook as, bundled against the cold, he coated the upper deck of Hull number 47 with fresh paint. "I just want to do my part to speed this war up," he said. "My son was doing his part. And when the war's over, we'll find out where he is and what happened to him."

The old newsprint quivered in Julia's hand.

Winter 1945

Accustomed to the only men she saw being dirty, middle-aged shipbuilders, Grace was startled by the handsome newspaperman in his expensive fedora, clean suit, and overcoat. She hung back, watching him talk with Lena, hoping he wouldn't notice her — she was filthy. But after he'd turned his attention to Violet, Lena came over. "You should talk to him," she said. "Tell him you're waiting for Derrick, too."

"Oh, no, I couldn't," Grace said. Worse than facing such a man in her current state would be seeing her name in black and white next to Derrick's.

Nearly three months had passed since his ship had gone down. The family had been writing to his friends, anyone he'd mentioned in his letters, to find out whether any had news. But since the only address available for the sailors and aviators was the ship

169

itself, there was no telling whether mail was even finding them. So far, only two men had replied, and all they knew was that Derrick had been safely catapulted off the flight deck in the Avenger with Lieutenant Nelson and the radioman Grabowski first thing that morning.

Nearly every night, Grace sat down at the table in her flat and wrote to him, short, heartfelt letters, always pretty much the same: *I'm thinking of you and hoping you're all right, and waiting to hear from you, and I'm so anxious for the day we can finally go dancing. Take good care of yourself, everyone here is praying for you and hoping you'll find your way home soon.* She'd begun to sign the letters *Love, Grace.*

Lately, though, she'd started to feel strange about dropping them into the mail slot, so she saved them in a shoe box. If news came, she would send them right away, and he'd see she'd been thinking of him the whole time. " 'The course of true love never did run smooth,' " Lena kept telling her.

Grace overheard the newspaperman say to Violet, "And where can I find your husband?"

Lena called out, "Grace will take you to him! She's on a break."

Grace hugged herself and sighed as Harry Mickelson turned to her, smiling.

"So, do you know Derrick Maki?" Harry asked as they walked.

"I've never met him."

"But you know the family pretty well?"

Grace wanted to tell him that he'd certainly gone into the right line of work: one look at his face and she wanted to spill everything. She wondered why he wasn't in the service; he looked healthy enough. She thought of Joe, then — she'd caught sight of him from a distance a few times, but she hadn't spoken to him since the day Derrick had gone missing. Maybe the newspaperman had an invisible affliction, like Joe's rheumatic fever. Or was it just that Harry was so good at tearing stories out of people that he'd been considered indispensable here? She averted her gaze and thus stopped herself from saying anything more than "Yes, I suppose."

"Does Lena really believe her brother is alive, or is she just trying to get attention?"

Grace looked at him again, and now the words rushed out. "Oh, my goodness, no. She has absolute faith he's alive. She has all kinds of theories. A water landing, a crash landing in the jungle. She's certain he's on some Pacific island, either being taken care of or maybe taken prisoner." She didn't want to mention: according to Associated Press articles that had been in the paper, all the survivors from Derrick's ship had been recovered.

Harry's mouth twitched. "Sounds like hell to me."

Grace yanked her jacket closed against a gust of wind. "Yes. Yes, it is."

They took a few more steps, dodging pipes and electrical cords and dirt-crusted snow piles. "And you don't know him at all?" Harry said.

"Oh, I mean for Lena and Violet! It's hell for them." But when she met Harry's eyes, she couldn't keep up the charade. She thought of that night she'd spent at the farm — how she'd felt locked in its embrace. "Well, I — we exchanged letters. Derrick and I. A lot, actually. But it's true that I never met him. Please don't put me in the article."

Harry frowned, watching his feet. "You know, nobody wants to admit it could happen to their son. Their brother. But everyone is somebody's son, somebody's brother. Unfortunately."

She led him around a stack of metal and toward the ladder. "This way," she said, swallowing hard as she began to climb.

They found Jago on the top deck. After making introductions, Grace waited a few steps away, looking out at the gray harbor and at Duluth rising on the distant hill.

She couldn't hear Harry's questions, but Jago's deep voice carried. First, his objection that he didn't have long to talk because he didn't want to take too much time from his work, then his explanation of the steps the family had taken to try to get information about Derrick. "It's something like if someone just cut off your hand and hid it. There's the bleeding and the panic and —" He stopped. He lit a cigarette, shielding it from the wind. "Don't write that, ay?" he said. "Maybe just say it's like falling. And there's no light and no bottom, only darkness, and you just keep on falling."

Grace blinked back tears, looked out at the harbor again. Jago's voice was lower now. "Well, yes, it's not the first time I've experienced this sort of thing. . . . No, not like my son, of course. A girl I planned to marry, if you have to know. Now that, really, you can't write. My wife doesn't know about her. . . . No, I never found out what happened to her. . . . I guess it does make this worse. Familiar."

Grace hid her face behind her collar, hoping Jago wouldn't sense that she'd overheard.

Later, after she'd led Harry down off the hull, bid him goodbye, and started trudging back across the yard, she couldn't shake the image of the water closing over her, of Derrick at rest at the bottom of the sea. It would be pitch-black, but somehow she could see him. She thought of Susan's awful prediction, and of the things Alex had been writing lately in his letters: how he wouldn't mind going to California after the war, if she wanted. She remembered Jago's secret, and wondered why he'd never told Violet; if she should.

No, she thought. *It's really not any of my business.*

Besides, Violet had enough to worry about in the present, without hearing of old troubles that had no bearing on anything now. The most important thing, Grace figured, was to keep Violet and Lena from realizing her doubts about Derrick. If they imagined she'd given up, they would surely think it the worst betrayal.

At home, Jago kept the grandfather clock wound. Violet knew that he and Lena were counting the quarter hours to themselves, too. At the shipyard, she would pull her watch from her pocket every chance she had, often to find that only ten minutes had passed. Sometimes, the realization would strike her like a hammer to the heart: that many more minutes gone from Derrick! Other times, she'd swell with hope, because surely he was that much closer to coming home.

Sometimes when Violet was melting metal to metal she would think, *Everything has its point of collapse.*

In John Tuomi's truck, riding home from work, she would sit on Jago's lap, grateful for his warmth, his arms around her waist over her heavy coat. Her eyes would burn from exhaustion and from the grit and smoke of the shipyard. Her muscles would ache from the hours of welding. Her feet would throb in their heavy boots. She was always sleepy because she never slept through a night. Yet her eyes would not close as she stared out the window at the houses rolling by, watching for service banners in the windows. She counted how many blue stars, how many gold; keeping track of odds, in her head. "Seventy-seven percent," Jago would whisper, so softly she sometimes thought she'd imagined it.

Lena was always cheerful this time of day,

saying today they'd hear from Derrick. Sorrow would rise in Violet's throat. Jago would stroke her hand; sometimes, she'd clutch at him. Other times, she'd snatch her hand away, thinking, *You! Your fault!* She still couldn't help thinking that Derrick would have been all right if only Jago hadn't signed that permission slip!

Once John had pulled in at the Maki farm, Lena would shove at Violet and Jago. Even as the two of them were stumbling, unlimbering stiffened muscles and middle-aged backs, she'd have broken past and be running for the mailbox, kicking up snow, framed in the pink light of winter evening. Violet would feel the creak of the hinges up her spine and watch as Lena took out the mail and flipped through. Then she would see her daughter's shoulders collapse, and she would know. *Not today.* And John's truck would back out of the driveway like a sigh and Jago would rest his hand on Violet's shoulder, and she'd shrink from his touch at the same time that she'd try to keep her spine straight and her head high. "Time to do the chores," she would say, walking out from under his hand, unbearably cold again, her boots crunching the snow, the frigid air choking her.

Derrick's absence was everywhere, like an

owl swooping. Even the house felt chilled and dark, like it had turned its back on her.

One night, Jago didn't come home. It was mid-afternoon on a Friday when he told Violet he was planning to work late, that he'd stay overnight in town with some co-workers. She eyed him suspiciously, but she didn't have enough fight left in her not to simply agree.

After that, every Friday he "worked late." Violet chose not to acknowledge the spark in his bloodshot eyes. He looked so jazzed and exhausted that she assumed he was winning. She trusted the phase would pass; at least, when he was home in the evenings now, he helped with the chores, then sat down to play the piano. Sad songs, and sometimes he would sing, his rich voice snaking through her, even as the log walls seemed to swallow the sound.

"Still, it isn't like the mines," Jago was saying, one Saturday night at supper. "We lost someone about once a week there." At the yard today, the news had come that a fifty-six-year-old welder had died of pneumonia after he spent an afternoon earlier in the week working outside in a bitter storm. Management was calling him a true patriot;

177

workers grumbled that he hadn't had much of a choice. "There were so many ways to die. You could lose your footing and fall a mile down the shaft. Into the darkness." Jago shuddered.

Violet got up to load the firebox. After the long day at work in the dampness, she couldn't seem to get warm; she imagined Jago and Lena felt the same.

"Every Saturday night, you know, we had dances. I'd play the accordion, ay. There'd be twenty-five people stomping and singing along, in houses no bigger than this one. The windows would rattle, and it would get so hot inside and stink like beer and meat and sweat." He poked his food with his fork. "But then, you could drink as much as you wanted and still on Monday you might be the one death would find. So you'd step out into the cold, from that hot little house, and it would be a dousing of reality. A relief. And a disappointment, ay."

Violet was holding her breath. It was the most he'd ever said about his past.

"What do you mean, Dad?" Lena prompted. "Tell us more."

He shook his head. His eyes had turned to mirrors. Lena cajoled, to no avail. She finally sighed. "Well, anyway, Dad, I don't want you taking any risks like that man at the yard did. You're no spring chicken yourself. You promise you'll watch it?"

Jago laughed. "Sure, kid. I promise." He glanced at Violet as she sat down. "The same would go for your mother, ay?"

"Mom's almost ten years younger than you."

Violet felt her mouth twitch in a sort of smile. She could feel in her aching bones and lungs how easily death could come, how it was waiting right around the corner.

"Still, I'd like to see her take care," he said. "Get more rest. You're looking peaked, Vi."

"It isn't as if I don't try," Violet muttered. "To sleep." He had been gone last night again. She wondered how much he'd won, what he'd lost. She was, out of habit, loath to ask. As if, if she didn't, it might not be real. So many years, he'd stayed away from his old demons. After the story he'd just shared of his past, she wondered if it was death he was trying to cheat. In any case, she felt as if it were her luck that had run out.

Sure enough, later, she lay awake again, staring at the ceiling, listening to Jago snore. The moon poked through the clouds outside and lit the bedroom like the shipyard floodlights. She finally got up, put on her robe against the chill.

In the living room, she pressed her fingers to the glass door of the clock cabinet. She could feel the motion of the pendulum.

She noticed that Jago had left his wallet on top of the piano. He must have taken it out of his pocket when he'd sat down that evening to play "Danny Boy" in honor of the departed shipbuilder. The wallet was shabby and paint-spattered already, though she'd just given it to him for Christmas. The man took good care of nothing. She reached for it. She couldn't continue to let him go, the way she had, could she? Shouldn't she at least try to get some sense of the odds they were up against?

She knew he'd cashed his paycheck yesterday. But now there was only one rumpled dollar in the wallet, and a folded, tattered piece of paper — an IOU, she hoped. Or maybe something from Derrick: Jago's own private prayer. It would be good to see that he was holding his son close.

She had not anticipated: a note in Jago's own bold, slanting handwriting. She read:

Darling J.,
I can't stand to be apart from you any longer. Can't we just forget our families?

Say you will. I have everything planned.

Your,

Jago

That was all. With shaking hands, Violet folded the note and replaced it in the wallet. She was careful. It had been wrong of her to snoop. She stumbled to the rocking chair. Suddenly, the house, the farm, this life they'd shared for so many years, seemed distasteful, like rotten fruit. And Derrick's absence was the spoiled cream poured over top of it.

Who was this woman — *Darling J.?* All Violet could think was to damn that sunny Saturday morning in 1922 when, with two of her co-workers, who'd begged ridiculously for her protection, she'd taken the streetcar across the bridge from Ironwood to the notorious town of Hurley. She'd worn her best lavender dress, her favorite white hat, its wide brim curving like a question mark. Her white canvas pumps had clicked on the boardwalk of Silver Street. And then a man all in white burst from one of the saloons and began leading her in a wild dance. Even in her horror, she caught his pleasing scent: a hint of cigarettes; of something tinny, like money; cloves. And when he stopped twirling her, she saw that his blue eyes shone, their whites shot through with pink like a white rabbit's ears.

She tore herself from him, hurried away. But one of her giggling co-workers called to him: "The Ironwood Hotel dining room!"

Some days later, when she saw him seated at a white-clothed table, the floor seemed to shift under her feet. She scurried past, scratching notes on her order pad, aware of him fumbling with his coffee cup, that he had opened his mouth as if to speak.

And she felt the odd thrill — the distinctive alarm — of having been seen.

Two weeks later, on a blue September Sunday at the park, she was walking alone, wearing her new coat with the fashionable fur collar. He was slouched on the edge of the fountain, smoking a cigarette. Why, she still had no idea. "Come and sit by me," he said, and his voice astonished her. In her girl's mind, it was the voice of a sultan, or maybe even of Rudolph Valentino, the silent film star, its resonant tones seeming to promise sumptuous riches, sensual pleasures beyond her dreams and suddenly alluring in their mystery. The effect was as if he were a magnet and she a small filing. "Tell me your name," he said. And she did!

He told her that, when their paths had crossed that first time, he'd just come from a poker game in which he'd won the deed to a farm. He acted sheepish about it. She disapproved, of course. Yet she was intoxicated by the fact that he owned property, free and clear. She'd never liked the idea of owing anyone anything.

So: Sunday after Sunday in the park. If he spoke of his past, it was in foreign languages that she didn't understand. Still, she pitied him; she relished his decadent voice. And one October afternoon (she could smell the coming winter), she blurted, "Marry me, and take me to your farm. We'd have a good life, I think."

He drew back like a man who'd touched his tongue to the raw end of a lightbulb. She jumped up; her footsteps sounded quick as gunshots.

But one moonless night not long after, he threw pebbles at her upstairs boardinghouse window. When she came out, he stepped so close she felt as if he'd wrapped her in a blanket. He told her he felt, at the end of some of his long nights, like he was descending to meet Charon at the river crossing to the underworld. He said he'd wanted to go to Chicago, even New Orleans, that he'd planned to, a couple of times, then gambled his ticket, or his money, away and let the thought disappear like a petal being tossed over a shoulder. *Loves me not.* He said he thought maybe she was the last petal that would be offered him, after all the others he'd so carelessly let fall, and that he hadn't put the farm's deed on the table after he knew it might mean the difference between having her and not having her. He begged her to help him. To come with him to the courthouse tomorrow.

"Of course," she'd murmured, perhaps considering herself the instrument of his rescue.

She realized now: he had never seen or wanted her at all. He had seen only some reflection of himself, as inaccurate as it was alluring. And she had been the fool to believe his lines.

All these Friday nights. He must be working on convincing the woman to run away with him for good. Did she give him the comfort he sought, that Violet had failed to give?

The clock tolled, jolting her; the noise of the hours chiming drove her from her chair. She thought of Lena: What would the poor girl do if her beloved father left them in favor of another woman, another life? Proving their whole existence a lie!

And how angry Derrick would be. Maybe Violet had been selfish in not doing more all along to discourage her son from think-ing ill of Jago. Now it seemed to her that, if Derrick returned, she would see in his steady blue gaze the truth of how foolish she'd been to stay with Jago all these taxing years.

She crept upstairs. She peered around the old red velvet curtain to watch sleeping Lena, finding solace for a moment in the rise and fall of the quilts, the soft noise of Lena's breath. She turned to Derrick's half of the room. In the moonlight, she studied the pictures that he'd hung on the low wall. Airplanes. Maps of the world. Some of the things had been hanging here for a decade. The most recent addition was a pinup of Rita Hayworth. Violet tried to smile, but her face only quivered.

Her eyes passed over the keepsakes on top of his dresser — there was the blue marble he had pretended was his glass eye. She closed her hand over it, savoring its cool smoothness on her palm. It reminded her of the other child she'd lost; that morning, the egg and the Cream of Wheat.

Shivering, she lay on Derrick's bed and pulled the quilt over herself. She held the marble in her fist, pressed to her heart. She stared at the maps in the moonlight, the red X of home.

Maybe she slept a little.

Then she sensed Derrick, sitting at the foot of the bed. She propped herself on her elbow. He was wearing his dress blue uniform and white sailor cap. He crossed one ankle over his other knee, and she could see the high gloss of his black shoe. "No!" she whispered. "I'm dreaming!"

He gave her a gentle smile.

She gasped and fell back, pulling the quilt over her head.

April 1945

Violet and Lena had never missed a day of work, not when they'd had bad colds and fevers, not even the day after the news had come about Derrick's being missing in action. But one gray Thursday morning in mid-April, they weren't there.

Grace's nervous fingers struggled to button her coveralls. She'd been extra-anxious for days, anyway: the Marines had invaded Okinawa and Alex was probably there. The newspaper, full of enthusiastic stories about the Allies' successes in Germany, contained almost no information about the war in the Pacific, and no matter how much she listened to the radio, it never told her what she needed to know.

And now she had to assume that Violet and Lena had received bad news about Derrick. If it had been good news, they would have come to work to share it.

The matron, Tess Olson, swept in the door. "Ladies, I wanted to let you know. Violet Maki's husband — Lena's father — was found dead this morning."

There were gasps. Grace pressed her knuckles to her mouth.

Tess Olson held up a hand. "Evidently he had a heart attack. The funeral is Saturday afternoon. If you'd like to attend, please talk with me. I wouldn't think you should all go — I know Violet and Lena wouldn't want their loss to affect our work. But if some of you could show your support, that would be nice."

Grace and Boots met eyes, then headed over to talk to the matron. The other women filed out, casting sympathetic looks.

Late that afternoon, Grace had just finished a weld when she felt someone whapping at her sleeve. She tipped up her helmet. "What?"

Sean O'Connor pointed at one of the loudspeakers, and Grace tuned in to the words crackling out over the yard. "Repeat, this afternoon President Roosevelt passed away at Warm Springs, Georgia. Vice President Truman has been sworn in as president. As we mourn the loss, let us not slacken our work to finish this war that our noble president led us through with such dignity and courage. Repeat, this afternoon . . ."

"That can't be true," she said, but no one answered. The men were pale. She felt tears coming. No more Fireside Chats! Another voice gone silent.

Russ squared himself. "We'd best get on with our work. The war continues."

Grace flipped down her helmet. Her hands shook as she fired up her stinger and drew the next bead.

That night, she and Boots dragged themselves downtown for supper at the Black Cat Café. It was unnaturally quiet, with everyone stunned by the loss of the president. Grace wasn't conscious of being hungry, but when her pork chop platter was set before her, she devoured every bite. She wondered whether Derrick would ever learn what had happened, what it would be like for him to arrive home to find his father dead. Sadness sat on the table between her and Boots like a cat, watching.

As they walked home, trying to shield their faces from a biting wind, Grace could hardly keep her eyes open. Boots plodded next to her in silence.

Just as Grace unlocked the door, the

phone rang. It was her mother. "I've been trying to call." There was a tremulous note in her voice.

Not one more thing, Grace thought. Her father? "We were out. What's the matter?"

"I wanted to drive over and see you, but it's getting so late; I have to put the children to bed."

"Is Dad all right?"

"Yes, he's fine. Grace, I hate to tell you over the phone. You'd better sit down."

Grace sank into a kitchen chair. She had started to tremble. "I'm . . . sitting."

"Grace, I . . . I got a call from Mrs. Kowalski. It's Alex. He's . . . he's been killed, Grace."

She didn't remember hanging up the telephone. Maybe she just dropped it and sat staring. Maybe she clutched her stomach and sobbed.

Maybe she did all of those things.

She didn't know what Boots said or how she got to bed or if she slept or what she dreamed.

At the shipyard the next morning, her eyes and throat were raw. She felt underwater again, heavy and weightless at once, too weak to stand, but the water wouldn't let her fall or quite breathe.

She made weld after weld after weld. *You want us to lose this war because of* you?

She could picture Alex's family. *You want us to lose Alex because of* you?

After work, she stumbled to her flat with Boots and got cleaned up, then phoned her mother to come and get her in the car. They went to call on Alex's parents.

The last time Grace had been to the Kowalskis' was three years ago, on that Sunday morning with Alex. The smell of the house — like oatmeal cookies and lemon furniture polish and simmering cabbage — brought the memory back to her: his nervous smile when he'd answered the door, the sweatiness of his hand as he'd led her upstairs.

Seated in the lamp-lit living room, she couldn't follow her mother's murmured comments. She avoided Alex's parents' tearful eyes. The clinking of china cups was like fingernails on a blackboard; when she took a bite of a cookie, trying not to be rude, it tasted like chalk. Finally, she interrupted to ask if she could go upstairs and look in Alex's room. His mother tilted her head, as if she hadn't understood. His father nodded. "First door on the right."

The little room was just as she'd remembered it. She opened Alex's closet, grabbing a fistful of shirtsleeves, bending close to savor the hint of his scent. She surveyed the adventure books on his shelf, the baseball trophies on his dresser, the rocks he'd picked up at the beach. She sat on his bed and held his pillow to her nose.

It smelled of bleach. There was no trace of the boy smell she remembered from the day she'd been in the bed. She threw the pillow back down, then fell on top of it and cried.

Saturday had been declared a national day of mourning for President Roosevelt, and many businesses were closed for the day, or at least the afternoon. But work at the shipyard continued, and Russ certainly didn't slow down any. Grace made every weld he asked her to, though her stomach and head ached like the worst hangover on record. She'd hardly slept; had kept remembering the smell of Alex's shirts, picturing the heartbreak on Mrs. Kowalski's face, and thinking, *What if I'd been faithful to him, like he deserved? What if I'd loved him more?*

At noon, she and her crew made their way to the yard's center for a memorial service for the president. Packed elbow to elbow with Sean and Russ and the others, she was grateful for the excuse to weep. She didn't hear a word that the priest or minister said; she thought about Alex and Derrick and Jago and her own father. She hadn't been as good as she'd intended about spending time with him since she'd moved into the flat with Boots. He seemed to be getting better, but what if he wasn't? What if one day she woke up and he was gone, too? She imagined Alex, dead on Okinawa. She'd seen photographs of dead Marines on beaches, so she knew exactly how Alex would have looked. She imagined the shallow grave far from home, the dirt being thrown onto his handsome face, covering his body. She imagined Derrick, rocking in the current at the bottom of the ocean, because how could she honestly believe anything else, in the face of everything that had turned out so wrong?

As the service ended, someone tugged her sleeve; she turned, expecting Lena. But it was Joe. "Grace?" he said.

She wiped at her eyes, too numb to feel anything at the sight of him, even if she had still been paying a bit too much attention to his small figure in the distance on the train and thinking a little too often of the warmth she'd felt from him the last time they'd spoken, that day she'd found out about Derrick's being missing. Almost five months ago now. Joe's face no longer had the same pasty look. She was glad to think he was recovering from his illness — at least something in the world was headed in the right direction. "Joe."

"I'm sorry, I thought it was you, but — Are you all right?"

She shook her head.

The crowd was dispersing; someone nudged Joe, pushing him closer. His hand cupped her elbow. "Is there anything I can do?"

She remembered the night they'd danced.

Now someone bumped her; she would have lost her footing if Joe hadn't caught her other elbow. They stood like two boulders on a beach of shifting sand.

His face had reddened. He shoved his hands into his coat pockets, and she missed his touch the moment it was gone. "Anything?" he said.

"There's nothing."

He mustered a spark in his eyes, a flirty smile. "Maybe a dance?"

She tried to blink back her tears, felt one trailing down each cheek.

"I'm sorry," he said, going pale. "I didn't mean . . ."

She hugged herself, shaking her head

again. "I'm just so cold."

He stepped closer.

She liked the gentleness of his eyes. "My . . . my Marine. Alex. He was killed."

His face crumpled, then set in a kind of anger as he looked past her, into the dissolving crowd. "I'm sorry, Grace." A deep breath; his eyes on her, soft again. "It's more than a person can stand, sometimes, isn't it?"

She nodded. Felt, strangely, more at peace.

She heard a deep voice call, "Hey, Hotshot! Let's go!" She saw Sean O'Connor standing some distance away, beckoning.

"That's me," she said, and the thought of leaving Joe seemed suddenly as unbearable as crawling out from beneath quilts on a below-zero morning.

He frowned.

She didn't think. She simply couldn't wait months to talk with him again. She couldn't tolerate any longer all her dreams feeling so distant and impossible. She told him where she lived, and that she'd probably be home after eight o'clock tonight. He smiled, and it was the first ray of light she'd felt touch her in days.

She hurried away, her arms pressed to her stomach, guessing she was probably immoral by the old standards — thinking how little that seemed to matter now, with the whole world turned on its ear.

Grace and Boots had received permission to leave work at two o'clock to catch a ride with John Tuomi to Jago's funeral. They'd brought their nice dresses and hats to change into. Walking out of the yard, Grace moved like a sleepwalker, trying to rub the remaining grime off her hands. She hoped Joe wouldn't visit tonight — she was such a mess. She didn't know what she'd been thinking, inviting him.

On the ride out, the sky was gray as dust, the weather wintery again after two seductive, fickle weeks that had suggested spring, and Grace fell asleep leaning on Boots. She dreamed that Alex was sitting next to her, that it was his shoulder she was resting on, and, when she woke up in Blackberry Ridge to find it wasn't true, she felt like someone had made tossed salad of her insides.

Still, she set her face for the funeral, wanting to be of some use to Violet and Lena.

"I tried to tell the sheriff, and he just laughed!" Lena whispered, clenching her teeth against the wind at the snow-dusted graveside, clutching Grace's elbow. The service was over and most everyone was walking away; only Violet stood looking down on the coffin in the grave. Lena had pulled Grace toward the trees; Boots had followed behind.

Grace couldn't fathom what she was saying. "You think your mother *poisoned* him?"

"She was reading my plant identification book last week. She's never read it in her life! And she closed it real quick when I walked in, so I couldn't see what page she was on."

"Kid," Boots scolded, "you've got to get ahold of yourself."

"He was only forty-nine years old! He was worn out lately, but not enough to *kill* him. Not like that other guy from work. No — he ate three pasties she'd just made. I was going to have one, and she said, 'Why don't you leave them for your father, they're his favorite!' And the next morning he was — dead!"

Grace tried to loosen Lena's fingers from her arm, realizing why the girl had said in the eulogy she'd given, *He was a man more sinned against than sinning.* "Lena, I'm sure Violet would never do anything to hurt anyone, especially not your dad."

"But you haven't seen her! How mad she's been! Ever since Derrick's been missing. She blames my dad. Because he signed that permission slip!"

Grace had never felt colder. "Lena, I know you're upset. But Violet would never have done anything like that."

Lena tightened her grip. "Why doesn't anyone believe me? Do you think I would just *make up* something like this?"

"Of course not," Grace said, finally freeing herself from Lena's bruising hand. "I just think you're upset. And I'm very sorry for your loss. But it's only going to make matters worse, accusing her like this. You two need each other now more than ever."

Lena's mouth trembled. "I don't need her. I don't."

Boots broke in. "Lena, you should know. Alex was killed. Gracie found out Thursday."

Lena caught Grace's arm again like an owl catching prey. "Oh, Grace. No." Grace tried to turn away; Lena put a cold hand on her face. "I'm sorry. I'm so sorry."

"Let's not talk about it," Grace managed to say. "We're here for your dad."

Covering her tremulous mouth, Lena glared at her mother again.

Grace followed her gaze. Violet looked exhausted, her eyes hollow, her jaw more square than usual, but she was as put together as always, her light brown hair set in perfect curls, her good gray coat wrinkle-free.

"We're going to give your mom our sympathies," Grace said. "Why don't you come with us?"

Lena just shook her head and hugged herself, rubbing her arms and shivering in the wind.

"Poor Lena," Boots said, when the two friends finally arrived back at their flat. She pulled the chain on the light over the kitchen table, flooding the room with a soft glow. "I guess it's hard to lose your dad like that. I guess it might make a kid a little crazy."

Grace was slowly removing her hatpins, setting them on the little shelf that stood just inside the flat's front door. "Yes, I suppose," she said, thinking of her own father again, remembering his pre-stroke voice and laughter, dancing with him to the *Hit Parade*. She finished with the pins and set her hat on top of the pile of them.

They'd spent what had seemed like the world's longest funeral reception at the farmhouse, keeping Lena from the neighbors and friends that had gathered, sequestering her in the attic, where she curled herself into a ball on Derrick's bed and shivered, even after they'd covered her with a whole stack of quilts. Grace, patting Lena's shoulder, had studied Derrick's maps until she found the place in the Pacific Ocean off Samar where his ship had gone down. She traced with her eyes the great distance between there and the red X that he'd drawn in northern Wisconsin to mark home and wondered if he'd ever find his way back.

Riding into town with an acquaintance from the shipyard, drifting in and out of a dream about Alex, about Derrick, she'd prayed Lena would realize that death was simply everywhere, random and irrevocable — just as Derrick had written.

Now Grace could hear in the distance the faint sounds of Saturday night. The tavern district, a couple blocks from the flat, had reopened after being closed for the afternoon of mourning for FDR, and people were back to drinking and business as usual: shouting, laughing, the occasional woman shrieking. It struck Grace as obscene.

"To think she'd think Violet could even imagine such a thing, let alone do it!" Boots said, hands on lanky hips. "Quiet little shrinking Violet!"

Grace sat at the table, lacing her hands together to keep them still. "Maybe we should have brought Lena here. Not left the two of them alone."

There was a soft knock at the door. "What now?" Boots said. Grace thought maybe Hat or Char had come to check on her; she stared at her beat-up hands as Boots opened the door.

A man's voice said, "Is Grace here?"

Joe. After the eternal-seeming day, she had scarcely believed it possible that this was the same night and he might still come.

When he walked in, she was surprised and ashamed to notice how good he looked. He was wearing his Army uniform dress pants, a white shirt, and a dark blue necktie under his unzipped leather flight jacket. He was clean-shaven, his dark hair freshly barbered.

Boots closed the door. "Guess I'll be off to bed, then, Gracie?"

"All right," Grace said, and Boots disappeared.

Joe had his hands in his pockets; he gave Grace a small smile. "Hello."

"Hello," she said. The sight of him was making her feel like crying again. Why had he come here? Why on earth hadn't he just written her off for the loon she was? "I guess I'll put on some music."

She walked to the radio and flipped on the noise, recognizing the strains of "The

White Cliffs of Dover." A song about peace, the war ending. She couldn't seem to pretend that even then this tiredness, this chill, would leave her.

Joe was still standing near the door.

"Will you dance with me?" she blurted.

He smiled; his cheeks flushed. "I thought you'd never ask."

She wanted to tell him she'd been kidding, *honestly!,* but when she opened her mouth, no sound came. He took off his jacket and hung it over a chair.

When he reached her, the hopeful look on his face reminded her again of that long-ago night they'd met. One more step. He put his hand on her waist. She caught the scent of his aftershave. Touching his shoulder, she felt his heat through his shirt.

Clumsily, they began to dance. She felt tears coming again.

"Are you going to be all right?" he said.

She leaned her forehead on his shoulder.

"Do you want me to go?" he said.

She knew she should say yes. But she didn't think his sympathy was pretend, and she didn't want to be alone. "No. Please."

She felt his chest rise and fall. "I'm sorry, Grace. About everything. I really am. I've been hoping I'd see you, but I really didn't want all this to've happened to you. I had this idea I'd try to win you over on my own so-called merits."

She looked up; his deep blue eyes unraveled her. *I'm sorry,* she said to Alex in her mind. *Forgive me,* she said to Derrick. "What merits do you have?"

"You have to ask?"

Her laughter astonished her.

He leaned down and kissed her, and she let herself be lost in him.

The house seemed so quiet: only the ticking of the clock. Violet was washing dishes. All the pans the neighbors had brought. Then, scrubbing the chopping block, scrubbing and scrubbing, as if she could erase the last four days, the last half year.

But time kept on. Jago was in the ground, in the darkness. Derrick was in the air.

Lena came in, wiping her face on her sleeve. "You're not going to get away with it," she snapped, as the porch door swung closed behind her. She had been like this for two solid days.

Violet scrubbed. She said what she had said before, voice quavering: "He ate too much and drank too much and smoked too much and he gambled. So he died. People die. I'm sorry. For you. I am. I lost my father, too —"

"I saw you with my plant book."

"Lena! Honestly! I would not. Could not! Take him from you. From us."

"You hated him. You did. I'm going to find evidence. I promise you."

"Lena! I know you're upset, you're tired. But, please! The two of us — we're all we have left. Us and this farm. *Please.* Sit down. I'll make you some tea —"

Lena scowled. "It's just like Dad always said. You want things the way you want them. He warned me."

"Lena, no."

"He told me! So many things you can't even imagine! And I don't care if Derrick thinks you'd never do anything wrong, or if you've never cared one bit about me and Dad and what we think. When Derrick comes home, he'll see me and Dad were right about you all along, and then you'll be sorry!" She turned and ran.

"Lena, wait! Come back."

But the girl was already gone, her footsteps echoing as she scampered upstairs.

Violet was shaking. She prayed: with some rest, Lena would come to her senses. Tomorrow would be better. *Maybe Jago can calm her down,* she thought, before she realized her mistake.

Later, staring up into the darkness, she

wished for his voice, his counsel; even, God help her, his snores. There was no sound but the clock's chiming, and the bed was still and cold.

Spring 1945

Only when Grace awoke in the morning to find Joe gone did she begin to lament what she'd done. "I don't . . . want . . . to take advantage," he'd said, even as his hands were everywhere, and she'd whispered that she didn't mind; yes, she was sure, she didn't mind.

She guessed she'd wanted to make a new memory to cancel out the old one that would never be again. She'd wanted to forget everything she'd ever lost.

How foolish to think that Joe could take her away, just because he rode the train out of the shipyard every day. For a while last night, he'd taken her away from who she thought she was, that much was true, and it had been a float out to sea on the most pleasant of days. But now she'd awakened to reality, on the couch in her dreary flat, undressed and askew, having succeeded only in adding one more thing to her stack of things to regret. She doubted she'd ever see him again.

Alex had deserved so much better. She thought of Derrick's attic room, the maps on the wall. He would be so disappointed in her, that she was so weak; that she'd stopped believing in him and in the dreams they'd decided on.

She wished for a drink: anything to help her forget.

But she wasn't the type to start drinking at eight in the morning. Anyway, she didn't want to be. Alex and Derrick wouldn't have wanted it, either.

She wrapped herself in the blanket and went to her room for her robe, almost wishing, despite her exhaustion, that she could go to work. At least it would get her mind off things. She'd often thought it unfair that men worked seven days a week, while women were allowed to work only six. It meant that the men made so much more money, never mind that lots of girls had to support themselves.

At that thought, she felt sick, remembering Susan's long-ago comment. *If one of them dies —*

She had to do something; decided maybe she could stand to face the day if she had a good cup of coffee.

Walking past the kitchen table, she saw a note. She picked it up and read:

Dear Grace,
I really wanted to stay, but I had to go to work, and you looked so peaceful sleeping that I didn't want to wake you. I'll stop by tonight, if that's all right. I hope you'll forgive me for last night. I already can't wait to see you again.

Joe

The day crawled. A cup of coffee. A hot bath. No one to write a letter to. Trying to sew, for the first time in months; callused fingers catching on fabric, seams going crooked.

Wondering: *Will he really come back?*

Dinner at her parents' house, like every other Sunday. But she couldn't follow the conversation, could barely eat, and her young siblings were shy of her. Over the dishes, her mother's questions about her plans, now that Alex was gone. Her mother's arched eyebrow, as if she somehow sensed what Grace had done last night.

She left the minute the last glass was put away, making excuses.

Back at the flat, she took a fitful nap on

the couch, smelling Joe everywhere, trying to stop waiting for his knock at the door, and fighting off dreams of sinking into icy water, of the train puffing into the distance trailing smoke, of Lena's tearful eyes. She awoke sweating, remembering the younger girl at the graveside yesterday. Lena'd really looked like she believed Violet had poisoned Jago! Grace decided she should phone out to the farm, see if they were all right today. But just when she'd nearly mustered the will, her mother called to tell her that the memorial service for Alex was to be next Sunday.

Grace staggered back to the sofa and lay there staring at a snaking water mark on the plaster ceiling. She guessed she'd been deep down hoping there'd been some mistake.

At six, there was a knock at the door. She scrambled up, smoothing her hair and realizing too late that she should have at least tried to do something with her face. She supposed she hadn't really believed he would come.

"Grace," he said, when she opened the door.

For a moment, she was conscious of nothing but her happiness at the sight of him.

"I brought you something," he said, holding out a small paper sack that was loaded down like a sandbag.

She looked inside. "Sugar! You must have used all your ration stamps!"

"Well, I don't use it very much, and I thought you might like it. Or maybe you'd bake me a cake or something."

"A cake!"

He smiled, and it was as if sparks were raining from metal, catching on her and smoldering.

"Do you want to get some supper?" he said.

"All right," she said, and, as she stashed the little sack in the cupboard and went for her coat, she felt an unfamiliar spring in her step. The second she realized it, she made herself think of poor Alex, dear Derrick.

When they'd settled in a booth at the Black Cat and placed their orders, Joe asked, "So, how are you?" His eyes were welcoming, though there was a furrow of concern in his brow. Last night seemed to Grace like something she'd dreamed, and now she could scarcely believe he was sitting across the table from her, after all the times she'd watched him from so far away.

She couldn't think. "I tried to sew today," she blurted, "and it was awful. And I just have to keep my skills up, because, after the war's over, I'm going out to California to try to get a job at one of the movie studios." As soon as the words were out, she realized how hollow they sounded. *But I can't give up on everything,* she thought, even as she registered in his raised eyebrows, his thinning mouth and darkening eyes, that maybe he'd had a different idea of what hope she'd grab on to. Yet she'd spent so long thinking of him as a cad: she wasn't one of those girls who could hammer together a ship of dreams and launch it, all in the space of the twenty minutes since he'd knocked on her door. "Hadn't I told you?" she said, and her voice was more tentative than she would have liked.

"No."

"Well, you aren't nailed down here, are you?" That just popped out, and she was mortified: *Anchors aweigh, Hotshot! For Pete's sake.*

"There're different ways of being nailed down, you know, Grace."

"What do you mean?"

"Well, I am going to get out of this damn town, I'll promise you that. Out to the country. I'm going to get a farm, when the war's over and I can afford it."

"A *farm?*"

He nodded. "On the railroad, everything's about time — everything scheduled to the minute, weather and anything else be damned. I'd like to be my own boss, you know? Pay attention to the seasons. It's how I grew up. It's . . . home. And so's Wisconsin."

"Oh," she said, ruing that she'd gone to bed with him without stopping to ask what his dreams were. When he'd told her, years ago, that he'd left his father's farm, she'd assumed the move from country life had been for good. She'd always imagined him in motion, with the train, on his way somewhere different and new. "You really have your heart set on it?"

"I guess you could say I'm nailed down," he said. His mouth twitched in a little smile. "It's getting a little bit set on something else, too."

She shifted in her seat. His face had reddened to the shade of a peony.

Fortunately, just then the waitress came and set their steaming meals before them. The smells of fried chicken and mashed potatoes made Grace realize she was ravenous.

And she was almost ashamed of it: that she was still so alive.

■ ■ ■ ■

As they walked home, she worried over what she'd say when they got to her flat. He'd want to come in, of course, despite how their supper conversation had faltered.

She simply had to tell him that last night had been a mistake. She couldn't succumb to the temptation to lose herself in him again. Too much had already been lost. And there was California, she had to remember.

At the door, she still could seem to find no words.

"Well . . . good night?" he said.

She nodded, disappointed that he hadn't tried to get invited in, though of course she'd been planning to deny him.

He leaned in and kissed her. She felt herself starting to bend.

She pulled away. "Maybe you could come in for just a minute? There's something I have to tell you!"

He agreed, and she unlocked the door, trying to keep her hand from shaking, which seemed impossible with his eyes on her.

When they were seated on opposite ends of the sofa, she found herself caught in his smile again. "Joe, I . . . I think you're really nice," she sputtered, before she could lose her will. "Really nice. But, last night . . . I mean, I shouldn't have."

He looked away, rubbing his hands on his knees.

She felt smaller and smaller: had he considered it a mistake, too? She'd expected him to protest.

"It was my fault," he said. "Do you think you can forgive me?"

"It's just that I feel bad because . . . because of Alex! And Derrick. And I . . . I hardly know you."

"I know," he said. "I'm sorry. I just . . . well, I never could forget you." Then a lopsided grin. "Even if you had lied about your age."

"Well, I had no idea the predator you'd be! I thought it was all in innocent fun!"

He laughed. "That was Hank's fault, not mine, all right? I would never — I mean —" He blushed, evidently recalling what had happened last night on this same sofa. "Anyway, when I saw you last fall, I figured I didn't have a chance. And I was sick, besides. But still . . ."

She found she liked him much more than she wanted to. "It's just . . . I feel just awful," she managed. "I can't do this. Not right now."

"Is it because of you? Or — because of

them? Or . . . me?"

"What do you mean?"

"You know what I mean."

She chewed on her lip. "Because of them."

"What did you promise them?"

Her eyes widened. "Well, nothing specific, I guess. It's just —"

"Then can we . . . get to know each other better? Can I still see you? As friends?"

She wanted to crawl into his arms again. She was like a girl without skin, just now, and he was so appealing. "Not . . . often."

"So we can be *occasional* friends?"

She knew she should turn away; she reached for his hand, scooted closer to lean her head on his shoulder.

"I want to see you," he said into her hair. "I'm gonna go crazy if I don't."

He was turning out to be much better than she'd assumed him to be. "Every now and then," she said.

He put a finger under her chin, tipped up her face, and kissed her. And then he pushed her gently away, stood, and said good night. She could see by his crestfallen look that he was as disappointed to say it as she was to hear it. But now it was she who didn't protest; she walked him to the door.

After he'd crossed the threshold, he turned

and smiled. "Is tomorrow long enough to wait?"

They went out dancing. While he was away in the service, he'd learned the jitterbug and the Lindy Hop — he told her she'd been the motivation, how the two of them had had to sit out all but the slow songs that night they'd met. She didn't think she should believe him; wondered about all the girls he'd probably danced with, all that time away. He sure didn't dance like a farmer anymore. Every time he took her hand, she felt heat thrumming between them, and when he held her and spun her and tossed her in the air, it seemed like time itself was running on ice or sand, slip-sliding and falling and standing still when he caught her and lowered her to the ground and step, step, swing step, lost in his fathomless eyes.

Boots's certainty helped to ease Grace's mind. "Gracie, you've got to live your life," she said. "Alex and Derrick would think so, too. Anyone would." Still, Grace didn't tell Lena or Violet about how often she and Joe were going dancing, going out to eat, sharing looks. The mother and daughter were too engrossed in their own fight anyway.

Every morning and evening, like a record skipping back into its same groove, Lena would tell Violet that she couldn't stand to live with her after what she'd done, that Violet would have to leave the farm because Lena never would, not while Derrick was still coming home, and Violet would answer, "What happened wasn't my fault. I am not leaving you. I am not giving up on you." Grace felt helpless to break through — demoralizing, given her promise to Derrick. The arguments began to seem like one of her recurring nightmares, especially as she grew increasingly sleep-deprived, lying awake imagining the heat of Joe's hands, resisting with this indulgence falling into guilty ruminations or into sleep and her waiting nightmares of Alex and Derrick. In an attempt to quiet the echoing of their names in her mind, she'd asked Joe his full name, and he'd laughed when he told her, and now she often sounded it out, *Joseph Anthony Mosckiewicz,* liking the friendly mix of the harsh and soft sounds of it, the way it seemed to suit his bright eyes and cheerful nose and thick arms and the calluses on his soot-blackened hands.

When it came time for Alex's memorial service, she bore the glimmering stained glass of St. Mary's with Boots on one arm and her high school friend Hat on the other, her mother and sister, Char, Violet, and Lena trailing like bridesmaids. There was no body; he'd been buried on Okinawa. She wished the service could be one of her bad dreams, or some terrible mistake. But there was Alex's mother, in tears, and a priest, speaking of God's will and patriotism and sacrifice, and Grace finally shook with sobs, and Lena, seated behind her, rested a gentle hand on her shoulder.

That night, she cleaned up and went out dancing with Joe again, grateful for the way his smile shone in the dim red light of Lonny's Cabaret, for the indubitable heat of his hands on her waist, for the way he spun her until she was dizzy. Having her feet swept from under her was an unexpected relief, and her hollow feeling seemed to ease, even as she wanted to fall deeper and closer into him, to lose herself entirely in his heat.

In the next days, every time she met Lena's smoky eyes, she had to turn away.

I'm thinking of you and praying you'll be found soon, and that we'll meet and go dancing and everything will be just as we'd planned, she wrote, most every night. And then: *Where are you? Are you staying away on purpose? I know you didn't want to come home. You wanted to see the world. But oh, how I wanted to see it with you! Have you forgotten? Are you lost? Forever? But how can you be, when I so, so wanted — and dreamed —*

But she realized then that it didn't seem to matter anymore what she'd wanted, what she'd dreamed. And then one night she was too tired to write, having been out late dancing with Joe, and then three nights had gone by, and she tried to write a long letter to make up for missing — and found she didn't know what to say. *Are you really gone? How can you be?*

"So, mission number thirteen, my crew?" Joe said, one night at the Black Cat. She didn't know why, after all the nights they'd had of fun and laughter and trying to forget, he'd started telling her tonight about what he'd done in the war: based in England with the Army Air Forces, he'd flown twelve missions as a waist gunner aboard a B-17 bomber. Around mission number nine, he'd come down with a bad sore throat, and, finally, with his crew heading off to London on liberty, an officer ordered him to the hospital, where the doctors diagnosed him with rheumatic fever. Next thing he knew, he was on a flight back to the USA, and, after four more months in an Army hospital, he was given an honorable discharge and told to go home and rest. Now he took a sip of coffee and scowled. "Mission number thirteen, my crew was shot down." His voice trembled in a way she'd never heard. "I heard from someone they saw six parachutes open. That's six out of ten. Some of those six might have lived. They might be POWs now."

Grace's fork dangled above her half-empty plate, suddenly purposeless.

"I think about it all the time," he said. "I go to confession every week. But I don't know what to confess. I'm guilty, though. I mean, I'm glad to be alive. I'm glad to be home. Getting to know you. The dancing we've done."

They met eyes; his were as agonized as she felt, and her face was hot with shame.

He broke the gaze, set down his fork. He rubbed his hands on his knees under the table. "There's no way I should be here. I deserted them."

"But you didn't, Joe," she said, and her own dismay was forgotten in her rush to comfort him. "You didn't know. You would have stayed, if you hadn't gotten sick."

"I just don't understand it. Maybe God saved me. But why would He choose me, out of all of them? I can't stop questioning it, and that's a sin, too."

"Joe."

"I just wish I could find out which of them had made it. They were my best friends. Now I can't walk down the street without someone glaring at me. People whisper behind their hands. They think I'm a slacker."

"But, Joe, they don't know." She hated remembering that she'd thought the same thing when she'd first seen him working on the train.

When he walked her back to her flat, she invited him in.

His face flushed. "I shouldn't."

She touched his arm. "But I want you to."

She just didn't want to think of how close he'd come to dying, too, or of the gold star hanging in the Kowalskis' front window, or of Lena and Violet with their unending grief and uncertainty and Lena's wild theories, or of her nightmare of Derrick at the bottom of the sea, or of the maps in his attic room and the distance between that red X and Samar, or of all the letters she'd written and not sent. She didn't think that certain sins were as bad as others. And she wanted that feeling of pleasant waters again, of the sunshine on her face.

May 2000

Julia had been young when she stopped asking about her grandma — or her grandpa — because at any mention of them, her mom, Marty, would go straight for the liquor cabinet. So she'd had no idea that Lena had ever had a brother, much less a twin who'd gone missing in the war, the way this newspaper article in her hands now said. She almost didn't believe it, but there it was in incontrovertible black and white, the newsprint as real as the old chicken coop and the trunk open inside it, as real as the antique shoe boxes and shipyard photos spread before her on the shabby greening grass.

She wanted to leave it all where it was and take off for a long, mind-clearing run — but night was coming on, and besides, when she pictured the old woman asleep in the house, she knew she had to dig further. In the next box was a stack of brittle, folded maps, along with a note in cramped handwriting. As if the newspaper article hadn't been unsettling enough! The note was addressed to the great-uncle she'd never known she had and signed, *Love, Lena.*

Sept. 1964

Dear Derrick —
I wanted to be sure you'd have these when you come back. I always bet you were the only sailor who'd ever heard of some of the places your ship ended up — Espiritu Santo, Eniwetok, Tulagi — words that had stared back at you from a map on the wall!

Memories come to me in snatches — the marble that was the color of your eyes — remember how we pretended we were pirates and it was your glass eye? You saying, "I don't even need a patch, now!" & me telling you, "It looks very real."

I want to have it buried with me, but I can't find it anywhere — did you take it with you? Is it with you still?

I remember Dad's eyes, too — After you went missing, they were bloodshot all the time — he didn't have my same faith in you, but I know he wanted to. Sometimes he stayed out all night. I didn't blame him — she treated him like he was one of the spiders she was always trying to broom down — & one night (it was not long before the end & later I had to wonder if somehow he knew it was coming, if he knew what she would do!) he was playing one of Artie Shaw's songs, "Any Old Time" I think it was, and when he'd finished, he said to me — "If anything happens to me, I want you to have it. It's the only thing I ever managed to hang on to."

Of course I asked what it was — but he was starting in on "When You and I Were Young, Maggie," and only said, "And don't tell your mother." I laughed at him, then, and reminded him how nothing was going to happen to him, how he'd promised to be careful, but he just started singing again (can't you just hear his voice? — "I wandered today to the hill, Maggie . . .") and we never talked about it again and I guess I'd forgotten all about it until suddenly he was gone — & then I couldn't help but wonder if she knew there were other things he was keeping from her, not just you —

I have not been able to determine the *exact* plant that she used to poison him. But, you see, she thought you were dead and she blamed Dad because he'd signed those papers. Of course, that was irrational, and would have been, even if you really had been dead! I guess I don't have to tell you, I was sick to my stomach until I plain couldn't be sick anymore. How I wanted to talk with you! I knew you would know what to do — I wrote to the War Department, the Secretary of the Navy, and President Truman, but no one could tell me where you were.

I used to wonder — did you think this was the only way to "see the world"? — just to disappear — to let us think you were really gone? But you wouldn't have hurt us like that, I know — and you would've realized that I'd feel you were still *there* — so I think you must have lost your memory, and when you get it back you'll find your way home.

"People die, Lena," she would say to me, over and over — (& how I hated her for that, because it was as if she meant *you!*)

I looked & looked, dug & dug, for what Dad had left us — sometimes almost laughing to myself that it was like we were still playing pirates! — always just as sure of its existence as I'm sure that you *live* — something "larger than life," just like him! — & always knowing, too, that the only thing more important than what he'd left was *our home* — no matter what! (Even though Mom said he'd lost everything — I couldn't believe he'd have left us with nothing.)

Grace, on the other hand! — she said she still loved you, she was still writing you letters, saving them in a shoe box! But her eyes were as hollow as caves — & when you read the letters you'll see she wasn't quite as faithful as she made herself out to be! I still remember the first time I saw her with him at the shipyard, standing close up against the stopped train — they did a couple of jokey dance steps & they were laughing. I didn't confront her — I thought, when you came home, then she'd be sorry — she'd see what she'd been doing — I couldn't bear to think how it would break your heart — her being so untrue — the way you loved her —

Suddenly desperate to shed the dust she could feel like a film on her skin, Julia shoved the old papers and boxes back inside the shed, slammed the door shut on its darkness, and ran into the warm light of the house, straight into the bathroom. Could any of it be true? *Lena was certifiable, wasn't she, isn't that the only explanation?* To think there'd been a poisoning — a murder — in the family! Julia couldn't believe it, especially if that frail woman in the bedroom now was Violet. Clearly, Lena had just been unhinged by Derrick's disappearance, accusing her own mother of such a thing — not to mention harboring a grudge for twenty years against his old girlfriend Grace because she'd moved on.

Julia was starting to understand why her mom and Alice never wanted to talk about the past.

Thinking of the photograph of Grace, of the inscription on its back obviously intended for Derrick — *To my darling, If you insist!* — she turned on the shower as hot and high as it would go and retrieved her blue silk robe from the hook on the back of the bathroom door. And then the silk under her fingers made her recall that morning after the accident, her hair dripping on the rug in front of Ryan's dresser and making small, wet dots on the blue sleeve, while she looked in his sock drawer and found, buried at the back, the diamond ring she'd exclaimed over in a store window a couple months earlier.

She'd had the strange impulse to swallow it.

Instead, she'd removed it from its cushion and slid it onto her finger.

But the next day, his mother had noticed, cleared her throat delicately, and said, "You know, since he didn't actually propose, and the charge is outstanding on his credit card, I'd have to pay for it out of his estate, and I'd *really* rather set up a scholarship fund in his name. I know you've never worked for a living, but Ryan worked hard to get to where he was, and I just know he'd've liked to help other deserving young people. Will you please give me the ring so I can return it to the store?" Julia had been too stunned to fight.

Maybe the way Violet was, when Lena accused her, Julia thought, feeling suddenly so tired, recalling how sliding the ring off her finger had felt like drawing a wire through a vein, deciding maybe this Grace person *had* been a bit shallow, to console herself with that railroad man.

Were Lena's accusations the reason Violet had left and stayed gone so long? But why had she come here now looking for Grace, not for Lena? And had Lena ever found what her dad left for her? It seemed unlikely; if Julia had the dates figured right, Lena had died shortly after writing that letter.

Hating the way the house was beginning to feel so haunted, when she'd tried so hard to rid it of its dust, Julia let down her hair and stepped into the tub, into the pouring water, bracing her hand on the wall like an old person — like Violet — might do.

June 1945

"So, are you looking forward to unemploy-
ment, girlie?" Sean O'Connor said, nudging
Grace as they walked toward the rod shack
one sunny morning.

She glared. Maybe she shouldn't have
been in such a foul mood — the mid-June
weather was gorgeous, the water a glisten-
ing blue and the breeze an occasional sigh
— but Joe had stayed with her last night,
and around three he'd awakened her with
his thrashing and yelling: another nightmare. After soothing him back to sleep,
she'd stayed awake, her mind racing over
the question of what she was going to do,
now that layoffs had begun at the shipyard.

The government had canceled its order
for Hulls 53 and 54, so, after the ship that
was to be launched next week, only two
more were under construction. The work
would dry up entirely by August, and the

230

shipyard would shut down. No more ships rising out of the earth, no more launch celebrations with their marching bands and radio announcers and patriotic bunting and bleachers packed with hysterical crowds. When Grace tried to imagine the ghostly silence, to envision a life without her work there, she felt — well — unmoored.

As much as she'd talked about going to California, when she thought of it now, she couldn't help remembering how her once much-beloved glossy photo of Tyrone Power had ended up curdled by a wet glass she'd set on it in her distraction when she was getting dressed to go to the senior spring dance with Alex. She couldn't deny that lately she'd found such tangible satisfaction in the neat folding of metal into metal, the gorgeous, sturdy filling of cracks. And in dancing with Joe.

"I've got a job lined up through the union already," Sean said.

"Good for you," Grace snapped, and she was already wistful for her crisp paychecks in their SUPERIOR SHIPBUILDING CO. envelopes. No one was going to be hiring women welders in peacetime. Thank goodness, of course, that Germany had surrendered, and that the march continued in the Pacific. She just wished the yard could go on building ships.

But the last thing she wanted was to get stuck in this town, with all her old dreams curdled like that once-prized photo, so she'd written away to a design school in Los Angeles. She'd liked Chicago, but a school near Hollywood would get her all the connections she needed to go into the movie business — or so the glossy brochure promised. And if the dream wasn't quite what it once had been, at least it was something to grab on to, something to help pull her from the magnetizing forces of her family, Lena and Violet and waiting for Derrick — even Joe, with his gorgeous eyes and warm hands and sweetness.

Suddenly, her stomach tied itself in a knot. She clapped her hand over her mouth and ran toward the ladies' room. She didn't make it. She dropped to her knees behind a pile of steel beams and threw up.

She heard Sean's voice behind her. "You all right?"

Humiliation crawled on her skin. "Fine!" she said, standing.

Too quick. She wobbled.

Sean grabbed her elbow and frowned. "You'd better go to the nurse."

"I'm fine. Let's go." She didn't know what

she'd eaten to upset her stomach, but she really did feel fine, now that whatever it was was out of her system.

Sean wasn't convinced. He pressed the back of his hand to her forehead.

She brushed him away. "Sean."

A sudden grin split his face. "Hotshot!" he said. "Have you been enjoying extracurricular activities in the evenings?"

Her eyes widened.

"And I don't mean bowling," he said, with a wink.

She swallowed.

"If only I'd known you were that kind of girl . . ."

"Be quiet!" she said, pushing past him, heading for the rod shack. *It couldn't be.* She and Joe had been careful.

Her stomach was upset, that was all. She tried to remember when she'd last bled. She'd been irregular since she started work at the shipyard. Missed periods had been a blessing, in fact, since it was no picnic having to deal with cramps on top of all the other pains that came with the job — not to mention the wisecracks from the men when you asked too often for restroom breaks.

Sean caught up with her. "Really, Hotshot. You should see the nurse. I mean, is there a chance . . . ?"

"What would you know about it?"

"My mom had eight kids after me. You get to know the signs."

"I just got sick," she said. "That's all."

But when the same thing happened the next morning, Sean said something into Russ's ear. Grace, who'd sat down on the ground to tighten her bootlaces, wanted to scream, watching Russ's eyes widen, his face soften.

He came and crouched beside her. He spoke softly. "I think you'd better go see the nurse."

She shot a death glare at Sean. "I'm fine."

"Anderson, if there's any chance, I can't risk you getting hurt. Tell me the truth. Is there a chance?"

Sean was watching, his look almost sympathetic. *Ask your men if they're getting screwed on the weekends,* Grace wanted to tell Russ. She yanked a double-knot into her bootlace.

Russ sighed. "You've got to go to the infirmary and get checked. I can't let you back to work until you do. Take a couple sick days." He stood, brushing off his knees. "Come on, fellows, the day waits."

"It's crazy," Grace told the nurse. "The idea of it."

The nurse raised an eyebrow.

"Well, all right, not strictly *crazy*. Not *impossible,* I guess! But —"

"I'm not equipped," the nurse said, "to test you here. You'll have to see a doctor." She sat down at her desk, began writing.

"Can't you just say I'm *not?* Let me go back to work? Isn't that your *job,* to make sure everyone's working who can be? I'm not *sick.*"

The nurse tore a sheet of paper from a pad, handed it to Grace. "Four days should be enough for you to get your test results. Give this to your supervisor; he'll file it with the office. Go today to the doctor. Don't wait."

"For Pete's sake," Grace said. The note in her hand, on shipyard infirmary stationery, read, *Miss Anderson is excused from work for four days for feminine trouble.*

That was putting it mildly, she thought.

She walked downtown and straight to a doctor's office. Not her regular doctor: he would have immediately called her mother.

"I'm so embarrassed," she told the new doctor, who was a large man with a gray walrus mustache. "My wedding ring got washed down the drain. I was washing dishes and it just slid right off and I didn't

235

realize and I let out the plug. My husband was furious, of course — it happened right after his last leave — but he says he'll buy me a new one, but until he gets home, I guess I'm just a scandal."

"Well," said the doctor, with a wink, "I'm sure he'll forgive you if you give him a nice, healthy boy."

"Do you — um — have a basin or something? I'm . . . not feeling very well."

She told everyone she had the flu. She refused to see even Joe. He called every night, wanting to bring her soup. "I don't want you seeing me like this," she told him. She'd been chewing her nails, the ends of her hair. "Besides, I can't keep a thing down." That was true in the mornings. In the afternoons, she was ravenous, and sneaked out to the Black Cat for fried chicken platters, thinking of the rabbits in the doctor's basement. The doctor had explained that he would inject one with her urine and, after three days had passed, he would dissect it. If he found that its ovaries had been stimulated, then he would know that certain hormones were present in Grace's urine — in other words, that she was pregnant. "Dissect?" she'd asked him. "You mean . . . ?"

"Let me assure you, dear, the rabbit doesn't suffer," he'd told her, patting her hand.

He called on the fourth day. "Congratulations, Mrs. Anderson!"

She imagined the rabbit sliced open in front of him on a cold steel table, his bloody hand clutching the phone while he grinned under his mustache. "Oh," she said, and gently hung up.

"Jesus," Joe said, when she told him that night, seated on the couch in her flat. He shrank from her like she'd said she had a communicable disease. She squeezed one hand in the other and watched the thoughts marching across his face: *How did it happen? Is it mine?*

Remembering all the nights: *Of course, yes, it's mine.*

And finally, again, the fear of God.

"We're going to have to get married," he said. "As soon as possible. When can you?"

She was astonished, though perhaps she shouldn't have been. She supposed she'd sensed his guilt, hovering on his skin like a bruise that hadn't yet turned purple. Maybe that was how she'd gone so far without precisely wondering about his intentions — had she known, deep down, that he would

237

"do the right thing," if it came to that? She liked to think so. But maybe her efforts to forget her losses had simply been so consuming that she hadn't considered anything else — at least until these past few days.

Now being told how things would be was some relief. *Of course, this is the right thing,* she thought, though her hands felt clammy.

She could hear Hat, teasing her about "Hollywood dreams": *Look at the way this town pulls at you, sucks you down.* She imagined what her parents would say, foresaw the long lifetime of being under her mother's thumb. She envisioned Lena; almost couldn't bear to, and shut off the thought of her, of Derrick's long-ago letters, of Alex.

Joe was waiting; she choked out a laugh. "My calendar's free. Except for my scheduled event next February."

He took her hand. "I'm sorry it turned out like this. Not quite what we'd intended."

She shrugged, not wanting to say that nothing had been what she'd intended since that autumn three years ago when she'd ridden the train north out of Chicago, watching the leaves drift to the ground and imagining her father up and dancing before Christmas.

"But, you know," Joe said, "I was going to

ask you to marry me, anyway. When I got settled. I was hoping . . . The first time I saw you — Have I told you? Everyone else in the room disappeared. And it's been like that, always, ever since."

She tried to smile. Tears started. Tomorrow, she'd go to work one last time and clean out her locker. She'd throw that glossy design school brochure into the fire. She'd have to tell Boots and Violet and Lena. She'd lose Lena's friendship, for sure. Her life as she knew it was over, and it was her own fault, for succumbing to her need to feel alive, for imagining that there would be no lasting consequences.

Given everything that had happened, she really didn't know how she could have even begun to imagine such a thing.

He pulled her close, stroked her hair. "Grace, I love you. Don't ever doubt it, all right? Even if this isn't . . . isn't the best way to start out. Like I said, from the first minute I saw you, I think I did."

She raised her head.

"I can't think of anything better than marrying you. You're going to have my baby."

She realized: part of her had still suspected him of being a cad. She supposed she'd feared he would burn her, the way Alex and Derrick had, through no fault of theirs. But she'd been wrong. Only that he was good and sincere to his core could account for the warmth of his eyes in this moment. She felt her disappointment collapsing, and a tentative anticipation springing from its dust, even as she wanted to weep anew at crossing the threshold from knowing to believing: Derrick wasn't coming back, and Alex, too, was gone, and the only comfort to be found was that they would never know the many ways in which she'd betrayed them.

"Of course," she said to Joe. She trembled a smile into place and kissed him.

At first, with Jago gone, Violet had slept like she was sinking to the bottom of the sea. No matter how she missed his heat and his voice, or how Lena had twisted the knife of her accusation on any given day, physical exhaustion would drag her down like an iron clasp around her ankle. She had accustomed herself to the silence, to the absence of his snoring, his jabbing elbows.

But then she'd begun to dream of walking into her bedroom to find him lying there dead. Or, sometimes, not there at all: just gone. She would feel again the panic, the helplessness, the wanting to fall down and weep. Lena would be there sometimes, saying, *Did you think I wouldn't know?* And Violet would run out and look in all directions, see nothing but the mist. She'd turn back to find the house gone, also; even Lena. And then Violet, too, was disappearing in the fog.

Tonight, with her nightmares beginning to seem more and more like premonitions, she couldn't sleep at all.

She wondered if Jago had told Lena about the post office box he had in town. If Lena knew all the so-called motives Violet might have had to poison him — things of which Violet herself had been unaware.

"He never wanted you to know about this, I guess," the postmaster had said, muddy boots planted on the farmhouse stoop, when he stopped by one evening last week. He was scratching his bald head. He handed over the stack of envelopes stamped PAST DUE. "But I finally thought you'd want to wrap up his affairs, and all." Avarice shone in his eyes; everyone in town would want her reaction. Violet shut the door in his face. She sat down at the kitchen table with the stack of letters from the First National Bank of Hurley.

Jago had mortgaged the farm on September 26, 1922, for six hundred dollars.

Before we were married. When I was meet-

241

ing him in the park on Sundays!

It was never mine at all.

He'd been paying on the mortgage haphazardly, these many years, it seemed. A dollar or two or three at a time. Sometimes five or ten dollars, as if to get the bank's hopes up. They'd been lenient with him; he must have had a friend in the management. A handwritten letter in the latest notice confirmed it. *We haven't heard from you in some time, Jago, and sincerely hope all is well with you and your family. We would hate to have to impose penalty fees on your account, so do let us hear from you soon.*

My egg money, she realized. *And all those times he left me. It wasn't just that woman he was cheating me with.*

She'd imagined that "Darling J." would have come out of the woodwork when he died, trying to stake some claim on him, but "Darling J." must have known better than Violet how he had nothing left to claim. Before Violet had married him, he'd told her he *hadn't put the deed to the farm on the table.* Maybe that was true. But he'd lost it anyway, before the deed had even cooled in his hand. And lied to her! And now, after almost twenty-three years, he still owed a hundred and seventy-six dollars on it.

He could have paid the mortgage off with about two weeks' earnings from the shipyard.

The next day, she found out from hangdog shipbuilders why he hadn't: there really had been card games on Friday nights. He'd lost every penny he'd earned. (When, she wondered, had he found time for "Darling J."?)

Then Lena let it slip that Jago had been borrowing money from her, too. "I didn't mind! He was going to pay me back. It doesn't matter." When Violet pressed, Lena admitted she'd given him more than two hundred dollars. The way Lena wouldn't meet her eyes, Violet feared that might not even have been the whole truth.

At the bank, the manager blushed to tell her that Jago had cleared out the family savings account. Violet was sick. Why hadn't she had the brains to put the money she'd earned into a secret account? Even after looking in his wallet that night! Why hadn't she realized? She'd been such a fool, yet again, to think that this could have been like any other time, after what had happened to Derrick.

For a moment, she pitied him. *He must have been so desperate to win.*

Then the insurance company informed her that his life insurance policy had been cashed in three months before he died. Her heart cracking like hot glass in sudden cold, she felt she might not have been an orphan until now. And then she hated him — how she hated him, for leaving her this way!

And now, today, a letter had arrived from Aviation Ordnance Man Second Class Percy Franklin.

Dear Mr. and Mrs. Maki and Lena,
Your letter of last November finally reached me. It is difficult to know what to say in a case like this. I hope you will have already received word from someone who knows more than I do. What I can tell you for certain is that Derrick and I spent many hours together in the ordnance shack onboard ship, making up machine gun ammunition, etc. He would have us all laughing with his stylish renditions of popular songs. He was one of the top gunners in our squadron, winning most target practice competitions, beating yours truly time and again.

But — on the Day in question, Oct. 25. After the Jap fleet was spotted, I was on the flight deck when Lt. Nelson's aircraft (with Derrick as gunner) took off. As I was climbing into my aircraft, I heard someone say that theirs had been low on gas. We were all in quite a hurry, since the Japanese fleet had been sighted only a few miles away, a few minutes before.

After we had all made runs at them, we were circling back around and saw an aircraft smoking. Shortly, it nosed into the water. After the crew got into their life raft, we dropped dye markers and a float light. We circled around, waiting for another aircraft to join up, but none did. The crew in the water waved to say they were fine. They were approximately thirty miles out from shore. My pilot reported their position, and we went to make another run. I can't say with absolute certainty, but we were pretty sure it was Lt. Nelson, your son, and ARM3 Grabowski that we saw in the water. None of them have been seen since that day, to my knowledge.

I wish I could tell you more. You've probably heard that the fellows who were aboard our ship when she went down were in the water for approximately 40 hours, waiting for rescue. You surely know that many of them were lost during this time. So although I don't want to be glum about the fate of your son and the others, it is honestly difficult to say for certain what would have happened to three men on a life raft in an isolated position. Though, like I said above, all three appeared in fine health when we last saw them. I hope and pray they are alive and well, and that by now you've heard more news than what I can offer. I hope you'll tell me, if you have.

Derrick was a fine friend to me and a sailor you can be proud of.

Sincerely yours,
AOM2 Percy Franklin, USN

As soon as she'd read it, Lena had crowed, "He's alive! I knew it!" She'd clapped and laughed and burst into noisy tears.

Violet read the letter again, trying to make sense of it. She couldn't focus. Phrases jumped out. *They were fine. None of them have been seen since. It is honestly difficult to say . . .*

She sat down across from Lena's happy tears. Yet what began to leak from her own eyes were tears of anguish. She imagined her little boy, on a small raft in the vast ocean, waving bravely to the plane above that would fly off and leave him there.

"I have to call Grace," Lena said, grinning, wiping her face on her sleeve.

Violet tried to object. She could find no words.

Lena placed the call. There was no answer.

When Lena hung up the telephone, Violet managed to say, "We still don't know."

"We know his plane landed in the water, and he was fine. All they had to do was get the raft to shore. He's out there somewhere!"

Violet wished Jago were there, to help try to explain to Lena the odds.

As it was, she didn't dare mention the hazards that would face three boys on one small raft in the ocean. She didn't dare remind her daughter that this Percy Franklin wasn't even certain that the crew he'd seen was Derrick's — or, if it had been, how far out they'd been from any shore; how there'd been a battle raging in the sea and air around them.

She hadn't dared mention how all of Percy Franklin's descriptions of Derrick had been in the past tense.

But tonight, trying to sleep, these were the only things she could think of.

She didn't remember falling asleep, but she awoke when Derrick came and sat on the edge of the bed again. She saw him in the moonlight, and he smiled a little.

"Derrick?" She raised herself on her elbows. She was not as frightened this time.

His sweet little-boy expression was achingly familiar. Like the last time, he was wearing his dress blues and his bright white sailor cap. And just as he'd done before, he crossed one ankle over his other knee so she could see the high gloss of his black shoe.

"Are you all right, Derrick?" She was afraid that if she reached for him, he would disappear.

He looked peaceful, sitting there. At least he wasn't angry with her.

"Derrick? Are you all right?" she said again.

He gave her a little wave, much like he'd done at the depot when he left for the last time. There was a trace of irony on his lips. *Like his father,* she thought. "I'm sorry!" she told him. "I've been trying my best!"

But he seemed to be telling her he was all right, everything was all right. He seemed to be absolving her of everything.

Sobs were rising within her, but she didn't want to upset him. She swallowed hard and watched him until her elbows wouldn't hold her up any longer. Then she sank into her pillow and her eyes drifted closed and she slept.

■ ■ ■ ■

In the soft light of early morning, Lena slammed the kitchen drawer and brandished a spatula. Bacon sputtered in a frying pan, scenting the air. "I don't care what you think! It was just a dream! It was your own mind telling you something to ease your conscience! You just don't want to believe you killed Dad for nothing!"

"No, Lena, no," Violet insisted. No matter how it sickened her to have Lena believe such things, Lena was her *child* — and she needed to understand the truth. "It was Derrick. He wanted to tell me we have to let him go. And he *believed* me. Why can't you? Please!"

Tears coated Lena's ravaged face. "You're making this up! You're making it up!"

"Lena, please. I don't say this to hurt you. I don't want to believe it any more than you. But he's at peace. I could see it!"

"What kind of a *mother* are you?" Lena cried. "Giving up on him this way? When we just got that letter! Which *proves* he survived!" She hurled the spatula at the wall and banged outside, slamming the door behind her as the spatula clattered to the floor.

Violet stood still until the reverberations of Lena's private earthquake had ceased.

She had to work to breathe.

Then, though her hands shook and her legs didn't want to carry her, she picked up the spatula, brought it to the sink to scrub it clean, and went to tend to the bacon.

Sitting between John Tuomi and Violet, Lena was like a storm cloud; John stopped trying to make conversation and just drove. Violet's head pounded. She closed her eyes and tried to rest, but all she could see was Derrick's face in the moonlight. All she could hear was Lena's voice: *What kind of a* mother *are you?* Violet didn't know. She tried to remember her own mother, Hannah, but the only picture she could invoke was of Hannah arranging purple flowers in a vase. In the memory, Hannah's shirtwaist was lavender; her skirt, royal purple. She was humming a tune, while little Violet stood on a chair, thrilled with the beauty before her.

But most of life wasn't beautiful, and this memory was the only model of motherhood Violet had had. It probably wasn't even real — she'd been just two when Hannah had died. Was it any wonder that she hadn't known what to do for her children, beyond providing material needs? That she didn't know what to do now?

At the shipyard, Lena hurried ahead to the locker room. By the time Violet walked in, Lena was sitting on the bench facing Grace and Boots. Grace was smiling; Lena must have told her about Percy Franklin's letter. In Lena's mind, it had been good news.

But when Grace saw Violet, confusion passed over her face.

Is my doubt so obvious? Violet thought. *No wonder Lena hates me.*

Then she noticed that, although Boots was already dressed in coveralls, Grace was in pants and a plaid shirt. Violet was irritated. Already Grace had taken four sick days — unheard of.

"Grace," she said. "Back among the living, I see?" Horror struck her, but it was too late to take back the words.

Grace flinched; her eyes darted to Lena. "Well, girls," she ventured. "I have some news."

When Grace told them, Violet didn't know if it was she or Lena who gasped so loudly. Lena jumped up and went to her locker, yanking out her coveralls and wrestling herself into them. Violet shot Grace a look of apology, thinking Lena would say something after she finished getting dressed.

But Lena walked out.

"Lena, wait!" Grace called after her.

"I'm sorry," Violet said, her voice unsteady. "I think it might just take her a little while to come around."

Grace was pale. "I'm sorry," she said. "Just when she was so hopeful. Now I've disappointed her. She thinks Derrick is going to be coming home." There was a question in her eyes. *Did Violet believe, too?*

Violet tried to swallow. "Grace, I . . . I saw him last night."

Grace and Boots drew in sharp breaths.

Violet thought, *How strange, one life ending, another beginning.* She prayed that the life growing inside Grace would not be lost. She thought she would do anything to make sure that it wasn't. "Lena thinks it was just a dream. But it was like he came to me." Violet crouched and took Grace's hand. "I know you did all you could for him."

"Oh, Violet," Grace said, pressing her fist to her mouth. "Oh."

"He'd want you to be happy."

"I'm sorry! I didn't mean to doubt — I wished so much —"

Violet shook her head. "Maybe I've always known."

"But Lena," Grace objected. "Lena said she's sure he's alive. Just now, she said that. I was hoping I was wrong!"

"But *I* know . . . it wasn't just a dream, last night."

Boots stood, pulled Violet to her feet and hugged her tight. Violet pictured herself shattering into a thousand pieces, collapsing into a pile of dust.

Later, the three of them walked out to the yard, Violet and Boots in their coveralls, Grace with her gear under her arm, heading to the office to sign out for the last time. Violet gathered herself enough to ask, "Now, when is the wedding? I'd like to be there, if I could."

"Yes, Violet, I hope you can. In about a month, I think. I'll let you all know." Grace squared her shoulders.

"Joe has a good job, doesn't he? After the war, too?"

"Oh, yes. Yes, thanks. He wants to buy a house. He has some money saved."

"Good."

Grace smiled. Surprising, this glimmer of happiness — Violet had been on the verge of forgetting what it was.

Grace said, "He's hoping to find a farm, actually, Violet. Can you imagine — me, a farmwife? Named Grace Mosckiewicz?" She chuckled, and when she looked at Boots, Boots started, too. And then the two laughed together like a hard rain pounding dry ground.

But Violet just nodded to herself, thinking of Jago's unpaid debts, of everything she'd lost. Thinking, *I guess I thought it was mine and he was mine but nothing ever was.*

She realized: Lena didn't understand. *That we're the only ones left who are tied together by our same blood. That everything else I thought I had has turned to dust.*

She realized: she had no choice. She had to do what she could, to save what remained.

■ ■ ■ ■

PART THREE: DUST

■ ■ ■ ■

Summer 1945–Winter 1946

Grace and Joe moved in at the farm the day the atomic bomb was dropped on Hiroshima, which was the same day that Major Bong, the famous flying ace who'd thrilled the crowd at the shipyard last year, was killed in California while test-piloting a jet, breaking the collective local heart.

Grace was three months pregnant, and Joe wouldn't let her lift a thing.

They'd had a courthouse wedding a couple weeks before, attended by Grace's family and a few friends. Grace had dreaded telling her parents her news, and their reaction had been every bit as disaffecting as she'd feared. They were kind enough not to mention how quickly she'd apparently rebounded from Alex's death. At the wedding, her mother made a show of her acceptance; her dad stood by, wavering, it seemed to Grace, between resignation and small surges of optimism.

She'd been startled by Violet's offer of the farm. But, after Violet had explained that she wanted to start over with Lena in a place that was theirs alone, where they wouldn't every day be reminded of their losses, Grace had understood.

"What does Lena think?" she'd asked.

Violet had frowned. "It'll be best for her. The farm has such a memory. And she'll never leave it on her own."

"But does she know? That you're selling?" Lena was barely speaking to Violet; the idea of them moving away together to start fresh seemed idealistic, at best.

A pause. "I haven't told her. But, Grace, if she stays on that farm, she'll never stop . . . mourning."

Grace hated to see Violet so sad. Deciding that buying the farm could be a way of keeping her promise to Derrick, she remembered how she'd felt the first time she stepped into the house, like it had swallowed her — for better and worse. As Derrick had written, it was a feeling of inevitability, of knowing where you belonged. Still, she wasn't sure it wouldn't be just the place to remind her of her own losses, every moment of every day.

But when she told Joe about it, he grinned

and got out his bankbook to check his savings account balance. "When can I look at it?" he asked.

She didn't want to quash his excitement. He said he was sure that, if he lived in the country again, his nightmares of the war would cease. If only! And if only he could know the fates of his old crew members. He'd heard nothing so far, though the POW camps in Europe had been liberated.

Violet had said they could visit the farm any time while she and Lena were at work. Still, when Grace and Joe walked into the unlocked house one hot July day, Grace couldn't help feeling like a trespasser. She remembered the cold night she'd spent here last November, sleeping in Derrick's bed, and the gray afternoon of Jago's funeral: Lena's tears, Derrick's maps.

But Joe, rushing through, declared the place perfect.

"Don't you think it's kind of . . . rustic?" Grace asked, trailing him, thinking for the first time of really living there. Romantic notions of Derrick aside, she was used to her parents' house in town — the modern appliances, the central heating, the polished woodwork. The indoor bathroom. The farm was all rag rugs strewn over plank floors, whitewashed log walls, an old wood-burning stove in the living room for heat, another in the kitchen for cooking. And was that an actual pump at the sink, rather than a faucet? She'd forgotten. *No wonder Violet wants to get away,* she thought. Besides, remembering the bad things that had happened to the Makis, Grace couldn't suppress a whir of superstitious misgivings about starting a new family here.

But after Joe proclaimed the barn "a diamond in the rough" and the chicken coop "serviceable," they wandered into the strawberry patch and crouched between the rows where Derrick had spent so many hours as a child. Joe picked a sun-warmed berry and fed it to her. Loving Joe's smile, she remembered Derrick writing that fresh strawberries were among his favorite things. She caught the scent on the air: *hay that's just been cut,* he'd said, for summer. She thought of tending this garden. Although they'd never met, they'd be forever connected.

Anyway, it was Joe's dream, and hadn't she signed on to give him everything? Wasn't that what love and marriage *meant?* So she handed over her war bonds and the money from her savings — even from her California fund, and she had the sense of *good riddance* that she'd grown out of that silly glossy-photo phase and was a *grown-up* now, a *wife* and soon a *mother* — and they came up with the fifteen hundred dollars Violet had asked for. They had both been saving for a long time.

One hot afternoon, two weeks after they'd moved in, the telephone rang. Immersed in mending a pair of Joe's pants, Grace kept the sewing machine treadle pumping while she listened to the party line ring: two long, one short. That was hers, she was pretty sure.

As she stood, it struck her how little had changed since she'd visited the Makis here. Violet and Lena had left the furniture and taken only personal things: sheet music, books, scrapbooks, photographs, dishes, linens, clothes. It had seemed convenient at the time. Grace and Joe hadn't had much, and Violet and Lena were going to be living in Grace's old flat with Boots until their jobs at the shipyard ended, then — according to Violet, anyway — heading off who knew where. Violet had said she wanted to travel light.

Now only the corner with Grace's sewing machine was different, and she couldn't help feeling that the Makis' return was still as inevitable as Derrick had suggested.

More than once, when Joe had kissed her awake in the morning, she'd been mortified to have been roused out of a dream of Derrick. Every time she'd decided he was really gone for good, doubt and hope would seem to creep in. The fact that his empty bed remained in the attic didn't help. Sometimes, when the days got long, with Joe always gone at work or outside doing chores, she would steal up there and sit, running her hand over the pillow where Derrick's head had lain, letting her eyes drift over the maps on the wall and linger on California, on the empty place in the ocean off Samar. She thought of how she'd watched Joe on the train, imagining he was actually getting somewhere, when it seemed now that all he'd been doing was looking for a square of mud to plant his boots in. It was strange, she thought, the things a girl could imagine.

Thank goodness, really, that she had to run like crazy to keep up with the housework. It kept her from thinking too much. Except sometimes she couldn't help thinking that everything on the farm had been paid for with the California money that she'd earned at the shipyard. And sometimes she couldn't help thinking of dancing in a flowing gown, waiting at a dock in San

Diego for a ship that somehow Derrick was on.

The kitchen needed modernizing. That ugly old wood-burning stove. Joe had promised, smiling in that way that threw sparks, the minute they had enough money, she could get a new stove, and they'd add an indoor bathroom. Of course, now that they'd spent their savings, and Grace wasn't working anymore, and Joe wasn't putting in the extra-long hours that he had during the war, that wasn't going to be anytime soon. They hadn't been dancing since long before their wedding.

She answered the phone mid-ring. "Hello?"

"Grace? It's Lena."

"Oh!" Grace felt her face heat up. Lena hadn't spoken to Grace since Grace's announcement that day in the locker room. Even at the wedding, when Grace and Joe had lined up to receive congratulations, Lena had only met Grace's eyes with a stony gaze and kissed her cheek quickly before moving away, leaving Grace in her new petal pink suit and veiled hat feeling like a convicted felon. By that time, Violet had told Lena that Grace and Joe would be buying the farm.

And now here was Lena on the phone,

her voice breathy, far away. "Listen, Grace, I was wondering if I could come out to see you? Tonight?"

"Oh! All right." She'd just assented.

"I'll ride out with Mr. Tuomi. Probably get there about seven. Tomorrow's our last day of work, you know? We've been laid off."

"Oh!" The shipyard seemed as distant as another country; Grace had forgotten about the imminent layoffs. She thought of Russ, of Sean O'Connor.

"I'd better go," Lena said. "See you tonight, then?"

"Yes, all right. But wait — What . . . what do you want?"

But the line was already dead.

She scurried around, dusting every surface. She swept and washed the floors, blacked the stoves, finished off her stitching and folded away her sewing machine. She picked a heaping basket of tomatoes, cucumbers, and onions from the garden. As though, if she could only prove to Lena how *capable* she was, Lena would cease being angry over the farm, cease being angry at Grace.

But what to make for supper? Lena and Joe would have working men's appetites — Grace remembered what that felt like. She looked in the icebox: lettuce, bacon, eggs, milk, cream, a square of butter, the produce she'd picked. Where did the time go? She'd planned to walk the three miles to the co-op for groceries today, but the laundry and mending had taken much longer than she'd expected. If only she were at her mother's house, or at the flat, where there was a market on every corner!

She remembered the crate of new potatoes in the cellar. She'd make boiled potatoes and wilted lettuce salad with bacon dressing, and serve pickled cucumbers and sliced tomatoes on the side.

Not enough, she realized. If it had been just her and Joe, she might have gotten away with it. But she didn't dare show the cracks in her façade to Lena. There had to be meat.

In the backyard, several hens were in sight, waddling and pecking at the ground. Grace had never imagined she'd live in such close proximity to chickens, much less a cow and a passel of cats. So far, Joe had been tending to the animals before and after work, selling the leftover milk, cream, and eggs at the co-op on Saturdays. Grace dreaded the day when she would have to do the milking, but she was certain it would come, at least after the baby arrived.

She had even less desire to butcher a chicken, but it seemed her only option. She remembered Violet pointing out the butchering ax, which leaned in the back porch's corner. At the time, Grace had taken no more than a passing interest, as if it had nothing to do with *her.* The polished blade shone; red paint was half worn away from the handle. When she picked it up, she was surprised by its weight.

How to catch a chicken had not been explained. She tiptoed up behind one, but it let out a squawk and ran. "Oh, come on!" she yelled. It didn't look back.

The air was heavy; the grass emitted a moist heat. She decided not to carry the ax with her; the chickens probably knew, somewhere in their tiny brains, what it meant. She leaned it against the stump near the garden where Violet had said the butchering was done.

She set off again toward the nearest chicken. "Come here, California," she crooned. Suddenly, they were all named California.

She hated how she sweat, how she was getting fat. Nearly four months pregnant, she imagined she was starting to waddle like the laying hens. Joe was hoping for a boy, to be named Joseph Anthony, Junior. He was hoping to quit his railroad job in the fall in favor of "the woods" — she'd have a lumberjack for a husband. A lumberjack who sometimes smelled like a farmer, like alive things: yeast, manure, chicken feed. She didn't know why this all appealed to him so much. They could have had a nice little house in town. Even a big house, with the money they'd saved. But no, he'd wanted this dirty old farm. And how could she have refused his smile? (*I'm sorry,* she said to Derrick in her mind. *It's just — look at me! Could you ever have* imagined? *And you never told me about the manure smell; the dirt!*)

And soon there would be soiled baby diapers, making more unpleasant smells, not to mention endless laundry. She'd had enough of that as a big sister: at twelve years old, she'd been changing her baby brother's diapers; even at eight, her baby sister's.

"Here, California," Grace called to the clucking red hen, whose tail feathers switched and neck stretched with each step, one direction or another, as if in desperate debate where to turn. Oh, it was hot, sweat making Grace's too-thick legs and arms sticky, as she thought back to the cold winters and the hot torch of the welding machine, the slow rhythm of fusing metal to metal along a seam. If she'd found the rhythm to that, she could find the rhythm to walking up behind a chicken and snatching it — where? By the neck? The feet? Would it try to bite her? Peck at her? Would it draw first blood, before she could get it to the stump and the ax?

All right, make it walk in that direction, then. A white hen had come wandering toward her, pecking along the ground. Grace turned to fall in behind it, letting the red one go. She was surprised by her good fortune when the white one kept moving in the right direction. She urged it on with her apron, imagining grabbing its neck, rehearsing in her mind the heft of the ax, noticing the way the white feathers folded so gracefully over the body — *did chickens have fleas?* Watching the tail feathers switching, the head bobbing toward the earth, the beak seeking bugs, or something else that Grace couldn't fathom, in the grass.

She was close now, so close. The senseless hen actually stopped. Had found something delicious in the lawn, evidently. Grace crept closer. She crouched. Reached out. Closed her hand around the white neck.

The chicken screamed, a terrible shriek that made Grace's spine constrict. She heaved it off the ground, and it was heavier than she would have imagined, and stronger, too, beating its wings, kicking its talon feet, struggling to get free. But Grace had spent months hauling welding equipment around the shipyard. She got both hands on the writhing neck and ran, gripping the screaming hen like a guidon in front of her, to the stump.

Sweat dripping, she wrapped her left hand in her apron and managed to grab the feet. The smell of wet feathers was nauseating. She slammed the chicken onto the stump, picked up the ax and swung it. She only nicked the neck. Blood trickled on white feathers; the ax blade lodged in the wood. The hen squawked. Grace yanked out the ax and chopped again, harder. She missed. The doomed chicken croaked, pleading. Grace raised the ax again and brought it down, and this time the head flew off; Grace staggered, releasing the feet, and then the bird was up and running, blood spurting from its neck. Grace dropped the ax and vomited into the grass and sobbed, while the hen ran out its life and finally dropped and went still.

"Hello?" came a voice.

Lena? Already? Grace thought, though she didn't know how long she'd been lying there in the grass. A few minutes? A half hour? *Get up,* she told herself, but she couldn't seem to move. She hated the thought of that hen, sprawled dead and bloody on the other side of the stump.

"Grace!" Footsteps, running.

A pair of smudged pants knelt next to Grace's head.

"Are you all right?" Lena said. "Is it the baby?"

Grace rested her hand on her belly. She didn't think she'd hurt the baby, swinging the ax, fighting the chicken. She hoped.

"You're bleeding!"

So much for not showing Lena the cracks in her façade. "Chicken," she managed to say.

"Oh!" Lena leaned back on her haunches and finally laughed. "Your first?"

Grace nodded.

"It's hard to say who got the best of the other, here," Lena said.

"It's dead," Grace said, though she didn't feel much like joking about it. "I'm only wounded."

Lena laughed. "Come on," she said, holding out her hand. "I'll help you up."

Grace thought she should pluck the hen herself, but Lena insisted on carrying it into the kitchen, and the smell when she dipped it into hot water to scald the feathers made

Grace gag. She ran outside, taking deep gulps of fresh air. Lena called after her, laughing, "Guess it's a good thing I got off work early!" Grace sank onto the stoop, using all her powers of concentration not to throw up again. She felt pathetic, but nothing could make her go back inside, not until that bird was butchered.

Later, as they set the table, she couldn't help recalling the last time she'd done this with Lena — less than a year ago, when they'd first gotten word about Derrick going missing. Tonight, Grace felt ghosts in the room: Derrick, Jago, watching. Alex?

"Listen, Grace," Lena said. "You'd tell me if you got any mail for us out here, wouldn't you? Anything about Derrick? Or from Derrick? I mean, if by mistake it didn't get forwarded?"

"What? Oh! Yes, of course. Of course I would. I'd tell you the minute there was anything."

"Now that the war's over, I think we'll hear from him any day. As soon as he gets word, I mean — if he isn't too deep in some jungle . . ."

"I would tell you," Grace said, feeling nauseated again. "But I —"

Lena interrupted. "I know I haven't been the nicest to you lately. My dad wanted me

271

and Derrick to have the farm; Mom had no right to sell it. So she paid off the stupid old mortgage — who cares? I didn't care about the money he borrowed from me, either. She keeps trying to pay me, and I won't take it!" She sighed. "But I've thought about it, and I understand you were just trying to do what you thought was best for you."

Grace straightened a knife. "Your mom told me that Joe and me buying the farm would be best for you, too."

"This is my home."

"But she wants you to start fresh. She wants you to move away with her — pursue your dreams."

"My dream was to live here. Derrick was going to build a house on the other half of the property. I was going to take care of my dad when he got old."

Grace sat. "I'm sorry."

"She's taken everything from me. My dad. My home."

"You don't really still think she poisoned your dad?"

Lena's mouth trembled. "I see it in her eyes every time I look at her."

"Lena! Your dad was working so hard, out in that weather all winter. It was just too much for him. Your mom would never have done anything to hurt him. She loved him."

"She supposedly loved me and Derrick, too, and look what she's done to us. Sold our home. Made it impossible for Derrick to find *me,* let alone her."

"Lena, if he sent a letter, or showed up here, I would make sure you found each other! I'm not heartless."

"But Grace, you were my best friend. You took our home from us! How can I possibly trust you? All I can think of is when my brother gets home to find that not only does he not *have* a home but the girl he had his heart set on has taken it from him — with another man her husband!"

Grace couldn't quite breathe, looking into Lena's kitten eyes.

There was the sound of the back door opening. Lena's face brightened.

"Hello, sweetheart," Joe called.

Lena closed her eyes: *Not Derrick.* Grace shuddered.

Joe peered around the corner. His surprise at the sight of Lena showed on his face.

"Hi, Joe," Lena chirped then, blinking away tears. "We've got a chicken roasting for you — should be done in about an hour."

"All right," Joe said, cocking his head a moment. He shrugged, came over and bent to kiss Grace, his hand hot against her face. He smelled like creosote, sweat, and coal dust. When he straightened, he held her head to his hip, smiling down. She tried to smile back, was still too stunned.

"I guess I'll go get the chores done, then," he said.

"Oh, can I help?" Lena said, wiping at her eyes. "I'd love to see our cow and our chickens and our cats and our barn and — just everything!"

That night, Lena slept in her old bed in the attic.

Downstairs, Joe curled around Grace. "It sure was nice to have some help with the chores," he sighed. "Your friend's funny, too. Not like what I thought, when I met her before."

Grace lay staring at the wall, her hand on her belly, waiting for movement.

She awoke to the smell of bacon frying. Outside, the sky was just beginning to lighten. She reached for Joe; he wasn't there.

Why hadn't he woken her? He always did, so she could make his breakfast — at least if he hadn't already woken her in the middle of the night with one of his nightmares, which seemed to her not to have lessened.

There had still been no news of his crew.

She got up and put on her robe. A light burned in the kitchen; Lena stood at the stove. Joe was sitting at the table with a cup of coffee, and he looked sheepish when he saw her. "Morning, sweetheart. Lena was already cooking when I got up, so I thought I'd let you sleep."

Lena turned and smiled. "Good morning, Grace. Are you hungry?"

"Coffee," Grace said, going for a cup.

Lena shooed her away. "Let me get it for you, Hollywood. It's the least I can do. To repay you for your hospitality." She winked. "You take it black, right?"

Grace nodded and sank down at the table, too tired to object; Lena set a steaming cup in front of her, then turned to the stove to dish up breakfast.

Grace looked at Joe, wondering if he was angry about her dereliction of duty. But he smiled and reached for her; she felt a flicker of warmth. She squeezed his hand in hers.

Lena set heaping plates in front of them. Bacon, eggs, sliced tomato. The sight and smell made Grace's stomach somersault. "Oh, I couldn't, Lena," she said, pushing away her plate, as Joe dug into his.

"You'd better," Lena said, sitting down with her own meal. "That baby needs food."

Joe nodded, chewing. He washed down a mouthful with a slug of coffee. "You should eat, sweetheart."

Grace just reached for her coffee and took a sip. It was about ten times better than the coffee she'd ever managed to make on that stupid old woodstove.

After a moment, the sight of Joe and Lena eating so enthusiastically made her feel left out. She picked up a piece of bacon and bit a little off the end.

After Joe left for work, Grace sat on the stoop with Lena to wait for her ride. It was a pretty morning, not too hot yet, even as the sun climbed the eastern sky. "Your last day of work. Are you sad?" Grace asked.

Lena shrugged. "Oh, you know. Times change. It's fine. I don't guess I'll miss it."

Grace missed the shipyard every day. That feeling of accomplishment, of skill. Of her work actually mattering.

"Listen," Lena said, "I didn't want to say anything around Joe. But are you getting along all right? The icebox is almost bare. I used up the last of the bacon."

Grace smoothed her dress over her lap. "I'm fine."

"I just thought, if you were having trouble, I could help you. I'm unemployed after today! And you need to save your strength for when that baby comes."

"I'm fine, Lena. You forget, I took care of my whole family when my dad was sick and my mother was working."

"Yes, but you've never lived on a farm before," Lena said. "And, I guess, to be honest, I don't have anywhere else to go."

Grace's pulse quickened.

"I mean, my mom's begging me to move away with her. She says we need to 'start fresh'? But I'm not going anywhere. She just wants to leave so the sheriff doesn't catch up with her. She thinks I'll just let it go, what she did."

"Lena," Grace snapped, "the whole reason she sold this place was so you could have a new start. And she didn't *do* anything — she's not trying to get away from the sheriff! You've got to go with her."

Lena scowled. "Well, I hate to think what Derrick would think, if he got home and me and Mom and Dad were all gone."

"Lena, I told you, if he came back, the first thing I would do —"

"I'll probably look for a new job," Lena interrupted. "Unless you need me? The garden's coming in. Do you know how to can?"

"I can can," Grace said. She'd learned the

basics in home ec and helped her mother once or twice, that was all. Her mouth twisted. "Not to mention do the cancan."

"If you don't do it right," Lena insisted, "you'll end up running out of food in March, if not before. It's not easy out here, in the winter. It isn't as if you can just run to the store any old time you feel like it. You have to really plan. I can show you what we always did."

Grace remembered where her pride had gotten her yesterday: prostrate on the ground opposite a dead chicken. Certainly Lena would have useful advice to give. Still, it didn't seem like a good idea to invite her back onto the farm — especially not when she continued to be so delusional over Violet's supposed poisoning of Jago. How would Lena ever move on, the way she needed to? How would Grace?

But she didn't want to hurt Lena's feelings; the girl was so fragile just now. Grace was trying to think how to turn her down gently when John Tuomi's truck pulled into the driveway.

"I'll come on Saturday," Lena said, patting Grace's knee, and she was up and gone before Grace could object.

Grace spoke to Violet on the phone the next

day. "She said you asked for her help," Violet said.

"Well, not exactly. Though I'm sure she will be helpful. There's so much to do. I don't know how you ever managed it."

Violet sighed. "I just worry about her. If I could just get her to come away with me. We could be a family again. That damned farm never was our home, excuse my language. We thought it was, but it was a lie. And she won't adjust to the changes. I know it's hard. I'm trying to be here for her. We've lost everything except each other."

"I'm sorry, Violet," Grace said, resting her hand on her belly.

Lena bought a car so she could come to the farm anytime she wanted. As the August heat gave way to a mild blue September, that was almost every day. She said life in town was dull and crowded, and she wanted to keep busy; she wasn't accustomed to having time on her hands.

"How's your mom?" Grace asked one day. "I haven't talked to her lately." She'd been meaning to call, but the time always seemed to get away from her.

Lena shrugged. "I haven't seen her in a while. I guess she left town."

"What? Lena! My God! What did you do?

What did you say to her?"

"Nothing!"

"She told me she wasn't leaving you for anything."

Lena blinked. "I guess she changed her mind."

Lena would say nothing more, only that Violet hadn't left an address. "I guess she'd write you if she wanted to hear from you, Hollywood."

Grace didn't believe it. She was certain Lena had made some threat, done something to cause Violet to run. Or . . .

No, she couldn't let her mind go to the bizarre idea that Lena had done something to harm Violet physically.

Still, Grace wanted to tell Lena to stop coming to the farm. That they couldn't be friends any longer.

Yet, when she called Boots to ask what had happened, Boots encouraged Grace to give Lena a break. "Vi never said anything to me about leaving — I went off to work, and when I got home she'd packed up her things and was gone. Just like smoke. I mean, you have to wonder a little, don't you? Much as I never would think it of her, of course."

"Boots! No, I don't wonder about Violet. I just think Lena must have said something to her. Some kind of last straw kind of thing. That's all I can think of."

"Well, I guess we can't prove anything one way or another. But one thing I'll tell you is, whatever happened between them, Violet was telling me just a couple days before she left how glad she was that Lena had you. The kid considers you a sister, you know. You've got a shine on you like a silver dollar, in her eyes."

Grace sighed. She supposed she should be happy that Lena seemed no longer to be holding a grudge. "Well, I did promise Derrick I'd look after her. After them both, really. I never thought Violet would up and leave like that! I guess I'd better do a better job with Lena. And maybe there'll be some news of him soon. There has to be, doesn't there? It's been almost a year."

"I hope so, Gracie."

So it was settled, and Lena continued coming to the farm, sitting by the mailbox each afternoon to wait for the postman. He would hand the mail to her, shaking his head sadly — nothing from Derrick, no news — and Lena would kick her way to the house, riffling through the envelopes, in case he'd missed anything. A cloud of sorrow would enter with her, and she'd hand the stack to Grace: "Maybe tomorrow." The whole routine dispirited Grace, prickled her. Even as her swelling midsection made the passing of time irrefutable, she couldn't help feeling that Lena was keeping her mired in the past. Still, she had to believe that, if news did arrive, Lena would bounce back to being the sweet kid she'd once been.

Anyway, Grace didn't think she could stand being on the farm day after day with only the wind for company. Joe was always away or busy. Besides, there was more to do than she could seem to manage, so she was grateful for the help, and, before long, Lena would surely get a job in Superior and not have time to come to the farm anymore. So there was no real reason to push her out now — even if she did sometimes go overboard assuming Grace a complete idiot about anything farm-related. Whenever Grace defended herself by mentioning who had been the more capable welder, Lena would just laugh and say, "Welding and farming aren't the same thing." Grace would bite her tongue, reminding herself how much Lena had been hurt, how Derrick wouldn't want to see anything cause her more pain.

She just wished she knew what had happened to Violet. It was too much, all these people who'd up and vanished. She hoped

Violet would write to her or to Boots, but nothing ever came.

Then Lena got hired at Ma's Kitchen café in Blackberry Ridge, where Violet had worked for all those years before the war, and she rented a room in a widow's neat house within town limits, and that was the end of the idea that she wouldn't have time to visit. She worked from 5:00 A.M. till 2:00 P.M. Monday through Saturday, and, every day after work, she hopped into her car to hightail it out to the farm. She'd stay the afternoon, and the supper table was always set for three. The minute Joe's truck pulled into the driveway, the meal would be steaming on the table, and Lena would have done the outside chores, too — even the milking; the cream and milk would be separated and cooling in the icebox — so he could sit right down to eat. Grace had to admit it was a big improvement from what she'd managed on her own, even if she did start to wonder when it would ever be just the two of them, her and Joe, again.

Nevertheless, Joe was happy not to have to do the milking. And each evening, after Lena had helped Grace with the supper dishes and given her a quick hug goodbye, Grace would watch for the beam of her headlights to swoop over the house, and then she'd go lie down on the couch with her head in Joe's lap. They would stay there for an hour or two, listening to the radio, Joe resting his hand on her in case the baby kicked. If not for Lena, they'd have never had this time to tell each other things they hadn't talked about before, to discuss possible girls' names. The only subject that made Grace squirm was when he would talk to her about converting to Catholicism; what they would do about the baby's religion was a topic they soon came to steadfastly avoid.

Joe had decided to continue his job on the railroad for another year. With his seniority there, a lumberjack job wouldn't pay as much to start, and he wanted to make sure Grace and the baby had everything they needed. He'd started kissing Grace's stomach good night, calling the baby Joey. He'd also started to complain about the long-distance bill, so she didn't call her mother or Boots anymore; they didn't call her, either. Clearly, life in town went on without her.

By some silent agreement, Grace and Joe never spoke of Lena or Violet or of the strange cloud of Derrick that hung over the farm. She certainly never told him how often Derrick was in her dreams. And she never shared how, most days, in the late afternoons, she'd see Lena hurrying toward the woods with a shovel in her hand. Grace — who was pretty sure the girl wasn't digging a drainage ditch, the way she'd claimed — didn't want to think about it; the couple of times she was tempted to follow Lena out to see what she was up to, the heaviness of her middle and the pain in her overwhelmed feet put a quick end to the impulse.

Anyway, for a while, that was how it was, as the frosts came and then the snow, and the nights grew longer and colder, and Grace, her wrists and ankles thickening, her belly swollen beyond recognition, spent the snow-muffled days inside the house, throwing more wood on the fire, trying to keep warm.

At one o'clock on a frigid Wednesday in early February, with the sun shining on the deep snow outside and throwing bright light into the kitchen, Grace was sidled up close to the hot stove, ironing one of her dresses, when her water broke.

For a moment, she stood looking at the mess on the floor, surprised, confused. *I'm going to have a baby!* The knowledge felt new and alarming. She shuffled to the phone. No one was on the party line, thank goodness. Joe was out on the train for the day; she asked the operator to connect her to Ma's Kitchen café. Lena said, "I'll be there in ten minutes! And I'm calling the doctor."

"Please," Grace said.

"You just rest, Hollywood. I'll take care of everything when I get there."

Lena got the rubber sheet onto the bed and helped Grace into her nightgown. She cleaned up the kitchen floor, called the depot to leave a message for Joe. She started a pot of soup and stoked the living room stove hotter than it had probably ever been. Then she came to hold Grace's hand through the pains that had begun. She said the doctor had told her to keep him posted — an outrage, Grace thought. She might die! But Lena didn't seem afraid, and her presence helped to calm Grace's fears.

Between the pains, Lena told stories to make Grace laugh. Everything from the way she'd shooed all the men out of the café this afternoon after Grace's call to stories from her childhood, about the farm and her dad and Derrick. She said that Violet had been standing at the ironing board in the kitchen, too, just over twenty years ago, when her water had broken with Lena and Derrick on the way.

The sunset cast pink light over the snow outside the bedroom window. Lena lit the lamps.

When Joe got home, he peered into the bedroom. Lena patted Grace's hand and left them, scooting past Joe in the doorway.

"How are you doing?" His face was pale, except for a bright flush on his cheeks.

"Fine," Grace said, trying to smile. She was happy to see him and hoped she didn't look too terrible. Her high school graduation picture sat atop his dresser in its frame. He'd insisted she inscribe it for him — and so she'd written: *To my darling, If you insist!* — and now the girl she'd been seemed to be watching her current plight with sad eyes and a trace of laughter.

A sudden pain gripped her; she clenched her teeth.

He stepped back. "I'm going to call the doctor," he said. And was gone.

Through the long, dark night, Grace imagined herself aboard a ship cutting through dense fog and intermittent storm surges. She tried to imagine having "sea legs" like

Derrick must have had. And there was Lena, holding her hand. Joe, peering in the door in the quiet times. The doctor, his smooth voice encouraging her. Were they all aboard the ship with her? And from the galley, the smell of coffee, chicken soup. Then the smell of Lena's skin, Grace's own sweat. The flickering of the lamp. The splitting feeling down below. She'd stopped trying not to scream; her voice grew ragged.

"You can do it, Hollywood," Lena said, over and over, squeezing her hand just as tightly as Grace was squeezing hers.

And then, at last, there was a final-feeling pain, and Grace felt the baby slide out. She was so relieved that she began to sob. She heard the doctor: "It's a girl!" And the baby cried. It was three o'clock in the morning, February 7.

Lena washed the baby and wrapped her in a blanket while the doctor kept an eye on Grace. Grace and Joe hadn't yet decided on a girl's name, but the minute Lena passed the baby to her and she saw the squeezed-shut eyes and the pursed little mouth, one of the names they'd talked about seemed right.

When the doctor and Lena finally let Joe into the room, he smiled down on Grace and on the baby in her arms.

And Grace said, "Let's call her Alice."

Fall 1946

It was a crisp fall evening, almost five o'clock, the sun pouring its light like melted caramel out of a pan onto the fields outside. While Grace sat at the sewing machine, pumping the treadle and watching the threads form an even line, her arms and shoulders sore from a long day of canning, her neck sticky from sweating all day in the kitchen, Lena had the baby down on the living room floor and was watching her crawl, encouraging her. "That's right! Come to Auntie Lena! There you go!"

Then Grace's stitching went too far. She stopped the treadle, flipped up the presser foot, yanked the fabric out. She felt like throwing something. That she should be so out of practice!

It had been months since she'd tried to sew; the spring and summer of Alice's infancy had passed in a fog of exhaustion and incredulity. Grace's flesh had felt as dense as packed mud; life had seemed to unfold behind wavy glass. But Lena's prompting had made the summer's work unavoidable, and the motion had coaxed Grace from her dark mood. Sensation had returned to her fingers; her mind was again able to have ideas of its own. Finally, last week, she'd had a dream of a dress that she couldn't deny, using the purple fabric Lena had given her so long ago. But now, staring at the mangled wreck of it, she realized the dress was just the type she might have worn to go dancing with Derrick.

She snipped the threads, loosing the material from the machine. To even think of sewing such a thing! When she was stuck out here on the farm and never saw anyone except Lena and the baby and, in the short evenings, Joe, who was always so busy playing with Alice that Grace might as well have been invisible. The only time she got out of the house was to work in the garden or milk the cow — and how she hated that job, the squishy feel of the udders in her hands, the warm squirts of milk filling the bucket, the dusty, alive smell of the barn, the swishing of the cow's tail.

She figured the cow would have about as much appreciation for a purple dress as Joe would have interest in taking Grace out dancing. He loved the damn farm so much that, when he wasn't at work, he only wanted to spend time at home, even if all the chores were done. Which, often, they were, because, most days, Lena did the milking.

Because who was Grace to keep the girl from checking the mail? Who was she to say she didn't care anymore what had happened to Derrick? If anything, her dreams of him were becoming more frequent, more vivid. Her dreams and her nightmares, both.

But she'd just spent several days trapped in the steamy kitchen with Lena, canning a hundred quarts of tomatoes and fifty quarts each of pickles and beans, and Lena still wasn't above laughing at Grace's inexperienced moves with the tongs, just as she'd done last year.

As Grace ripped out stitches, the sound of Lena's laughing with Alice made her livid.

She remembered the shipyard, the view from on top of the hulls. The feeling of building something that lasted, of actually getting somewhere.

She'd already put a roast and potatoes in the oven for supper; Joe wouldn't be home for an hour. She shoved the dress aside — she would see, later, if anything of it could be salvaged. "Lena, do you mind if I go for a walk? You'll watch the baby, keep an eye on the roast?"

Lena smiled. "Sure, Grace, that's a wonderful idea. You get some fresh air."

Grace picked up Alice and kissed her forehead, then handed her to Lena. As usual, Alice didn't fuss. Grace grabbed one of Joe's wool shirts off the hook near the back door, shoving her arms into it as she walked outside, letting the door bang shut behind her.

She walked west along the county road, heading toward the sun. She remembered Derrick writing, so long ago, about the tree stand he'd built in the woods, how he'd gone there to be alone in peace. She hadn't been alone — really alone — in months. How was it possible that she felt so lonely?

Last Sunday, her parents and brothers and sister had finally come out to the farm for dinner. Her mother had insisted they leave early so they'd get home before dark, as though they were visiting a foreign country. Her sister, Susan, thirteen now, had been horrified at having to use the outhouse. "How do you *live* like this?" she'd said. Grace had had to laugh about that. Thank goodness, at least, that her dad was doing well. He still wasn't able to form words, but he'd held Alice for most of the afternoon, making happy faces, tickling her, encouraging her to grip his fingers.

Meanwhile, Grace hadn't talked to Hat or Char in ages. She supposed they were still disgusted with her for marrying Joe so soon after Alex had died. She guessed she couldn't blame them, but she did wish they'd at least asked if she really loved him. Maybe then they'd have understood. And she'd seen Boots only once, last month, when she and Joe had taken Alice on a rare outing, into Superior for the county fair. Boots admitted she'd never been good at keeping in touch.

The whistle of the freight train sounded in the wind from the crossing in Blackberry Ridge; Grace felt yearning in her chest. The only part of any train she saw these days was the dirt that came home on Joe, that she had to scrub out of his clothes every Monday.

She had a weekly schedule. Lena had helped her devise it. Wash Monday, iron Tuesday, bake Wednesday, mend Thursday, clean Friday, bake again Saturday. Then there were the meals to plan for and prepare, the diapers to wash, the bed to be made and floors to be swept each day, and the seasonal work. She and Lena had finished the canning today, but now the potatoes would have to be dug and wood chopped, to prepare for winter.

There was simply no end.

"Well, that just isn't life, Grace," Joe had said, smiling at her like you'd smile at a child, when she'd made such a complaint last week. It had been some time since she'd felt the pleasant stirring that used to come when he was near, the warmth and the light. But there was always a shadow in him now; he was angry that she'd refused to have Alice baptized as a Catholic. She'd held fast, insisting that Alice be Lutheran, *like her mother!* They'd had several fruitless yelling matches, and now the issue simmered beneath their skins. "This is just the way it is."

"Well, I don't have to like it," she'd said. Then, seeing the concern on his face, she'd laughed, as if she'd been joking.

In the evenings, he was always reading *Farm Life* or *Farm Journal* or *Hoard's Dairyman.* He wanted to get two more milk cows and put three acres in hay next year. Which would mean a lot more work for Grace, spinning all that whole milk through the cream separator, churning the cream into butter, bottling the milk and packaging the butter to take to the co-op to sell. *Thank goodness for Lena,* she thought, dreading the day when she'd have to do all the milking herself.

But obviously, Lena couldn't share the work forever. If Grace never put her foot down, Lena might just take over entirely.

Soon, she told herself. *Soon, I'll talk with her. When I feel stronger again.* She didn't want to think about it.

Listening to the paper rustle of the leaves drying on the trees, she remembered Derrick's place of peace. If only she could find it. But as she was about to turn in to the woods, she saw a car coming. Recognized it as a neighbor's. She stopped, waved as they passed. Fearing they would sense that her heart wasn't in the right place, that there were chores left undone at home and she was out wandering in search of the past, in search of a freedom she would never have, she forced herself to head back toward the house, keeping to the road.

"I don't think you need to feel ashamed," Lena said, when Grace finally confessed her discontent, around Thanksgiving time. "This is pretty different from what you'd imagined for yourself. Besides, you aren't even that good at it — being a 'farm wife'!"

Grace retorted as she always did: "Well, at least I could weld!"

Lena laughed.

A few days later, when a storm blew up and the snow was horizontal in the wind, Lena came into the house rosy-cheeked, stomping her feet. "California this ain't!" she said.

Grace sighed. "Oh, I wish you wouldn't say things like that. You know how I hate the winter."

"Well, at least we aren't out welding in it, right? And thank goodness we've got the cellar full of goodies." Lena laughed. "Of course, we haven't got any oranges or olives or anything."

Grace didn't like olives, but the thought of a sun-warmed orange hanging on a tree somewhere in California made her ache. She could imagine a swimming pool, a white two-piece bathing suit and a broad-brimmed white hat, the sun on her skin, a warm breeze rustling palm trees. *I hate her,* she thought.

She shoved another stick of wood into the firebox, then buttoned the last two buttons of her tattered sweater and held out her hands to warm them.

The wind blew as if it intended to clear the

land like a broom would a porch. The incessant sound of you-are-not-welcome-here bothered Grace even more this winter than it had the last. She imagined herself trapped inside a lidded pot, the snow piling atop it, heavier and heavier each sunless day.

Every Monday she lugged the wet clothes outside and hung them on the line to freeze, every Monday night she wrestled the stiff things inside to put them by the stove, where they would soften to dampness, and every Tuesday morning she ironed them dry, the steam rising.

And every afternoon, Lena was there to say, "I'll bet it's sunny in California." She'd brought her father's old ukulele back out to the farm, and now she spent the afternoons, while she watched Alice and Grace did housework, playing and singing the most aggravating selection of songs: "Down Among the Sheltering Palms," "Hello, Frisco," "California, Here I Come," "In the Good Old Summertime," "Wait Till the Sun Shines, Nellie," and on and on. Once, Grace went out to the living room, intending to yell at her to stop, but then she saw Alice, clapping her little hands and grinning with delight. So she let Lena play on.

The music reminded Grace of the movies. It had been ages since she'd seen one. She didn't even know what was stylish this year, or who the new stars were.

But what did it matter? The only things she wore anymore were housedresses, with her oversize wool sweater, and her big rubber boots to go outside. Sometimes, if she ever had a moment to herself, she would take out of their box her pretty navy blue, open-toed pumps, the ones she'd had since her days working at Roth's. Unfortunately, she'd always end up thinking how she'd probably never be able to buy such a pair of shoes again. Let alone wear them! Even if she had the chance to go shopping, she didn't have any money of her own. A shock, after all those years of working! And Joe would never approve of buying shoes for their beauty alone. She could picture begging and pleading and saying, "But don't you love me?" and him looking like he was passing a kidney stone, and her finally giving up.

She'd never considered what it would mean not to have her own money. To see Joe, month after month, spending every last dime on chicken feed and milk pails and bottle brushes and butter churns, a new bell for the cow, a new air filter for his truck. Not anything the least bit beautiful. But she didn't mean to begrudge him any of it; she still wanted to see him smile. She tried to content herself with running a hand over a blue shoe, the bow that curled above the open toe, the swerve of the high heel.

"Have you ever thought," Lena said one day, helping Grace haul in Joe's frozen laundry from outside, "it's kind of like Joe has two wives!"

"You don't have to help me," Grace snapped. "With anything!"

"Oh, I don't mind, Hollywood!"

Lena had begun asking Joe to do little things for her. First it was to help her get something down off the high shelf in the pantry. To carry the full milk pails to the house, though, before, she'd always been perfectly capable. Another time, she claimed her car was making a strange noise, and would he look at it? They were outside for forty-five minutes, while Grace kept supper warm.

She couldn't believe that Lena honestly would think she'd share Joe in any fashion. She gave her what she thought was a stern talking-to.

Lena's kitten eyes went soft with hurt for a moment; then, a smile trembled onto her face. *"Manu on työnsä tehnyt, Manu saa mennä,"* she said.

Grace snapped, "I don't know what that means, Lena."

Lena tilted her head, a heartbreaking reminder of Derrick's snapshot. Despite the dirty shell of the farm clothes she wore, Lena was becoming a beautiful woman. Grace was suddenly jealous of the younger girl's luminescent skin, the clean angles of her petite features. When had Grace stopped seeing her, not to notice she was no longer a child?

"I just would think you'd realize you'd be lost without me," Lena said, and she shrugged into her ragged coat and went off to the barn.

Nothing ever seemed to wear her down, whereas Grace felt constantly like she might just scream.

That night, Alice was asleep in her crib and Grace and Joe were in bed, propped on their pillows with the lamps on so he could read *Farm Life* and she could read *Look*. But the words on the pages blurred; she could only think of Lena. Finally, she whispered, "Joe, I'm not sure if we should keep letting Lena come out here every day."

"What are you talking about?"

Without mentioning Lena's obscure beauty — if he hadn't noticed, she certainly didn't want to get him started looking — she told him what Lena had said about him having two wives.

"Jesus," he said, closing his magazine. "Well, you know I don't think of it like that. It just seems like you . . . like you've been having a hard time? Do you really think you could handle all the work without her?"

Grace pouted at his lack of faith — justified or no.

"I'm sorry, sweetheart. I know maybe this isn't your . . . your ideal life. But I think it'll get easier for you, in time. When Alice gets a little older? I don't know if you realize how much Lena does on the yard, too, plus helping you in the house, and with Alice? I'd say we're lucky to have her."

Grace remembered Derrick's promise that he would never tie her to the farm if it wasn't what she wanted, and she bit back what she wanted to say: that she didn't know why on earth Joe had wanted this stupid old farm anyway, especially if he'd known it would be too much work. Though she did know that his nightmares had finally begun to ease; that he loved the space around him, loved watching things grow. He even loved how the changes in the seasons affected their lives. She would have preferred to continue to ignore them,

particularly the winter, and suddenly she wished that her love for Derrick had never seduced her into thinking she could live this life.

But Joe couldn't know that had been her reason. Besides, hadn't it been his smile that had persuaded her, too? "Lena said I'd be lost without her."

"I know it's hard, sweetheart. But as long as she's willing to help out, I don't see why we'd turn her away. She really loves you, that's why she's doing it. And Alice, too."

"Lena's not doing it because she loves me or Alice. It's because she loves this farm. And she's flirting with you."

"No," he said, ducking his head, drawing out the *o* sound. But Grace could tell from the color that had come into his cheeks that he knew it was true.

"Yes, she is. She has it all planned. She's going to get rid of me, and you're going to marry *her* instead." A sudden lump rose in her throat.

"That's ridiculous," he said, too loudly. "She's your *friend.* And mine, too, now."

Grace shushed him. She couldn't meet his eyes. "I'm *extraneous.* The two of you could handle everything without me."

He sighed. She stared at the pattern on

the wallpaper, the darkness outside the window.

"But, Grace, I love *you,*" he said, and then he was leaning over her. He threw her *Look* onto the floor and kissed her, his hand slipping beneath the quilts.

"We have to be *quiet,*" she said, embarrassed with Alice in the room, not sure she wanted him to touch her at all.

"I know," he whispered, reaching to turn off the lamp, and she relented. And in the relenting, to her surprise, unearthed a lost joy.

But later, after he was asleep, she lay staring into the darkness. She thought about how he hadn't denied that he and Lena could make do without her. And the way he'd emphasized the *you* in "I love you" made her wonder if he hadn't once or twice thought about what it might be like to love Lena instead.

On a clear day shortly after New Year's, Grace was in the kitchen feeding Alice lunch when she was startled by a knock at the back door, and there was Boots's grinning face in the window. Grace jumped up, leaving Alice to make a mess with the spoon and mashed peas.

After exclamations and hugs, Grace put

fresh water on to boil in the coffeepot and went to join Boots at the table, Alice between them in her high chair.

"The kid's looking good," Boots said. "Course, I didn't remember her being so green."

"Oh, dear," Grace said, wiping Alice's face with the bib.

"Looks like you got a knack for this mothering stuff," Boots said.

Grace gave her friend a skeptical look. With the sticky spoon, she scooped up more peas, tried to get them into the baby's mouth.

Boots said, "Well, it feels like a crime I haven't been out here to see you and the kid."

"Oh, that's all right," Grace protested, though she sort of agreed. Boots had only seen Alice that once, last summer at the fair.

"Course, I've been busier than a one-legged man in a butt-kicking contest. Working six days a week, you know. And I was dating that fellow for a while; that went the way of most things, the son of a biscuit. Beg your pardon, Alice."

Alice cooed, reaching for the spoon.

"And then, of course, I haven't got a car. Excuses, excuses, right?" Boots laughed. "But today I said to myself, I've got to see

Gracie before I leave. Yesterday was my last day of work. So I borrowed my dad's wheels and came on out."

"You're leaving?" Shocked, Grace left the spoon dangling just out of the baby's reach. Alice fussed for it. Grace adjusted. Alice smacked her lips.

Boots said, "I'm going to New York City, can you believe it? Got an old high school buddy out there, and she needs a roommate. I leave day after tomorrow."

"New York City! What are you going to do there?"

"Whatever I can find, I guess. I wanted to see a bit of the world."

Grace sighed and scooped up another bite of peas for Alice. She'd seen Judy Garland and Lana Turner in *Ziegfeld Girl.* New York — Broadway! — was the next best thing after Hollywood, as far as she was concerned.

Boots seemed to sense her thoughts. "Maybe you can come visit me someday, Gracie."

"Yes, sure," Grace said, pouting. Alice batted the proffered spoonful of peas away. The spoon clattered to the floor; green mush sprinkled the stove, the table, Grace's legs. Alice clapped her hands, but Grace wanted to cry.

Boots laughed. "Kid's got an arm, doesn't she?"

"Oh, yes!" Grace got up and put the spoon into the sink, then used a towel to swipe the peas off of everything. The water in the coffeepot was boiling; as she mixed a scoop of grounds with an egg and dumped the mixture in, she forced a happy tone. "You have to tell me more. Where does your friend live? Is it near Broadway? Tell me everything!"

But when Boots left three hours later, having had a chance to visit with Lena, too, Grace stood at the front window holding Alice and watched her go. And when Lena came inside from seeing Boots off and saw the look on Grace's face, she said, "Well, it looks like someone's been bitten by the green monster."

Dismayed, Grace rubbed at her face. Did she still have mashed peas on her?

Lena winked. "You and I both know it, Hollywood. You wish it was you going and not her. You know you don't belong here."

Grace would have been offended had it not been for the soft look on Lena's face. As it was, she was simply too taken aback to protest.

Lena reached out. "Can I hold Alice?"

And Alice held out her chunky little arms

to Lena, and the transfer was made. Grace stood rubbing her elbows, watching Lena whisper to the baby, some secret Grace couldn't pretend to understand.

One night soon after, the temperature dropped to forty below zero and the wind was rattling the windowpanes. When Joe got in from the barn, he didn't remove his coat and boots on the porch, like he normally did. He came right into the kitchen, tracking snow, his face flushing from the sudden heat, his hands stiff as he stripped off his frozen gloves. Grace helped him with his coat, rubbing his hands between hers to warm them, while Lena carried supper to the table, clucking over the weather, saying, "One time Derrick and I got stuck out in a blizzard. It had been warm and the storm came up so quick, while we were walking home from school. We couldn't see our noses in front of our faces! My dad came along and saved us."

"Well," Joe said, taking his hands from Grace to hold them up to the stove, "I don't think you should go into town tonight, Lena. I know it's only three miles, but if you went off the road, you'd be a dead duck. That wind isn't fooling around. You can sleep on the couch; the attic'll be too cold. Maybe it will have died down by morning and we can caravan in."

"Well, if you insist, that's fine by me," Lena said, putting Alice into her high chair.

Hanging Joe's coat, Grace couldn't help thinking, *This is just what she's been waiting for. She may never leave at all now.*

But Grace wasn't inhumane. She wouldn't send Lena out into the storm to die. For Pete's sake, she wouldn't do *that.*

Exhausted from the cold, Grace dropped straight off to sleep, despite the roaring wind. She didn't know how much time had passed when she was startled awake by Lena bursting into the bedroom, lunging to raise the window. A blast of icy air came in like a train. "Lena!" Grace yelled, yanking the quilts up. She could see Lena silhouetted against the moonlit snow outside. "What are you doing?"

"Lena?" Joe said groggily.

Lena had snatched up Alice from her crib and was wrapping her in a blanket. Alice started to cry.

"Grace had the draft almost closed on the stove," Lena snapped. "The smoke fumes could have killed us. Thank goodness I woke up and caught it."

Joe cursed. Grace clutched the quilts in

both hands. She'd loaded the stove just before bedtime; Joe and Lena had had to go out to the barn to check on the animals again. But she was sure she hadn't touched the damper.

"Grace, what were you thinking?" Joe said.

"But I . . . I didn't —" she stammered. *Had* she touched it? Maybe she just didn't remember. Her parents had a coal-burning furnace in town. She did still have trouble adjusting the stove from time to time, didn't she?

"You could have killed us." Lena stood righteously by the window, holding the whimpering baby with her hand cupped over the back of her head. *Protecting her from me,* Grace realized, horrified. Hotshot, indeed. Maybe she was destined to die by fire after all.

"You should know better," Joe said.

"I'm sorry! But I really don't think I —"

"Jesus, it's cold," he said, getting out of bed.

"I've got the living room open, too," Lena said.

"Thanks, Lena. Is Alice all right? Let me see her."

"She seems fine."

Grace saw the two shadows exchange the baby.

310

It was them against her. It had never been clearer.

She pulled the pillow over her head, tears burning her eyes. Oh, she was tired. So tired of it all. She didn't know how she would bear it much longer. How any of them would.

May 2000

In the morning light, the old woman's face clouded over as she climbed out of Julia's Corolla and surveyed the tiny graveyard. Julia had been in the barn mucking out a stall — it was the first time in all these months she hadn't minded the chore; anything seemed preferable to being in that house with the old woman, with the place feeling so haunted — when she heard an engine roar to life. Recalling the ER doctor's judging eyes yesterday, she ran out screaming for the woman to stop. Met with frowning annoyance, the weathered hands clutching the pickup's steering wheel like a threat, Julia finally surrendered and said she'd drive the woman to the cemetery.

Now everything she'd been trying since last night not to think about — the newspaper article she'd found in the trunk; Lena's crazy letter with its hints of family treasure and menace and the faithlessness of that woman Grace — was seeping through her mind, even as she realized, *It really is her, my great-grandmother, because why else would she have wanted to come here?* But Violet seemed fine; evidently, her long rest overnight had done her good.

Julia could not believe this tiny old woman a murderer.

Violet's shoes left a trail of Ked-shaped reliefs in the dew, and Julia hurried behind, realizing that she'd visited this place once, as a little girl, and that Lena was buried here — at the top of the hill? Did Violet even know she was dead? "Are you sure you feel up to walking, Violet? We can always come back later!"

"I'm fine."

Words stuck in Julia's throat, and all she could do was follow. Violet's jeans had creases pressed into them, and the swishing noise they and her bright blue windbreaker made with each purposeful stride seemed to forbid argument.

When Violet finally stopped at a particular stone — just short of where Julia thought Lena's was, thank God — Julia read the inscription: JAGO MAKI MAY 8, 1895–APRIL 12, 1945. "Oh! It would have been his birthday today! A hundred and five."

"He was a long way from that," Violet said, the map of lines on her face crumpling. "I felt older then than I do now. Life is strange. I'm going to be ninety-six in July. If I make it."

Thank goodness: she seemed to be back in the present.

She went on. "They've found spots. Shadows. On my lungs, of course, on one of those strange scans? They say it's cancer, that I may only have a couple months."

"Oh!" Julia felt suddenly as if she were the one who could make no sense of time.

"Now, you must know where Grace is," Violet insisted. "You said her daughter, Alice, lives here. I need to see if Grace knows where Lena is."

"What?" Julia said, wondering again, *Isn't it her, really? Alice is* Lena's *daughter!*

"I have to make sure Lena understands that it broke my heart, selling the farm, taking our family away from it. How I had to break my heart to save what was left of us. Like setting a bone."

"You never sold the farm, Violet," Julia said, because it was one thing she knew for sure. The farm had always been in the family. Her grandma and grandpa had lived here their whole lives, then it had gone to their daughters, Alice and Marty, and now

Alice and George had lived here for decades. *Why would Violet make these things up?*

Violet's brow furrowed. "Yes, I did. To Grace, when she was pregnant with Alice."

"Alice . . . is Grace's daughter?" Julia said, even as she thought of how Marty was five foot two, small-boned and dark-haired, while Alice was five foot eight, broad-shouldered and blond — like the woman in the photograph. Like Grace. For a moment she wanted to believe — *Derrick! Alice was Derrick's child!* But then she remembered the railroad man and the "jokey dance steps."

She guessed that would explain why Lena had been so mad. Still, it didn't seem possible that, all these years, everyone had lied.

And, if Alice was Grace's daughter, what had happened to Grace?

"But I don't understand. I mean, Lena lived here until . . ."

"Until?"

Julia surveyed the rows of gray stones, the wooded hills rolling into the distance beyond them, the sky resolving from pink to an even softer blue, the sun climbing above the greening trees, the rain clouds rolling in the distance like a behind-schedule train. She touched Violet's arm and led her up the hill, finding the grave with Lena's name

315

on it and the dates. "I'm so sorry, Violet," she said, and the words sounded painfully hollow.

Violet's face was the color of ash. She withdrew her hand from her jacket pocket to reveal a blue marble trembling on the lined surface of her tissue-paper skin. "But I brought this for her," she spat.

Julia remembered Lena's letter, the pirate game. "Derrick's marble?"

"Yes — how did you . . . ?" Violet stopped and stared down at Lena's name. And then one white Ked shot out and kicked the stone.

Back at the house, Julia pulled Alice's address book from the kitchen drawer. Violet had been limp, nearly too exhausted to get out of the car, when they'd returned from the cemetery, and Julia helped her to bed, the panic she'd felt at Lena's grave stoked by a new, flickering loneliness — alarming in itself.

She'd wanted only to calm Violet, so she'd kept to herself the story she recalled Marty telling once: how Lena had lingered a long time with breast cancer when Marty was thirteen or so; how, toward the end, it had been autumn and everything had smelled of apples, and Lena had been so tiny, so wasted away, she'd barely indented the bed; how, the only times she'd gotten up, she'd spent all her energy "packing, like she was going on a long trip, and looking for something that she would never say what!" (And then Marty had shaken her head and laughed and poured another drink.)

Packing the trunk, Julia realized, *and looking for . . . whatever Jago had left for her?* She hated to think how Violet might react.

Her younger brother was the only person she could think of to call. Not that he'd have the first clue what to do with an unhinged, sick old woman, but Danny was Alice and George's godson, their favorite, and he'd spent something like seven summers at the farm, growing up, after he'd become "too much" for Marty to handle alone, and Julia had to wonder if Alice had confided in him about not being Lena's daughter.

Julia hadn't talked to him in years, but she remembered Marty saying that his Army enlistment was almost up, so she dialed his and Nicole's home number in South Dakota. She was shocked when he answered; maybe she'd expected empty rings, a futile sense of *at least I tried.* Sounding as surprised as she was, he said he'd gotten home a few days ago, and he was looking for a job.

317

"I'm not calling to check up on you," she said, though she was touched that he'd felt the need to explain himself. "I just need to know if you know anything about this." She started haltingly, but she was soon pouring out the whole story, and it wasn't like her to share so much so quickly, but his incredulous cursing seemed to spur her on. Finally, she reined herself in. "So, you didn't know about Alice?"

"Fuck, no. Listen, I think I'd better come help you. If she's as sick as you say . . ." His voice was rough, like an old smoker's, and she worried what he'd been up to since they'd last spoken.

"Oh, my God, Danny, I didn't mean — Anyway, you just got home — you can't leave Nicole and Josh like that, right away."

Silence, and then: "You ever heard that song 'The Highwayman'? That's me, Jules. Might as well be, anyway."

She didn't know what he meant. "Danny, forget it, really —"

"Listen, Jules, this is, like, the first time in the history of the world that I've heard you say you don't know what to do. Besides, she's my great-grandma, too. And it's about time I got back to that farm — it's been too long. I'll be there tonight," he said, and hung up.

She pulled the phone from her ear to glare at it; yet she felt the sudden slackening of a strong wind into which she hadn't quite realized she'd been leaning.

She went out to the barn. It always needed more cleaning, and the work usually cleared her mind, but today she didn't know whether to feel bad for Alice or to hate her for lying, and the uncertainty consumed her, along with the problem of what to do about Violet.

When she finally went inside, she thought she heard a noise upstairs. A thump. There it was again.

She thundered up the steep steps just in time to see Violet, crouched in front of the armoire, reaching into the drawer, pulling out the camera that had been nestled with Julia's sweaters all winter. "Violet, what are you doing! You're supposed to be resting!"

The old woman looked over her shoulder, eyes innocent.

Julia hurried to snatch the camera from Violet's shaky hands. "That's mine."

Violet sighed. She gazed into the drawer like it was a crystal ball from which she was trying to divine something. "I thought my twins' things might still be up here. And then I found this was the only drawer to look in. Everything's gone."

The weight of the camera in Julia's hands felt strange and familiar. "You shouldn't even be climbing stairs, Violet. You're going to give *me* a heart attack, at this rate."

"My heart is fine," Violet mused. "I wanted to donate it, but they wouldn't take it. I told them if it hadn't quit by now, after everything, think how strong it must be. I told them: it's a good heart. But they said no one would want it, it was so old. 'Experienced,' I told them."

"Violet, seriously, you should go back to bed."

"I didn't know about Lena being gone, though," Violet went on. "We'll see how my heart stands that now. And Grace. I should never have gotten her involved. Why do you keep your camera hidden in the drawer?"

"What?" Julia's macro lens was on it still, for extreme close-ups, but she couldn't recall what her last subject had been. She remembered how, when she'd bought the lens, she'd imagined it would change her life, this new perspective. But it seemed to her now that it had only kept her from seeing the long view. "I guess I just — My boyfriend died. My fiancé, I mean." She couldn't believe she'd said it out loud, and so casually; a pressing pain between her eyes that she hadn't been conscious of suddenly eased. "We were planning to go out for a special dinner, that Friday, but he died on Thursday. I was going to say yes." He'd worked late that night, and she'd attempted pasta sauce, knowing there'd be some crucial seasoning she'd neglect and, when he got home, he'd laugh and hug her and then add the perfect spice. She'd just sampled a spoonful and thought, *What do you know, he might actually be impressed,* when the phone rang.

She realized: even now, when she ran, with every crunch of a shoe on gravel, she imagined the smash of metal on metal and glass. And all she could do was keep running, keep sanding and stripping and repainting the little house. There was still the kitchen to do, and the bedroom, and the marathon she'd signed up for was next month already. It would be her first, and, though she hadn't come close to running that far in one shot, every day she was feeling it a little more possible that she *could.*

"So you put your camera away?" Violet demanded.

Dust motes floated between them, sparkling in the light. "Well, there was no need to prove the concept of permanence anymore," Julia snapped, but she was thinking of Derrick and Grace and Lena, as if they were hovering in the dust, too.

Violet insisted on going out to explore the south section of woods, looking for a tree stand Derrick had built. Nothing Julia said could dissuade her, not even offering to search alone and report back if she found anything. Now she was gritting her teeth at Violet's slow pace, and the ground was uneven, littered with fallen branches, and Julia's neck was stiff at the thought that the old woman could fall. "I can still see him," Violet was saying, "carrying boards out here. He'd finally gotten old enough to tell his dad what was what, but he wasn't very big, even then, so he could only carry a couple at a time. Jago had his stand in the west section, so Derrick claimed this one for himself."

"Well, where is it, Violet?"

"I don't know. I never got out to the woods when I lived here. I was so busy with everything I had to do. But Derrick liked to come out here to be alone. Like his father. You know men, they never feel comfortable in a house." Then she stumbled; Julia lunged to grab her, steeling herself against the feel of the old arm, Violet's slick jacket. The old woman just kept on talking, saying she couldn't believe Lena had been gone so long — she could hardly comprehend how that time had slipped away — and commenting on the green smell of the air and how she'd thought she wouldn't see spring again, much less spring in Blackberry Ridge. Julia felt a trill of sympathy at that, but she didn't want to say that she, too, had imagined the season would never change; that her lungs, too, had been gray and shadowed with the winter and with loss.

Yet, as her shoes squished damp earth through the floor of dried old leaves, the burgeoning of new life all around was so insistent that she couldn't help breathing it in, and Violet suggested they pick fiddleheads, young ferns, to eat, and she pointed them out and Julia picked them and went back to holding Violet's arm, the bouquet of fiddleheads in her other hand. She could feel energy thrumming in Violet's bones, and she sensed it was through sheer will that Violet had lived so long — long after her muscles had begun to weaken, long after her cells had begun to decay, still her good heart was beating and she was pressing on. Decaying, but regenerating, too, like the forest in its seasons.

But they found no trace of Derrick's tree stand. Finally, Violet admitted to being tired, and they started the long walk back, Violet quiet now, her feet dragging, and Julia wondering what it would be like to have such old memories, to feel so certain of where you belonged that the smell of the air was the smell of home even when you'd been gone more than fifty years; wondering if the sense that the farm was uniquely exempt from time had been why it had so appealed to her at the beginning. (Yet, that sense was so clearly wrong: that old grandfather clock, no wonder she'd hated its endless ticking and chiming!)

Still, the place had whispered to them all, pulled them all home: Violet; even Danny, on his way now. And Julia suddenly wanted to think it possible that Jago really had left something for his children to find. Lena had believed it: she'd rooted herself here on the basis of that faith and on the faith of Derrick's inevitable return. (Had Grace and the railroad man died or vanished, leaving Alice to Lena along with the farm?) Julia, inhaling the scent of new leaves and damp earth and picturing the white spray of roses on Ryan's silver coffin, her father's motorcycle roaring away when she was nine, could hardly imagine the comfort of knowing that your loved ones hadn't forgotten you, that they really hadn't left you at all.

And then she thought: Jago's tree stand.

Her shoes crunched the muddy gravel in a quick, pounding rhythm, and when she finally glanced back, the house looked like the afterthought of a landscape artist against the sky. She'd helped Violet back to bed and run out, guilty and relieved at leaving the old woman alone with her pain, the idea of the tree stand pulling at her like gravity.

At the far side of the pasture was a shadowy thicket of brush and spring-thin trees. *The west section,* Violet had said. Julia's shoes slid in the mud, carrying her down the hill, and she pushed aside the branches that snatched at her.

And then she tripped and fell, scraping her palms on the earth, on last fall's twigs and dead leaves.

Pain shot through her wrists, but, thank God, her ankles were okay, her feet. But she was shaken, and she felt alone but also found out; strangely, near tears. Jago had died fifty-five years ago; there was nothing for her in these woods. She turned around and walked back, trying to scrape the dirt from her palms.

And a man was sitting on the stoop, a cigarette burning under the wide brim of his cowboy hat.

■ ■ ■ ■

At first, she thought, *Derrick?*, and she hadn't known how much a part of her wanted to believe that Lena's sense that he was alive could be as credible as Violet's that he wasn't; that he could have gone out exploring, seeing the world, maybe lost his memory the way Lena had imagined; that he could be alive, even now.

But how could she be so foolish? She had seen Ryan in that silver casket, had watched it being lowered into the ground.

A familiar gravelly voice sang a Johnny Cash tune, greeting her. ". . . 'I ain't seen the sun shine, since I don't know when.' "

She couldn't get over it: her little brother, Danny, looking about ten years older than the last time she'd seen him, nearly four years ago at his wedding, when he'd seemed pathetically young, bright-eyed and grinning in his tux. Her little brother, a hardness to his face, his gray eyes like polished river stones, his smile as bony thin as the rest of him. Grinding his cigarette under the heel of his boot, like some outlaw, when he'd stood to greet her, and it was still strange that he'd outgrown her.

326

"So, you seem . . . attached," he said now, his eyes crinkling, amused. They were hauling the trunk from the shed across the yard, everything glowing in the sinking gold light of the sun. Not knowing what else to say, she'd filled him in on Violet, the visit to the graveyard this morning, their exploration of the woods.

"Well, I don't think she's here for my *amusement,* like some people seem to," she said. He'd admitted to peeking in on Violet and said she looked like a relic from another time. Julia hadn't told him that the whole place was starting to feel that way; that she was feeling a little that way herself.

He laughed. "I'm just surprised to see you caring so much. Miss Independent. Miss Break-up-with-him-first-before-it-crosses-his-mind-so-you're-never-the-one-to-get-hurt."

Julia felt her face heat up at that. She'd made the mistake once in high school of sharing her dating philosophy with Danny. "Listen, I don't think you understand the importance of what all is going on here. And that was a *long* time ago, anyway. More recently, I was just about engaged to Ryan, remember."

His face sobered. "Hey, listen, I'm sorry —"

She interrupted. "Besides, it's hardly the same thing, with Violet." *Sorry you never even called?* she was thinking.

"I just mean you're like Superman would be, if every other human was made of kryptonite." He smiled. "I mean that as a compliment."

"I haven't seen you in, like, four years. How do you even know what I'm like?"

"My point exactly," Danny said, starting backward up the steps.

"Smartass," she muttered, struggling to hold her end aloft.

"Somebody was quite the shopper," he said, once they were settled on the dining room floor in front of the open trunk. Julia had grabbed the lamp from the living room so they'd have plenty of light. "All these shoes."

"That's not the point," Julia said. "We need to find out what happened to Grace."

"But what do you think happened to the shoes?" He examined one of the labels. "Some of them look like they were kind of hot, from the drawings. The Esmeralda model. Like that vampire chick who used to host the movies on TV, Saturday nights or whatever."

"That was Elvira, you dork." Their dad had let them stay up and watch, those rare weekends they'd spent with him.

She noticed a box marked DAD. Would there be something in here about Jago's death, Lena's suspicions, the treasure he'd left behind?

Danny was digging into his own box, so Julia said nothing. She sorted through the crumbled remains of dried leaves, a rumpled red silk bow tie, gambling chips, a deck of cards, a rusty fishing lure, 1945 pay stubs labeled SUPERIOR SHIPBUILDING CO., and several snapshots of Jago, usually holding either a dead fish or the antlers of a just-killed deer. Julia could see his aging over the years, the thickening of his waist. She thought he looked like a man with secrets. But he looked kind, too. Too kind to have motivated anyone to murder him, certainly, let alone his own wife, Violet.

And then Julia found another note from Lena:

I couldn't find what Dad had left — & it felt like one more thing I'd lost — & (I guess!) losing one more thing was one more thing than I could stand! & I could hear in my mind — like a scratched record — Mom and G. telling me they wanted me to have a "different life," to "start fresh" — but they couldn't tell me how it would stack up against everything I'd lost — no one could.

& then — one gray afternoon — I found G. sitting at the kitchen table — she was sipping a cup of coffee & wearing a wool cap down over her ears — & in the other room, Alice was screaming — but G. didn't seem to hear, she didn't even look up when I came in — I had to say her name 3 times — & when she turned, her eyes were like the slush that forms when a lake starts to melt in the spring.

I ran for the baby! — I saw right away a diaper pin sticking her — & I fixed her up — thinking — how sad! My good friend "Hotshot," who'd had so many dreams! You wouldn't even have known her — you'd have been ashamed this was your girl!

I carried A. back to the kitchen — she was making terrible little snorts, nestling on my shoulder — & all G. said was "Do you want some coffee?" — & it was suddenly so *clear* — if it hadn't been before! — how *much* I had to protect them from each other!

I asked how long A. had been crying — & G. said she'd "tried everything" to get her to stop.

"She stopped when I picked her up," I said — !

& G.'s mouth trembled (I remember!) — & fat tears rolled down her cheeks — "I thought this was supposed to come naturally."

I hated to see her cry!

I thought — already I love her — I do! —

"What happened to your hands?" Danny said, jarring Julia from her reading, from wondering what Lena had been up to. Had she *done* something to Grace, *taken* Alice? Did Alice even know that Lena wasn't her mother?

In the lamplight, she could see how badly her hands were torn up, how filthy they were. She'd forgotten to notice the stinging. She wished she could reach Alice, ask her what was true. "Nothing. Just . . . being stupid, I guess."

He squinted at her from under his hat. "I've got a karaoke machine in my truck," he said. "Don't make me use it."

"Why would you — Oh, never mind." She got up to wash her hands, deciding, even if Danny was a smartass, at least he was here. At least she wasn't alone with these ghosts and mysteries. So, when she sat down again, she told him about the tree stand, about Lena's conviction that something waited for her in the woods. "I don't *think* she ever found it, whatever it was. But I thought, what if it was 'larger than life' in value, you know, not in size? What if it's, like, up in the tree stand, somehow? But then I fell, and I thought I was just being an idiot." She realized: maybe she'd been thinking, *If there's nothing, then I'll just say that Lena was crazy, that Violet is right about everything being already gone. That the most you can do is just try to bear it.*

Danny shrugged. "I know where the stand is. Violet'll be all right for a few minutes, right? Let's go see."

"You'll have to show me where." Julia grabbed the flashlight and followed him out the back door, thinking of Lena and Derrick and their pirate game.

In the dusk, they rock-hopped across the narrow, babbling stream to start up the hill again, and Danny pointed: on one of the larger trees in the distance, weathered boards were nailed across the trunk crosswise, rising to make a ladder. Julia's eyes followed them to the platform above. Danny had said he used to hang out here sometimes, those summers he'd spent at the farm as a kid. "There's a little compartment in there where George keeps his shells. That's all I know of."

"I'm going to take a look," she said now. "You'll kill yourself if you try to climb in those cowboy boots."

He smiled. "Stylish, though, aren't they?"

The boards were rough as she climbed, and the platform was old and weathered, but it seemed sturdy enough, well constructed — two-by-fours were sandwiched on their sides between top and bottom layers of flat boards. "Wow, the view from up here!" She could see the city lights of Duluth sparkling on the hill that rose some thirty miles in the distance. The sight made her long for her camera, though she didn't know if she could capture such vast and distant beauty, so different from what her typical subjects had been.

"Don't get distracted, Jules."

"Right." She ran her hands over the boards, felt a protrusion. And there was a rusted hinge, a little knob opposite of it. When she pulled, the board opened upward like a door. *Like a treasure chest.*

Inside the platform was nestled a narrow wooden box, handmade, rough, old-looking, built to fit in the space. Julia fished it out and found inside it two boxes of shotgun ammunition — mostly empty. "George's shells," she reported, shining the flashlight into the box's nest. Its borders were only an inch high, allowing access to the rest of the platform's hollow space. "Have you looked further inside here?"

"Felt around a little. Didn't find anything except a mouse's nest."

This was no time to be squeamish. Julia reached in, flattening herself, stretching her arm as long as it would go. She moved aside the old, chewed-up leaves and paper and — fabric? "Got something!" she yelled. She tugged the frayed thing closer, pulled it out. It was an old flour sack; inside was something hard and rectangular: a small tin box.

And inside that was a tiny oval ring box.

She heard Danny call, "What is it?" She couldn't speak.

But the ring box was empty. Just a silk lining with some printing on it that she couldn't make out, and an empty little pillow with a slot where the ring would have gone.

Despising the idea that someone might have exchanged it for cash, she searched with the flashlight as if the ring could have fallen inside the tin box, but there was only a piece of yellowed newspaper. The text was in Finnish, the bold headline reading, 83

MURHATTU! The date was DEC. 26, 1913.

Why would Jago have left his daughter an empty box and an ancient newspaper clipping? Was this what Lena had gone to her grave in search of? Imagining it was something "larger than life"? How sad! Were *both* of them crazy?

Or was Julia, because she couldn't help thinking that because there *was* something here, maybe Lena could have been right about Derrick, too?

"Julia?" Danny called. "What did you find?"

She hadn't cried in a year and couldn't seem to manage it now, even at the sight of the empty box. She searched again inside the platform, but there was nothing else, no matter how she cursed the mouse that had filled the space.

Finally, she shoved her find into her pocket and climbed down to Danny. "I found something," she told him. "But I don't think it's our treasure. I mean, it can't be."

The flashlight beam led them to the house, to the warm glow of the porch. Julia clutched the little box in her pocket, eager to get inside to see if she could decipher the newspaper article. But when they stepped into the kitchen, Violet, in her nightgown and robe, was leaning against the refrigerator, holding the phone to her ear. "Who *is* this? You woke me up, you know, calling just now . . . I asked you first. Who are you?"

"Violet!" Julia said, aghast. "Please, give me the phone."

But Violet said, "Oh! Alice! How wonderful to hear your voice, finally. This is Violet Maki. I came here to look for you. Or, well, for your mother, Grace."

"Oh, my God," Julia breathed, thinking nonsensically, *I thought she was in the wilderness!* Thinking: *So much for breaking this gently.*

Alice didn't believe Violet — at first, she didn't even believe that Violet was Violet — and Julia took the phone and tried to explain. Alice had clearly had no idea about Grace. There was heavy silence on the line, and then, finally, Alice, sounding shell-shocked: "I just wanted to find out how my babies were; we only camped one night and then George's knees were bothering him from all the hiking, and when we got back, he said, 'It's too late to call,' and I said, 'She'll still be up . . .'" Her voice faded. Then, she added, "My earliest memories, my mother — Lena — she's there! She was always there. And my dad, too!"

"I'm going to find out what happened," Julia promised, and when she hung up, her hand left a sweaty print on the phone.

She was still getting her mind around Alice's shock — it was a relief not to have to hate her for lying, but terrible to think she'd never known — when Violet looked Danny up and down and said, "You look just like Grace's husband, Joe, used to look. Except you're skinnier."

Julia leaned on the counter, steadying herself. "You're confused, Violet," she said, remembering the portrait of her grandpa, the one Marty had kept on her dresser and never spoken of. Joe in a military uniform, his eyes squinted, his smile slight — like Danny's. Julia had thought of Joe as so dashing — and as so far gone as to have nothing to do with her, since he'd died long before she was born. "Joe was our grandpa. He was Lena's husband."

Violet frowned. "Lena's husband?"

Danny touched Violet's arm, and his face softened, and Julia was amazed at his tenderness and at how close he was willing to get, when he'd just met her. *He's a father,* she realized, really for the first time, though of course she'd known all along, and she was ashamed that she'd never met her nephew, who was already three and a half years old. "Violet, our mom, Marty, was Lena and Joe's daughter," he said. "Our mom was your daughter's daughter."

"Oh, dear," Violet said, and she wandered off toward the bedroom again. "I'm beginning to see."

Julia glared after her, disgusted by the innocent fluff of her hair.

"I was waiting for the perfect moment to tell her," Julia said. Danny had brought beer, and they were sitting on the stoop in the cool darkness; the moon was just past new, and stars arrayed the black canvas of the sky.

"I don't think she understood anyhow," he said. He blew out smoke; Julia waved it away. Having lived with her mother all those years, she was a firm believer in not drinking alone, which meant she hadn't had anything to drink in months, and she was beginning to feel the effects after just half a beer; she'd drunk it too quickly, relishing the bitter taste.

"Well, I guess Grace must have passed away," she said. It was the only possibility she wanted to entertain. "Then Lena married Joe. They must have figured it would be easier if Alice didn't know. But — poor

Grandpa Joe: losing his first wife, and then his second wife turns out to be obsessed with her missing brother and then *she* dies, too."

Danny smoked and reached for another bottle, popped the top.

Julia couldn't keep her fears at bay. "Except I can't help but wonder if Lena . . . I don't know. If she *did* something to Grace, you know?" She told him about the letter she'd found. "Violet said something today about how she shouldn't have gotten Grace involved, but I didn't know what she was talking about. What if our grandma Lena was, like, some monster?"

"I don't know, Jules."

Some help he was. Julia sipped her beer, finding herself yearning for the computer she'd left behind, the Internet connection at Ryan's apartment. The comforting ease of a search engine. As if anything or anyone could be found with a few simple keystrokes, the faith to strike the Enter key. Maybe she could locate Derrick, or at least some information about him. She couldn't help feeling he'd be the one to set everything right. She wanted to believe that, if she'd had a sister like Lena — not to mention a dad like Jago, with his empty boxes stashed away — she might have stayed gone, too.

Then she realized: she'd been so concerned with the past and with Violet that she hadn't thought to ask Danny how things were going, despite the trouble she'd sensed on the phone with him this morning. She set down her beer to pull the sleeves of her fleece over her hands. "So, um, what did you mean on the phone about that song, the highway robber or something?" she said, and it was plain ridiculous how nervous she felt. Her little brother! She lifted her beer and took another swig; some went trickling down her chin, and she wiped it away with her sleeve.

He laughed. "You'd better slow down, there, Jules." He sang: " 'Well, I was *drunk* . . . the day my mom got out of prison . . .' "

"You're going to wake up Violet," Julia objected, though she liked the sound of his voice.

He quit abruptly, cursed, and smoked. "Nicole's seeing someone else," he said.

"Oh, my God." Julia felt a twinge of gratification that her poor opinion of Nicole had been vindicated, and she thought of Lena, believing so strongly that Derrick understood — or would understand, anyway — everything about her, and she about him, and that they always would. She thought again what it might be like, to be so certain you were never alone. "Are you gonna talk to her? Do you still love her?" She remembered how happy he'd seemed at his wedding.

His mouth twisted. "My boy hid behind the fucking sofa when I walked in. The first night, I tried to put him to bed and he wouldn't stop screaming till *she* came in."

Julia felt her skin tighten. *And his heart, too, how will he . . . ?*

"She never would leave Devil's Bend because her sister's got leukemia, you know? But I thought she wanted me to reenlist for the money — not because she was fucking this other guy."

Julia winced at his bitterness, could find nothing to say.

He blew out a long stream of smoke. "I know what it's like to think your dad doesn't give a fuck about you. I'd die before I'd make Josh feel like that. But it's like she's not giving me a choice."

They'd spent so many years never talking about their father; Julia hated to think Danny had felt this way all that time and she'd done nothing to help him, or even anything to share his pain. "Well, you can't just give up," she said, trying to sound hopeful.

"It's complicated," he said, and there was a note of *case closed* in his voice.

"Right," she said. So much for trying to share his pain.

"What about you?" he said then. "Have you decided what you're gonna do when Alice and George get back in the fall?"

She looked into the distance, where the light faded to blackness, surprised and embarrassed he'd think to ask when he was neck-deep in problems of his own.

"You know," he said, "I don't think being alone has been that good for you. You've been here since, what, last fall? Mourning? Do you ever get out? See friends?"

"I was doing fine until Violet showed up." She chewed her lip. She didn't like the taste in her mouth, and the cool air was crawling up her neck. She added, in her defense, "You don't know what it's like to lose someone."

His face clouded over, and he smoked.

She decided then: it was ridiculous to think that they could ever be as close as Lena and Derrick had been — that had pretty much been in Lena's head, anyway! — or that she could do anything to help him. She couldn't even help herself. She stood, started up the steps.

She heard Danny's voice. "I doubt he even

really knew you, Jules. You don't know what it is to lose somebody you actually *had*."

She turned back, wobbled. "Look, Danny, I'm sorry Nicole's cheating on you, but don't put your shit on me, because Ryan knew who I was from the beginning. Did I tell you how we met? I was naked! Posing in an art class."

He snorted. "Nice, Jules. Very classy. I'll bet he made a *beautiful* drawing."

She folded her arms.

"But did you ever let him actually see you — beyond the surface shit, I mean?"

"I let him see *everything,* and I *told* him everything."

Danny dropped his cigarette, ground it out under his boot. "Did you tell him how you never bothered to meet your nephew?"

"Danny! I . . . I was busy. And you weren't there, and Nicole and I never exactly got along . . ."

"You never even tried."

"Well, you never called me when Ryan died! And don't tell me Mom didn't tell you; I know she did. At least I send Josh birthday presents! December twenty-first, every year!"

His eyes narrowed. "Right. Well, I guess we're fucking even, then." He stood and walked off into the darkness.

■ ■ ■ ■

In the morning, just as the sky began to lighten, Julia brushed her teeth three times to clear her mouth of the rotten taste of last night, then sneaked out through the back porch quietly so as not to wake Danny, who'd set up camp out there without ever coming back into the house. He moaned and burrowed deeper under his blankets, and the cool silence outside calmed her as she went through the familiar motions of feeding the horses and letting them out to the pasture.

She was working up a sweat cleaning a stall when Danny came out and said Violet was up and needed her. His face was rough with dark stubble; his eyes, shadowed under his hat, were inscrutable as stones again. She handed him the pitchfork and her work gloves, and headed for the house.

In the kitchen, the smell of coffee assaulted her nose. Violet, in pressed-looking jeans, a denim shirt, and her Keds, was standing at the stove, pouring steaming, dark liquid from an antique-looking pot — God knew where she'd found it. "Violet, there's a Mr. Coffee right there on the counter!" Julia cried, wanting to snatch the pot from those shaky hands, fearing turning the impending disaster into an actual one. Steam rose from a cast-iron skillet where fiddleheads were wilting in butter, their green smell scenting the air. "Danny let you do this?"

"I can't stand that drip stuff." Violet finally set the pot down; Julia exhaled, though her anxiety lingered like hot air after a summer tornado. "Is that his name?" Violet said, picking up a spatula to stir the fiddleheads. "Danny? He's a nice boy. It's amazing how much he looks like Joe, honestly."

Julia wondered if Violet remembered what Danny had told her last night. "You're supposed to be *resting*. You have your doctor's appointment at noon today, remember."

"Doctor's appointment?"

Julia explained, but Violet seemed to recall nothing of her arrival Sunday or the trip to the hospital. She finally said, "Well, we're going to have to cancel that. I don't need more tests. I've got my doctor at home. We need to find out what happened to Grace. I feel I'm responsible — I'm afraid it's because of this place, the hold it has on everyone. I realized far too late."

Julia finally conceded and called to cancel the appointment, remembering how dark her mother's eyes had always gone whenever the past, or the farm, had come up in conversation. Julia knew now that she didn't want to be like that, but, in the morning light, she'd begun to wonder if there was any escaping it. Not only could Julia and Danny not seem to get along for five minutes, but the past was casting this deep shadow over the farm, and Violet still hadn't acknowledged that they were related. Yet — Violet surely wasn't well enough to go back to Minnesota and live alone, was she?

But, God, the last thing Julia wanted was to be stuck with some old woman who didn't even know what they were supposed to mean to each other.

Just as Julia hung up, the phone rang again, and Violet brightened, and Julia looked at it shaking with the noise of its bell and thought, *Derrick!*

But it was Alice. "I've been thinking about what you said about that woman, Grace," she said, and her voice sounded raw. "I have to tell you what happened with my dad."

Spring 1965

Alice was nineteen years old, and she was washing the supper dishes, watching her reflection in the kitchen window become clearer as the sky outside darkened and a cold rain fell, coating standing piles of old snow. Her thick hair, the whitish yellow of fresh-churned butter, and broad shoulders and hips had never convinced her to consider herself beautiful, especially not when compared to her small-boned, dark-haired little sister, Marty, who had always been their mother's favorite. Alice didn't blame Lena for that. Marty demanded attention the minute she walked into a room, while Alice inched in, hoping no one would notice.

Though Lena had been dead for six months, Alice could still hear her voice.

She didn't want to think of it; she turned her thoughts to George, which made her

347

smile. Only two months until their wedding. It would be awkward to live at the Tuomi farm with George and his brother and sister and aunt — his parents had been dead for years, killed in a car crash when the kids were little — but at least there wouldn't be so many memories. Here, every time she walked past her father's bedroom, she would swear she could smell those long months of her mother's dying, and she would remember Lena's pale face, the way her head had barely indented the pillow that Alice would fluff for her. Alice hoped that, after she got married, she would remember Lena as she'd been when she was healthy and strong, before her activities had devolved into the packing of old letters and things in empty shoe boxes and layering them in a trunk. (When Alice had wondered where all the shoes had gone, Lena had laughed and said, *Where useless things go!*) Lena told everyone that, when Derrick came home, he would want to have these things, these reminders of their childhood, these tokens of her not forgetting.

Everyone else, even Joe, thought Derrick was dead — he hadn't been heard from in twenty years — but they humored her. When a person was dying, that was what you did. They all promised to keep the trunk, and not to open it, until Derrick came home. Now, every time she went in to make her father's bed, Alice would see it, there in the corner of the room, as if he harbored plans for it.

The back door opened, and her father came in. Alice smiled at him, though she worried at the eggplant-colored half-moons under his eyes, and at his hair, looking grayer every day. It seemed a bad idea, leaving him and Marty alone.

But, to her surprise, he smiled and asked her to sit at the table with him. His mouth twitched — she couldn't recall seeing him nervous before. She wondered if he was going to invite her and George to live with him. She knew immediately: she would do it, if George agreed. Though she'd been looking on the bright side of leaving the bad memories of her mother's dying, she didn't at all want to leave her father.

Instead, he told her he thought she was a very responsible girl, that she'd been a big help to him. She basked in the rare praise, until he said, "Alice, I need to take a trip."

Like a needle prick, that sentence! He'd never left the farm, had scarcely taken a day off from work on the railroad. Now, wiping his hands on his knees, he said he'd be gone for three weeks, and maybe George could help her with the outside chores. He needed to go to California.

As Alice floundered on the waves of an interior storm, Joe looked down at the table and told her: he had a good friend there from the war he'd lost touch with, and, since Lena had died, getting back in touch with this friend had become all he could think of.

Alice swallowed. She tapped the table with her finger. "A woman?"

There was heaviness in his eyes. "Yes. A woman." He took a breath, like there was something more he wanted to say. "I should tell you . . . ," he began. But then he closed his mouth and looked down again.

Alice flounced up. She sank her hands into the cooling dishwater, found something to scrub. "I don't want to know," she said. "I don't!"

"It's nothing against your mother," he said. "Against Lena, I mean."

But she didn't even care, for once, if she'd hurt his feelings, though, in a moment, the sound of his chair screeching back from the table, his quiet footsteps leaving the room, made her scalp ache and tingle the way it had, long ago, when the boys at school would yank her braid, trying to make the quiet girl yell.

■ ■ ■ ■

Alice and Marty took Joe to the train, and three weeks went by. Snow melted, birds sang, and the pussy willows came, along with the mud and the robins. From a distance, the birch and poplar trees looked like they'd dressed in light green tulle for a ball; the pines stood among them like men in black overcoats. George came each morning and evening to help with the chores. He planted the potatoes. Every night, he ate supper with the two sisters. They got letters from Joe every few days. *Things here are taking longer than I expected. I miss you both very much.*

Alice was disgusted. Her scalp throbbed.

Yet, she postponed her wedding, waiting for him to return.

Mid-July, George's Aunt Margaret finally put her narrow foot down. She'd been keeping the house company-ready and baking a wedding cake every Thursday, as the wedding got pushed from Saturday to Saturday to Saturday. She told Alice it was beginning to seem Joe might not come back.

Alice didn't want to believe it, but, furious at the thought, she agreed to go through with the ceremony.

She realized her dismay and emptiness only as the neighbors stared at her standing alone in the Tuomis' living room door, ready to process behind bridesmaid Marty, while George's aunt played the "Wedding March" on the out-of-tune piano.

She wrote Joe with the news; two weeks later, a letter arrived, with money enclosed. He'd never forgive himself, he wrote, for missing walking her down the aisle, but now, with the wedding accomplished, he'd decided to take his pension from the railroad, stay in California, and continue looking for his friend. He wanted Alice and George to consider the farm theirs, and Marty to join him in California, if she'd like. The money was for a one-way train ticket for Marty and a round-trip ticket for Alice so she could visit any time she wanted. He hoped that, by the time she came, he would have found his friend, because he really wanted the two of them to meet.

Alice stuffed her father's money into her pocket. She crumpled the letter and threw it into the trash, dumping the morning's coffee grounds over it.

She was not going to give him the satisfaction of sending Marty out to be with him.

Just what Marty needed — to be completely uprooted, when she'd already lost her mother! What could he be thinking? To imagine that a fourteen-year-old girl could be expected to comprehend that her father had been waiting for her mother to die so that he could go in pursuit of his one true love? Because surely that was the only explanation for his bizarre behavior in searching for this "friend," this woman.

It would simply have to be that Alice and George and Marty would be a family.

She wrote Joe: *Marty doesn't want to move out there, and don't ask her about it again, she was in tears for hours until I told her she didn't have to go. George and I will keep her, don't trouble yourself about it. I'm afraid I can't spare time to visit. You know how busy the farm is in the summer and then I'll be starting classes again. Here is your train ticket money back. George will be pleased about the farm.*

She wrote: *As for me, I'd rather have my father.*

Then she scribbled over that sentence until she was sure it was illegible and just signed her name.

She told Marty that their father was starting a new life in California and it was up to them to take care of the farm now. And then Marty was, in fact, in tears for hours. Alice crooned, "It's for the best, Marty, don't you see?" Rubbing her sister's back, bringing her Kleenex to dry her tears.

May 2000

Julia shuffled through the messy stacks of pictures and stray papers that she'd unloaded from a shoe box onto the kitchen table, random images and scribblings she could seem to make no sense of.

"Then she wasn't dead!" Violet had said to Alice on the phone, certain that it was Grace that Joe had gone to find, and that Grace never would have willingly abandoned her child — that Lena must somehow have precipitated it. "You're in California anyway — you have to try to find her! Please, Alice. These connections mean everything." But, as far as Alice was concerned, Lena had been her mother, and Grace clearly hadn't wanted her, and, besides that, Joe had never found Grace when he'd looked, years ago.

Neither Julia nor Violet mentioned to Alice that Lena might not have really wanted

Alice (or Joe, for that matter) — she might just have wanted the farm. Julia had been sad for Alice — it was almost more heartbreaking to think that Grace had up and left than to believe that she'd died — and Violet, too, had seemed dejected, going to lie down again, leaving the buttered fiddleheads to congeal in the skillet. As she'd shuffled away, Julia had found herself grinding her teeth. If the old woman went back to Minnesota, it seemed it would be like sending her off alone to die.

Now here was a stack of square snapshots date-stamped on their white edges: '58, '59, '60 . . . A young, earnest Alice with her thick blond braid; dark-haired little Marty, usually with an up-to-no-good grin; handsome, fit Grandpa, his eyes always somehow in shadows; Grandma, still looking so young for one who wasn't destined to live much longer. And another note from Lena:

Here are the girls — over the years you've missed — I told them all about you! I told them that without you and boys like you, they would have *nothing* — they rolled their eyes! Not understanding I was *serious.* So I told them about your ship — crisscrossing the Pacific through those hard middle years of the War — regardless of the danger — fighting to keep the world safe from tyranny — & how brave you were (over and over!) to get into that tiny airplane that was going to be as helpless as a pebble in a slingshot going off that catapult, the *faith you had* to be latched inside and to brace yourself there, knowing how many had gone up & — so many things could happen! — never made it back onto the ship's deck — or maybe you didn't think of it — maybe you just knew *what had to be done.* & I told them about the battle — your tiny group of "escort carriers" facing the entire Imperial Navy — how if your group had turned tail there was no telling what might have happened to *us* back home. Because — I told them — "Back then, there were no *guarantees!*"

So don't think they don't know! Tho' — "teenagers!" Got a little tired of my stories, I guess! M. — "I don't care, I don't want to hear any more about him! Why don't you ever want to talk about *me?*" Ah, "how sharper than a serpent's tooth!" (I don't recall us being "smart" that way in our day — or am I misremembering, ha ha —) But Derrick —

how she'll love you — when you finally meet!

So this was why Marty and Alice had never talked about Derrick: they'd already had their fill. And why Marty had infused Julia with hate for the naïve condition of hopefulness. "Don't *ever* think he's coming back," she'd said when Julia's dad had left without prelude or explanation; Julia was nine. "Don't even *imagine* it!"

Yet — he had come back, from time to time; not to stay, of course, but to visit. To talk. To ask how she was doing and to tell her a few random things, too. She'd always found his efforts inadequate, but now she had to concede: what he'd done had been better than doing nothing. It was disconcerting to think that her scorn for the past hadn't been her own idea, and she hated that she hadn't tried to call her dad all year. She'd never even told him about Ryan, because he'd always been flustered and useless in times of crisis anyway, typically starting in on some crap about healing your aura or something, and now he didn't even know she was at Alice and George's, they'd been out of touch that long.

Stashing the old papers back in the shoe box, all she could think of was how Alice had lied to Marty when Marty was just a kid, had made her think her dad didn't want her when, really, he did.

Danny banged inside, and with him came a whiff of fresh air and the lingering odor of cigarette smoke. Julia wrinkled her nose, watching him fill his coffee cup from the antique pot. "Boiled coffee," he mused. "And what's this? Spinach or something?"

"We're going to have to figure out what to do," Julia demanded, "about Violet."

He turned; she felt a flash of disgust at his impassive eyes. So he was just going to give her the stone face forever, pretend they'd never bonded before they'd fought, pretend they were nothing to each other at all, just as they'd been pretending for so many years. "Well, I guess I could drive her back to her place, if you want," he said. "At least that way she wouldn't be on the road by herself, and she wouldn't have her truck, so we wouldn't have to worry about her driving after she got back there. I mean, I should really head home, anyway, or there'll be no fucking chance with Nicole."

"Oh," Julia said, and she was surprised at the depth of her sudden dismay. *So confronting his cheating wife is preferable to staying here with me — and I did say I didn't want to be stuck with Violet, didn't I?* Well, she was not going to cry — of course not — and she wouldn't, even if she could, not in front of Danny. "Well, I guess it would be best for her to be near her doctor. But I mean, I don't think it's the best idea for her to be alone. And if she didn't have her truck, what if there was, like, an emergency?"

The phone rang.

Julia jumped up, thinking Alice might be calling back with more to tell about Joe, or more to ask about Grace. But Danny grabbed it, and it was Nicole. He took the phone out to the porch, closing the door behind him, all but a crack to leave room for the cord.

Julia went back to the photographs, trying to drown out the murmur of his voice. *Alice and her daddy,* said the handwritten caption on the border of one that showed Joe holding baby Alice in his arms, and Julia said to her grandpa, *How could you?* Then she heard Danny yelling. Something about an (expletive) guy with an (expletive) Harley and Danny's (expletive) paycheck and "Don't think you're gonna fucking take him from me!" She felt like she was having her eyebrows plucked, not knowing just where the next little sting would come.

Alice and her ~~mommy.~~ Baby Alice in the arms of smiling, beautiful Grace.

Danny came in and slammed the phone onto its base; the bell jangled. "I never thought I'd be fucking divorced!" he said. Then he was gone again, and Julia was left staring, her ears ringing from the bang of the door or the sudden silence, or both.

Then she heard Violet's voice: "What's all this ruckus?"

Julia turned. Violet's hair stood on end like a dandelion gone to seed. "Sorry, Violet. Danny's . . . upset, I guess! He didn't mean to wake you."

"I wasn't sleeping. You know, you kids are awfully free with planning my life. I am not leaving my truck here."

"Oh!" Julia hadn't thought: on the other side of the kitchen wall was the bedroom.

"I'm perfectly capable of driving myself home, when the time comes. If we can find out what happened to Grace, with Lena gone, there's no reason for me to stay after that. If we can just get Alice to try to find her!"

"Oh, but Violet, remember, when you got here, you ended up having to take the ambulance to the hospital!"

Violet stiffened. "I did not."

"You did!" Julia said, hating that Violet didn't think she and Danny were reasons to

stay. Not that she should have been surprised!

Violet frowned.

"Well, listen, Violet," Julia snapped, "if
you're going to be leaving us so soon,
there's something I have to show you." She
was tired of being so sensitive about Violet's
supposed delicacy, when it seemed Violet
was probably stronger than she was, anyway,
and clearly didn't care about her or Danny
besides.

When Julia handed her the little package
from the tree stand, Violet seemed to
crumble. Her old eyes, squinting behind her
glasses, couldn't make out the tiny newsprint, so Julia, softening, sat down across
from her and explained about the article
and where she'd found the things.

"I've never seen this before," Violet mur-
mured. " '83 Murhattu.' I don't know much
Finnish, but I'm fairly sure that means '83
Murdered.' "

"Oh, my God. Seriously?"

"This must be about the Italian Hall
disaster up in Michigan. I remember the
date. I was a little girl when it happened.
Jago grew up there, in what they used to
call Red Jacket — it's Calumet now — but
he never said . . . Only that he left town
because of the strike."

"Well, do you think this could have been what he meant when he told Lena he'd left something on the farm for her? I mean, except it's an empty box. Do you think she would have taken the ring and left the box behind?"

But all Violet said was "He should have told me. If he was there."

Julia shuffled absently through another bunch of old papers. She felt the whirring of discontent, somewhere between wishing she had some idea what to say to soothe Violet and wishing she could go back to the comforting scrape of sandpaper, to her life as it had been, before she'd known this exasperating old woman existed.

Then she came across an envelope addressed to Lena in an angular handwriting she hadn't seen before. Return address of *B. Stanwood* in *Nyack, N.Y.;* date of June 2, 1950. She unfolded the thin paper and scanned it. "Oh, my God, Violet, listen to this." She read out loud:

Lena,
Well, I knew you were a shrewd cookie, but this takes the cake. You're a peach to congratulate me on my marriage and thanks a million for sending back the birthday card I intended for our "friend"

Grace. I guess if I wrote more than once every 3 years I'd have kept up with the developments. I will say I don't know that I'd give a bushel of rotten apples for your version of "events." I suspect you may deserve a good slap across the face, on behalf of Grace and Violet both. I'm only sorry I encouraged her not to give you the boot years ago when she thought you were up to something. But don't worry, I won't tell your little secret. In fact, I intend to wash my hands of you, and I'm not kidding about that. I am sorry that you still have not received any news of your brother. (And yes, I do remember all the times we had together at the yard and beyond. Seems to me the real question is, do you?)

                                    Boots

Violet's face had regained some color. "Boots! We need to call her. Maybe she'll know where Grace is. Maybe she'll know what happened."

"This letter was written fifty years ago," Julia said. "What are the odds she's still in the same place?"

"The odds!" Violet laughed. Her eyes glinted. "We have to try."

■ ■ ■ ■

Julia called information in New York: the only listing for a Stanwood in Nyack was for a Robert. Hanging up, she asked Violet, "Could that be her husband's name?"

"Try it."

Julia dialed. The ringing on the other end of the line seemed to go on forever. Julia felt a pinching pain between her eyes. Finally, a woman answered. Julia was so surprised that she just said, "Boots?"

And the woman said, "Yeah?"

January 1947

Four days after the incident with the stove, the cold snap broke. Grace was amazed that afternoon when she looked at the thermometer outside the kitchen window and saw it was thirty above — seventy degrees warmer than it had been. Thank goodness! She'd really begun to wonder if they would survive. The poor animals in the barn. And poor her, having to run to and from the outhouse all the time! Not to mention that Joe had been coming home from work nearly frozen solid. No matter what the temperature was, no matter how the wind blew, he had to walk the length of the train all day long. She guessed he had it worse than she did, at that. Besides, he'd just received a letter from one of his old crewmates with the news that only three of them had survived the war, and there was nothing she could say to make color return to his face; it had gone the pasty shade it had been back when he'd been his sickest. She worried he was going to relapse. He wouldn't call in sick to work and he couldn't seem to sleep, and he said he was loath to try anyway, because of the dreams that would come — which she understood.

As there seemed nothing she could do for his misery, she wallowed in her own. The endless work for no reward. Joe's glowering. Lena's unceasing critiques, veiled though they might be with humor. Defending herself against their cutting comments about the stove episode in particular had seemed hopeless, so Grace had given up trying. Here Joe already thought she'd consigned their baby to hell by "delaying" her baptism (as if it were inevitable that Grace would finally consent to going Catholic!), and now she'd just about killed her, too. Grace found even the endless cries from Alice, who always needed something, wearing. No one ever asked Grace what she needed, what she wanted. She was hard-pressed to keep from screaming at Joe, "I never wanted this stupid place, anyway! I never even really wanted *you!*"

Though, of course, that wasn't true. It just felt like it, these days.

As soon as Lena arrived, Grace asked her

to watch the baby. "I'm going a little stir-crazy," she said, forcing out a laugh. "I've just got to get some fresh air."

"No problem," Lena said. "It's beautiful out there! Enjoy it!"

Grace put on a pair of snowshoes and set off, heading west down the county road. The world was white, and the air felt soft on her skin.

When she reached the woods between their property and the neighbor's, she thought again of Derrick's tree stand, of the view from up there that he'd said had made him feel at peace.

It couldn't hurt to try. Besides, seeing the vista from the top decks of ships had always made her feel restored when she'd worked at the shipyard. Maybe, if she could find the place, it would make her feel better. When Joe had mentioned in the fall that he'd been hunting from it, she'd bitten her tongue, wanting to say, *How dare you?*

There was no traffic coming; she veered into the woods. The snowshoes kept her weightless atop the snow. Trees dropped chunks of white, loosened from branches by the heat of the sun, like children letting go of water balloons.

She hadn't walked far when she saw the thick tree with the ascending boards nailed across its trunk, leading to a platform about twelve feet in the air. She unstrapped the snowshoes so she could climb. The wood creaked under her weight. Standing on the ladder, she brushed the snow from the platform; her foot slipped as she climbed onto it. But this was nothing compared to clambering over icy steel beams at the shipyard.

From the top, she could almost make out Duluth in the shimmering distance. Funny that Derrick hadn't mentioned that. Not caring that her pants might get wet from sitting on the crusted remains of snow, she leaned back on her hands.

Through her gloves, her hand felt a protrusion. A handle of some kind? She turned, yanked on it. It was frozen. She dug out snow and ice with her finger. Finally, a section of the board lifted up on a hinge. There was a box inside. She pulled it out.

A pack of cigarettes. And Joe had promised he wasn't smoking. With his rheumatic fever, it could really kill him. Blinking back tears, she tossed the pack over the edge, hoping it would disappear into the snow.

Wondering what other awful secrets he had hidden, she reached in and patted around, then lay on her stomach to reach farther.

There! Way in the back corner, fabric of some kind. She tugged on it until it came toward her.

When she saw the ruby and diamond ring in its little oval box, she was astonished. *Derrick?* Joe had spent nearly his last dollar on the farm and, though diamonds had become popular lately for couples getting engaged, he'd given her only a plain wedding band. Until seeing this ring, Grace hadn't thought it mattered.

Could it be that he'd purchased this and intended to surprise her with it? He'd always had that way of being better than what she assumed.

No, it couldn't be Joe's, she decided. Or Derrick's. Too old-fashioned-looking. She remembered: Jago had had his own tree stand. This one must have been his.

She felt the crush of disappointment. And suddenly she just couldn't stand it. Losing Derrick over and over again, every single day, this boy that she'd never even had, losing him every afternoon when Lena with her sad, gray eyes brought the mail in.

She tried to breathe. There was a folded piece of newspaper in the bottom of the tin box. Something in Finnish, dated December 1913, and she remembered that cold day on the top deck of Hull 47 at the shipyard, when Lena's dad had told Harry Mickelson, the newspaperman, that there'd been a girl Jago intended to marry when he was young, and the girl had disappeared. Had Jago saved the ring for that girl all these years? Grace studied the yellowed article, but she didn't know Finnish and couldn't get anything from it.

Poor Violet, she thought. She put the ring back into the oval box, then the oval box into the tin box, and the tin box into the flour bag. Then, she shoved the whole thing back into the platform, right where she'd found it, and sat there, hugging her knees and shivering.

May 2000

"Holy mackerel," Boots kept saying, as first Julia, then Violet, explained. "Holy mackerel."

Finally, they were able to get some information from her. Last Boots had heard, twenty-five years ago, Grace was alive. "I never have been the best at keeping in touch," Boots admitted, but she was happy to share the most recent California address she had — especially when she learned that Alice had just discovered the truth about her mother. She said Grace never would talk about what had happened, how she'd lost Alice and Joe to Lena. "I have my theories," Boots said darkly, "but she never did say. If I'd've pried harder, she might've, but I didn't want to stir old coals, you know."

Boots had been married for fifty-one years and had five children and eleven grandchildren. "Can you imagine?" Violet said to

Julia afterward, looking the happiest Julia had seen her. "All that family!"

Violet insisted on trying Grace's old phone number before they called Alice at the campground. "If Alice knows she wants to see her, it will be better," she told Julia.

But this time, when Julia called, the voice on the other end of the line said she had the wrong number. "You've never heard of a Grace Mosckiewicz?" Julia pressed. "What about Grace Anderson? Anyone named Grace at all?" But even when Julia described Grace from the photo that was hanging in the living room, the person in California had no clue.

"You have to try to find her, Alice," Violet was saying into the phone. "The number's no good, but maybe if you go to the address, someone there will know something. You'll always regret it, if you don't *try*. I didn't want to tell you how Lena . . . how much she wanted this farm, after I sold it to Grace and Joe. She would have done anything. I don't know what happened, but I can tell you, no woman wants to lose her child! Please, take a lesson from me and Lena and all the mistakes we made!"

Julia had the sense that Violet was fighting for her life: for her life to have some meaning, at least. She imagined it must be hard to be so old, to have the certain knowledge that nearly everything was behind you. All the mistakes you'd made. All the things you'd managed, through neglect or misfortune or arrogance or the simple passage of time, to lose.

Then Julia thought she heard Alice say, *But — my father!*

Julia grabbed the phone. "What about Grandpa Joe, Alice?"

"I — I don't know what happened to him."

"He died, Alice," Julia said, wondering if they'd all gone straight off the deep end. "Mom said —" And then she realized: Joe wasn't buried next to Lena. Why had she never asked anyone why not?

"I *told* her that he died," Alice said. "But it wasn't true."

Julia banged outside, a rushing fury in her ears, the cool breeze cutting through to her skin as she ran, accelerating until her whole body thrummed, and she found she was thinking of her dad, the few random times they'd spent together — at least they'd been *something.* Her mom had been denied even that.

Alice had explained: she'd thought Joe was

looking for some old girlfriend; she'd been cold every time he called. Finally, he'd stopped calling. And when, about a year later, she'd tried to reach him again, the number had been disconnected. And this betrayal had been even worse than the first, because it was as if he'd abandoned her again. Seething, wounded, she'd told Marty he was dead. "I thought: I don't need him anymore! *We* don't! I thought: Clearly, family means nothing to him!" And then there was no taking it back.

"He was my grandpa, Alice," Julia had snapped. "And Danny's. And Josh's great-grandfather! What right did you have to take him from us?"

Alice had had no answer.

Now, her feet pounding the road, her anger beginning to steam off with her sweat, Julia wondered why there was such a family tradition of people disappearing. She guessed her dad would say there was something karmic going on. But what would it take to stop it? Or were they all just destined to keep falling from the face of the earth?

"There's a spider in the corner," Violet said, pointing, when Julia dragged herself back inside later, drenched in sweat and exhausted enough that she didn't care. "I've been watching it weave its web."

Julia squinted, pulling the Brita pitcher from the fridge. "How did you even see that, Violet? I thought your eyes were bad, even with your glasses."

"Well, kill it," Violet snapped. "We can't let the place go to heck like this."

Shaking her head, Julia grabbed a paper towel, kicked off her muddy running shoes, and boosted herself onto the counter, balancing on the edge in her socks. "Well," Violet said, "if she finds Grace, I'll finally believe it, I guess. That lost things can be found, sometimes."

"I hope so, Violet," Julia said, knocking at the web, not sure she believed it herself.

"I called information," Violet blurted. "You'd done it for me. There are twenty-six men named Joseph Mosckiewicz listed in Los Angeles. I'm afraid I didn't have the fortitude to write them all down. But maybe you'll want to call back."

"Oh!" Julia tried to process that. It was hard to imagine finding anything, anyone, just now. She was so angry — at Alice, at Lena . . . And Grandpa Joe: well, he'd clearly been a selfish son of a bitch, leaving his daughters and running off to California the way he had.

Squishing the spider in the paper towel,

Julia couldn't help it — part of her still thought that even Grace had probably just up and left, and never cared enough to come back.

When it was nearly six o'clock and Violet hadn't gotten up yet from her afternoon nap, Julia peered in and found her lying in bed with her teeth clenched, tears streaming from her pinched-shut eyes.

Julia screamed for her brother.

January 1947

Grace sat in the frozen tree stand, hugging her knees and trying so hard to appreciate the view, trying so hard to leave Jago's little ring in its hiding place.

But the air was too raw to let a person daydream on pleasant things, and the view was colored only in the shades of the season she'd always hated. Her mind wandered to the night, five years earlier, when she'd shivered on her parents' front porch waiting for her first kiss from Alex; and the night before that one, when she'd first met Joe.

If only she hadn't so loved to dance; if only his hands hadn't been so warm, and the darkness outside so cold.

But there were so many if-onlys. It would be impossible to list them all.

Ever since she'd watched Lena pass the baby to Joe on that awful night with the stove, it was hard not to imagine the worst.

She was sure she'd seen Lena's eyes brightening, her mouth softening, whenever he was in the room. Maybe Lena actually was falling for him. Had Joe noticed her simple beauty, her ease and comfort with this life?

Grace felt sick at the thought.

She remembered Lena saying, *You could have killed us.* And maybe it was true. She always had been reckless: Wasn't that what everyone used to say at the shipyard? Wasn't that what "Hotshot" had meant?

She retrieved the little box from inside the platform again and held the ring between her thumb and finger. The ruby was the color of blood; the diamonds winked in the sun.

Every night when Joe walked in the door, his joy at the sight of the baby was obvious. Whenever he looked at Grace, his eyes dimmed, and the hollow feeling he'd once helped to ease in her grew deeper and more gaping.

She slipped the ring onto her pinkie — the only finger it fit. At the sliding sensation of the metal on her cold skin, she shuddered. Tears started.

And when her anguish had wrung itself from her as much as it would, she wiped her face on her sleeve, put her gloves on over the winking ring, and shoved the package back into the platform. She made her way down the ladder, careful not to slip, though she was trembling. *What would Lena think? What would she do?*

She strapped the snowshoes onto her feet, and lifting one heavy foot, then the other, she tramped back to the house, to where Lena waited with Alice.

May 2000

In the hospital waiting room, Danny paged through one magazine after another, obviously not reading a single word, while Julia chewed on a pinkie nail, staring at the *Highlights* that was still on the table, seemingly right where she'd left it on Sunday. It couldn't be the same issue, could it, after all that had happened? She didn't want to look to find out.

"Listen, I'm . . . sorry —" she ventured once, and Danny just shook his head and kept flipping pages. She felt lonely for his raspy voice, for an old country song.

Finally, the doctor with the gelled hair emerged, chart in hand; he didn't smile as they stood to meet him. The tag around his neck, which Julia hadn't noticed Sunday, identified him as Dr. Eric Hanson. "She was able to tell me the name of her doctor back home, so I spoke with him," he said. "I'm afraid the cancer is developing quickly, and she's refusing treatment. I gave her some pain pills to make her more comfortable, but she's still talking about going home to Minnesota, and, I have to say, that's not advisable. She's going to need constant care. A long trip could be a death sentence. It's a miracle she made it here to begin with."

"Does she need to be hospitalized?" Julia asked, and her voice was unsteady.

"At this point, I'm recommending hospice care, or a nursing home. Assisted living, at the minimum. Our staff can help with placing her. She's probably been in pain for some time. She said she's been questioning, in some way, whether it was real. She thought it was her mind, playing tricks. But I think tonight it finally just became too much for her."

"Thank you," Julia managed.

He nodded. "I'm sorry I can't give you better news." He directed them to the desk for more information, then he turned and was gone.

Julia closed her eyes. She hadn't conceived of how there would be such a tightening around her chest, as if Violet were attached to a cord on the other end, walking away with it looped to her, tightening and tightening. "I can't do this," she said. "Seriously. Put her in a nursing home?"

"We have to, Julia," Danny said, and his voice was like an old man's. His hand came to rest on her shoulder; she found it was a comfort.

"I don't really know why I'm calling," Alice said, her voice sounding dim and light-years away. The phone had rung again just as Julia and Danny were helping a woozy Violet back to bed. "I guess I just wondered if I imagined it all?"

"No," Julia said. "You didn't." She didn't bother to temper the news that Violet was dying. "She thinks everything is her fault, Alice." She couldn't resist adding, "Even though *you* were the one who cut off Joe."

Alice sniffed.

Julia sighed; being nasty hadn't helped. "Alice, seriously, it would make her feel so much better if you could at least meet Grace, before she dies. If there could be some connection there. Won't you at least *try* to find her?"

"Violet," Alice remarked coolly then. "But she's no relation to *me,* isn't that what you said?"

"Alice, come on — you owe us this, at least."

But there was a gentle click; the line went dead.

Julia thought for a second she really might cry: but no.

In the darkened bedroom, Julia pulled the rocking chair next to Violet's bedside to keep watch. Finally, as the pain medication wore off, Violet noticed her and said, "What's happening to me?"

Julia leaned on her knees and explained haltingly that they'd made a "reservation" for her to go into a nice "home for older people," that they would move her there as soon as there was an opening. Danny had tried to tell her as they'd driven home from the hospital, but Violet, loopy from the medication, had only laughed, and Julia had had to turn away.

Now Violet seemed to take in the information; she drew herself up, indignant. "Well, that's ridiculous. I can't stay here. At some old people's home? I have my farm in Minnesota to take care of. The neighbor can't watch my dog and cats and chickens forever."

Julia took a deep breath and reviewed for Violet what the doctor had said.

Violet frowned. "It's worse than I thought. Not to get to see my farm again?"

"I'm sorry, Violet. But, for what it's worth, I . . . I'm glad you came here." Julia was getting used to the idea of Violet being with her for a little while. Even Danny had promised to stay a couple more days to help, though he'd made it clear he was planning to leave for South Dakota soon, to try to work out a visitation arrangement with Nicole. All Julia had managed was to wish him luck. Her throat had felt so dry.

"I hope you don't mind the idea of staying too much," Julia told Violet now. "We'll figure out what to do about your other farm."

"I should have known this place would be the place where I'd die." Violet sighed, leaning back into her pillow. "But I suppose he can find me. He's found me before."

Julia felt the tightening again. Violet had said she'd dreamed so many times over the years of Derrick coming to sit on the edge of her bed. He was always young, always in his dress blues and white sailor cap and polished black shoes, and it seemed to Julia that time had healed nothing; that they were all only moving in circles, back again and again to where they'd been. To empty boxes, to placing calls that no one would answer. She thought of her dad, imagined him laughing, saying, *Karma's a bitch.* "I know

385

you'll miss your farm, Violet, but, listen, you can visit here anytime. The place you'll be staying is only a few miles from here." Julia found herself reaching out to touch Violet's gnarled hand; her fingers were astonished by its heat.

Violet seemed surprised, but then her bony fingers curled around Julia's: a concession. "Well. You have to promise you'll make Alice look for Grace. And tell me, the minute there's any news."

Julia didn't want to say how Alice had hung up on her, how there seemed to be so little hope.

But Violet seemed to sense it. "Alice believed my Lena was her mother," she said. "And she learned from Lena how to cut people off — even if she didn't realize it."

"But, Violet, Alice took Joe from us."

"Yes, and Lena called the sheriff to come and question me."

Julia flinched at that.

"He knew she wasn't in her right mind, but, well, she had that way about her. That was why I left. I suppose I didn't know what to do. I thought somehow it was me that was provoking her, after everything. I thought, if I was gone, Lena could find a way to heal. I tried to make the best of it.

"Life is like quicksand," she said. "Take

out a shovelful, and the rest creeps in and fills the space. Pretty soon you think it's always just been that way. Look at Alice and Joe." A tear snaked down her wrinkled cheek. "I tell you, the *last* thing I wanted was to leave Lena an orphan. But I knew Grace would never let her be truly alone. And oh, how she loved Grace! I honestly hoped they might be happy. They might be a family. I should have known better, I guess! I should have known. But — I hoped!"

And Julia realized: it hadn't been Violet who'd stopped believing. It had been Lena who'd been so caught up in thinking of what she wanted and wished for that she'd forgotten to appreciate what she had. It had been Lena who'd never been able to forgive. And she'd kept them all in her unrelenting grasp, all this time.

The next afternoon, Violet, seated between Julia and Danny on the bench seat of Danny's stale-cigarette-smelling truck, was medicated again and seemed not to understand what was happening. Julia was having trouble comprehending it herself: the nursing home had called already this morning to say a space had opened up. Just when they were all getting settled at the farm!

Arriving, Julia and Danny helped Violet find her room and unpack — she didn't have much: her one suitcase, plus the little package from Jago's tree stand and Derrick's blue marble, both of which she put on her bedside table. As they set out to tour her around the place, she was beginning to seem like herself again. "A fine way to treat *family,* shipping a person off alone like this," she said, trying to walk, at first, with them holding her arms, and Julia's heart skipped: *Does she understand?* The halls were long, and finally Violet consented to Danny's pushing her in a wheelchair. "Faster, faster!" she kept telling him, like a jockey astride a racehorse.

With the tour complete, Violet gathered them before her in her room. "Now, I've been hating to ask," she said, her blue eyes clouding behind her glasses, "but I have to know. There really never was any news of my Derrick, was there?"

Danny dropped his head, nudging the floor with one pointed toe of a boot. Julia tried to think of some shred of hope to mention, but there was nothing tangible: only Lena's undying belief, her own ridiculous illusions. Violet had said that, in her dream, Derrick always seemed to want to check up on her, to make sure she was all right. Julia didn't know how she could have been, honestly, after everything.

But if he really was dead, what could he have done? From what Julia had learned, he didn't seem like someone who would blithely stay absent from his family for fifty years. Surely he would have realized that their fate was inexorably woven with his.

The way she was only beginning to realize now. "I'm so sorry, Violet," she said, "but I don't think they ever did hear anything."

Violet nodded, staring into some middle distance of memory. "I knew it . . . the way he came to me . . . and yet . . ." She sighed, focused again. "You will try to find Grace, won't you? And Joe? He was a good man. My Lena wasn't bad, either. She'd just . . . well, she'd had more than she could handle, I suppose. I'm sorry for that."

"Of course, Violet," Julia said, though she had no faith she could bear up under such hopes, and she wondered how Violet could be so forgiving toward the woman who'd made such outrageous accusations, who'd driven her away.

Violet picked up Jago's ring box. "I wonder if Lena knew about this." She sighed. "He was always . . . distant. Dreamy. Looking for something. He was my only husband. I'd like to know the story of this. It's the story of *my* life and it's a mystery to me."

"I know, Violet," Julia said, deciding she would open every shoe box, if she had to, to find out something to tell Violet, to tell everyone. All their fates *were* woven together, with Jago and Violet the linchpins. Even if Violet never comprehended their biological relationship, finding out the whole truth might be a way to free the family from the mourning that had permeated it for so long. At least, Julia's dad would say so — and why not try to take some comfort where it might be found?

Then Violet looked up and said, "Did you say . . . did you say my Lena was your grandmother?"

Julia felt her heart quicken.

"That's right, Violet," Danny said, and Julia could hear the expectation in his voice.

Violet's eyes brightened with hope and almost delight; a smile quivered into place. "I thought I had to be dreaming when you said it before. I was so sure Jago had left me with nothing. I was so sure I had no one left."

■ ■ ■ ■

PART FOUR:
HOME

■ ■ ■ ■

May 2000

It was difficult to be riding in Danny's truck without Violet sitting between them, and Julia hated to think how empty the house was going to seem, especially since Danny was planning to leave, too. When they'd told Violet he intended to return to South Dakota to see his son, Violet had asked him to go to Minnesota to check on her farm. She wondered if he'd bring a few things back for her, including her dog and cats — if they could stay with Julia, so Violet could visit them. He was to give the chickens to the neighbor who'd been taking care of things. "And," she'd said, "get my egg money out of the cookie jar. It should be enough to pay for a couple months here. That should be all I need, if that sourpuss of a doctor can be believed."

Julia, her shock having given way to thrill at the sight of Violet's smile, hadn't been able to decide if the old woman was extremely sharp or totally out of her mind. "Your egg money is going to pay for two months here, Violet? That could be a few thousand dollars."

Violet had gotten a faraway look in her eyes again. "I guess I always imagined there was a hole in the bottom of the jar, even when there wasn't anymore."

Now Julia took a breath. Even if it turned out to be too late to find anyone who'd been lost, or patch the things that had been torn, some things had to still be possible. "Danny, are you really getting divorced?" she asked her brother loudly, over the wind and the road noise.

His face twitched like she'd pinched him. "So she says."

Julia pressed on. "Well, what are you gonna do about Josh?"

He clenched the steering wheel.

The truck lurched over a bump; Julia grabbed the door handle. She was trying not to think how Alice had hung up on her. "Because I was thinking . . . what if you came back for the summer and brought Josh? If Nicole will let you have him? I mean, Alice owes us, right? Maybe if you stayed for the summer it would give you time to figure out . . . I mean, you told

394

Violet you'd bring back her pets anyway, and I still have to do the kitchen, which is gonna be a *huge* job. . . . And we have to find out about Grace and Jago. If we can. And you know all about the horses, right, from when you spent those summers as a kid? I mean, I could use the help. With everything. And you could spend time with Violet — think how much she'd love that, and she'd get to know Josh. . . . You could go to Devil's Bend and get him, go to Violet's, and then come back and just . . . stay. For a while."

He looked at her, and the hope pooling in his eyes made her smile.

Nicole put up a fight. She said she'd pay money to see Danny try to handle Josh for a day, let alone a summer. But, finally, she said she'd been wanting to take a trip with her boyfriend on his Harley anyway, and if she didn't have Josh for the summer she could help her mom and sister more, besides.

Danny left right away; he was going to drive all night. He wanted to get to his son.

Julia, not relishing the prospect of absolute silence once she was alone, had made Danny help her move the old stereo and boxes of LPs back in from the shed, and now, in his honor, she put on a Johnny Cash album, the music filling the dim, empty room. She *hoped* Danny wouldn't change his mind about coming back; she decided to remain optimistic. And then she found herself drawn to the photograph of Ryan's back that hung on the living room wall, all shadows and silver. She touched the glass, brooding on the ring she'd found at the back of his sock drawer. She would never have given it up for anything, if she'd had a choice. If there'd been a ring in Jago's little box to begin with, what could explain why he'd let it slip away? And if he'd given the ring to someone, or lost it, why would he have told Lena there was something waiting for her to find?

Poor Lena. There was hanging on to things and there was letting them drag you down. Julia thought of the trunk. She didn't want to go near it just now. But, as Johnny Cash sang about flames going higher, she took the frame of Ryan's picture in her hands, lifted it from its hook, and carried it upstairs. Pulling open the bottom drawer of her armoire, she took out her camera from where it nestled in her sweaters. She laid the photo in its place and pushed the drawer shut, then stretched out on her futon, letting her camera rest on her chest, feeling her heart thump against its weight, listening to the faraway music about fire going wild. She pointed her camera at the ceiling and pressed the shutter on the place where the evening light faded into shadows; the sound of the image being captured made her shiver. She remembered Violet — *Lost things can be found, sometimes.*

Even if Derrick was really gone, even if Alice refused to look for Grace, and even if Julia never could find out the story of Jago's little box, she realized there was something more that she *could* do. She went downstairs and called information again and took down the numbers of all the Joseph Mosckiewiczes in the Los Angeles area, wondering if there'd once been a girl Jago had meant to give the missing ring to; if maybe Grandpa Joe had been the one to stash that photograph of Grace in the attic with the magazines: his own secret dream of what he'd once had and lost.

It had taken Alice only an hour to get from the campground to the address Violet had given her. In the speed and congestion of the rush-hour freeway traffic, her foot pressing more and more heavily on the gas pedal, she'd been afraid to take her eyes off the road long enough to look at the speedometer, so she had no idea how far she'd traveled, only that the journey had been so terrifying she'd imagined it would last forever. But then it had been over sooner than she was ready, the exit for the city coming at her like a hurricane.

She took the exit, stopped at a gas station, and bought a detailed area map. Her heart had already committed the address to memory.

George had said she'd regret it if she didn't try. And they were so close: it would be so easy. "You said already it explained so much," he'd told her. "Imagine if you could meet her."

It had been petty to hang up on Julia yesterday. But there'd been such a rushing in her ears; she'd barely heard what Julia had been saying. She knew that she herself might have said something rude before she'd hung up, gently, hand trembling. She didn't recall.

But she hadn't dared to dial the number again. She only kept making things worse.

And it seemed that time had such a way of calcifying mistakes. It didn't take long before every day you started waking up and saying to yourself, *It's too late*. And, of course, every day was later than the previous day. So if yesterday had been too late, then today certainly was.

She just hadn't understood — maybe it had never occurred to her — that, through her deception about her father, she'd done damage to Julia and Danny, too. Not to mention Danny's little boy, Josh.

She supposed she'd been trying to hurt her dad the way he'd hurt her, but she hated to think that she could willfully harm another child. Even through cowardice, selfishness. Bad enough what she'd done to Marty! There was just no excuse. Not after the way that she, herself, had been hurt. Not even knowing it! Only having had the sense, her whole life, whenever she walked into any room in Blackberry Ridge, that people had been talking about her, whispering behind her back: the puzzling veiled comments from people at church, at school, that Alice didn't now exactly remember, only knew they had made her feel she didn't know quite *who she was.* That maybe everyone else knew something she didn't.

She'd looked so different from her own family, with her awful big bones and her big chest and hands, her butter-colored hair. How excruciating it had been, not fitting, and trying so hard, always trying so hard.

(And always Lena had been there to laugh

and say: *Nice try!* And her father, with his halfhearted smile, that distant look in his dark blue eyes.)

And her mother — Lena! — she had said that the trunk was for *Derrick,* of course, so Alice had never dared to open it. Maybe she'd considered it her job, not to give up on him. And then she couldn't help just plain wanting to forget. So, after her dad had gone, she'd shoved the trunk into the corner of the attic and never looked at it. *In* it. She'd scared everyone else away from it. Had she known all along that the truth of her was inside? Had it been her own pounding fear and regret that had kept her from it?

Now, as she pulled the car out of the gas station parking lot, struggling with the map in one hand and the steering wheel in the other, she wished she'd asked George to come along, so she wouldn't feel her aloneness so bottomless and vast, her dark self so irredeemable.

Parking next to the curb of the gently winding road, she studied the house in the distance, a compact, low box in the desert sand, surrounded by strange plants: cacti, palms, some spike-leaved things low to the ground with bright flowers blooming. The

memory of the freeway seemed an impossible nightmare on this quiet street; she felt the strange thrill of the stakeout. She wondered if the woman (her mother!) by any chance still lived here; if she was home, if she would come outside. If she would seem, in any way, familiar.

Alice didn't know, now that she was here, if she had sufficient courage to go to the door.

Though: the phone number had been invalid! This way, she could tell them all: *I tried!*

She got out of the car. The door creaked, slammed. So loud, on this deserted street!

All those years ago, Alice had encouraged Marty (she could still see her sister's bewildered gray eyes, the delicate curl of her lip at that very moment when she transitioned from a girl with the possibility of sweetness into a faithless adolescent) to think that her dad plain had no interest in her. She wasn't sure why she'd done that. Was she just jealous of the way Lena had preferred the younger girl? She'd never planned for her juvenile pouting to fend off her father — for good! She'd had no plan at all, no sense of potential consequences. She'd only wanted to make him suffer, to wait. He was looking for that woman, in preference to being home on the farm with his daughters!

She remembered how, whenever he'd called, those first couple of years, she would sit with the phone pressed hotly to her ear, waiting for him to apologize, waiting for him to say he was coming home. She remembered he would say, trying to tease her, in a false-jocular tone, "Don't you want your old dad to be happy?" And she wouldn't even answer him! A couple of times — she thought now, looking back — he might have tried to tell her. And she'd cut him off: "Gotta go, Dad — chores!"

Yet: if only he'd told her that, really, he'd wanted his family all to be together again!

Her hand was shivering its way toward the doorbell.

She lunged, heard the bell sound.

If she'd had the strength, she might have run away.

Grace stood in front of the bathroom mirror putting on pink lipstick, with effort holding her hand steady to do the job. For her dinner date with her friend Patty this evening, she'd chosen white linen cropped pants, a cobalt blue silk shell, and a patterned, tailored jacket that picked up the cobalt shade, mixing it with other blues. They were planning to go to a wine bar that reputedly served "fusion" food, a concept Grace didn't pretend to understand. She'd never been there, but Patty had sworn that dozens of eligible, silver-haired gentlemen in brass-buttoned blazers hung around the bar like butterflies in search of a flower to land on. "And the flower, that's you," she'd said. "In case you were wondering."

"Very funny, Patty," Grace had said. Since they'd met at the costume shop a few years before Grace's retirement, Patty, who was thirty years younger than Grace and happily divorced, had never ceased trying to play matchmaker, one time encouraging Grace to pursue a handsome older actor who'd needed a pair of pants tailored. "Just measure his *inseam*," she'd advised, the rest of the imagined scenario written in her wide eyes. To her, it was all so easy.

Grace hadn't bothered to correct Patty's assumption that she'd never been married, since the perceived tragedy of it seemed to satisfy the younger woman. "And you so beautiful!" Patty would say, shaking her head. "We may not need a husband to keep, but every woman should be given a great big ole diamond just once in her life, at least."

Grace would think of the ruby and diamond ring she'd found in the tree in Wisconsin, and hear Lena: *You* can't *have your cake and eat it, too.*

Now, putting on her lipstick, she tried not to mind the lines around her mouth, or the way her eyes seemed to have receded while the skin around them puffed and wrinkled like a lightly roasted marshmallow. She wasn't about to go the route of some of her friends and have those injections in her face. A few years ago, she'd let her hair go white. It seemed unlikely that any of the men at the wine bar, silver-haired or not, would be interested in a "seasoned" woman like herself — and that was fine with her. She just wanted to have a nice dinner with Patty, maybe try a few wines, and come home early.

Padding across the smoke blue carpet of her bedroom to the closet, she turned on the light to survey her shoe racks. Her eyes fell on the navy blue pumps that she'd brought with her from Wisconsin so many years ago. She hadn't worn them even once, here in California, but they were the base of her collection; her ruby slippers, in a manner of speaking. *No place like home.* But where, after all, was that?

She selected a pair of flat sandals with cobalt leather uppers and flipped off the light, trying to anticipate the wine bar, the comfortable noise of the chatter, the new, bittersweet tastes. In the kitchen, she poured herself a glass of milk, watching the white pile up like snow. When her doctor had advised her to get more calcium, she'd remembered the shipyard and being required to take a glass of milk each evening. She'd disciplined herself to return to the habit, and most days, as she stood drinking her milk at the sliding glass door looking out to her sunny patio and backyard, she'd recall that cold, exhausting, filthy work. To her surprise, after having spent over fifty years trying not to think of those times, she'd found, lately, that she liked remembering the headstrong girl she'd been, dragging that welding equipment around the shipyard, standing up to Sean O'Connor, dreaming about the train, taking care of her dad, fighting with her mother, bonding with Violet and Lena and Boots, writing letters to Derrick and her forever-young Alex. She even liked remembering Joe, swinging himself up onto the side of a boxcar, and the way she'd had so much faith that everyone was going to be all right.

Ever since, faith had been as tremulous as the strings on Lena's ukulele.

The telephone rang. Grace set down her glass and picked it up.

"Oh, Grace, you're home! This is Betty Jacobs."

"Hello, Betty!" Betty and her husband, Ed, had purchased Grace's old house from her in 1980; since Grace had been moving only a mile away, they'd promised to be friends. Both had made feints over the years, but the friendship had never come to fruition. Now Grace remembered: she'd told Betty she would consider joining her book club, Defining Women. Betty's amorphous description had left unclear whether the group's members were dictionary lovers or women determined to define their place in society; Grace had found herself unable to decide about committing to membership, and she hated to say she'd do something and then end up fading from it. Besides, she was so busy with her extended family, her nieces and nephews, Susan's and Ted's children, who all lived nearby and referred to Grace as their number one aunt. She felt keenly the pressure to live up to the title. "I'm so sorry I haven't gotten back to you about the book club."

"Oh, no, that's all right, Grace."

"You sound strange, Betty. Are you all right? Is it Ed?"

"No, Grace, we're fine. It's just — there's someone here asking for you. She said this was the most current address she had? But I didn't want to give her your information until I called you. She said she used to know you back in Wisconsin? She said her name is Boots."

Grace laughed. That would be just like Boots, to stop by out of the blue at an old address, not having written or called in twenty-five years. "Boots! That's great! Sure, send her over. Thanks, Betty." She was already picturing Boots at the wine bar with her and Patty — great fun.

But when Grace opened the door a few minutes later, her smile faded. She didn't recognize the tallish, strong-looking, blond-going-gray woman standing there with her hair back in a thick braid; a stoic, sun-wrinkled face. Her arms were crossed; her shoulders in their plaid shirt were broad, her jeans and shoes unfashionable. "I'm sorry I'm not Boots," the woman said, as a smile trembled into place, then faltered. The depth and luster of her blue eyes was un-nerving. "I didn't know if you would see me."

And then Grace knew.

And out from the jumble of her emotions stood the crystalline thought: *Has she forgiven me?*

January 1947

When Joe's truck disappeared into the rising pink of the morning sun at the place where the cold winter sky met the rolling white landscape, Grace began to pack, whatever she could fit into her biggest handbag and her small suitcase.

It wasn't much. A few pairs of underwear, her toothbrush and comb, a couple snapshots of Alice, her old drawing portfolio, two changes of clothes, her favorite nightgown, the autographed napkin Derrick had sent, and the beautiful navy blue, open-toed pumps. Everything else, she would buy new when she got to California. But leaving behind so many lovely pairs of shoes, the ones she'd accumulated eons ago working at Roth's, all in their boxes in the attic — it pained her. Even worse was the shoe box full of her letters to Derrick. She considered burning them, but the thought brought on a cold sweat. She didn't think Joe would snoop, and if Derrick ever did come home, she wanted him to know she'd meant what she said, even if it hadn't turned out to seem that way. She taped the box shut and labeled it FOR DERRICK ONLY. She stopped her work frequently to pick up Alice and squeeze her, hating the memory of kissing Joe goodbye this morning, how guilty her lips had felt, savoring the last taste of him.

When she'd come in from the woods yesterday, she'd asked Lena to give her a ride to the train today, to keep an eye on Alice for the afternoon; she'd said she wanted to see how her parents had fared in the cold snap. "Oh, and don't mention it to Joe tonight, would you?" she'd asked, swallowing hard as the ring in her pants pocket pressed her leg like a wayward dance partner. "Otherwise, he might insist on driving me in when he goes to work, and I don't want to spend *all* day with the folks."

Lena had given her an arch look at that, but all she'd said was "Sure."

Lena showed up in the kitchen at two fifteen. "You look spiffy."

Grace, dressed in a traveling suit and short boots and a hat, holding Alice in her arms, blinked and said, "Well, I can't have my

409

folks think they've completely lost their stylish daughter to country ways!"

Lena raised her eyebrows when she saw the suitcase at Grace's feet.

"A few things to bring to my mother," Grace lied.

"Oh." Lena had that suspicious look again.

Well, Grace wasn't about to tell her. And get an earful all the way to the depot about how Lena had known this life wasn't for her? No, thanks!

She'd left a note in the bedroom for Joe, under his pillow, hoping he wouldn't find it until late tonight, when he went to bed, after Lena had gone. Grace didn't want her to be there when he read it.

Dear Joe,
I am so sorry. It isn't that I don't love you. This life just isn't for me. Please forgive me for not being what I should, for you and our Alice. This is the only way I can see to stop hurting everyone. Lena will obviously take better care of you than I can. "Three's a crowd," as the saying goes. I'm so sorry for *everything.* I hope someday you can forgive me.

She hadn't known what to say. The only

thing she'd been certain of was that he would never forgive her if she took Alice.

The baby liked Lena better anyway.

And at least Lena wouldn't be so reckless as to burn the house down, set everyone on fire. Watch them all go up in smoke.

"Well, we'd better get going, I guess," Lena said, not meeting Grace's eyes.

Grace thought: *She's not going to stop me?*

"Don't want to miss your train, do you?" Lena said.

So Grace got her coat on, and Alice's. Lena carried Grace's suitcase to the car. Grace carried Alice, and held her the whole ride, pointing things out to her through the window. Alice babbled and laughed.

I can't do this, Grace thought. *Leave her!*

Lena turned on the radio. Music washed over them; Grace didn't recognize the song. *This is all her fault. I would have figured it out. We would have made a life.*

But — a life I never wanted, and never would want!

She was tempted to tell Lena that she was going to pay for her ticket to Minneapolis with the ten-dollar bill that had been stashed in her jewelry box for going on three years with the note *DERRICK! DANCING!* attached. *I gave up! What do you think about that?* But the thought made her want to weep — Derrick, really gone! — and besides, she didn't want to confide in Lena: not one more thing.

When she got to Minneapolis, she would pawn the ring that had belonged to Lena's father and that Grace now had stowed in the lining of her purse; surely it would bring enough money to get to California.

So what if she was stealing something that should have belonged to Lena? Lena was stealing from *her*.

But: something I never wanted, she reminded herself, even as the image of Joe's smile in the smoky red light of Lonny's Cabaret flashed in her mind.

She squeezed Alice so tightly that Alice tried to shove her away.

She thought of her mother and dad, her brothers and sister, hating to leave without saying goodbye. But her parents would be so ashamed! They would make her try to stay. They would never understand.

Still, what if Dad . . . ? He hasn't been well for so long . . .

She couldn't finish the thought.

And then the ride was over and Grace was handing Alice to Lena and buying a ticket, and then she was hugging them goodbye, and Alice was crying, so Grace couldn't help it, tears began to stream as she kissed the baby's cheek, rested a hand on her silky hair.

"You're only leaving for the afternoon," Lena said. Her smile seemed almost to tremble. "I'll take good care of her, I promise!"

"I know you will. I know!" Though the thought flashed in her mind: she was making a deal with the devil.

The call came: *All aboard!*

"I guess you'd better go," Lena said. "If you're going to go."

Grace felt she was drowning. Yet she knew this would be her only chance.

She touched Alice's hair again.

And then she was aboard the train and it was pulling out of the station with its great puffs of steam and there stood Lena and Alice on the platform, Lena holding Alice's arm and helping her wave goodbye.

May 2000

Grace reached for the woman's arm.

The woman shifted away.

And Grace's hand fluttered, purposeless, then landed back at her side. She took a step back. "I'm sorry. I'm so sorry. You're . . . Alice? Aren't you? How did you . . . ?" Regretting the questions immediately — but what else to say? She felt so small, faced with this formidable woman. Recalling the day at the depot — she could almost smell the choking steam and the cold, the metallic scent of the train, the baby's hair. Hard to imagine: this woman?

But Alice, too, appeared to be trembling.

Grace reached out again. "Won't you come in? Please, please, come in."

Alice's vivid eyes filled with tears.

Grace could think only: *I can't let her get away!* She curled her fingers around Alice's hand and gave a little pull. And Alice

414

stumbled over the threshold.

Seated on the couch next to her daughter. Grace's mind could hardly register the fact, even as her body seemed to recognize the connection, her knees angling toward Alice while Alice's pointed straight ahead.

Grace felt an amorphous hurt, fear like crashing surf.

She had quickly called Patty to cancel; she wasn't sure how she'd explain it later. *My daughter . . .* Oh, Patty would burst a seam.

The only conscious thought that had formed was that Lena must recently have died. Grace had always hoped that, when that happened, Joe would tell Alice the truth. She'd tried to have faith that he was, at heart, a good man. "Did your father help you find me? He must have known how much I'd want to see you! How much I've wanted to see you, all this time!"

"Dad never told me anything." A tear escaped Alice's eye. "He came out here to look for you a long time ago," she said. "After Lena died."

"What?" Grace was thrown from the treadmill of her constant imagining: Joe content with Lena and still so angry with Grace; a grown-up Alice coming home to the farm to see her "mom and dad," a holiday dinner in the dining room, everyone laughing, snow falling gently outside the windows. She'd been resigned to it — though she couldn't count the days, the years, that she'd sat hunched over her sewing machine at the costume shop, thinking of writing to Alice, trying to decide what to say, and always coming to the same conclusion: *I've no right to turn her life upside down. She probably doesn't want to hear from me, anyway, even if Joe and Lena have told her the truth.*

She remembered Lena's last letter, in 1948, warning her never to bother them again, saying Alice would be the one to suffer if Grace did. *Imagine her heartbreak — knowing you chose another life over her!*

"Did he ever find you?" Alice said.

"What? No. When — ?"

"He was looking for you when I last heard from him. Nineteen sixty-seven."

"What?" Grace said again.

"I didn't know — he never told me you were my mother. He left me on the farm. I thought Lena was my mother and he came out here to look for some . . . for some old girlfriend from the war he couldn't forget."

Grace squeezed her eyes shut. She saw Joe again, swinging himself onto the side of a boxcar, his jaunty wave and grin. How lucky she'd felt, knowing she'd see him at the end of the day, that he'd come to her flat to take her dancing.

Oh, the pain of opportunity, of seeing that tiny ring in its box — of knowing what she had to do, to save herself. Yet she had truly believed that it would be best for everyone! "You must hate me, Alice," she said, with effort. *He must have died out here. Looking for me?*

"I don't know," Alice said. Her hands were clutched together, knuckles white. "No one told me anything." She confessed what had happened with Joe, what she'd told her little sister.

Grace felt she'd fallen into deep water and was sinking down and down.

Alice wiped at tears. "I've regretted it the rest of my life. And he's never written, or — And I've stayed! I've stayed on that farm, waiting. Like my mother — like Lena, I mean, like Lena waiting for Derrick! And now I don't even know if Dad's alive. This is what's happened to our family. The only reason I found out about you was because of Violet and Boots." She explained.

Grace almost couldn't believe that Violet was still alive — any more than she would have believed she was dead. Without thinking, she reached for her daughter's hand: a lifeline. She remembered that evening on the couch in her flat, after supper at the Black Cat, when she hadn't been able to keep from reaching for Joe.

But Alice jerked away, said her husband would be waiting, worrying. She sprang to her feet.

Grace scrambled up, too, asking: Would she come back tomorrow? Maybe bring her husband?

Alice sank her teeth into her lip. "I can't help but feel it's your fault. Or mine, I don't know."

"Oh, no, Alice, please. If you'll give me the chance to explain! Tomorrow, let me explain!"

Finally, Alice nodded: one quick bob of the head.

And Grace could breathe again. They made the arrangements.

At the door, Grace couldn't stop herself. "Alice, I'm so sorry to bring this up, but I really — I don't — I mean, I was wondering, did Lena ever hear anything about Derrick?"

Alice winced. "No. No, we've never heard anything. She was still waiting when she died. I guess we've all been waiting, all this time."

"Oh," Grace said. "Oh, I'm sorry. I'm so sorry. I'll . . . see you tomorrow!" As Alice turned away, Grace blurted, "You don't know how much I've wished — how I wanted to come for you — I did!"

But Alice was already gone.

Grace stood, hand on her aching throat, watching out the window Alice getting into her car, turning around in the neighbor's driveway — she backed over a curb, her tires smashing a corner flower bed, and was gone. Grace wondered if she'd ever see her again, or if she'd dreamed it to begin with. The answer to her prayers!

And yet it seemed now that what she wanted most (maybe she hadn't quite realized!) — Alice's forgiveness — was a more distant hope than ever. And that Alice would blame herself — and how Alice had cut off Joe from *both* his daughters. There was more to despair over than Grace had dreamed.

And Joe, she thought, overcome with memory.

No: he'd probably come to California to look for her only to chastise her, maybe to see if she'd like to connect with Alice. Surely not to declare any lingering love for her!

She wondered if there was any way he

could be alive, if he could be nearby; if he'd
been nearer than she'd known, all these
years.

No, no, no: because he'd loved *Lena,* after
all, hadn't he?

Wasn't that what she'd been telling herself, all this time?

May 1951

The day after her mother's funeral, in the afternoon, Grace drove her mother's car out to the farm, without having exactly planned to. Her coat wasn't warm enough; the sky was flat gray. She drove with both gloved hands clutching the steering wheel, not knowing what she would do when she got there.

It was Susan, seventeen now, who had called her last week, crying. Their mother had had a heart attack and died. Their father had been dead four years already: Grace's worst fear coming true. What a fool she'd been, that day at the shipyard when she'd ridden the ship down the ways with her friends, to think everything was going to be all right. She remembered the train ride in 1947 out to California: her traveling suit, her short boots, her leather gloves tight over her hands; the brown-suited man with the expensive hat and stained teeth who'd sat next to her for a couple hundred miles, a seeming eternity, flirting with her even as she'd pleaded exhaustion and leaned her head on the window. How she'd wished that she hadn't left her wedding band behind, though she'd imagined it would be needed, with her note, to show Joe that she was serious.

She had missed him so much on that journey, wishing for his shoulder to lean on, imagining she'd shatter if she didn't soon press her cheek to Alice's silky hair. The train was dirty, rollicking, crowded. She barely slept for four days. The air grew drier, colder, thinner; then, finally, alarmingly warm. When she stepped off at Los Angeles, she squinted in the hot sun and thought, *January?*

And felt the little thrill of it, despite everything; despite at the same time wanting to cry for home.

From the depot, she wired her parents: I AM SAFE IN CA STOP SO VERY SORRY TO HAVE LEFT WITHOUT GOODBYE STOP WILL WRITE SOON STOP

And Joe: ARRIVED CA SAFE STOP SO VERY SORRY DARLING STOP PLEASE KISS BABY AND TELL HER I MISS HER SO STOP

Looking back, she supposed the telegram

had probably struck him as flippant in light of what she'd done. But she'd meant every word.

No wonder he'd hated her, had set out to punish her.

She hadn't been able to go home for her father's funeral; she hadn't been at her job long enough to accrue vacation. This time she'd put in for a three-week leave and boarded the train the very night Susan called, and then there'd been too much time to think of the mistakes she'd made, writing her mother only about the California weather and her latest pair of shoes, never trying to explain herself or show any sympathy for her mother's point of view. *Thanks to your selfishness, my grandchild is a lost cause,* Helen had written, when she'd tried to visit Alice at the farm and Lena and Joe had told her to stop coming around, they didn't want Alice to get confused. Grace hadn't answered the accusation — what could she say? — and after that Helen and she had settled for shallow talk to ice over the depths of their fury.

Grace wondered how she could have watched Violet and Lena disintegrate before her eyes and not have learned a damn thing.

She'd supervised the funeral, the sorting of a lifetime of her parents' things, putting the house up for sale. It had been like auctioning off her own internal organs.

Now, arriving at the farm, she parked on the east-west county road, far enough away that she thought she'd be out of sight from the kitchen window. She shut off the ignition and blew warm air into her gloved hands, shivering despite the car heater that had been running until a moment ago. She considered walking up to the door. What would she say?

Facing her again.

Lena would be the only one there — Joe would be at work — and sitting here now, Grace knew more than ever that she didn't want what Lena had taken: not that life, certainly not the farm, and not even any piece of Joe — not after how he'd been! When she thought of the life she'd carved out for herself — her work in the studio costume department, her apartment, her own money, the ability to do what she wanted whenever she wanted to do it — the idea of giving it up made her feel like her clothes were four sizes too small.

But: Alice!

She imagined going to the door and demanding that Lena give the girl over to her. But Alice would be five years old and wouldn't remember Grace, would probably be frightened at the sight of her. The idea stilled her.

Selfishly, she thought, *And then my life wouldn't be my own.*

Then, in the distance, she saw her! A small girl in a purple jacket and denim overalls with chin-length blond hair, running from the house down the driveway. For a moment, Grace dared to imagine: Alice had seen her! Was running for her, wanting her!

But now, behind Alice came Lena, unchanged, except, to Grace's shock, hugely pregnant, her belly protruding from her unzipped jacket. Even in the distance, Grace could see Lena's smile, see her calling after Alice, Alice turning. She imagined she heard laughter. Lena's belly like a beach ball on her small frame.

So Joe had made his deal with her, too.

Grace supposed she'd known it. Lena had written her three years ago that Joe and she wanted Alice to have a "quiet, normal life" with a "normal family," without the "disturbance" of a far-off "mother" (Lena had put the word in quotation marks) in California. They'd already spoken to the neighbors, Lena wrote, and everyone had agreed that the little girl would be better off not knowing she'd been "abandoned." Grace had argued, writing over and over that abandonment had never been her intention (*I told you from the beginning I wanted her to spend summers with me when she gets older!*), but Lena was insistent: *We're going to have her* baptized. Lena had converted to Catholicism. *You* can't *have your cake and eat it, too, Hollywood. Don't ever bother us again. Don't write, don't call. We will provide her with the happiest of lives, without your selfish influence. You* don't know *what it means to* love.

That was the last Grace had heard from them.

In her head, she asked Derrick, *What would you have me do?*

She'd known that Joe was furious with her — his signature on the divorce papers had been a dark slash, and he'd let Lena take care of the correspondence after that. Grace supposed she couldn't blame him, after she'd forced him to go against everything he believed, with the divorce. She didn't even blame him for marrying Lena: she presumed he'd done it for Alice, for the farm he loved. And to stanch the bleeding of his heart. And she regretted having been the largest cause of his undoing. *If only I could have borne it* —

But that he would make a new baby with Lena!

But why should Grace have been surprised? Had she flattered herself — and him — that he'd resist the girl whom no one else could?

Alice ran back and grabbed Lena's hand, impatient, tugging, but Lena could only move so fast, could only laugh and, Grace imagined, say, *I'm coming, Alice!*

And Grace watched them walk to the mailbox. They were chatting and laughing.

Lena took out a stack of envelopes, flipped through them. Alice jumped expectantly. Lena's shoulders drooped; she shook her head. Alice looked at her shoes.

Grace wanted to gun the car forward the hundred yards, reach out the door, and sweep Alice into the car, away to California, away from this awful place! But, hands fumbling, she couldn't get the car to start. It made a sound like a scratched LP record.

The noise drew Lena's attention. She shaded her eyes and frowned.

Don't let her know it's me! Grace prayed, the weight of Lena's belly seeming to rest on her lap as Lena watched the car, as if perceiving a threat. She put her arm around Alice's little shoulders and guided her back toward the house, throwing a distrustful scowl over her shoulder.

Grace watched until they were gone, tenting her gloved hands over her nose and mouth. Then she lowered them and took a breath. Carefully, she started the car, put it into gear. Her foot trembled as she pressed the accelerator. She turned south onto Blackberry Ridge Road and didn't look as she passed the farm, heading for the highway.

Two days later, having made arrangements for Susan and Ted to come to live with her when the school year ended, she left Superior for the last time, driving her mother's car, spending the hours and days on the road trying to remember dance steps, trying not to think of all she'd left behind again, all she'd chosen again not to fight for. Trying not to think at all. In the middle of Nebraska she had a flat tire and she was changing it when a man stopped to help her. She was wearing her newest checked suit with its long, narrow skirt, plus a new pair of pumps, and he was tall, with a nice smile, soft brown hair, a cleft in his chin, and milk-chocolate sweet eyes, so she handed him the wrench and stepped aside, maybe out of loneliness telling him, as she gazed at the horizon, "It gives me the creeps, the way you can see forever out here, and all this wind." As he tightened the lug nuts and she admired the flexing of his tattooed forearm, he started telling her about why Nebraska was the place for him: how he'd been in the Navy and his ship had gone down in the Pacific and he'd been in the water for more than two full days, watching the battle for several hours until it was done, and then floating off, he and nineteen other men on a raft, utterly alone in the vast sea, and his best friend had been snatched by a shark and never seen again and he himself had gone delirious and thought he'd seen land, and he'd almost swum for it and would have, had another man not grabbed him and tied him to the raft, where he'd gotten sunburned to the color and texture of a lobster and his tongue had swollen to fill his mouth, and after the war he'd decided he wanted to get as far away from the sea as he possibly could, and stay there.

"What was the name of your ship?" she asked, shielding her eyes from the sun.

He looked up and said the name.

"Oh!" She reached for him, not quite touching his arm. "My . . . my good friend! Derrick Maki! Aviation ordnance man second class? Was on that ship! Did you know him?"

He squinted his chocolate eyes. "Don't think so."

Still, once the tire was fixed, she followed

429

him to the next town, where, at the café, coffee stretched into supper and he thought finally, after she showed him the photo of Derrick that she'd found at her mother's house and stashed in her handbag, that maybe he did remember him, maybe they'd played cards together once or twice, though he said the aviation fellows generally kept to themselves. "Did he make it?" he asked.

Grace looked at her hands. "He's . . . still missing." The past couple of years, she'd been hoping that he'd been found; that she just hadn't heard, because she'd fallen out of touch. But now that she'd seen Lena and Alice at the farm's mailbox, she knew that wasn't true. They were still waiting to hear. It was likely he'd, by this time, been officially "presumed dead," though of course Lena wouldn't believe it. Grace thought of Derrick's long-ago letter about his friend being swallowed by the sea, about staring at the empty spot in the ocean and not believing there could simply be no trace of a person left.

The ex-sailor with the chocolate eyes — his name was Jack — nodded and, frowning, lit a cigarette.

There was a jukebox against the wall in their booth, and, after they'd stretched supper into dessert and another cup of coffee,

Jack put in a nickel, selected "Stars Fell on Alabama," and said, "Want to dance?" There was no dance floor, but she nodded, and they slid off their benches to come together at the end of the table, the waitress rolling her eyes as she dodged them going back and forth, as outside the windows the sunset painted the horizon shades of pink and purple and Jack said into Grace's hair, " 'Stars Fell on Nebraska,' I think it should be called," and she rested her cheek against his broad chest and her eyes filled as she felt his heart beating.

When the song was over, she stepped away and said she had to go. He objected: it was too late, almost dark, what if she had another problem with her car? There was a motel just up the road; he'd take her there to get her settled.

But she insisted, filing Derrick's picture back in her handbag. Finally, he paid the check and walked her to her car. The sky was nearly full dark now, and he slid his arm around her waist, pulled her close, and kissed her, pressing her against the car with just the combination of insistence and gentleness to make her tremble. Then, still so close that she could feel his coffee-and-cigarette-scented breath on her mouth, he said, "I did know your friend. I'm sure of it now. I remember him. I think he might even have shown me your picture, one time. I remember seeing him get into his plane, that last day. These are the things you try to forget. But I remember it now. I remember seeing him."

She looked up and saw the tears in his eyes.

"I'm sorry," she said. "I'm sorry I made you think of it."

"Don't go."

"I have to."

"It isn't safe out there for you, babe. Please."

But she nudged him away and got into the car, fumbled in her purse for her key. Hands shaking, she started the car. She unrolled the window, and he leaned down. He looked desolate. "I'm sorry," she said again and shifted into reverse.

She watched him in the mirror as she drove out of the parking lot; his silhouette showed his dejection. And when she passed beyond the town limit sign, accelerating toward the dark horizon and the stars, she began to cry, great, hollowing sobs.

May 2000

Surveying the tire tracks in her neighbor's flower bed — restitution would be needed; such easy damage to undo! — Grace decided she needed to speak to her old friend Violet. Maybe Violet could tell her she wasn't crazy, it hadn't all been her fault!

She called information for the farm's number, listed under the name of Alice's husband, George Tuomi — the grandson of John Tuomi, Alice had said. *So many years,* Grace thought, dialing. *I could have been calling her here, if only I'd known!*

It pained her to think how often she'd remembered that long-ago night in Nebraska and wished she'd asked for Jack's address. But Joe was the one she'd loved — really loved, in flesh and blood, despite their differences, despite how they'd hated each other, too; despite that she couldn't have lived that life with him for one more day. To quiet her regrets, she would remind herself of how much she'd liked so many elements of her new life: the near-constant sunshine, the chaise lounge on her patio, the flowers and palm trees, her extended family.

Though always would linger the memories of Joe's eyes and Alice's hair; of winter, the snow piling on the roof of that little white house. *Not* her fault, she hadn't been able to breathe!

She wondered if Joe had ever felt that way, living there with Lena.

She wondered why she'd never met any man since to inspire her truly to give her heart.

She had not thought in a long time of the heat of his hands, but now it seemed she could think of little else. Of him and Alice. Her family.

A young woman answered the phone.

"A *ruby?*" Violet said, when Julia visited the next morning and told her what Grace had said.

"She wanted to call you, she was so upset to hear you were sick, but I told her she should let you sleep. She'll call you later today, I think." That there'd really been something Jago had valued enough to hang on to thrilled Julia.

She'd imagined Violet would feel the same, but learning that Jago hadn't gambled the ring away seemed to infuriate the old woman. "I can't believe he had a ruby, all that time. All that time my Derrick was gone. When all I ever wanted in my life was to keep my children safe."

"Finders keepers, I guess," Violet said brusquely; her voice on the phone struck Grace as eerily familiar. She could picture the way Violet had looked during the war, that rose-red bandanna above her smooth face, and wondered what she looked like now.

Grace had hardly slept last night, anticipating talking with Violet, seeing Alice again. Worrying. Wondering if Joe could still be alive, if she should try to find him. Was everything really her fault, the way Alice had said? And what could she do to stop Alice from blaming herself? But Violet had pounced on the subject of the ring nearly the moment their voices had greeted each other.

"I'm sorry, Violet, I can pay you for it, I got forty dollars for it then, so now —"

"What I don't understand is, if he was engaged to the girl, why did he still have the ring?" Violet said. "Why did he hide it for you to find?"

"I don't know. I'm really sorry. I shouldn't have taken it."

"But I can't believe he didn't gamble it away. He'd lost *everything.* Everything we ever had." Violet's sigh rushed like a winter wind. "And to think, all this time, I've been picturing Derrick's bones, washed clean at the bottom of the ocean. It's the only solace I've had. Because, when you're bones, nothing can hurt you. And if he's been in the salt water all this time, then he's come back to me, to where he was born. To me and to Lena. We were there with him at the beginning." The line crackled. "The only thing I've ever wished is that I could have kept them safe."

"I know, Violet," Grace said. She'd never pictured Derrick just as bones — it was dismaying that such an image could comfort Violet. But: how few years Violet had had with her twins, out of the great span of her life. Who was Grace to judge what got her through? Especially now that there was some chance Grace might be granted more time with Alice. If things went well today, she'd ask if Alice would stay for a while.

"I'm so sorry, Violet. About the ring and Lena and . . . and that you never got any word about Derrick. Alice told me nothing ever came. I can't imagine what it's been like." Though she had known longing of her own. Even last night, wishing for Alice to return, wondering if Joe might be near.

There was silence, just the buzzing of the line. Then: "I had a few good years. Go long enough without eating, you don't feel your hunger anymore. You might still be starving to death. But you don't feel the pain of it, not all the time."

Grace didn't know if Violet was right about that. She remembered those winters at the farm, Lena singing: "Wait Till the Sun Shines, Nellie." "Down Among the Sheltering Palms." Grace asked, "Where did you go, Violet? Why did you leave and never write?"

Violet explained: she'd gone first to Minneapolis, and, just in case the sheriff whom Lena had made to question her ever decided to subscribe to the girl's ideas, she'd given her name as Amelia Carlson — her middle and maiden names, so not jarringly unfamiliar. She'd found a job as a hostess at a department store tearoom. She'd worn white gloves every day, eaten alone each evening in the tiny apartment she'd found, and gone for long walks, like she had as a girl back in Ironwood. She'd imagined herself an orphan again, and it didn't take long for her to come to believe that her time with her family had been the aberration, that maybe she was meant to be a solo act.

Still, years went by that she had not intended. She kept telling herself, *Maybe next year, maybe then I'll go back and try to find her, to talk with her.* "I always supposed she'd keep in touch with you, that you'd be able to tell me where to find her," she told Grace. But when her war bonds came due, she found herself buying a farm in central Minnesota. Better soil than in Blackberry Ridge, slightly earlier springs. She couldn't complain. She worked part-time at the local café and kept a huge flock of chickens, a few cows and pigs every year, a big garden for the farmers' market; for many years, a roadside stand. She sighed. "I guess I just never knew what I'd say to her. You see, I . . ."

"What, Violet?"

"I, well . . . it was confusing times, wasn't it, Grace?"

"Oh, Violet. I didn't mean to be so reckless, honestly. I didn't mean for anyone to get hurt. But I just — I wanted so *badly* —"

"I know, Grace," Violet interrupted. "I understand, believe me. But, honestly — this girl. Did Jago say anything more? Who was she?"

"I don't know, Violet. It was all so long ago."

"Well, I wish he'd told me. It might have changed everything, if I'd known. Or maybe Derrick could have told me. But he never says a word! Don't get me wrong, I'm grateful for the company. But . . ."

Grace was troubled, until she remembered that long-ago day in the locker room at the shipyard when Violet had sworn that Derrick had come to her. She thought of his bed in the attic, his maps on the wall. The ten dollars she'd used to buy her train ticket. "Do you think she'll ever forgive me, Violet?" she asked, her voice lilting with hope.

"She's her mother's daughter," Violet said, and Grace had no idea what she meant by that, whether or not to be consoled.

Julia thought she'd looked through everything in the trunk, and she was dejected to have found nothing more concerning the ring or Jago's mystery girl. But, as she was about to replace the stacks of old shoe boxes, she noticed two that were completely encased in withered masking tape and labeled, FOR DERRICK ONLY.

The first box had been cut open once and then resealed. *Sorry, Lena,* Julia thought, *but*

439

time doesn't stand still, or even cycle around — it just goes on and on. She got a knife and sliced through the tape.

She found a note on top in Lena's familiar handwriting: *Disingenuous. It is unclear who she ever really loved. She left these behind when she left.*

The letters inside were from Grace to Derrick, written after he'd gone missing in the fall of 1944 and continuing for a full year. The early ones were all much the same: *I think of you all the time and pray that you'll find your way back home.* But the later letters were more like diary entries; Julia read only about half of them before forcing herself to put them away. Maybe someday she'd ask if Grace wanted them, but not right now, not when Grace and Alice had just been introduced. It would do no one any good for Alice to learn that Grace's heart, too, had belonged to Derrick.

The second box was also full of yellowed envelopes, with a note on top addressed to Derrick:

It broke my heart when she got on that train! Maybe I didn't believe she'd really do it. Maybe I thought — how would she?

But I'd seen her suffering all those

months — & her pain sat on me like a boulder — & when she was gone I felt lighter — & more hollow, too — but I knew it was meant to be this way — (& it was clearer than ever how wrong I'd been, how she *didn't deserve* you!) — & after that it was just a matter of time — (I'm not without my "charms" — ha ha!) — Time & commiseration & proving he couldn't succeed at this life without me & this was the life he'd always wanted & telling him he ought to give her the divorce she was begging for in her letters, saying she wanted to be "free of the obligation which I've already smashed anyway!" — some attitude, I thought! But I was glad of it, too, & I told him — when you love someone, you do what they want you to (& anyway, look at what she'd done! — why would anyone want to be married to someone who would do such a thing? — to someone who didn't know that "obligation" was a sacred part of *life*) — & I told him the church would view him as justified since he & the baby had been abandoned — & after he'd signed the papers (finally! — she wrote he was being "archaic," that our "whole generation" had rushed into the "wrong thing" because of the war, and everyone was getting divorced so why shouldn't they) I told him "what will Alice do without a mother and what will you do with no mother for Alice" (G. *didn't* want her! — how could she? She'd left her!) & "here I am & already *I love her*" — & "everything I have is yours & everything you have is mine & everything we ever wanted is *right here*" —

The only resistance was in his eyes — they had the look of a man trampled & I did feel bad about that. But she'd been so clearly unhappy with him! (& he with her — they'd made such a mistake, from the start!)

& I thought — (I *was* beginning to care for him!) — I can make it up to him, everything she did to wrong him, & then too — every little thing I do for him will avenge — piece by piece by piece — all that she did to wrong me (& *you*) — & *A.* — the way she left us *all* so easily when all we'd ever done was *love* her —

So don't think it's all been "sacrifice" — he's steady & we've been happy, in our way, with the girls, & I still sometimes wonder — *how* could she have walked away!

(& I am *not* proud of everything I've

done! — such as not showing him these letters — but what I did that I *am* proud of was I gave them a *family* — & it breaks my heart to be leaving them so soon — yet I hope they'll forgive me, knowing it's "out of my hands" — I so tried to protect them from disappointment — from feeling like everyone they loved had left them — I so tried to make a life where everything they needed — whether or not they *knew* it — was *right here* — I so tried to make for them a *home* —)

In the box was another series of letters from Grace, begging Lena and Joe to grant her some rights to Alice, accusing Lena of using Joe and Alice to get back the farm. *Maybe you're right that it would be "easier" on her to have a "normal family" and yet don't you think she'll have some memory of me? You say that since I'm so happy with my work I obviously don't want her, but you're wrong! Yes, I fit Hedy Lamarr with a dress — who wouldn't be thrilled!? But even though this work is my passion and I couldn't set it aside (I thought you understood — you were the one who bought me the most beautiful purple fabric I've ever seen!), I do miss her more than you can imagine. . . . I was not sane at*

*the time that I left, surely you must under-
stand! I am grateful that you love her and for
all the care you've taken of her. But how can
you feel justified in cutting me off completely?
I am sorry about D. but haven't I been punished enough?*

Julia stacked the boxes back in the trunk.
Alice had called earlier, apologizing for
hanging up on Julia and expressing bewil-
derment over her meeting with Grace. As
dismaying as it was to learn of Lena's
schemes, Julia looked forward to telling Alice the truth of how Grace had felt —
maybe it would help the two forge the connection that Violet so wanted them to have.

It was also a relief to know that Grandpa
Joe had been unaware of Grace's letters.
Maybe he hadn't been as terrible and selfish as Julia had imagined. She hadn't told
Alice that she'd spoken to two strangers in
Los Angeles named Joe Mosckiewicz before
she'd lost her courage to try more. Even if
she could find him, would he want to be
found? He'd been away for so long. . . .

With the boxes stowed, she paged through
*The Complete Works of Shakespeare. Jago
Maki* was scrawled on the frontispiece, and
a passage from *Romeo and Juliet* was underlined and dated *March 1945:*

Love is a smoke rais'd with the fume of
  sighs;
Being purg'd, a fire sparkling in lovers'
  eyes;
Being vex'd, a sea nourish'd with lovers'
  tears:
What is it else? a madness most discreet,
A choking gall, and a preserving
  sweet. —

Reading the lines, Julia had to believe that, when Jago had underlined them, he'd been thinking not just of his lost girl he'd saved that ring for all those years, but of his family: Lena and Violet, Derrick and Grace. *They meant just as much to him as they did to Violet. He didn't want to lose them. He didn't want to lose anything — but, somehow, he'd already lost so much.*

Violet blinked to clear her ever-blurrier vision — one more indignity — and saw the old people at her table beginning to drool as they took their first bites of the dining room's pasties. These things were probably from the cooler at the supermarket and warmed in the oven; Violet used to make pasties from scratch, back on the farm in Blackberry Ridge.

She hadn't made or eaten one since that

night Jago had died. They'd been his favorite, not hers.

Still, she was curious. She took a bite, chewed.

Terrible. The taste of children's craft paste. Yet enough of the essence came through that a picture flashed in Violet's mind: Lena, reaching for a second pasty that April night in 1945, saying she was still hungry after the long day at the shipyard. Violet's heart thudded at the memory: the way she'd pushed the plate from Lena, toward Jago. "Why don't you leave them for your father? They're his favorite. There's peach pie for dessert I made last night from canned peaches. I'll get some for you."

"Oh, thanks, Mom! That would be wonderful," Lena had said, her eyes alight, so unusually pleased with Violet that Violet had been taken aback.

And Jago, too, had grinned, finishing up his third pasty, shoveling that crusted mix of meat and potatoes and rutabagas into his mouth, his eyes admiring her.

She'd jumped up, run to the kitchen for Lena's pie, veins humming with shame.

Everything has its point of collapse.

It was just: whether by God's design or nature's whimsy, a glimmer of spring had come early that year. Violet had collected a

few wild mushrooms from the mossy part of the woods. She'd imagined they'd give the fresh batch of pasties an earthy flavor. Jago might not notice a thing. She and Lena would eat warmed-over ones from the last batch.

She'd carefully matched her find to the illustration in Lena's plant book. This variety of mushroom was known to be fatal only occasionally. She didn't know the percentages, the odds.

She'd used her sharpest knife, mincing the fungus into tiny pieces, thinking of Derrick's enlistment papers, of her ever-vanishing egg money; of the letter she'd found in Jago's wallet to *Darling J.* She was not that fool who'd succumbed to him: *not anymore.*

He was going to lose everything for her, *everything,* if she didn't stop him.

With the knife blade, she plowed the capricious morsels into a neat pile. She was ready to toss them in with the meat and potatoes. Her little gamble with God.

But the mushrooms blurred before her.

She was not a murderer. She was not.

She scraped the tiny gray pieces into the fire and watched them smolder.

She scrubbed the chopping block and the knife. She rolled out the dough, scooped the meat mixture onto the circles, pinched the edges, and put them in to bake. She cried a little; thought, *You fool!*

Still, later, at the table, when Lena had reached, Violet had been struck: What if the chopping block had retained traces of the poison? And she'd rolled out the dough on it! And why had she burned the mushrooms in the cooking fire? What if there'd been fumes? She didn't know the possibilities. But she wouldn't test them on her daughter.

The next morning, he hadn't awakened.

As he might have said, what were the odds?

But surely no trace of the mushrooms had remained in what he'd eaten. She'd been so careful! Besides, she'd read in Lena's book that victims of that particular species tended to suffer for days before succumbing; Jago had died overnight. A heart attack, obviously, brought on by his bad habits, by the sorrow of the uncertainty over Derrick.

By the time Violet had awakened Lena that morning and told her the news, she'd already been convinced of her innocence, of the terrible coincidence.

She realized now: she would never have been able to go through with it. Because, whatever else Jago might have done or not done, he had stayed with her. Always, he had stayed, and they had made a family.

Yet now there was this ring that Grace had found: another reason why Violet might have wished she'd had the stomach to go through with it. The fact that there was a girl who had meant more to him than she or the twins or their home ever had. Something he would hang on to, when he'd let everything else — everything that had ever mattered to Violet — slip away.

"You all right?" said a voice. The man across the table from her. He was withered with age; the liver spots on his jowls looked older than Violet had ever felt. But his eyes must still have been sharp.

"Fine," Violet said. "I was thinking about my husband, that's all."

"Is he gone? I'm sorry." His eyes had seemed to brighten.

"A long time ago; it's fine. But — I just found out he'd kept a ring for another girl. A ruby ring. When he lost everything else we'd ever had, gambling." She didn't know what had caused her to spill the beans to a stranger. Maybe she was just getting too old to hold things in.

The man frowned. "I used to play a little poker," he said, "back during the war, when I worked at the shipyard. I remember a guy told me a story about a ruby ring. He was the most addled man you'd ever met. His son had gone missing in the war. I'm ashamed to say it now, but I bought a car with what I won off him."

Violet felt her throat closing, felt she might choke. She raised her napkin to cover her mouth. Pain blazed in her lungs. She picked up her glass of water; her hand was shaking, and the liquid spilled onto her pants, seeped cold through onto her legs. She set the glass down. Couldn't seem to swallow anyway.

The man's eyes were focused on the table. "We were drinking at the bar," he said. "It was a hard time. He said he'd never told anyone. That it weighed on him all the time."

"Tell me," she said, feeling the cold bleed through to her bones. "Tell me what he said."

1913–14

The cage hoisting the dust-coated miners from the darkness of the earth ran on a cable more than a mile long, and Jago Maki was looking up, yearning for light. He'd descended into the mine this morning when the sun was just peering over the horizon, and his longing for it now took his mind off the burning of his muscles and the swaying of his body in the climbing cage. Had he not been packed in with thirty men who stank of garlicky, cabbagey sweat, he might not have been able to keep on his feet. Clutching his empty dinner pail, Jago had to think that breathing was coming a little easier than it had all day in the humid corridors below, where fumes from explosives and dust and human waste lingered. Now he was certain he sensed cool, fresh oxygen snaking down the shaft.

He was imagining the company bathhouse

— a clean towel, clear water, the scent of soap, the relief of the warm flow over his aching muscles and of scrubbing the grit and stench from his skin — when the cage jerked to a stop.

The impact threw the men; for a moment they were like worms in a bait bucket, boneless and twisted. Jago felt a lurch of panic, trying to right his body, as the men around him cursed in their various languages. "Goddamn strikers!" said the last man to speak, and then they all looked up for the light. But they were too far down the shaft.

Jago felt hot, new dampness under his arms. In his two months working at the mine, the cage had never made an unscheduled stop like this one. "What's going on?" he said to his best friend, Dominic Barinotti, who was standing next to him.

Dominic, brown eyes wide, shook his head.

The only sound was the heavy breathing of the upward-gazing workers; somewhere, a measured dripping of water. A lantern flickered.

Jago thought: *I'm too young to die.*
And then: *Or am I?*
He was highly conscious of the many ways a man could meet his end. Crushed by falling rock, caught in the path of the unstop-

pable hoist, falling from a narrow passageway into nothingness. He had dreams of falling into darkness, falling down and down. Now, if the hoist cable snapped, the cage would crash three thousand feet to the bottom and there'd be nothing left of Jago and the others to haul up but their broken bodies.

Jago tried to think of music, of Josie Barinotti's brown eyes. Dominic's younger sister; Dominic didn't know that Jago planned to marry her. Neither did Josie. He really had never spoken to her. *Saturday night, I'll ask her to dance. Enough of this goddamn being scared. Nobody lives forever, nobody.*

"Hey!" one of the miners yelled up the shaft. "Hey, let us up!" Soon they were all screaming it, in their different languages.

There was fresh air and grass and sky just two thousand feet above. But the only image in Jago's mind was of his father's ice blue eyes this morning as they'd sat at the kitchen table in the company house where Jago lived in the downstairs front room with his parents. Several Siankivich and Pietala children swarmed; the two other families lived in the three rooms upstairs. Jago's mother was busy at the stove with Mrs. Siankivich and Mrs. Pietala. The trio was uncharacteristically merry, though, as always, the kitchen smelled of boiled cabbage, charred bacon, and spoiling milk, and only one tiny window admitted the weak morning light.

But, this morning, four dinner pails remained shelved above the stainless-steel sink. Jago's, his father Eino Maki's, Mr. Siankivich's, and Mr. Pietala's. Usually, by this hour the women had them packed with Jago's mother's homemade pasties. Some days ago, the union had asked the mine owners to negotiate; the owners hadn't dignified them with a response. So, last night, the union men had met to declare the strike, and today, Mr. Siankivich and Mr. Pietala hadn't come downstairs yet. On the bright side, this left Jago free to steal glances at Mrs. Pietala, who, in the joy of the morning, had blithely forsaken the top three buttons of her shirtwaist. Meanwhile, Eino delineated the miners' demands, striking the table softly with the flat of his hand: "The union recognized. Shorter hours. Better wages. Two men always on the one-man drilling machine."

Strange to see such passion in a man who typically plodded through life with the imagination of a packhorse, seemingly resigned to his inevitable death in the mine, seeming to know it a matter of just time and chance. Only on occasion did Eino revolt against this fate with the excessive consumption of alcohol, and his hands, in which were located all the rebellion he possessed, would reach out to cuff a too-smart boy on the ear, or twist a nagging woman's arm until she screamed and beat at his chest with her free hand.

Jago didn't like to think about these things. "Guess I can earn more working than I can sitting on my duff on strike, ay," he told his father.

Eino pointed a finger. "You will see," he said: a command, not a prediction.

Jago shrugged. "Ma, I need dinner packed, ay. I'm going to work."

The women and children fell silent. But Jago had never feared being contrary. What he feared was never hearing Josie Barinotti say his name in the unmistakable way he imagined; never making enough money to marry her and take her out of Red Jacket, Michigan, to someplace where life wasn't so damned grim. He didn't intend to work for the mine forever; he'd always had more interest in literature and music than in metallurgy or machining. He thought he might like to go to college, someday — an idea he hadn't mentioned to Eino. Anyway, he'd thought maybe the strike talk would blow over, and he didn't want to get into trouble for being absent from work.

But now, stuck halfway up the mile-deep shaft, clutching his dinner pail like a child would a toy, he guessed he should have listened to his father.

Then there was a whirring sound and the cage shuddered back into motion. Some of the men began to chatter, already relieved, but Jago held his breath, praying they'd make it to the top this time.

As the cage slowed and finally emerged, inch by inch, from the ground, Jago was so anticipating the light and fresh air that he didn't immediately hear the crowd. But then he saw a thick forest of dirty boots, set in wide stances. Hands, many holding clubs or rocks, others balled into fists. Then the flushed, pinched faces. And the mouths, flinging curses as the cage lurched to a stop. The engineer who ran the hoist had blood trickling down his ashen temple; a man stood over him with a pipe.

"We should have let you die down there," snarled one of the mob. "Then we thought, no, we teach you what happens when you work with a strike on."

Jago's feet were lead. "Now, hold on, fellows," pleaded the man inside who was nearest the gate.

Later, it would all be a blur: the whispers about making a run for it, the quick fingers of the man at the gate unlocking and swinging it open, knocking one man outside down, and then the mass of them scrambling out. Jago grabbed a handful of Dominic's jacket and dragged his friend along; they slipped between broad shoulders while men swung for bigger targets, fists and clubs thudding. Then something slammed Jago's side and he fell, dropping his dinner pail, his knees and hands scraping the ground; Dominic fell on top of him. Then came the heavy boots aiming kicks at their midsections. Dominic tried to get up, but each time he almost made it, he'd get kicked, and all his weight would land again on Jago's back. Finally the kicks stopped; Dominic sprang up, and so did Jago, snatching his dinner pail. They broke free from the crush and ran.

They sprinted through the dust toward town. Finally, both hurting, looking over their shoulders, they slowed to a limping, fast walk and headed for Jago's house, past the rows of identical company houses on the bleak, treeless streets.

No one was home. Jago couldn't remember that ever happening. In the kitchen, he set his dinner pail on the shelf next to his father's. He told Dominic to hand him his, too. He opened the faucet and thrust his hands under the flow of water, washing the gravel out of his bloody palms. Every time he took a breath, pain shot through his side.

All Jago wanted was to get to the bathhouse. As he and Dominic made their way downtown, trying to walk normally so no one would know how they'd been kicked and beaten, it seemed the town's entire population of forty thousand was out in the streets, everyone pushing and shoving and laughing like there was a party going on. And, in fact, in addition to the wildness caused by the strike, the Fireman's Festival was proceeding as scheduled: shrieking children devoured cotton candy and played tag and waited in line for the Ferris wheel. Jago wondered what he would do, the next morning. Always his father had told him work was a man's first responsibility. Yet these were his father's friends, beating up the men who would work.

His father had told him that he would see, but he didn't.

A group paraded in the street, holding

458

signs above their heads, chanting. Jago and Dominic stepped aside to let them pass; Jago saw his father. His father saw him, too, and gave him a skewering look. Jago felt it worse than the blows he'd taken up at the mine. He tugged a passing man's sleeve. "Where do we sign up, ay?"

The man gestured for them to join the march.

So much for getting a nice bath.

Since the age of fourteen, Jago had spent just about every Saturday night playing the accordion at whichever boardinghouse in town was having a party. Everyone gathered: men and women, boys and girls, stomping to the music Jago and others made, drinking beer, eating kalamojakka and ravioli and cevapcici, and forgetting, for a moment, everything but the joy of dancing. These magical Saturday nights were, in Jago's mind, the only things that made life in Red Jacket bearable.

Now, though, no one was playing music or dancing. No man was working, above or below ground. Pumps, which had always run day and night to keep water from rising in the mine shafts, were silent, while crowds boiled and chanted in the streets, coexisting uneasily with the plague of rats that had emerged from the flooding shafts; the constant squeals and skittering reminded Jago of stories he'd read of the underworld. National Guard troops arrived on train after train and set up camp in every available green space; many miners and their families boarded these same trains and left, off to find more peaceful work elsewhere.

When Jago wasn't parading with the strikers, he was watching the soldiers drill, watching them stage rat fights with rodents they'd adopted. He imagined, if he'd been in Pompeii, he'd have watched the ash raining down, too.

One night, he and Dominic went to a meeting at the stadium. In winter, the building was an indoor ice skating rink; as popular a pastime as that was, Jago had never seen the place so full. People were packed as tightly as miners in the cage, and the various contingents — Croatians, Finns, Italians — roared their approval and pumped their fists when their men on the platform spoke their native languages. Jago understood enough to know that the speakers were saying pretty much the same thing. He was bored, and irritated with the man next to him, who kept bumping Jago with his sign, which read THE ONE-MAN DRILL —

OUR AGITATOR.

On the platform, a man was speaking English: "Stand with your arms folded for the next ten days and then they'll not talk of a blacklist. They'll be asking you fellows to save the whole conglomerate lode from caving in, and you'll do it, when they treat you right!" A massive cheer went up.

Ahead of him some distance in the crowd, Jago recognized the red bow Josie always wore in her hair. His stomach lurched with expectation and the simultaneous realization that he was not capable of fulfilling it.

But, for the rest of the meeting, he watched to be sure she wouldn't disappear. As the last cheers dissipated, he elbowed Dominic, pointed, and said, "Isn't that your sister?"

Dominic looked; his face went pinched. "I will have to see her home." Jago followed him through the crowd, trying to keep a smirk off his face.

Josie's eyes widened at the sight of her brother. But as Dominic scolded her, her fear gave way to anger. "Mama said I could, and I'm with Beatrice and her brother, and Papa's here, besides," she said, pointing to a girl and an older boy moving off in the crowd.

Dominic shook his head. "How will you

461

find Papa in this mob? And Beatrice's brother couldn't protect you from a cat. I will take you home."

She glanced at Jago, so briefly he'd have thought he'd imagined it, but for the tiny shiver down his spine. "All right," she said to Dominic. "Let me just tell Beatrice."

Jago wished that they had farther to walk, that the streets weren't so crowded, that Dominic would slow down.

Except: he and Josie couldn't keep up with Dominic (not that Jago was trying), and when someone in the crowd bumped her, Jago grabbed her elbow. She looked up at him with those large, dark eyes.

Carefully, he smiled down at her (she was shorter than he'd realized). Had she turned sixteen yet? He hoped so.

Now someone nudged him into her, and the contact felt like when dynamite exploded underground, the way it shook your whole body and pieces of huge rock went tumbling down and down. "Sorry," he mumbled, glad the sun had nearly set so she wouldn't see the color he could feel rising in his face.

The crowd was thinning; Jago slowed his step, gathering his thoughts. Soon, Dominic was ten paces ahead. Jago leaned down and

murmured to Josie, "An outstanding escort, is your brother."

She laughed and looked away.

A woman on the other side of the street shrieked. "A rat!" It was scurrying toward them. Josie screamed. Jago wanted to: the thing was the size of a rabbit. He swept her into his arms. Just in time! The rat raced past his shoes and vanished into the ditch.

He could feel her trembling but couldn't tell if she was laughing or crying or both. He was shaking, too. Dominic was running back. "What is it?"

"Just a rat," Jago said, trying to sound like it hadn't bothered him.

"It was enormous!" Josie said.

"Yes, yes," Dominic said, "flooded out of the mine. No dinner scraps to eat down there now, and plenty of water rising without the pumps."

"Are you all right?" Jago said to Josie. Her face was inches from his. He wondered if she'd consent to stay in his arms the rest of the way to her house.

She pressed a hand to her chest. "Of course," she said, "other than a small heart attack." There was a spark in her deep eyes that he'd never seen before.

He smiled, as molten relief and fear and hope pooled in his fingers, his wrists, his knees and toes. "Me, too."

It was difficult to find excuses to see her. Dominic had already commented — maybe he suspected something — that his father considered Josie far too young for courting, so there was no point in asking permission for that. Besides, Jago didn't know how she felt about him, and that seemed to him the more important question. But how would she fall for him if he couldn't see her? And he hated to skulk around just trying for a glimpse of her.

One afternoon, as he and Dominic were passing the National Guard camp, cursing the unfaithfulness of the group of girls in white dresses who were laughing with some young soldiers at the camp's periphery, Jago recognized Josie among them. Dominic hadn't seen her; he'd already turned back to Jago and changed the subject.

Jago didn't want Josie to get into trouble for fraternizing with the enemy; strikers had been shot and beaten by these same soldiers. But he didn't want her getting mixed up with some other fellow, either. So he pointed and said again to Dominic, "Isn't that your sister?"

Dominic looked. His jaw set. He marched over and grabbed Josie's arm. "They would

464

as soon shoot me, and you cavort with them!" he yelled, dragging her away while she hit at him. Jago trailed behind, swimming in equal parts joy and shame.

Back at the Barinottis', in their too-warm kitchen that smelled of garlic and the spicy tomato sauce simmering on the stove, Josie's mother and father shouted at her while two young girls and a boy screeched in and out of the room. Jago recognized Josie's expression from experience with Dominic: determination pushing toward anger. He didn't want to think that her family's loud objections would increase her interest in the soldiers. He caught her eye, gave her a sympathetic smile and shrug. The corner of her mouth twitched in response. Finally, her mother snapped in Italian, "I cannot look at you. Go out and pick the tomatoes."

Josie took a basket off a hook near the door; Jago slipped out behind her, watching the red bow in her black hair bounce as she ran down the steps. The sun was hot, and, as they made their way down the rocky path, Jago caught up to her. He could think of nothing clever to say. He gave her a little smile.

"Are you mad at me, too?" she said.

"No."

She smiled. He followed her into the garden, behind the tall beans climbing wooden poles and a cross-hatching of twine, next to the row of staked tomato plants. When she reached for a tomato, he rested his hand on hers. She looked at him. His other hand rose to move her hair off her neck. "You . . . won't do that again, will you?" he said.

She blinked, then picked the tomato, pulling her hand from under his, placing the tomato in her basket. She moved down the row. Regret stabbed him. The scent lingered on his hand as something already lost. But she looked back over her shoulder and smiled. "Romeo," she teased.

He'd played Romeo in the school play last fall. Had she seen the girls shadowing him at school, the way they'd giggled, the way he'd teased them? Did she think he viewed her as just another in the string of them? "No," he said, crestfallen. He'd made so many plans — ideas he'd never even briefly entertained about any other girl or woman.

"Perhaps Romeo could make himself useful," she said, indicating the many ripe tomatoes.

When he brought several to her and placed them in the basket on her arm, the mischief on her lips made him feel he was underwater, being tossed about by the force of the waves. It was painful, and he couldn't breathe. But there was so much to see, and sensations were so heightened, he didn't care if he ever surfaced again.

The problem perplexed him into the fall, as the nights became crisp and the leaves tinted with gold. It had taken all Jago's powers of persuasion to convince Dominic he'd followed Josie out that day only to escape the noise in the kitchen. Friends were turning against each other for lesser reasons than their sisters' honor these days. Shots were being fired into houses at night; mine deputies had killed a pair of men that way. Jago had marched in the martyrs' extravagant funeral procession, looking for Josie but not seeing her.

Jago's father berated his lack of passion for the cause; Eino had been at the forefront of several demonstrations, arriving home with bruises and, once, a weeping welt on his forehead. Jago had had enough of being beaten the first day, though he hadn't told his father — Eino would say he'd gotten what he deserved, having been on the wrong side of things. Jago thought maybe his father was getting what he deserved, too, and just wished that the fighting would stop, that

Saturday nights could be the same again.

But when his mother and Mrs. Siankivich worked themselves up to go with a group of neighborhood women to accost "the dinner-pail brigade" — those men who'd gone back to work as the strike dragged on — Jago tagged along to make sure she'd be all right. To his surprise, it was she who lashed out, grabbing the pails from two flabbergasted workmen and dumping the contents on the ground; other women, jeering at the "lousy scabs," did the same. The next day, in the brilliant golden light of autumn, the women returned with eggs and rocks in their pockets, carrying brooms they'd dipped into backyard privies. Jago watched with horror as his mother flung a broomful of shit at a passing dinner-pail man, an egg from her pocket at another. The workingmen lost patience and soon were scuffling with their attackers, same as they would have with men. Jago's mother was knocked to the ground; the man who'd hit her kicked her in the ribs. Jago sprang into the melee and beat the bigger man until the man fell to the ground, blood congealing in his mustache. Jago looked around at the mob, at his mother and the man who'd hit her, groaning side by side on the ground, and thought, *Now this, surely, is what hell must be like.*

Then he picked up his mother and helped her home.

He put her to bed and sat with her, staring at his scraped-up knuckles, clenching and unclenching his hurting fist. The minute his father got home, he ran out and headed across town for the Barinottis'. He went around to the back. His luck was good: Josie was in the garden, picking the last of the beans. He slipped through the back gate and into the garden, into the row with her. Only then did she hear him and look up. Fear flashed across her face, then surprise, and then pleasure.

"Hello," he said, taking a step toward her.

"Hello," she said.

Next to her, he cupped her face in his injured hand and leaned down and kissed her. She was stiff at first, but then she dropped the basket of beans onto his feet, and her arm circled his neck as his arms enfolded her. When she pulled slightly away, he opened his eyes and said, "Josie." And in her brown eyes was the light he'd been waiting for, and she said, "Jago," just the way he'd imagined it.

His mother wore a black eye like a badge as it faded from purple to yellow, and Mrs. Siankivich began leading a band that spent its days going from house to house of the nonunion men, terrorizing the wives with taunts and threats. Her sons spearheaded delinquent gangs, vandalizing workers' homes at night.

Jago spent part of every day behind the withering bean vines in the Barinottis' garden with Josie. She told him her dreams of living in a six-room house all her own, of teaching her children to sing. He shared his frustration over the strike, his anger at the violence and the fact that it was beginning to seem it would all end up being for nothing. Well, not exactly nothing: the workers got the eight-hour day. But management refused to recognize the union, and now many families were destitute, literally scraping by on the very last from their gardens, unable to get credit at the markets. The men were desperate to go back to work. Jago would have gone, too, if not for his father's murderous eyes, but at least he'd managed to keep twenty-five dollars socked away in his mattress, and he wasn't about to let his mother know, or it would go for groceries. He couldn't lose every shred of a chance of taking Josie away.

"I don't suppose your parents would allow me to marry you if I was a piano player in a saloon, would they, ay?" That slipped

out one day; he'd been considering apply-
ing for such work, though his mother had
slapped the idea down as immoral. He'd
wanted to ask how she could justify throwing brooms full of shit at people. He knew
the answer, anyway: anything for the cause.

"I'd only do it to save enough money to
take you away," he told Josie. "So we could
have a better life. I'd get you your house
with the six rooms."

"You want to marry me? And take me
away?" He nodded. She bit her lip, then
pushed him and ran out of the garden. The
slam of the house's back door was a shock.
He went out that night and spent two of his
last twenty-five dollars getting drunk.

But when he returned the next day, head
pounding, she was waiting for him. "Do you
forgive me?" she said. "I had to think. It
means leaving my family. But I will." She
smiled; he realized his mouth had fallen
open. He clamped it shut and grinned.

"Yes, I will, Jago," she went on, wrapping
her arms around him. She pressed her cheek
to his chest. "Next year, when I'm seventeen. Can you wait for me? My father would
kill you if you asked before that. And you'd
better not work in a saloon, or he'll never
give us permission."

Jago kissed her.

■ ■ ■ ■

In October, Mrs. Barinotti insisted that Josie cut the bean vines down. Now Jago was only able to see her downtown a couple of times a week. She would hurry through the marketing and he would carry her basket and they would sneak into the Catholic church, up the stone steps to the bell tower, and look out across the crowded rows of houses and steeples to the brown, frozen land in the distance, holding each other, dreaming. Jago dreaded the sound of the church bells striking the hour, her turning to him to say she had to go home; he dreaded descending to the ground, when for those moments in the tower he would almost imagine he could fly.

Strangely, the snow didn't come. He couldn't remember another year when there hadn't been several inches in November; usually, by December, the town was buried. He prayed it would come: all of it had to be shoveled from the streets and walks, loaded into sleds, and driven out of town with teams of horses. When the big snows came, two or three feet falling in a matter of hours, a hundred men were needed. He'd worked the night shift when he was in high school, and he was sure the boss would take him back, if only the weather would cooperate. He wanted to buy Josie something to show how much he loved her. He wanted to eat — something other than potatoes and cabbage from the root cellar. He was tempted to go back to the mine, but he thought his parents might actually kill him if he did.

But it was Mr. Barinotti who threatened him, meeting him at the door one cold, rain-streaked afternoon. "My wife, she notice the way you look at our Josie. You come here to eat our food, you call my son your best friend, and yet you would dishonor our family."

Jago protested: "I wouldn't —"

"She is too young. You are not welcome under our roof again. You try to see her, I make you wish you were dead." Mr. Barinotti slammed the door.

Jago stood there shivering. He heard a quiet tapping on the window. Through the rain-dappled glass, he saw Josie. She pressed her palm to it. Her eyes were large and sad. Someone pulled her away.

They didn't let her leave the house anymore, not even to do the marketing.

By December, nearly all the mine shafts were up and running again, and those three thousand men still on strike were told daily in the newspaper and elsewhere that their position was "folly." The union leaders were rumored to have left town.

When it was announced that any man who didn't return to work before January first would lose his position for good, Jago decided this was it. As long as he had prospects, and some money saved, Mr. Barinotti couldn't turn him away forever.

But when he told his father, Eino said, "I have not sacrificed everything for this cause to have my own son defy me. You go back to work, you find your own roof to live under, and you don't come here again."

Jago's mother was spooning meager portions of boiled cabbage onto their plates, a stony look on her face. Her belly was swollen under her apron. Evidently, his parents were going to replace him with a freshly minted brother or sister. Strange, after he'd been the only child for eighteen years.

His feelings were hurt. He felt he had no choice.

The mine manager agreed to take him back starting the day after Christmas. He found a room in the Rambletown neighborhood, arranging to move in on January first. He might end up sleeping in some alley for a few days, but he'd endure it.

Meanwhile, Dominic had revealed (with a nearly imperceptible wink) that, on Christmas Eve, Josie was going to bring some of the little Barinottis to a Christmas party that the union's auxiliary was putting on at the Italian Hall. The children would get gifts there; at home, there would be only what Mrs. Barinotti had managed to create out of thin air and old scraps. With Dominic and Mr. Barinotti still striking, the family had no money.

That morning, Jago dug into his mattress for his remaining nineteen dollars and went downtown to the jeweler's. He chose an intricate gold ring with a deep red ruby at its center and two small sparkling diamonds on each side. It cost seventeen dollars and fifty cents. As he walked home, clutching the tiny oval box inside his coat pocket, his teeth chattered. He was going to give her the ring today, then convince her to stand with him before Mr. Barinotti, who would have to see that Jago's intentions were honorable, that he truly intended to give Josie everything he had. Jago dreamed that Mr. Barinotti might permit them to marry right away.

At home, he dressed in his cleanest clothes and shaved at the kitchen sink. The Pietalas and the Siankiviches had already left for the party; Jago's mother sat at the table, wrapped in a shawl, her hand on her swollen stomach. Eino was out somewhere. "You sure you don't want to come to the party, Ma?" Jago asked, praying she'd say no.

She waved a bony hand. "Oh, no, that's for the children. I think I might lie down awhile, as long as it's quiet."

"Sounds good, Ma, you relax, ay." He wiped his face with a towel, folded and stashed his razor, kissed his mother's icy cheek, threw on his jacket, and was out the door.

The day was gray and cold; a recent, insignificant snow dusted the frozen ground. He walked fast. He hadn't seen Josie in almost a month, and he thought about how she would look when he gave her the ring. He tried to determine the best time to give it to her, how to get her alone.

The street in front of the Italian Hall was crowded; Finnish and Italian exclamations punctuated the air. Jago made his way through the throng, under the great arched doors, and up the wide stairs to the second floor, the noise of the party growing louder. At the top, a man standing in the vestibule admitted him with a nod. In the main hall, children swarmed and squealed; adults clustered on folding chairs, their many languages commingling in a loud, happy babble. Jago scanned the crowd for a red bow in long black hair. Finally, he saw her. Her back was to him and she was talking with a friend; children circled her like gulls, intermittently tugging her hand or skirt. Ignoring his nerves, he went up behind her and said, "I hope you haven't given up on me, ay."

She turned, startled, but grinned when she saw him and, shocking everyone, stood on tiptoe to kiss his cheek. "Jago!" she said, and he felt whole again.

They found seats and got Josie's brother Paolo and sister Rosa settled around them; three-year-old Marcellina insisted on sitting in Jago's lap. Up on the stage, the program started — some danced, others sang carols in Croatian and in Finnish. Every time Josie looked at him, Jago wanted to reach into his pocket for the ring. He contented himself with squeezing her hand, hidden under Marcellina's flowing skirt.

The audience grew restive. Babies cried. Several youngsters left their seats to scamper up and down the aisles. Marcellina squirmed; Jago locked his arm around her middle. The crowd's noise began to drown out the performers. Finally, a woman directed the children to line up to receive their gifts.

"Ready for your present?" Jago asked Marcellina.

"Yes!"

"Let's go, then, ay." He picked her up and slung her over his shoulder, spinning around and around; she held out her arms like a thrill seeker on a carnival ride, shrieking with laughter. He saw Josie smiling, bringing the other children behind.

The line was long; the room, as noisy as a stockyard. Holding Marcellina, Jago leaned down to ask Josie whether they could leave the children to wait and go for a walk. He had to repeat himself three times before she heard. She smiled but said the children were too young to be left. He was getting a headache, and she didn't seem to understand how important it was for them to be alone. He tried to hide his impatience as she scolded Paolo for pulling Rosa's hair and Paolo laughed, dark eyes dancing.

They were nearing the stage, about to climb the steps, when Dominic appeared. The little ones jumped and squealed. Jago started to sweat. Dominic took Marcellina from Jago; the girl grinned and circled her tiny arms around her brother's neck. "It's a madhouse here, no?" he said to Jago. "I came to see the children home."

"We can't leave now," Josie said, with an anxious glance at Jago. "They haven't gotten their presents."

"We can't leave!" Paolo emphasized, his younger sisters joining in.

Dominic scowled. "I'm going to go get cigarettes. Then I'll be back. Maybe it will be quieter then. Want to come, Jago?"

Jago looked at Josie; she nodded. Both knew that Dominic's questions tended toward demands. Besides, she'd probably realized that Jago wasn't enjoying himself. "We'll be back soon," he told her. Risking Dominic's ire, he leaned down to kiss her cheek.

Dominic said nothing, just handed Marcellina to Josie.

"Dom'nic," Marcellina scolded, folding her arms across her chest.

"We'll be back," Dominic said, turning away. Jago winked at Josie and followed. Halfway across the crowded room, he looked over his shoulder to try to catch her eye again, but she was busy with the children.

They were gone longer than planned because they ran into a couple of boys they'd known in school, who got started talking with Dominic. Jago, stamping his feet to keep warm, was distracted by the thought of getting back to Josie, by the weight of the ring in his pocket. But the fresh air and relative quiet of the downtown street was a relief after the bedlam of the hall, so he didn't complain. His headache was fading. He hoped to convince Dominic to take the little ones home, so he could walk alone with Josie.

He heard shouting in the street. A man was running toward them, his face a mask of horror. Jago couldn't understand the exclamations until he heard the word *"Tuli-palo!"* Fire.

Dominic grabbed the man's sleeve. "Where? Where's the fire?"

"The Italian Hall!"

They were running before he'd finished saying it.

When they got there, they saw no smoke, no flames. The front doors were open wide, but no one was coming out. People were scattered in the street: women with fists pressed to mouths; a few screaming children, clutching their mothers' skirts; flushed-faced men, yelling "Let us in!" as they scuffled with the mine deputies who blocked the doors. Upstairs, people leaned out the windows and shrieked for help, terror on their faces.

"What's going on? What's happened?" Dominic shouted as they approached.

"Someone yelled 'fire' and there was no fire!" someone cried. "So many people are trapped!"

Jago and Dominic rushed closer; a big deputy clotheslined them with one ham-thick arm, knocking them down. They sprang up and rushed him again. He grabbed their shirtfronts, one in each hand, and plowed them into the street. "Boys, you have to stay back! No one can go in."

Jago could make no sense of what he was seeing inside the open doors. Arms. Feet. Hands. Protruding from a tangled wall of bodies that reached from the bottom of the stairs nearly to the ceiling. Three men were at work in front of that wall, tugging on limbs, cursing, sweating. There were terrible sounds from within: children whimpering, women and men moaning.

"My sisters, my brother, are in there!" Dominic cried, but the big deputy continued to hold them. His mouth was a sneer, but his dark eyes were kind and full of sorrow. Jago choked back the sob rising in his throat. *Maybe she's all right!*

The men who'd been working inside the doors ran out, eyes gleaming with mad light. "We can't budge a one! We're going up top." They disappeared into the space between the Italian Hall and the building next door.

"We'll stay back," Jago told the deputy. "I promise we'll stay back." Fire engines clanged up, horses' traces jingling. The deputy let the boys go and went to help extend the ladders. Jago pulled Dominic behind him into that hollow space between the buildings. People were descending the fire escape like rats running from water. The boys had no choice but to wait, lifting crying children down, praying to see Josie and the little ones. They didn't. When the path was finally clear, they clambered up and in the open door.

Inside, chaos. Women and children screaming, sobbing. Deputies blocking the doorways, shouting, "There is no fire! No fire!" Women crying, "They're trying to kill us all!" Some still pushing their way toward the stairs with babies wailing in their arms, the men shoving them. "Get back, get back, the stairway is blocked! There is no fire!"

"Josie Barinotti!" Dominic screamed. "Josie! Paolo! Rosa! Marcellina!"

No answer, just random yelling, crying, other people shouting for their families.

Someone yanked Jago's arm. "Come on," said a man. "We need you." Dominic had gone ahead, and Jago didn't see him again.

Jago was led toward the vestibule at the top of the stairs and pressed into service. The deputies and firemen would hand him the bodies from the crush in the stairway and he would carry them into the hall and lay them on the floor, by himself if they were small children, with other men if they were larger people. Most of the ones near the top were alive, just bruised and scared. He patted their hands and rushed back, praying to find the Barinottis soon, soon. Or praying that they were already outside, maybe already home. Maybe Josie had become exasperated waiting for him and Dominic and left the party. *Please*, he prayed.

And then the bodies they began to hand him were limp. Dead. Now many who'd been helping to release the sufferers remained in the main hall, comforting those in pain on the floor, not wanting to face the horrific work as the rescue inched toward the stairs' bottom. But Jago continued: he had to see if Josie was in the tangle.

■ ■ ■ ■

He'd been carrying the injured and the dead for what seemed like two weeks and was maybe forty-five minutes when someone handed him Paolo, dead. His knees almost gave way. When he set Paolo down next to the other bodies, he couldn't stand up again. But he had to. He had to get her out.

And yet the next body was a stranger's. And so was the next. And the next. He began to carry them faster and faster, as though digging for buried treasure.

When all the bodies were laid out on the floor, there were more than he wanted to count, rows of them, and still he had not found her, or little Marcellina, or Rosa.

He hurried once more down the terrible stairs, pushing through the men who had congregated, hats crushed in their fists, through the gray-faced couples making the long march up to identify dead children. He ran into the street, calling her name.

And then she was there, rushing to Jago, holding him, crying. "Dominic found us hours ago and we couldn't find you, and they wouldn't let us back in and we haven't found Paolo! He went to play with some boys after we'd gotten the presents and I couldn't find him in that madness and I had to take the girls out the back! You have to help us find him!"

He felt a hundred years old. He looked into her wide brown eyes and said, "I'm sorry."

Altogether, more than seventy — some said eighty — people had died, most of them children like Josie's brother. At the funeral service, there were so many caskets that Jago and Josie didn't know which one to touch to bid Paolo goodbye, and so many mourners that they couldn't get close enough to touch one anyway. Grief pooled in Josie's eyes as the coffins were lowered into a mass grave, long rows of strangers.

Jago didn't go back to work. He couldn't, not in light of the rumor that it had been someone on the mine owners' side who had burst into the room full of strikers' children and hollered "Fire!" It was murder, some were saying; some even said the owners had directly sanctioned it. Jago couldn't work for a company that might be responsible for Paolo's and the others' deaths, for that horrible scene in the stairwell that he tried and tried to forget.

He wished he could leave town, but he wasn't going anywhere without Josie. The only thing he could think of was proposing to her, convincing her father of his sincerity.

But he didn't want to seem vulgar or self-absorbed so soon after the funeral; he decided to wait a couple days, though he sent a letter telling her that he had a Christmas gift for her which he hoped, despite her family's sorrow, could still mean something. He got no reply. He hadn't seen or heard from Dominic, either. On the third day, he went to their house, the ring in his pocket. He had no job, only a dollar and fifty cents to his name. Still, if she would just agree, and Mr. Barinotti would consent, he was certain he could figure something out. He'd written a note to pass to her, in case he couldn't get her alone: *Can't we just forget our families? Say you will. I have everything planned.* (Not exactly true, but the appearance of confidence seemed imperative.) Fat snowflakes drifted to the ground, leaving a fluffy coat of white to kick through.

When he got to the Barinottis', his repeated knocking on the front door had a hollow sound. He turned the doorknob; it was unlocked, and he poked his head inside.

The front room was empty. He thought: *Do I have the wrong house?* All the houses on the block were exactly the same. Maybe in his distraction he'd climbed the wrong steps.

But when he backed out and looked at the number, his stomach started to hurt.

Inside, his footsteps echoed on the bare wood floors. The kitchen was cold and, though the smell of garlic and herbs and lemon lingered, there was nothing on the stove.

"Hello?" came a voice. It was one of the upstairs neighbors, a handkerchief crumpled in her work-reddened fist.

Jago somehow spoke a question. The neighbor shook her head. "They had such heartbreak. Mr. Barinotti, he sold his father's gold watch. They took the train last night. West, I think. He and the boy will look for new work. A new life."

Jago saw Paolo's face, knew the feeling of lungs being crushed. He ran down the back steps and kept running, past the snow-covered garden, through the rickety back gate.

He thought she would write — or at least Dominic would — but no letter came. He knocked on the doors of all the neighbors;

no one could say where the family had been headed. Someone thought Montana; another said maybe Nevada. West, it was generally thought: someplace where Mr. Barinotti and Dominic could find work. Jago thought of sending letters to every town where there was some kind of mine, but the odds of something ever reaching her were slim to none — and even if a letter found the family, her parents might not give it to her. Even if by some miracle (and he did envision it!) he could show up on her new doorstep, they would likely turn him away. Or Mr. Barinotti would kill him for his insolence. The more days that passed, the more trying to find her seemed a foolish plan. The idea smoldered and burned and then raged: if she loved him, she would write. His longing for her began to feel like a heavy cape worn foolishly in the heat of summer. He started to wish he knew how to shed its weight.

He spent most of his time at the pool hall, racking up a tab he couldn't pay. And then, in the middle of one dark night, his father called out from the other side of the blanket, waking Jago from a nightmare of bodies laid in a snowy field in a never-ending row. He was running along them, panicked, stopping at each one, trying to find Josie.

"Jago," came his father's voice. "Go to get the doctor for your mother."

Even just waking from his nightmare, Jago sensed an unusual edge in the voice. He jumped up, pulled on his clothes, and ran out, his feet pounding the street, cold air burning his skin. He knew this was too soon for the baby to be coming.

Later, he waited in the kitchen with his father, the wavering lamplight casting shadows on the walls. Mrs. Siankivich and Mrs. Pietala had come downstairs to help. The two families had been busy thanking God they'd lost no children in the disaster; another calamity seemed unthinkable. Finally, as light began to creep through the tiny window, Mrs. Pietala, tears in her eyes, brought in a towel-wrapped bundle. "I'm sorry," she said in Finnish, passing the bundle to Eino, who took it in clawlike hands, horror on his face.

Two days and two nights went by, and Jago's mother was still in bed, feverish, delirious. When they summoned the doctor again, he said that she had an infection, that time would tell. He didn't think she was sick enough to go in the hospital. Those beds were needed for men who worked, not the wives and mothers of men who were still striking.

Three days later, never having had a lucid moment to bid Jago or Eino goodbye, she died.

After the funeral, Eino said he was moving to Detroit. "Ford pays five dollars a day," he said, starting to pack his few belongings.

Jago's head hurt. He had made less than $2.00 a day in the mine; his father, after years of service, had made $2.70. "What about the union, ay? The 'goddamned capitalists'? The cause?"

"The cause is as dead as your mother. I will not break my back for nothing any longer."

There was no way Jago was moving to Detroit, no way he was leaving town. She might still write. The image of the dead bodies laid in a row raked at him — as much as the image he held in his mind of her dark eyes, the red bow in her hair.

He shook hands with his father on the depot platform; Eino gave him five dollars. "If you change your mind, come," he said. But his eyes were ice again, and Jago didn't think he wanted to be followed — maybe setting off alone reminded him of coming over from Finland, when he'd been young and all had been possibility. The train cars clattering, couplings snapping, whistle howling, and steam expelling made the word come to Jago's mind: *orphan.*

He started playing piano at the pool hall to work off his tab. He spent three of his father's five dollars on a gilded volume of the complete works of Shakespeare. The other two, he put on the table in a poker game and turned into ten, then lost and got it back again. To lose felt comforting, familiar; the ease of winning, intoxicating, strange. Sitting down at the table felt as inevitable as descending into the mine. He relished entering that different world, even while the ring stayed heavy in his pocket, as day after day he lost and won and lost again.

In the fall, a man approached him at the piano to say that he owned a large, classy saloon in Hurley, Wisconsin, with a revue of dancing girls; he would pay three times whatever Jago was making now, plus provide him a furnished room upstairs. Jago had heard that Hurley was a good place for a man to forget his troubles. He felt the feeble light in him finally flicker out. Maybe she really was dead: fever or fire or some terrible accident. Such things happened every day. And if she was alive, she didn't feel about him the way he felt about her, or she would have written. She would have found a way.

He left on the train with the man the next day, the ring tucked into his coat pocket. Standing out on the vestibule in the crisp air and the noise, he watched through the steel grating the earth blur under his feet. He smoked, bracing himself against the motion, trying to quell the cold burning inside him, as the church steeples of Red Jacket faded into the distance. He took out the tiny box, intending to throw it overboard.

Instead, he watched it stay still in his palm, even as his home and everything he'd known slid from under his feet. He had no fight left in him. It had gone out of him piece by piece when he'd carried the bodies out of the stairwell, when the Barinottis had vanished, when the doctor had let his mother die, when his father had abandoned the cause and Jago and ridden that train out of town — and with every day that had passed without a letter from Josie. Any good that had been in him was gone. But at least this ring would remind him of when he'd known what it was to hope, of when he'd worn his heart on his sleeve.

May 2000

"Violet keeps asking about you, and she can't wait to meet Josh," Julia told Danny on the phone. She'd been visiting the nursing home every day; to her relief, Violet had found contentment there, after one of her fellow residents had turned out to know the story behind Jago's ring. Julia had listened in astonishment to Violet's recounting of the tale, and, ever since, she'd perceived within herself the springing of a tentative, if incomplete, optimism. At the farm, the air smelled fresher, as if the dust that had lingered was finally dissipating. Violet, too, seemed to feel that her burdens had been eased. She'd even said her pain was tolerable, and, one day, she'd happily reported having her familiar vision of Derrick the night before. She was also looking forward to a "real" visit from the granddaughter she'd never met.

Marty had been shocked, on her arrival back from Spain, to hear all that had transpired. She and Alice had had a long and painful talk, and now Marty was officially not speaking to her sister. "Someday, I will, maybe, but — not yet!" she'd told Julia. She'd said she wanted to search for Joe, that she was gathering her courage. Julia didn't mention the steps she'd already taken, the fruitless calls she'd made.

At any rate, Marty was coming to visit the farm — and meet Violet — in mid-June. She was even planning to stay to watch Julia run the marathon. Julia, covering longer distances each day, was finally beginning to feel that she was running not from anything — not even her memories of that gleaming silver casket — but toward the marathon, the mini–family reunion.

Now she told Danny, "She gave me a list of things for you to get from her farm."

"Why don't you tell me when I get there? I'll call you," he said, and he, too, sounded happier than she'd heard him. He'd said he was giving Josh time to adjust to the fact that Danny was "Dad," but he thought he'd be back as early as next week.

Every night now, Julia put on Ray Charles and turned him up loud; the first couple times, she'd felt like crying, but after that, she just danced and danced. Then, with Johnny Cash playing in the background, she'd call two or three Joe Mosckiewiczes, her voice seeming to echo in the lonely house.

She had started taking pictures of the horses, the farm, of Violet, and she'd converted the old pantry into a darkroom. She spent hours in there, savoring the biting smell of the chemicals and the underlying scent of old wood and cinnamon and cloves, watching images emerge. As she worked, she thought about Alice — forgiveness was a challenge, but Julia was doing her best not to perpetuate the family tradition of relentless anger, having realized that her stubbornness was aggravatingly like Marty's, Lena's, Violet's, despite that she'd always thought she was brand-new, that her messed-up parents were as good as strangers, with no bearing on who *she* was.

Alice apologized every time she called — and even if it did sometimes seem she was speaking a language that she hadn't quite mastered, it always sounded sincere. So one morning, Julia mailed her copies of some of the best pictures of the horses, in care of Grace; Alice and George had given up their cross-country odyssey for now and were staying put in Southern California.

That afternoon, Julia showed Violet the portfolio she'd been compiling. Violet said, "This picture of my . . . eye? This is 'work' to you?"

"Like Grace and her costumes, something you can't set aside," Julia said, and Violet, still studying the image, nodded.

And then giggled. "Modern life!" And she told Julia about the job she'd had waiting tables at the Ironwood Hotel. "I never thought about whether I was fulfilled, I guess!

"Listen," she said then. "I've called my lawyer in Minnesota and changed my will. I'm leaving my farm there to you and Danny. There're lots of things to take pictures of there! You can redecorate the house, if you want to. It's the least I can do for you. After the damage I've done!"

This was a burden Julia didn't want. "Violet, you forgave Lena from the beginning. Isn't it time you forgave yourself?"

"It won't bother me a bit, after I'm gone!"

Julia hated when Violet was so cheerful about her impending death. But that night, alone at the farm, her fruitless calls made, she was rolling coneflower yellow paint onto the bedroom walls when she realized that, by giving her and Danny a place to share, Violet was trying to be sure that the family wouldn't fly apart again, that none of them would be alone.

Not that Julia would settle at the Minnesota farm with her brother forever.

But maybe for a little while.

On the year anniversary of the day Ryan had died, Julia heard Danny's truck pull into the driveway, and she ran outside in time to see him lifting a dark-haired boy down from the cab. The truck bed was packed full and piled high, covered with a blue tarp, a rope crisscrossing it — Violet's things. A yellow Lab leaped out and bounded toward Julia; she laughed when it jumped to greet her. "Come in the house with me quick, you guys. I want to show Josh his room!"

Danny cocked his head and said to the boy, who was now hiding behind his leg, "Josh, meet your crazy aunt Julia."

The yellow walls complemented the navy blue cowboy bedspread and curtains she'd found at Target, along with the kid-size beanbag, the red bookshelf, and the reading lamp with a brown cowboy hat for a shade and red plastic boots for the base. She'd added her own touches, too, polishing an old saddle from the barn and arranging it on a stand in the corner, nailing onto the wall horseshoes in slanted pairs and a thick rope draped in an artful loop.

So what if it's just for the summer, she'd told herself, considering that when Alice and George returned they'd surely want their old room back, and they probably wouldn't go for the cowboy motif. *Any time can be like forever. Any time can mean everything.*

Then again, since Alice was with Grace in California, maybe she wouldn't want to come home so soon.

"Dad? Dad?" Josh said. "Can I ride the horse?" Indicating the saddle on the stand. Soon Danny was bouncing him up and down atop the saddle and singing an up-tempo version of "The Highwayman," which Julia recognized because she'd found it on an old Willie Nelson LP of Alice and George's. Josh's giggles were contagious; Julia found herself laughing, too. Danny took off his cowboy hat and put it on Josh's head.

"Danny?" Julia said. "Danny, you're not like the highwayman at all. You're not a ghost like Derrick. You're right *here.*"

Danny winked at her, still singing, and

the hat flopped down over Josh's eyes. All that was visible of his face was his grin.

"You called every Joe Mosckiewicz in L.A.?" Danny asked later, after Josh was asleep. "Did you tell Mom?" They were sitting on the stoop again, watching the map of stars emerge in the darkening sky.

"No, I haven't told her. I'm afraid he's dead." She sighed, leaning back on her hands. "We'll go see Violet tomorrow. She's so excited to see you and Josh."

"You know," Danny said, "there are a lot of other places in California where Joe could live." He got up and walked into the shadows, disappearing around the corner of the house. *Typical.* Why had she expected so much of him? She heard his truck door creak open — was he leaving?

No: the door slammed shut, and, in a moment, he was back, carrying a road atlas. "How much does it cost to call information?"

Two hours later, as she dialed the number for the Joe Mosckiewicz in San Juan Capistrano, Danny was brewing a fresh pot of coffee. But Julia's hope was wearing thin; soon it would be too late to call even to California.

When a man answered, she launched into her spiel like a telemarketer. "I'm looking for a Joe Mosckiewicz who was born in Wisconsin in about 1920 and lived on a farm near Blackberry Ridge from 1945 until 1965."

There was a pause, and then, "Who is this?"

Usually, the person at the other end of the line had either snapped at her or laughed and wished her luck. "His granddaughter."

Silence.

She pressed on, conscious of Danny watching her. "This Joe Mosckiewicz served in the Army Air Forces during World War Two. He had a daughter named Alice by his first wife, Grace, and a daughter named Marty by his second wife, Lena. They haven't heard from him since 1967."

A pause. "Whose daughter are you?"

"I'm Marty's daughter. My name is Julia."

"Jesus," the man said. "Julia."

She beckoned Danny closer.

Silence.

"My brother is here, too!" she blurted. "They say he looks just like you."

Danny got on the extension. For a moment, they all tried to talk at once.

Finally, Joe explained: he'd gotten tired of the silences and cutting remarks whenever he called Alice and Marty. He'd thought he'd find Grace soon and that, when Alice finally met her, she'd understand. "When Grace left, it was like . . . like my chute hadn't opened. Like I'd had to bail out and I was falling through the sky and my chute wouldn't open. We airmen have nightmares about that kind of thing, you know. They never go away." But, as more and more time passed without his finding Grace, it had started to seem too late to get back in touch with his daughters. "I was embarrassed, I guess. You can't imagine how many Grace Andersons there are in Southern California. I finally figured she probably got married again and changed her name. I guess I thought I wasn't meant to find her. That she was happier without me. She'd never wanted us to begin with, so why would she want us now? And the girls were so angry. I couldn't seem to think of how to explain."

Then he'd met someone else and gotten married again.

"Fuck," Danny breathed on the extension.

Joe went on, "Kathryn always encouraged me to try to get in touch with the girls, but . . . so much time had gone by. My whole life on the railroad, I had to keep such an eye on the time. I guess, out here, I started to think it was trying to get back at me, flying away the way it did. The way that even the seasons never changed."

"Are you still married?" Julia asked, reminding herself: Grace and Alice — and, according to what Joe knew, Marty — had rejected him; punished him, even. There were limits to what a human being could take. And he'd probably learned a few things from Lena, too.

"Kathryn passed away five years ago." He paused. "Will you tell them . . . tell them I think about them all the time? I know it's too late, but —"

Danny interrupted. "Not really."

"No, I don't think it's too late!" Julia agreed. She told Joe about Violet's return to the farm; about the letters from Grace fighting for Alice that Lena had hidden. How they'd been able to locate Grace in California, and how Alice had gone to meet her. "Would you like to see them? I'm sure we can arrange something —"

Joe had started to cry.

Julia and Danny managed to reach Alice at the campground. Alice said, "Oh, this is too much. Too much. What am I going to do? I — I thought, after Uncle Derrick, that no one would ever come back, that no one could ever really be found."

"He can't wait to see you," Julia assured her. "It doesn't matter what you've done. You're his daughter."

"I got the pictures you sent," Alice said. "They're beautiful. Home."

"Yes," Julia said. "Home. It's all right, Alice."

"Thank you," Alice said. She let out a long breath. "Thank you."

Next, they called their mom in North Carolina, waking her, and Marty wept, her brittleness falling from her like an ice cream bar's chocolate shell. She hung up to phone Joe, then called back to report. "We couldn't talk, we just cried and cried. I'm going to get a plane ticket and go see him — the first airplane they'll put me on! I want you both to meet him, too. When you can!"

Then she said, with her old bitterness, "I don't know if I can stand to look at Alice's face, but she's not going to have him to herself out there, not when she kept him from me for so long."

"I hope you can find a way to forgive her," Julia said.

"It's not going to be easy."

"You might as well give her a break, Mom," Danny put in. "She's the only sister you've got."

"*Half* sister," Marty snapped. But then she sighed. "Oh, I wish we could all be together. Not so 'scattered to the winds'! Well, at least pretty soon I *will* get to see you two — and Josh! And, good Lord, the grandmother I've never met! And maybe I *could* get my dad to come, too, to meet you all!" She laughed, astonished, thrilled; a little caustic. "That damn farm never seems to let us go!"

"Mom?" Julia said. She was hoping that, when Marty met Violet, Violet could teach her about forgiveness, too. "I'm going to invite Dad to come up to see me and Danny, sometime this summer. After your visit, I mean."

"Fuck, Jules," Danny broke in, "why even take the chance?"

"Danny, he's our dad. We can at least try."

Marty sighed. "Julia, just don't get your hopes up, as to whether he'll even respond. You know he isn't reliable, and look what happened the last time —"

"Mom, stop."

A breath. "Yes, all right. Just — call me? You two? If you need me?"

It was the best thing she could have said.

As they hung up, it occurred to Julia that there was no way to erase memory; instead, you could learn to bear the things that had been, to fold them into who you were and who you would be. You could learn to forgive the fates and move on, and find your way to the light, out from the long, dark shadow of the past.

She went into the living room. Danny was studying the portrait of Grace. "You all right?" she asked, moving toward the stereo.

He rubbed his face, coming back to the present. "Not too loud — you'll wake up Josh."

She put on Earth, Wind & Fire at a whisper. "Come on," she said, performing a *Saturday Night Fever* move to make him laugh. "Let's dance."

June 2000

In the four weeks since their initial reunion, Grace and Alice had been seeing each other nearly every day, though they'd quickly learned they had few interests in common.

Alice had humored Grace with shoe shopping — she'd even allowed the purchase of a pair of elegant white sandals. Not that she'd worn them. But at least Grace knew they were there, maybe slid under Alice's bed — if such a thing could happen in an RV — waiting to be worn and loved. And Alice, though apparently holding out final judgment, had paid careful attention to everything Grace had explained about those long-ago years.

Grace, meanwhile, had listened to enthusiastic tales about Alice's horses and the farm (she was her father's daughter, it was clear) and gone to the ocean more than she had in many, many years. It had always seemed to her like such a tourist thing to do, or a young-person thing — or maybe she didn't like to think of Derrick, at rest somewhere in it, under it — but now, with Alice and sometimes George, she loved going. Packing her beach bag with just the right piece of fruit, a bottle of sunscreen, a magazine, a chosen pair of sandals. They'd spend hours there, Grace on her folding chair under an umbrella, watching as Alice and George played in the water. To Grace's surprise, now she actually found it a comfort to think of Derrick somewhere in that ocean; she felt his warm presence with her constantly.

But her favorite part was when Alice would come running toward her out of the waves, hair and swimsuit soaked, grinning as if the sea had scoured away her fear, her reserve. And she'd be hungry, wanting to go eat, to try all the different kinds of seafood. Grace had never felt more content than she did watching Alice smacking her lips over crab legs and wiping melted butter from the corners of her mouth. George seemed to relish the sight, too, and his warm expression reminded Grace of his grandfather John Tuomi, those times she'd ridden with him from the shipyard out to the farm. But George gave them their space, too, gave the

mother and daughter time alone. Sometimes, they took walks along the beach, Alice barefoot, closer to the water so the waves
would wash over her feet, Grace on the
shore side in her sandals. Grace never
noticed the crowds; she was too intent on
listening, talking. Getting to know Alice was
like peeling an onion. Grace had learned
she had to be patient, take it one layer at a
time. She'd tried to get Alice and George to
move into her guest room; Alice had insisted
they'd stay in their RV, though they did
move to a camp that was closer to Grace's
house. Grace supposed she had no right to
ask for more. She still thought of trying to
find Joe, but something held her back: Her
own fears and reserve? Anger? Maybe even
selfishness. She didn't want to share Alice
with anyone just now, not when she'd
missed so many years.

She'd spoken with Violet a couple of
times, and though it was unclear how much
Violet was tracking these days, the thought
of Grace and Alice being reunited did seem
to cheer her. Grace had also called Boots
shortly after the first reunion with Alice,
and she'd been calling every couple of days
since. Boots had insisted, and talking with
her helped, when Grace got frustrated. She
knew Alice was keeping things hidden from

her, and she was desperate to find out what they were. At least there seemed to be new light in her eyes the last couple of weeks, and Grace wondered what might have put it there. Not *her,* certainly? "You've got to give the kid time," Boots would say. "She'll come around."

Alice did agree to attend a family gathering. Susan and Ted were there with all their children and grandchildren, who were Alice's cousins and second cousins, and who'd had no idea about her at all. Though she was by far the oldest, they quickly welcomed her as one of them, and Susan and Ted remembered their few visits to the farm, Ted saying proudly that Alice was the first baby he'd ever been allowed to hold. Grace thought that pleased Alice, though she wasn't entirely sure.

"Grace?" Alice said one afternoon, when they were walking on the beach. Grace hadn't pushed to be called Mom, though she would have loved to hear it, just once. She remembered Alice's baby voice saying "Ma" and supposed Lena had retrained her to refer to Lena that way before Alice's memory had even formed.

Those were the kinds of things she didn't like to ponder. "Yes?"

"Will you tell me honestly? Why did you leave? Didn't you love us?" Her voice caught.

They'd been skirting the topic for weeks; Grace wanted to throw her arms around Alice, stroke her hair, anything that might soothe her. But the couple of times Grace had hugged her, Alice had stiffened and not hugged back. She didn't seem to like to be touched. So Grace just kept walking, a bit stunned by the sudden directness. She wondered why the change, searched for what to say. "Alice, I did love you. Very much. Please, don't ever doubt that I did. And do! But it was . . . how can I put it? The times, I guess."

"Dad told me you'd said everyone rushed into the wrong thing because of the war."

"Oh, dear. Did I say that? I suppose he'd have remembered something like that. Well, I shouldn't have said that. It wasn't . . . it wasn't 'wrong,' Alice. It just . . . well, it wasn't the right thing for *me.*"

"But what about me? What about Dad?"

Grace realized: she'd been dreading that question for fifty-three years. Imagining meeting Alice, she'd never been able to come up with a satisfactory answer. Maybe that was part of the reason why she'd vacillated so endlessly — so unforgivably —

about connecting with Alice again. And why she'd been so cautious, these past weeks — even about so much as considering trying to find out what had happened to Joe. "There's no excuse, I know that," she said, to start, hating that Alice's eyes had dimmed. "But, please believe me, at the time, I honestly thought that you both would be better off with Lena. She was constantly telling me I was no good at anything around that farm. She had a knack with you. And your father and I . . . well, we weren't . . . meshing, I guess you could say."

"Lena told you that? That you couldn't do anything right?"

"Yes."

"She told me that, too."

"Oh, dear. Oh. I never — I guess I never thought she would take anything out on you. She seemed to love you so much."

"She did love me," Alice said. "I've thought a lot about it, and I know she did, in her way. I didn't have a terrible childhood or anything. She just . . . had her blind spots, I guess."

Grace laughed. "You can say that again."

Alice crossed her arms.

Grace sighed. "Alice, you do know nothing is your fault, don't you? Not one thing.

I don't want you to think it for a minute! So many things had happened and . . . well, maybe your father told you that I . . . I had a dream."

Alice nodded; a tiny smile flickered.

"I want to be honest with you, Alice. All I can tell you is that I didn't even realize everything that was happening to me. I just had this craving for freedom. Independence, I guess you'd say. I'd had a taste of it, working at the shipyard, and a lot of things had happened that had made me feel so upside down and backward, and I just clung to this old dream and . . . maybe didn't consider everything as carefully as I should have. I guess it's no excuse, but we didn't understand, back then, all the things that can happen in a woman's body when she has a baby, and sometimes, looking back on it, I think I just . . . wasn't quite right in the head, if you know what I mean. . . ."

Alice's eyes bore into her; she nodded once: a release.

She is so strong, Grace thought, proud and regretful at once. She looked down the beach at the children playing in the sand; the people in bright swimsuits laughing, throwing Frisbees, running in and out of the water. Seagulls swooped and cried. "I acted selfishly. I guess I thought that my old dream would be the only thing that would make me happy. And that you'd be better off with Lena, since I was such a wreck. And then, when I got out here, I realized that wasn't really true. I got what I guess I'd wanted, but I still felt so empty, because I missed *you.* But it was too late, because Lena and Joe . . . well, I don't want to speak poorly of them to you, but they decided I should be punished. They wouldn't let me have anything to do with you. And I wanted to!"

"Dad said he regretted it." Alice's eyes flashed up. "He was just angry with you for leaving. Because he loved you so much. I know exactly what he meant."

Grace took a deep breath; remembered dancing, so long ago. "Yes. Well, in any case. I'm sorry for everything. Please believe me. I'll do anything I can, now, to be here for you. For the rest of my life."

Another nod. And then, to Grace's astonishment, Alice reached down to clasp her hand. Grace looked over, but Alice was still watching her feet make indents in the sand, the water rushing up and washing over them.

So Grace just held on tight, and kept walking.

After a moment, Alice said, "There's

something I want to tell you. I hope you don't mind."

They were approaching one of their favorite restaurants. Alice gestured with her eyes — *do you want to go?* — and Grace nodded. They were to that point: communicating without words. It thrilled Grace. They turned toward it, away from the rolling waves. "What is it, Alice?"

Alice glanced ahead. A man stood at the bottom of the restaurant's steps, silver-haired, trim, compactly built, not tall. He looked about seventy-five but was maybe older, in good shape. There seemed to be something familiar about him. *Couldn't be,* Grace told herself quickly.

She looked at Alice again, wanting to know what she had to say.

And Alice, stifling a smile, looked again toward the man.

And then Grace (suddenly realizing, *If he'd never told her about me, how could he have told her all these things!*), seeing the tentative smile on his face and the warm glint of his indigo eyes, stopped walking and covered her mouth with her hand.

And then she grabbed Alice's arm and ran as best she could toward him, dragging Alice with her, her feet slipping in the sand, and time had stopped and time was lost and then nothing mattered but that they had found each other again.

Epilogue:
June 2000

"Well, here's the cause of my undoing!" Violet said, when she saw the old gambler. He was being pushed in his wheelchair by a tall young man whose hair looked like a cat's brushed the wrong way; Violet sat in her wheelchair before the chirping birds in the aviary, Julia nearby. The young man said, "Amelia?"

How strange: the child-doctor from the hospital. She remembered he'd been a sour-puss about the fact she was dying, not seeming to realize that, at her age, if it wasn't cancer, it would be something else.

But he'd been kind. "I don't go by that name anymore," she said. "I'm Violet."

"Dr. Hanson?" Julia said, standing. "Do you work here now?"

The doctor's face flushed. "No, I'm just visiting. This is my grandpa."

Violet smiled at that. "Did you know, young man, your grandfather was an inveterate gambler?"

"In my day," the old man said mildly. He never seemed to mind Violet's teasing; they'd taken to eating meals together. He'd told her again and again how sorry Jago had been for everything; how sorry the old man himself had been, later, to have taken Jago's money.

"Let's not bother with the modest apologies today," Violet told him. She could not, for the life of her, remember his name.

The young doctor looked down on her. "How have you been feeling?"

"Better than you imagined I would. I've outlasted your prediction, at least." She didn't want to say: the only way she'd managed to get through day after day, year after year, at all — the only way she managed it, still — was by resolving not to think of her lost children. Though sometimes, lately, she would find herself doing the new calculations. Without Jago, she had to do them herself. *Born 1925, Died 1964.* She still could seem to make no sense of it. She'd had longer to comprehend *Born 1925, Lost 1944; Conceived and lost, 1933.* Not that any of it was easy, how time slid like a ship down the ways, leaving you scrambling to keep your footing. And still, sometimes, against her will, she would find herself imagining how that never-born baby might have stood up for her, against Lena; enumerating the many ways she and Jago had failed to protect Derrick — and Lena. How vast were the promises you made to your children when they were born! And how slim the chances of keeping them.

The doctor laughed. "I should never have doubted you."

"This old man told me about the ring," Violet told Julia. "About 'Darling J.' "

The young doctor looked puzzled.

"An old family story," Julia said to him.

Violet couldn't help giggling. *This old man, he played one.* She didn't know why, these past weeks, everything had struck her as so funny. She would sit with the old man at meals and they would laugh and laugh over things they had never found humorous before. They'd laugh about work at the shipyard, the cold steel, the intolerable weather, how their paths must have crossed without their meeting. They'd laugh over how he'd taken all of Jago's money; how the other shipbuilders had been afraid to point him out to her as the main culprit. Violet didn't know why this tickled her so, but it did. They laughed over how old they were, how their eyes were going dim. She even chuckled about the constant aching of her belly and lungs, though the aching and the pills they gave her to fight it played with her memory and concentration in maddening ways. Her bones jutted from ever-more-papery skin. Sometimes, at the table, she'd pull up a sleeve to show a wrist bone and tell her new friend, *Bony as a bird, I'll grow feathers, wings, fly away.* And he would laugh so hard that liquid would dribble from his nose, and then they would giggle over that, how everything had simply escaped their control, and all they could do was to wait for the day when they'd finally be relieved of every concern. Not that they looked forward to it, exactly, but: well.

Now, the doctor looked at Julia. "I . . . don't think I ever got your name?"

"Julia." She sounded nervous; Violet tittered.

The old man looked at the ceiling and whistled a tune. Violet thought she recognized it: "For Me and My Gal"? She grinned at him and said to the doctor, "She isn't married, if that's what you're wondering. She's a wonderful girl. My great-granddaughter! You'd be lucky to get her."

"Violet!" Julia said.

The doctor looked puzzled. "Your . . .

great-granddaughter?" And then he must have decided the point wasn't worth fussing over, that Violet was just too far gone.

The old man winked at Violet; the doctor smiled at Julia. "Well, could I . . . call you sometime?"

Violet said, "She lives at my old farm. Corner of Blackberry Ridge Road and County E."

"Yes!" Julia said. "You can call me. Or — stop by, if you want, I guess."

They each fumbled for paper, a pen. They said goodbye. They said, *Nice seeing you; see you soon.*

Violet felt her wheelchair begin to move; Julia was pushing her away. "Goodbye," Violet cried to the men, laughing. "See you soon!"

Julia's running shoes squeaked on the linoleum; she leaned down close to whisper, "Violet, I cannot believe you!"

"You should thank me. Hard to believe a no-good old gambler like that would have a nice doctor for a grandson, but sometimes the apple does fall far from the tree. Like Derrick from Jago. He's a dish — and a doctor, at that! Life's short. Yet it does go on and on. Were you just going to leave it to chance you'd bump into him again?" She thought of that long-ago day in Hurley, Jago

bursting out of the saloon: a chance colli-
sion, if ever there was one!

"Violet, for God's sake. Besides, haven't
you said that old man's getting to be your
friend?"

"Of course, and he's an old bastard, too.
If it hadn't been for him, I might not have
had to sell the farm. Except Jago probably
would have lost his money to someone else.
You might as well go for the grandson.
Poetic justice, I'd say. Or something like
that." She had the sudden urge to tell Julia,
who was always commenting how Violet had
been so forgiving of Lena, about the mushrooms. That though what she'd said before
(how she'd left hoping Lena would move
on) had been true, it hadn't been the whole
truth. In fact, she'd allowed her anger to
weaken her; she'd gone so far as to mince
those poisonous things into tiny pieces. And
then she'd succumbed to her fear of Lena's
accusations, and she'd run away and never
come back. She'd told Grace she wanted
only to keep her children safe, but look at
what she'd done. She'd chosen to protect
herself rather than protecting her daughter.

How could she ever forgive herself for
that?

"I cannot believe you," Julia snapped
again, pushing Violet's chair on.

"Oh, you don't even know, dear." But Violet had already stifled the impulse to confess. No, she would not do anything to jeopardize the lost things she'd found at this late hour of her life, these imperfect, beautiful young people who proved it was her aloneness that had been the lie. Julia and Danny and that darling little boy of his. Not to mention Grace — finally reunited with Alice, and even with Joe, out in California. And Violet was going to be meeting her granddaughter soon, they'd promised. *Marty.*

Surely all of this was enough to justify her continuing to let everyone believe that Lena had been crazy. As Jago would have said, Violet couldn't control the way people felt about things. Besides, Lena *had* done plenty of crazy things, the poor, dear girl, and Violet had loved her as much as they'd all loved Derrick, yet somehow they'd all slipped away, as relentlessly as time.

She supposed that was what happened when you held things so tightly: so tightly that you squeezed the life and breath right from them.

It was time she learned to do a little letting go.

"Julia," she blurted. "There's something else I need." She reached into the pocket of her sweater and came up with the cool blue marble in her fist.

Violet and Julia clutched each other's arms as they picked their way across the muddy cemetery. The evening sun was sinking behind the trees, the air growing cooler, the sky purple. Danny and his little boy walked ahead, Danny carrying a trowel and a cross he'd fashioned by nailing together two scavenged pieces of wood, Josh waving a tiny paper American flag.

Violet had asked Julia to use some of her egg money to buy a tombstone. *Beloved son and brother, 1925–1944,* Violet wanted it to say. *Forever living in our hearts.*

By the time they reached the top of the hill, near where Lena was buried, Violet's legs ached and her lungs burned. She wanted to say something beautiful, but the pain was so bad that she couldn't think. Danny knelt, chipped a small hole into the earth, and planted the marble like a seed. Violet trembled, holding Julia's arm, as they watched him cover it and place the cross and the tiny flag. She managed to ask him to sing "Danny Boy." Jago would have wanted that. As Danny's voice rumbled, Violet stood blinking, trying not to fall.

She heard Julia sobbing; from the wet heat on her own face, she realized she was doing the same. Finishing, Danny bowed his head and touched the earth; little Josh mimicked him. And Violet loved them, then, for doing their best to remember, in whatever ways they could, her beloved boy, who'd left so long ago and never found his way back home.

And then it was time to go. Violet allowed Julia, who was still sniffing back tears, to help her into the car; her old body settled into the seat with relief.

Oh, her hand felt empty, without the marble; a fist of sadness clutched her heart. But it had been time. Though now it occurred to her: the grandfather clock at the farm had been silent. She wondered at what time the hands were frozen. She closed her eyes and thought of her own frozen hands, that long-ago day she'd crawled to the Tuomis'. The spiders weaving their endless webs; Derrick pinning up his maps; Lena with her scrapbooks; Grace at the shipyard, the happiness on her face when she'd talk about a letter from Derrick.

Violet could feel Jago's smooth hand on her face, even smell his scent of spice and money. She could hear his voice, its richness belying his inability to hold things.

Doors slammed. A key turned in the ignition.

She thought she might tell them to bury that little ring box with her, when the time came, so that it could be next to Jago, too, and with the twins. *Much as I hate it, that girl was a part of us!* That damned Darling J., leaving him like that, without even saying goodbye. Violet hoped the girl had at least had a good reason for never writing him, the way his heartbreak had strewn wreckage across the lives of so many. If Violet had known, would she have been more forgiving, understood why it was so important to him — and so impossible — to win? Might she even have understood why he'd signed Derrick's enlistment papers, why he'd believed it so important for their boy to leave home while he was still young and unspoiled?

Or would she have hated him even more, knowing that what she wanted — his whole heart — simply hadn't been his to give?

If only he'd given her that ruby! She might have had a chance, then, of protecting Derrick and Lena.

Although: every fact he'd kept from her would have hurt her. She liked to think that, in his own strange way, he'd been trying to protect *her.* Julia had told her about the

Shakespeare verse, had written it out for her in big block letters. Violet had studied it often, these past weeks. A sea nourished with tears, indeed.

Yet she had her memories; she had her family — even Grace and Alice and Joe, now. And they had their home, the farm. They had loved one another fiercely.

Her body was drifting into numbness. Even her pain was fading, as daylight into evening.

She found she didn't mind, not really. *I'll see them soon,* she thought, and her heart beat faster. *Good heart, you did your best. Forgive me; I forgive you, now, I do.* And then Danny and Josh were talking with Julia about something Violet couldn't seem to understand, and she felt a flash of irritation, but then joy overcame her that none of them was alone, as together they drove on, toward the bending of the light.

ACKNOWLEDGMENTS

I'm deeply grateful to everyone who has shared in the adventure of writing this book.

Many amazing and generous people have, with unstinting grace and candor, told me the stories of their lives or offered their time and expertise to help me find what I needed to know. This list includes: Sally Jacobson, Bob and Nancy Davis, John Kansler, Eleanor Groves, Dorothy Stafford, Larry O'Shaughnessy, Mary Robek, John Schimenek, Lewis Flagstad, Margaret McGillis, Joyce Erickson, Tim Schandel, Gina Sacchetti, Bob Fuhrman, Teddie Meronek, Davis Helberg, Wes Harkins, David Lull, Bob Murphy, Laura Jacobs, Richard Stewart, John Gaines, and Sparky Stensaas. Special thanks also to Captain Bill Peterson and Ken Gerasimos for giving me a tour of the Great Lakes freighter *John G. Munson* on a blustery winter day in the Duluth harbor, to Robert Gardner and Ryan Stokes of the

Minnesota Ballet for teaching me the Lindy Hop, and to Richard Ford for opening my eyes to new ways of perceiving words, phrases, sentences, and the writing life.

Many of Grace's experiences working on the special crew at the shipyard are based on episodes described in the written memoirs of Carol Johnson Fistler. I'm grateful to her for recording her story and to Kathy Laakso of the Douglas County (Wisconsin) Historical Society for pointing me to it. I also owe a particular debt to three fine books: *Death's Door: The Truth Behind Michigan's Largest Mass Murder* by Steve Lehto, *The Last Stand of the Tin Can Sailors: The Extraordinary World War II Story of the U.S. Navy's Finest Hour* by James D. Hornfischer, and *The Men of the Gambier Bay* by Edwin P. Hoyt. (Any errors — or creative license with facts — are, of course, my own.)

I'm so fortunate to have had generous support not only with coming to the details of the story but with finding the time, space, and motivation I needed to write it. My deepest thanks to those who provided me "homes away from home" when I needed fresh surroundings in which to work: Lonnie and Gary Vitse, Judy Cloninger, and Andy Anderson; Bob and Dianne Hess; Christine and Joe Skorjanec; Sonya Steven;

Audrey McGlashan and Rich Hurlbert; and Dan and Sharon Brown.

Thank you to Michael Radulescu for being passionately on my team and for never believing that Anne Wallace isn't real; to Pat Lull for providing me with out-of-this-world chocolate treats; and to Lara Zielin, Naomi Musch, Carrie Sutherland, and my mom and dad, Marya and Bob Farrell, not only for being stupendous friends to me in all ways but for reading my manuscript at various stages, often on very short notice, and always providing helpful and encouraging remarks. Many thanks also to the outstanding team at Random House, including Lindsey Schwoeri, Beth Pearson, Susan Brown, Annette Szlachta-McGinn, and Kenneth Russell.

I'm humbled by the generous heart of the man I married, Jay Baker, who spent hours brainstorming with me, celebrated milestones on the journey, and gave me the extraordinary gifts of his unconditional love and unflinching support.

Finally, my deepest appreciation to the world's best agent and editor, Marly Rusoff and Kate Medina, as well as the equally fabulous Julie Mosow and Millicent Bennett. These amazing women kept their faith in me (and in Grace) through many, many drafts, and they each lent countless brilliant insights along the way. Without them, this book simply would not be.

ABOUT THE AUTHOR

Ellen Baker has worked as a costumed living history interpreter, a curator of a World War II museum, and a bookseller and event coordinator at an independent bookstore. Her previous novel, *Keeping the House,* won the 2008 Great Lakes Book Award. She lives in Minnesota.